VEILED

SERAYA

VEILED

SERAYA

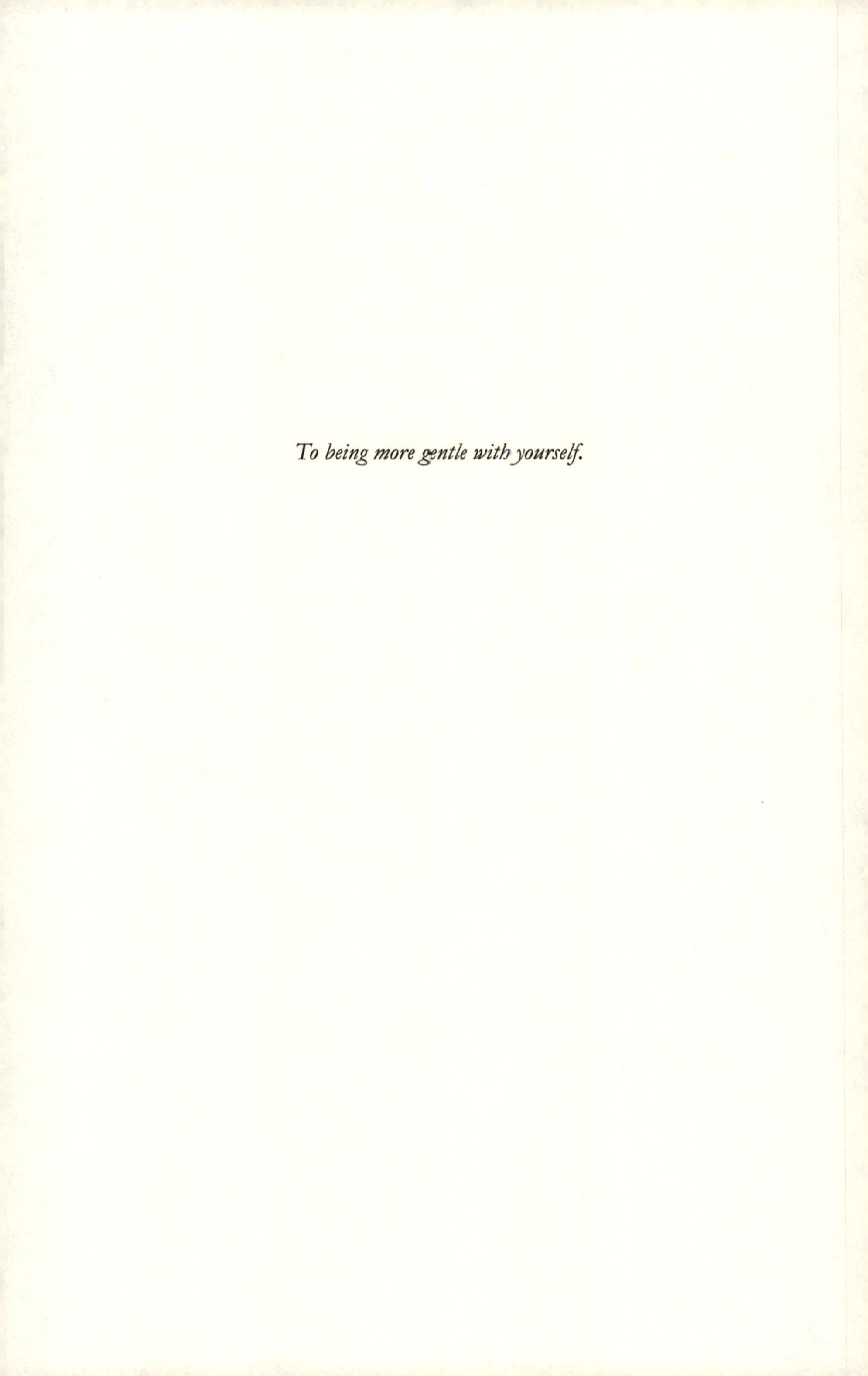

To being more gentle with yourself.

AUTHOR NOTE

Readers discretion advised. *Veiled* is a dark, contemporary romance and contains strong language, explicit sexual content, and topics that may be sensitive to some readers.

It is my hope that I've handled these with the care they deserve. For a detailed list, click here or scan the code below.

Disclaimer: The Sons of the Atlas Series is a series of interconnected standalones with an overarching plot. Veiled, Book 1 in the series, must be read first.

HOUSE OF THE ATLAS
YOUNG FAMILY TREE

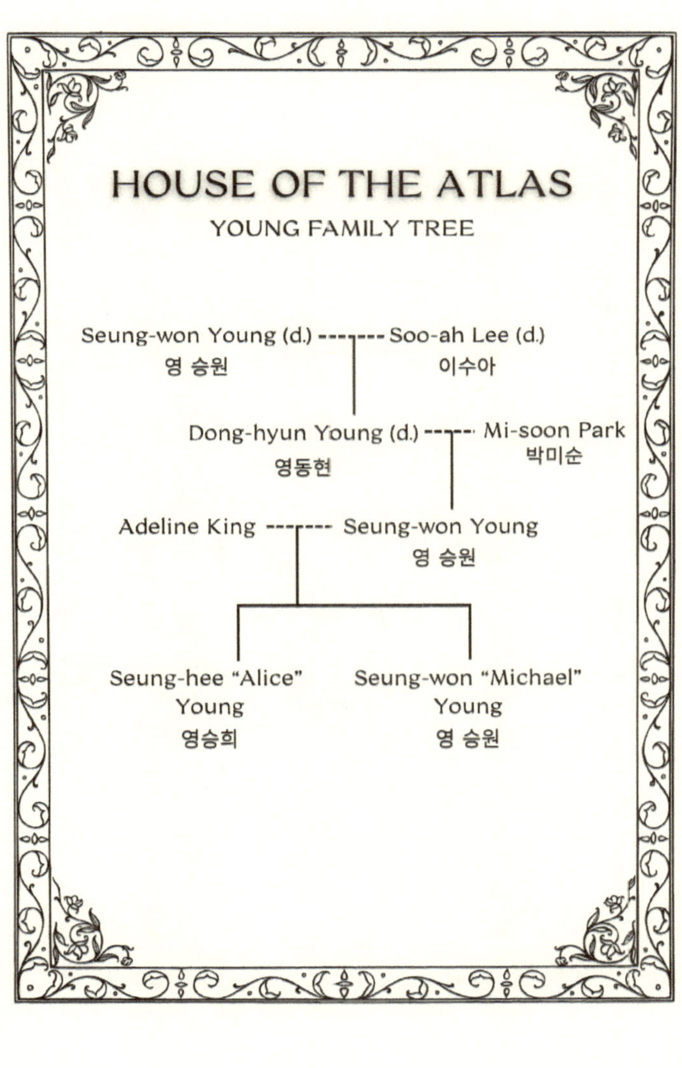

PROLOGUE

IF THREE MONTHS AGO YOU'D told me I'd be roaming the narrow streets of London in this bloody fucking cold—on my birthday nevertheless—as I followed someone who was a practical stranger, I'd have laughed in your face.

But three months ago, Young Seungwon was just another wealthy bloke in the city and my perception of who I was hadn't been completely shattered.

A group of teens in their school uniform, laughing, swarmed out of a local shop right in front me, snapping my attention out of my thoughts.

"Careful," one of the boys told the one who almost ran into me, reaching for his sleeve to keep him out of my way.

I ignored them and brought the hood over my head tighter around my face. Keeping my head down, I shielded myself and swerved past them as I kept trailing the golden boy.

The unexpected heavy raindrops from earlier thundered harder above me, drenching my thick black overcoat even further. Following someone in broad daylight seemed easy enough in theory, but tailing them through this weather was proving to be more challenging than I'd anticipated.

Especially when I wasn't much of a morning person.

And to my dismay, he was. Or I guess he had to be because of his job.

It was already afternoon, but I'd been awake since dawn yesterday because the precious doctor had been scheduled for an on-call shift this weekend which meant I equally barely slept.

But most of my days now consisted of little to no sleep, watching, and waiting.

Because all I could do was wait.

At least for now.

Young must have gotten a call from the hospital with how abruptly he'd left the late lunch he was having with his sister.

I'd been sitting at a cafe across from UMMA, the small Korean restaurant tucked away from the busy streets of London where he and his younger sister often came to when she was in town, when I saw him bolt out of the place. I'd quickly discarded my barely touched cup of tea and unfinished pastry before exiting the coffee shop.

He seemed to be on a mission as he quickly took a right turn onto Main Street. I slowed my steps and waited a brief moment before I took the same turn. I always maintained a healthy distance during my surveillance tours, always keeping each of them in view but never too close in case they decided to change course or peered over their shoulder and noticed me.

But none of them knew they were being tailed. That every single one of their moves was tracked by someone they'd never see coming.

Just the thought of my existence coming to light and having to watch the looks on their faces sent adrenaline coursing through my veins. The anticipation—albeit far away—fueled my steps despite the persistent rain drumming against my body.

Amanar General Hospital, commonly known as AGH, was the largest trauma center in the city and technically only a seven minute walk from the restaurant, but with this incessant downpour, it felt like ages.

Young wasn't starting there until the new year, but he'd been called in to cover another doctor's shift and of course, he accepted it.

He crossed the junction, weaving through the taxis already engaged on the turn despite their light still being red. I slightly hurried up my steps when I noticed the light turning amber to avoid losing him in the crowd forming as they filtered out of the Tube station, but as I chanced to cross over, an idiot driving a single-seater red Ferrari roared around the corner, its honk blaring as it doused me under a cascade of water in its wake.

I closed my eyes and let out a frustrated groan.

Bloody hell.

I stepped back onto the pavement, drenched even further than I already was. In a split second decision, as the light turned red, I jogged across the road and made it to the other side before the light switched to green.

Thankfully, Michael was too concentrated on making it to the hospital that he hadn't paid attention to what had just occurred.

I continued following him, passing the railway station, and took position across the street. Taking shelter behind a weathered brown brick building, standing in a small alley, I watched him run the remaining distance to AGH's main entrance.

The large entrance glass doors slid open, and he stepped inside, pulling off the hood of his black rain jacket. He ran a hand through his thick black hair, pushing back the damp strands that clung to his forehead from the rain. He then shifted, and I caught a glimpse of his face as he wiped the rain from it with his jumper.

After he disappeared inside the hospital, I waited a few more minutes before a gust of frigid air snaked beneath my clothes, sending a shiver down my spine. I finally stepped out of my hiding spot, the sun dipping below the horizon, and made my way to the nearest station.

Once inside, I wove through the busy concourse, the buzz of voices and the squeak of damp trainers against the tiled floors creating a now familiar backdrop. After spending so much time in the city, you eventually grew used to the chaos that came with it.

I made my way to the platform that would take me to the place I'd been calling home for the last few weeks. I'd had other plans for today, but with my current state of disarray from the relentless weather, it seemed best to retreat to my flat until later tonight.

I jogged the remaining distance and squeezed between the Tube's doors right before they closed. The southbound line that traveled to my area was generally quieter, but it being Friday, there were a few more commuters leaving work early.

I stood for the short ride and hopped off once the train reached my stop. My flat wasn't far from the station and by the time I climbed the short steps that led inside the weathered building I'd been living in, the rain had already turned into a light drizzle .

Once inside the one-bedroom I'd been renting, I shed my sodden clothes until I was down to my underwear and let them fall in a wet heap on the wooden floor by the entrance. I then grabbed a large, frayed towel from the small bathroom and headed down the pitch-dark narrow hallway that opened up to the space that served both as my living room and my bedroom.

I dried myself off as I flicked on the lamp on the end table, the soft yellow light casting a warm glow around the room. Running the towel over my head to dry my hair, I moved closer to the right wall, slowly taking it in.

Photographs and article clippings covered the space, some connected by a web of red strings crisscrossing from material I'd collected over the last ninety-two days.

The low hum of the heater finally kicked in, providing a slight respite from the chill that had settled in my bones. Tossing the used towel onto the sofa, I shuffled over to the kitchenette and while I waited for water to boil, I grabbed a jumper and joggers to slide on.

A pang of fatigue suddenly hit me from the long day I'd had, but I ignored it.

There was no time for it.

The sharp whistle of the kettle echoed against the walls and I moved to make myself a cup of tea, adding a splash of milk to it until I was satisfied with the taste. I took a long sip from the steaming cup in my hand, letting the warmth seep into my insides, and walked back to stand in front of my work in progress.

My eyes slowly trailed to his picture.

Young Seungwon. Also went by Michael Young.

Cardiothoracic surgery trainee at Orion University Hospital and soon to be consultant at AGH.

But most importantly, he was the oldest Atlas set to Ascend in just a few months.

Or at least, that's what he'd always been made to believe.

I set my mug down on the small cluttered coffee table behind me and picked up the worn notebook resting there. Flipping through the pages with scrawled notes and hastily drawn diagrams, I quickly jotted down the details I'd gathered today on a new page before I waited too long and forgot the small details.

After tucking the black pen back between the pages, I placed the journal back on the table and turned my attention again to the web of information. My eyes darted from one image to another, trying to piece together what I'd discovered in a short period of time and how much more there was still to uncover.

Because Michael wasn't the only name on my list.

You see, there's a group of people out there that secretly run our country.

A group no one knew about.

Their influence seeped into every corner of our city. So much so they were involved in everything, their names cropping up everywhere.

From sports to the Mayor's Cabinet.

They were the perfect monster of modern society, hiding in plain sight.

A group that was invisible to most people.

Except me.

These men played God without permission.

But now, they'd get what was coming for them.

My gaze shifted to another one of my targets just as my computer pinged with a new notification. I moved around the coffee table and sank into the second-hand couch I'd picked up from a charity shop last week. Since my scholarship funds wouldn't hit my bank account until next week—another courtesy of the failed system we lived in—I'd been making do with sleeping on the floor until I'd finally splurged and bought this old thing.

I grabbed my laptop, settled in, and typed in my password to access the encrypted server I'd been using.

A faint smile played on my lips. *There you are.*

I know you're probably wondering who I am, but giving you

my name would be a slippery slope and quite frankly irrelevant for the moment. It was only a matter of time before everyone involved discovered the truth.

Including me.

I'd been slowly shedding myself from who I once was and garnering a new veil.

They might be the Atlas kings of the city…

But I was here to ensure their legacy never saw the light of a new generation.

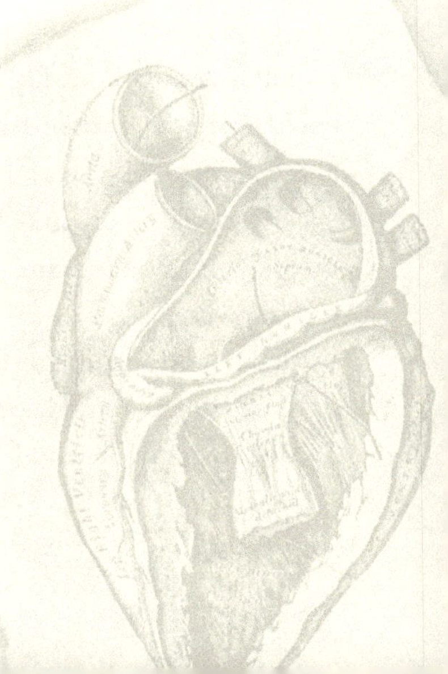

CHAPTER 1

AZARA

I STARED AT THE DIGITAL clock on my bedside table, watching the minutes crawl by agonizingly slow. I'd easily fallen asleep last night—which hadn't been an easy feat for the last ten years—but a nightmare I could barely even remember now woke me up and I couldn't fall back asleep after that.

It was currently 5:00 a.m. and I'd been lying here for the past thirty minutes, despite knowing I should be grabbing every minute of rest I could. Especially when I had a full day of scheduled surgeries ahead, and with how busy work had been lately with the holidays coming up.

It was like everyone's heart in the city failed and since I worked at the biggest trauma center in London, we always got the biggest influx of patients.

I'd hoped that if I'd shut my eyes, I could get a few more minutes of sleep but my mind kept racing through my endless list of tasks that needed to get done, and I ended up running through it instead.

I was still exhausted from my last shift, but when was I not tired? My whole life was dedicated to Amanar General Hospital, but just another year before what I'd dedicated my blood, sweat and tears—a lot of tears—came to fruition. Although my work wouldn't really end when I finally finished my training and I officially became a cardiothoracic surgeon.

My alarm went off fifteen minutes later, its shrill sound slicing through the stillness of the room and pulling me out of my thoughts. With a groggy groan, I fumbled for the snooze button, and silenced it with a frustrated swipe.

I lay there for a moment longer before letting out a resigned sigh and swinging my legs over the edge of the bed. The cold touch of the floor instantly ran up my spine and I grabbed the side of the mattress, mustering the courage to get on with my day.

I eventually got up and shuffled to the bathroom, every step feeling like a monumental effort. I flicked on the bathroom light, and startled at my reflection in the mirror.

I look like I need a large dose of coffee injected into my veins.

Rubbing my weary eyes, I reached into the shower and turned it on. While I waited for the water to heat—which usually took much longer than it should, especially with how much I was paying for this flat—I rummaged through my dresser for a pair of leggings, a sports bra and a chunky cable-knit jumper, laying them out on the bed to be ready after I showered.

Picking up my mobile from where it lay on the bed, I checked my blood sugar as I made my way out of the bedroom and found it within range. A small victory that I always appreciated in the morning, because it was too early to have to deal with my diabetes.

Especially after the night I'd just had.

Passing the living room, I flicked on the small lamp beside the cream sofa I'd gotten for my birthday a few years ago before I headed into the kitchen. I left my phone on the rustic wooden table and brewed my first—of many—coffee for the day.

Walking back to my bedroom, I glanced at the clock on my bedside table to confirm I wasn't running late before finally getting to showering. After a quick wash, I changed into my clothes and opted to leave the bed undone, like I did most days.

It was just so much more convenient to slip back into it after a long day at work.

Back in the kitchen, I downed another coffee and grabbed a piece of toast from the bread bin, spreading a thin layer of *amlou* on it. Then, with my toast in hand, I slung my work tote over my shoulder and grabbed my phone, inputting the grams of carbs into my app, as I headed out.

It was still pitch-black outside, like it was most mornings these days, as I walked briskly to the station. I quickly regretted not wearing a coat, my wool scarf and jumper barely cutting out the frigid air, but I couldn't go back home or I'd miss the Tube and be late to work.

I quickened my steps, my breath forming small clouds in the chilly air, and once inside the carriage the warmth of bodies slightly helped. Shoving the remainder of my toast into my mouth, I sat at one of the vacant seats and pulled out my phone, going through my emails and responding to any urgent ones.

I was in the middle of drafting an email when the doors slid open at the next stop, and in walked a couple, laughing and seemingly oblivious to the world around them. I glanced up from my screen to find them practically glued to each other—his mouth nuzzling her ear while she gazed at him with a nauseating affectionate glance before he planted a lingering kiss to her lips.

I felt my lips curl into a subtle frown.

It's 6:00 a.m., for heaven's sake.

They eventually settled into the seats across from me and she was practically in her partner's lap, completely unconcerned with the half-dozen grumbling commuters around them.

I found myself stifling the urge to roll my eyes and tried to refocus on my phone again, but their incessant PDA was hard to ignore. It wasn't that I hated affection or people in love, but I'd always thought it was a bit overrated.

The whole concept of love or finding *the* one was always shoved in your face—in movies, songs and now, apparently, even morning metro rides.

Fortunately for me, my stop came up next, and I slipped out of my seat, leaving the couple and any thoughts of their overly affection display behind.

It was almost 6:30 a.m. by the time I made it to work. I changed into the green scrubs the hospital provided and headed for the cafeteria. There were many things I loved about working at Amanar and being a surgeon, but my favorite part was the free coffee and food the hospital provided doctors.

I picked up my regular order of a matcha latte at the counter and spotted Houssam and Zainab at a table. I'd met the twins last year during a consultation in the emergency department where they were both working during their last rotation as junior doctors.

I wasn't exactly known to be the social type and tended to keep mostly to myself aside from when I spent time with my bestfriends Nakia and Hazel, but the twins reminded me a lot of my cousins back home. Since I hadn't been back to Morocco in what felt like ages, I liked to enjoy their company whenever our paths crossed.

Despite the early morning, they were already bickering over something I couldn't quite make out. Zainab looked up as I approached.

She used the loose end of her navy hijab to create a makeshift barrier between herself and her brother as I sat down across from them at the small round table.

"Please tell my idiot brother that he's wrong," she implored, though I had no clue what the argument was about this time.

These two future general practitioners were exceptionally bright and competitive, which often found them in predicaments like these where they argued about anything and everything.

I took a sip of my coffee, knowing better than to get involved. The last time I'd taken a side, I'd spent an entire week never hearing the end of it.

"You know I can still hear *and* see you," Houssam shot back, bringing his sister's hand down.

Zainab barely glanced at him, tucking the fabric of her hijab back into her blue scrub top. "Could have fooled me with the two brain cells you seem to have," she replied, before focusing her gaze on me.

"What's wrong with you?" she suddenly asked.

I frowned. "Nothing. Why?"

She narrowed her eyes slightly. "You're usually grumpy, but your energy"—she vaguely gestured her hand in circles in my direction— "Yeah, it's grumpier than usual."

I took another sip from my paper cup, unsure if I should be offended or not. I wasn't the most spirited person in the world, but I wouldn't call myself 'grumpy'.

Houssam sighed in exasperation and chimed in. "Don't listen to her. She always thinks she can read people better than she actually can."

Zainab ignored him and waited for my response.

I groaned, recalling the earlier email I'd received. "It's nothing really. I just found out we'll be welcoming a new consultant soon."

This morning, while checking my inbox, I'd found an email dated from two days ago from our medical director—who also happened to be my father— informing me that a new cardiothoracic consultant would be joining the team in the next few weeks and that I'd need to make a good impression. In other words, my father wanted me to welcome him with a radiant smile and be nice.

"*Oh,*" Zainad said suggestively. "Who is he? What hospital is he coming from?" she fired off each question in quick succession, barely taking a breath between each. "Is he good-looking?" she whispered the last question, hoping her brother wouldn't hear.

Judging by the eye roll he gave, it was clear he had.

Zainab had a knack for gathering any crumbs of gossip roaming around the walls of this hospital. Not that she would run around and spread it amongst the staff, but she liked to be in the know. Just in case it would be useful in the future.

I shook my head and let out a short laugh. "I don't know much, only that he was awarded his certificate for completing his training early, and I've heard he's unbearable."

Now, that last part wasn't entirely true. I'd never met Dr. Young, but the amount of gushing I'd overheard from the nurses after he'd covered one of my on-call shifts last month, when I'd gotten violently sick from whatever flu had been roaming around, had been enough to draw the conclusion.

"My favorite kind," Zainab said with a dreamy sigh.

I raised an eyebrow at her just as her brother stood up from his seat. "I'm not sticking around for the rest of this conversation." He gently flicked her over the head before bidding us both goodbye and heading back to work.

"You know, arseholes in real life aren't quite like the ones you like to read about?"

She got up and placed her hands on the table, leaning over it to bring herself closer to me. "Oh, I'm very much aware. But a broody and mysterious doctor sounds wonderful. Maybe it'll dislodge that stick up your arse."

Before I could respond, her DECT phone went off. "I have to run, but I'll need a detailed rundown on this Dr. Young whenever he arrives." She smiled at me before walking off, dropping her empty water bottle into the recycling and disappearing through the cafeteria door that led straight to the emergency room.

I sat there, staring at the spot where she'd vanished.

Ridiculous.

Before I could savor the last few minutes of freedom ahead of my morning rounds, I glanced at my phone and realized it was already time for my shift. I inhaled a deep breath before finishing off my latte, and heading upstairs.

To surviving another day.

"ZAYD, HURRY UP OR WE'LL be late," I called out.

"I'm coming," my younger brother yelled back, his head briefly poking out of the corner at the top of the staircase before he retreated back into the bathroom.

He'd been locked in there for the past twenty minutes. Ever since he turned fifteen last spring, he'd been spending hours getting ready, regardless of where we went.

Who needs this long for a simple trip to the park?

I was about to call his name again when he came barreling down the stairs, nearly crashing into me. My hands instinctively flew up to steady him.

"Oi, watch it. You'll hurt yourself."

He ignored my reproach and gave me a cheeky smile. "I'm ready." He put on his coat and grabbed a knitted hat from the closet, tugging it over his light brown, curly hair.

I rolled my eyes at him. "About time." Reaching for the front door of the townhouse I'd grown up in, I motioned for Zayd to head out first. "Why does it always take you ages to get ready," I huffed, locking the door behind us since our dad was upstairs, fast asleep, and wouldn't notice we'd left until much later.

"I was hardly in there for ten minutes," Zayd protested.

I turned to face him, raising an eyebrow. "More like twenty."

"But you'd wait an eternity if it meant spending time with your favorite little brother," he countered, flashing me another broad smile.

"You're the only one I have. Unfortunately."

He clutched his chest in mock indignation. "I'm quite offended by that." Zayd was usually rather shy around others, but his personality came out the moment it was just the two of us.

I shook my head at his dramatics. "Spare me," I said, placing the keys in my pocket and going down the few steps at the front of the house.

He slung an arm around my shoulders—yes, my fifteen year old brother was a giant—and we started the short walk from our home to Hyde park, the sun beginning to set on the horizon.

With my surgical training keeping me busy, I didn't get to see him as often as I'd like, but I'd made it a priority to have these sibling outings. And like every other year, we were heading to Winter Wonderland.

"So, will I finally manage to convince you to do a ride with me this year?" Zayd asked, his eyes shining with mischief.

I shot him a sideways glance. "What do you mean? I always join you on rides."

"The kiddie ones don't count," he deadpanned.

I swatted his chest and gently nudged him away, but he barely moved, only tightening his grip around my shoulder. "You know I'm not fond of heights," I explained.

My role at any type of theme park was to be present, hold belongings if necessary and eat all the food I could handle without spiking my sugar. Heights or adrenaline? Not particularly my thing. Unless the adrenaline came from performing surgery. But more importantly, I was far too old to risk a heart attack from something I'd willingly subjected myself to.

"Or you're just *boring*," he drawled, emphasizing the last word.

I rolled my eyes and chuckled. "Alright, Mr. I have no fear. I'll do the giant wheel with you, but that's it."

"First off, I'm not fearless and you are well aware of that. Remember the incident with the thing that ran away with me on it."

I threw my back, laughing, as the incident he was referring to took shape in my mind. On one of our summer holidays to Morocco, we'd taken a trip to the beach with some of our family and Zayd had implored us for an entire hour to let him ride on one of the horses. My dad and I had eventually agreed, just to get him to stop asking.

Everything had been fine until my brother decided it would be amusing to yank on the horse's mane. The horse bolted with a screaming Zayd still securely fastened on top of him. It only took the owner five minutes to get him back, but it scarred him for life. Even now, my brother could barely look at one—or even utter the name—without getting full body shivers.

Zayd spoke again, pulling me out of the memory. "Secondly, the giant wheel does not count. It's so slow, you barely even feel a thing."

"Take it or leave it," I replied as we made it to the blue gate, the queue for the entry stretching out before us. Thankfully, I'd bought tickets online so we didn't have to wait and were let in easily.

Once inside, we passed the ice rink and strolled through the Christmas market stalls, browsing through the various small businesses. Although our family didn't celebrate the holidays anymore, Zayd and I always went our separate ways and bought each other a gift—well, I technically bought both since I gave him the money to spend on mine.

After securing our presents, we wandered deeper into the park and we explored every corner for the next few hours. We raced through some of the Fun Houses to see who did it the fastest, walked through the Magical Ice Kingdom to look at this year's ice sculptures, before I spent the rest of our time there watching Zayd jump on every ride he laid his eyes on and eat twice his weight in food, while I nursed the same decadent hot chocolate from EL&N.

Then, to my misfortune, I'd had to honor my promise to climb into the giant wheel. I'd closed my eyes the entire time, gripping the edge of the seat so tightly, I could barely feel my fingers after the ride.

It was almost 10:00 p.m. when we sat on the front porch for our annual gift exchange. I briefly glanced back to find the living room lights on, which meant my dad was most likely engrossed in one of those Turkish soap operas that were broadcasted on 2M. Although he would totally deny watching them, and blame it on the fact that it was the only thing on at this time.

"Right, so who goes first?" I asked Zayd, turning my attention back to him.

He took off his hat and shoved it in the side pocket of his coat. "I've got the best gift, so you should go ahead. It'll be a gentler blow to your confidence," he replied with a wide grin.

I rolled my eyes but couldn't suppress a smile as I rummaged through my tote. "And I was told *I* lacked humbleness." I pulled out the wrapped parcel and handed it to him. "Here you go."

He wasted no time in tearing into the wrapping, his eyes widening in surprise when he registered what was inside. "Shut up!"

"Hey, language," I chided gently.

"Sorry," he mumbled. His hands roamed over the handmade leather sketchbook before he opened it up to explore the different compartments.

Zayd loved drawing so the moment I'd seen it, I knew I had to get it for him. It was made of distressed genuine leather, came with an assortment of pencils and hosted a few pockets inside for storage. The shopkeeper, a lovely older lady, had recommended it and since I didn't know much about art or drawing, I'd taken her word for it.

By Zayd's reaction, she'd been spot on.

My brother finally looked up, a broad smile lighting up his face. He hugged the sketchbook to his chest and said, "Thanks, Zizou. I love it."

I loathed that nickname, but it was worth it for the expression on his face.

"Think you can top that," I teased, nudging his shoulder with mine.

He grimaced at that, and gave me a non-committal nod, his earlier confidence waning. By the look on his face, I braced myself for what he'd picked for my gift.

He reached for the inside of his coat pocket and retrieved a thinly wrapped bright orange package. Then, he bent forward, presenting it with a flourish, "For you, dearest."

I narrowed my eyes at the horrendous color and grabbed it from his open palms.

"Don't judge until you open it," he said, sitting back.

I couldn't help but chuckle. "I'm not judging, but your earlier gloating doesn't quite match the size of this package."

He shrugged. "Yeah, well you know not to believe everything I say."

I unwrapped the paper to reveal a wooden bookmark engraved with the words "Best Sister Ever."

"Surprise," Zayd said, tilting his head to the side.

I held the bookmark up, feeling a mix of amusement and disbelief. "Really? This is what you came up with?"

He shrugged again, a cheeky grin spreading wider across his face. "Isn't it charming? And don't you like to read, so this is perfect so you can stop dog-earing your books which for the record, should be a crime. I'm not even a reader and *I* know that."

I couldn't help but laugh. "I don't even know what to say." I hadn't touched a fiction book since secondary school and the only ones I read now were textbooks or peer-reviewed journals so I didn't know how this would be useful, but it was the intention that mattered, right?

"A thank you would suffice."

I rolled my eyes playfully, and tucked his gift into my purse before wrapping an arm around him and pulling him into a side hug. "Thank you, little brother," I said, ruffling his hair.

"Azara, no. Not the hair," he protested, laughing as he pulled away to fix the unruly strands.

"Maybe that'll remind you next year to do better." Which reminded me. "By the way, where did the rest of the money go? Surely the bookmark didn't cost the full fifty quid I gave you."

He looked at me with a guilty expression. "Can we consider it a tax for being the best brother ever?"

I shook my head. "I would say yes, but I suspect you've already spent it."

Before he could confirm what I already knew, the front door swung open and we both startled at the sound of our father's voice interrupting us.

"What are you two still doing out here? It's nearly midnight," he scolded, his head poking through the door. "And it's bloody cold out here, you'll get sick."

He pushed his glasses up his nose, feigning authority. My father might look like he would put you in your place, but he had not a mean bone in his body—especially when it came to us, his greatest weakness.

The man I grew up with might have changed a lot over the last fourteen years, but on rare occasions, his old self resurfaced.

"Sorry, *baba*[1]," I said, standing up. He opened the door wider, and I moved to greet him. I planted a kiss on his cheek, the familiar stubble grazing against my skin. "I know it's a school night, we just lost track of time."

"Hi, *benti*[2]," my father said, his voice softening as he kissed the top of my head.

Zayd joined us, kissing his other cheek. "What she said," he added.

My father narrowed his eyes at him. "You should be in bed."

"Tomorrow's Friday and we don't have anything important scheduled." My dad didn't acknowledge his explanation and simply gestured for him to get inside.

"I'll see you next week," I said to my brother as he kicked off his shoes and shrugged off his coat.

He winked at me, already halfway up the stairs. "I wouldn't miss it. Thanks for today."

"Always." I smiled at him, before he took off to his bedroom in a hurry to avoid another scolding.

"That boy is giving me more gray hairs than I should have at my age," he grumbled, running a hand over his buzzed hair.

I let out a small laugh. "Well, you *are* old." When his eyes widened in disbelief at my comment, I quickly added, "But you look phenomenal for a sixty-three year old *excellent* father."

---

1 *Father (Arabic)*
2 *My daughter (Arabic)*

He gently tapped my cheek a few times. "Nice save." There was a short pause before he spoke again "Did you get my email?" he asked, changing the subject.

I should have seen it coming. I *had* seen his email, but still hadn't acknowledged it or the other five text messages my father had sent me about it since then.

"I did," I confirmed, hoping that would be enough for him to drop the subject.

It wasn't.

"And you'll be nice to Dr. Young. He's a great addition to the department."

"I'm always nice, *baba*."

He raised an eyebrow, clearly skeptical.

"I *will* be nice to Dr. Young," I promised, even though I wasn't entirely convinced myself. I'd never met the man, yet something about his arrival set my nerves on edge. It was most likely entirely irrational, but I couldn't help it.

Competition was an integral part of our field and I thrived in it. I loved the challenge it brought, and proving that I was the best at what I did, especially in a male-dominated specialty. The look on other surgeons's faces when I walked into a room was in my top three favorite things in the world.

But the idea of spending the rest of my career being compared to this Dr. Young every step of the way, wasn't something I wanted to be subjected to.

My father would retire one day—although he refused to ever discuss it—and I wanted his position. I'd worked hard to get where I was and I refused to let a newcomer, much less a man, take it from me.

"Good. It's quite late, stay the night?"

"No, that's alright. I have a shift tomorrow," I replied, giving him a soft smile. Besides, my Omnipod would expire in the next hour and needed to be changed.

"Alright, *benti*. I'll see you tomorrow, then." We exchanged goodbyes, and I crossed the street to where my car was parked, my father still lingering on the porch, watching until I climbed in.

As I drove home, replaying the day in my mind, one thought kept resurfacing, and I couldn't shake the feeling that this new arrival might change everything.

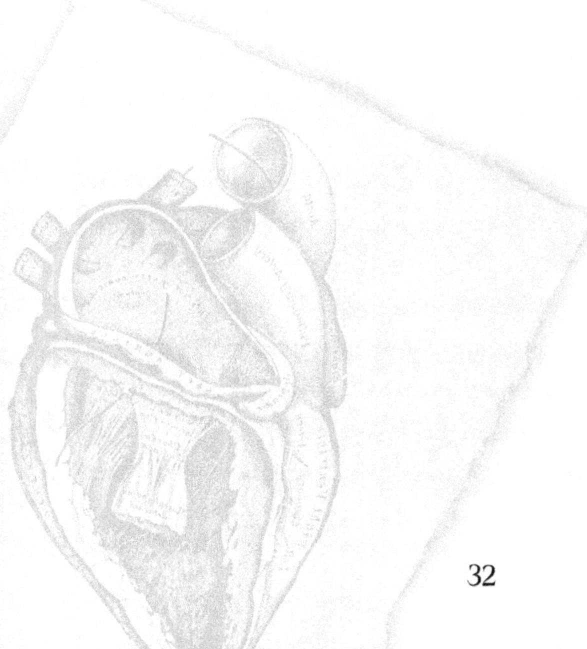

CHAPTER 2

MICHAEL

"LAST DAY?" A VOICE SAID, suddenly startling me out of my focused state.

Kaz dropped onto a chair, peering up at me from the nurse's station.

I glanced at him from where I stood at the counter. "It is indeed," I replied, finishing up a few exit orders.

Luckily for me, the few patients I'd operated on over the last week were stable and the past hour had been uneventful. And I could think that now without having to deal with the potential repercussions of saying it was too quiet.

"Just a few more minutes, and I'll be out of your way," I added.

He let out a dramatic sigh, tapping his fingers on the desk. "At last, we shall be free from our misery."

"Please. I was the best part of your shift," I shot back.

Kazim and I met a few years back when he started working on

12E as an ICU nurse, where I was a senior trainee in cardiothoracic surgery. We'd quickly become mates after bonding over our shared love of football and graphic novels.

He huffed and leaned back in his chair, crossing his arms over his chest. "Such a humble man you are, Dr. Young."

"Never claimed to be one," I replied as I finished writing my last set of orders and inserting the prescription into the patient's file. I stacked the binders and moved to put them back, but eventually Kaz stood up and grabbed them from my hands.

He must have noticed the confused look on my face. I usually only took one chart at a time, but knowing I couldn't be late to tonight's dinner, I'd taken all the ones I'd needed at once.

A rather foolish move, as it turned out.

Kaz rolled his eyes. "You've been here ten years and you still don't know where these go," he chided, placing them back in their proper slots.

"Hey, at least I tried," I protested, feigning indignation.

He scoffed playfully, standing beside the counter. "And you pride yourself on being the best."

"I *am* the best. At fixing people's hearts," I replied, leaning next to where he stood and checking my watch. "Not that I don't enjoy your *delightful* company, but my shift is now officially over."

His expression suddenly turned serious. "There's nothing I could say to convince you to stay, is there?"

If it were up to me, I would have never left at all.

I pushed that thought away and gave him a cheeky smile to lighten the mood. "You could just say I'm the best cardiothoracic surgeon you've ever worked with and you're going to miss me terribly," I quipped, nudging him with my shoulder.

"Oh, piss off," he replied, though I could see the corners of his mouth twitching in a suppressed grin. He shook his head. "Just don't be a stranger when you're off being a big-shot consultant at Amanar."

"Is that a compliment?" I teased as I headed for the lifts at the end of the hallway.

"You're too full of yourself," he called out.

I couldn't help but laugh as I pressed the down button. "Just don't miss me too much," I called over my shoulder just as the doors opened.

"The only thing I'll miss is your collection," he shouted back, referring to my extensive library of graphic novels, as I stepped inside the lift.

I waved him goodbye before the doors closed. Once on the third floor, I headed for the doctor's lounge and sank into the worn armchair I'd come to love lounging in over the years. I looked around the room I'd spent the last decade of my life in—from sleepless and frustrating nights to fond memories of successful days of surgeries.

I wasn't much of a sentimental person, but leaving this place wasn't something I was looking forward to. *I* had chosen to work here, another small rebellion against my father's wishes. Just like my sleeves of tattoos were or choosing a different specialty than what he'd expected me to pick.

But this time, I didn't have any other choice than to abandon the place I'd put ten years of work in for a new environment. Not when *the* infamous birthday was approaching.

It wasn't the novelty of Amanar that made me dread the change, it was the fact that I couldn't continue ignoring my duty. Not that the late night phone calls I got every other week to patch up someone weren't already a reminder enough that my life wasn't totally mine.

Although I wanted the consultant job, sometimes I wished I...

My 5:30 p.m. alarm rang, pulling me out of my thoughts and reminding me that I needed to get out of here. I discarded my used teal scrubs into the designated laundry bin and changed into the suit I'd kept in my locker. My flat was on the way to my parents, but with London traffic, I didn't want to chance being late.

Or I'd never hear the end of it.

Besides, if I stepped foot inside my place, the temptation to cancel our family's annual holiday dinner would become even more unsurmountable. We usually held the tradition on Christmas day, but this year, my parents were flying to my father's hometown in Korea for the holidays to visit my grandmother and attend to some business.

I was a street away from my parent's place when my phone rang, my sister's caller ID displayed on the dashboard. "Alice, you okay?" I asked, worried.

My little sister and I had a close relationship and we texted each other almost everyday, but she only phoned me if something was wrong.

"Please don't hate me," she replied, and my gut sank.

I let out a heavy sigh because I already knew what she was going to tell me.

"You're not coming to tonight's dinner," I grumbled, my fingers tightening against the steering wheel of my Rolls-Royce as I took a left turn.

"I'm sorry. You know I wouldn't leave you alone with our parents, but I'm still stuck in Edinburgh. I was supposed to arrive an hour ago, but there was a mechanical failure with the train and they're still working to fix it."

Alice's classes had wrapped up earlier this month, but she'd stayed back for a little longer so she could explore before heading home for the winter break. My sister had moved to Scotland back in August to start her first year at uni. She was pursuing a degree in education to become a primary school educator which was an ideal fit for her since she loved babbling.

I still found it hard to believe that my baby sister was now in uni. I still vividly recalled the day my parents had brought her home and I'd held her in my arms for the first time.

"It's fine," I lied, knowing that if she knew how I truly felt, it would only add to her guilt. "Are *you* alright?"

"Yes, I'm fine. They're nearly finished with the reparations. But I won't make it back to London until much later tonight."

"Do you need me to pick you up?"

"No, that's alright. Dad said he would send Alby to pick me up." Albert was my father's personal butler and his family had been with the Youngs for years.

"Okay. I can't promise I'll be there when you arrive, but do text me when you make it home."

"I will. I'm sorry again—I *will* make it up to you."

I shook my head. "You're fine. Just get here safely. I'll speak to you later, alright?"

"Later."

She hung up just as I parked in my designated spot outside of my parent's main property and turned off the engine. I lingered in my car for a moment, gathering whatever energy I could muster before I had to face our father alone.

Usually, with Alice around, my father was decidedly more agreeable. She also led most of the conversations at the table and steered the attention away from me, with my mother chiming in occasionally. Which meant I could just quietly sit there and nod in agreement when needed.

But without her here, I was already dreading how this night would turn out.

A knock on my window jolted me out of my thoughts. I glanced over to my right to find Albert standing outside, his hands behind his back. He opened my door before I could reach for the handle.

"Good evening, Seungwon," he greeted me by using my Korean name—a rarity, as only a handful of people did since my father and I shared the same one.

I stepped out of my car and fastened my suit jacket, light snow beginning to fall around us. Snow in London in late December was relatively rare, but perhaps we'd have a white Christmas this year.

"Good evening, Albert," I replied. "How are the kids and Kareena?"

Albert had been married to his wife Kareena for twenty-five years and they had the two most precious daughters, Divya and Rhea, who were five and seven respectively.

Kareena was an exceptional baker who owned a small bakery in Camden Town and when I was younger, he would sneak in some of her pastries whenever my father's back was turned since my dad thought sugar would hinder the growth of my brain.

"They're well, sir. Thank you for asking," he said, closing the door behind me and gesturing for me to walk ahead of him.

I paused for a moment, taking in the stucco-fronted townhouse where I'd spent my teenage years. I was born and raised in Busan until we had to move here. I once used to love this place, until I realized my true role in this family and I'd grown to dread it.

I climbed the two steps, and the second I reached the porch, the grand black wooden double doors swung open. "My darling son," my mother greeted with her arms outstretched, her face beaming.

I stepped inside, removing my shoes and changing into house slippers. I leaned down to give her a hug before planting a small kiss on her cheek. "Hi, Mum. You okay?" I asked, pulling out of her embrace.

"Yes, darling. I'm much better now that you're here." She placed a hand on my cheek, and I leaned into her soft touch.

"I'm happy to see you too," I replied, offering her a smile.

She gave my cheek a gentle tap before I followed her down the broad hallway that led to the heart of the house. I glanced over my shoulder to thank Albert in the process, but he'd already slipped away, probably to the staff quarters on the lower ground of the house.

Once we made it to the main entrance hall, my father came down the sweeping staircase, its steps carpeted in a rich, emerald-green fabric. His hand glided over the mahogany rail of the iron banister he'd had imported when he'd built this place.

His appraising gaze roamed over me and though we had yet to exchange a word, I already knew he had something to critique me over.

A man's suit conveys to everyone in the room who they're dealing with.

Stand up straighter, no one will take you seriously otherwise.

Fix your hair, you look like you've just rolled out of bed.

His usual remarks echoed in my mind until he came to stand beside my mother, his hands tucked into his pockets.

"*Abeonim*[3]," I greeted him with a curt nod.

"*Adeul*[4]," he responded, his tone cool.

He wore his signature and impeccably tailored black suit, a stark contrast to my mother's light pink vintage Chanel two-piece tweed suit. The Youngs didn't believe in casual family dinner. Being dressed up, even at home, was part of our world.

My father used to tell me it was for the sake of potential impromptu guests and we needed them to never see us vulnerable. I never truly believed his explanation, but defying my father hadn't been on my list of priorities.

Well, that was until I turned eighteen and went to uni.

"Shall we move to the dining room?" my mother suggested with a

---

3 *Father (Korean)*
4 *Son (Korean)*

bright smile, attempting to lighten the tense silence. She wrapped her arm around my waist and I placed mine around her shoulder. "I made some of your favorites and by the looks of you, you need it." She always complained about me not eating enough.

I pulled her closer and planted a kiss on top of her head as we made our way past the stairs, down the long corridor, and into the reception room overlooking the south-facing terrace that led to the vast gardens.

The dining room, draped in dark wood-paneled walls, was illuminated by a grand, ornate chandelier, a soft warm glow casting over the room. The ceiling was adorned with intricate moldings and decorative flourishes, mirroring the room's furnishing.

At the center stood the long, dark wooden dining table, its edges carved in delicate patterns. The high-backed chairs around it were upholstered in cream fabric, embroidered with baroque designs, their dark wooden frames matching the table.

My father followed closely behind us, and I could feel his eyes boring into the back of my head, his heavy sigh of disapproval indicative enough that my mother and I were being too informal for his taste.

Displays of affection were never much his thing.

How my loving mother tolerated him was a mystery to me, but despite his serious and cold exterior, I knew my father loved her—another rarity in our world.

Despite their arranged marriage, my parents had broken the curse the others had been plagued with and had gradually fallen in love with each other over the years. I'd often caught my father's casting tender glances at my mum, or the subtle touches they shared when they thought no one was looking.

My father took his place at the head of the table while my mother sat to his right and I settled in to his left. We mostly enjoyed each course in silence, my mother occasionally probing me about work and ordering me to eat more, while my father merely nodded when she attempted to engage him in our conversation.

This was precisely why my sister was essential at these dinners.

Eventually, after an excruciating hour, the staff came to clear our plates. I prepared to excuse myself for the rest of the evening when my father spoke for the first time since he greeted me at the door.

He wiped the corners of his lips with the cream napkin and stood, discarding the linen on the table. "Meet me in my office," he ordered, striding out of the room without sparing me a glance or addressing me directly, but I knew he'd summoned me.

I let out a resigned sigh and ran a hand over my mouth.

My mother patted my hand on the table and I immediately knew what she would say. "Don't take his demeanor to heart," she started, her expression softening. "He means well."

Her words were always meant to be reassuring and comforting, but it never worked. I knew why she came to his defense, he was her husband after all. Yet sometimes I wished she knew everything to understand where the strain between my father and I stemmed from.

However, I didn't voice any of that to her as I squeezed her hand once and left.

The chosen spouses of members weren't privy to the House and what it entailed, unless extenuating circumstances dictated otherwise. Families coveted being married into one of ours because of the power and wealth that was inherited with the title of being attached to us.

But none had a clue of how *deep* our influence ran.

My father's office was situated on the third floor, so I opted for the lift to avoid making him wait—an oversight he would surely add to his list of grievances. Once upstairs, I made my way down the corridor, passing two large rooms that housed my father's library, until I reached the last door.

I fidgeted with the gold ring on my left pinky finger, engraved with the House's crest, a symbol each of us wore.

After taking a deep breath, I finally knocked on his door.

"Come in," my father called out.

I entered and closed the door softly behind me. He sat behind his large, ornate desk, positioned at the center of the room. Floor-to-ceiling windows flanked the space, each framed by rich, royal blue velvet drapes trimmed in gold, that pooled onto the floor and complemented the dark wooden accents that lined the room.

"You wanted to see me?" I asked in Korean, crossing the room and halting a few feet from his desk.

A single lamp glowed from the corner of his desk, where he seemed to be reviewing one of his client's case files, piles of papers neatly stacked across the large expanse of his mahogany desk.

My father was the managing partner at Young International, London's top corporate law firm. He also served as legal representation for Atlas Capital and its employees—a multibillion-pound hedge fund run by the Oualis who were the lineage to the youngest generation of Atlas.

He peered at me over his reading glasses, lifting his gaze from the papers he had in his hands. "Have a seat, Seungwon." He gestured to the chair across from him.

Doing as I was told, I propped my right ankle on my left knee and rested my hands in my lap. Anxiety slugged in my veins, but I made an effort to suppress it to avoid letting it show.

My father exuded this quiet authority where his mere presence commanded attention. Even his full head of silver-gray hair that was meticulously combed back didn't have a single strand out of place.

I'd grown up envying him and desiring to be the same. But that admiration had quickly changed the moment I'd turned thirteen and made my debut into society. My relationship with my father had never been conventional, but that year, it changed dramatically as if a switch had been flipped. The father who used to play football with me in our backyard and take my cousin Isaiah and I karting, transformed into this cold, and calculated stranger who fixated on one goal.

Shape me into the perfect Atlas.

My father's almond-shaped, dark brown eyes, identical to mine, scrutinized me in silence. I stayed quiet, waiting for him to reveal why he'd summoned me.

He dropped his file onto the desk and leaned back in his high-backed chair, upholstered in dark leather, removing his glasses and gently tossing them on the hardwood surface.

"How are you?"

From any other father, this would be considered a benign question. But our relationship, and the society we were a part of rendered it anything but trivial.

"Fine."

He hummed in response, his jaw set in a hard line at my curt answer. Which I knew he didn't appreciate. I knew he expected more, but I wasn't in the mood to pretend I cared tonight.

"Are you ready for your birthday?" he asked, a hint of expectation in his tone.

We were less than two months away from me receiving my Order, which would allow me to Ascend next year on my thirty-third birthday. Although he couldn't hint at anything regarding the task I'd be given, it wasn't uncommon for him to do these "check-ins" to ensure I wouldn't fail him.

God forbid that would happen.

As the eldest Atlas, the burden not to screw up had been placed upon me the moment my mother saw those two pink lines on a pregnancy test. Because my failure would be the ruin of everyone else that came after me.

I arched a brow. "Haven't you prepared me for it my entire life?"

His jaw twitched. "Watch your tone," he bit coolly.

I stifled the urge to talk back. Despite how much I really wanted to, it wasn't polite. I might have my differences with him, but he was still my father.

"I'll be ready," I reassured him.

"Good."

That was the most encouragement I'd get from him.

"If that's all, would you care if I excused myself."

He nodded curtly, effectively dismissing me and returning to his files.

I rose from my chair and hesitated, expecting him to say something, but he remained silent. I shook my head ever so slightly, and glanced at him one last time before promptly leaving his office.

I took the stairs and headed to the first floor to my mother's drawing room to let her know I was leaving. On my way out, she handed me a bag filled with containers of leftovers from dinner along with a large container of *kimchi-bokkeum* she'd prepared earlier in the week—a recipe my paternal grandmother had taught to her.

With a final goodbye, I slipped out of the room and made my way toward the entrance, Albert already waiting at the door as if he'd sense I would be leaving. The cool evening air greeted me when I stepped outside, a welcome contrast from the stifling atmosphere inside.

As I walked to my car, I couldn't shake off the tension that clung to me. My upcoming birthday loomed over me like a dark cloud, and with each passing day, the weight of my father's expectation grew heavier.

I paused for a moment, taking a deep breath to steady myself, but it was no use. So I climbed into my car and pulled onto the road, navigating the familiar pathway to my flat.

The thought of leaving all of this behind and abandoning my duty had crossed my mind countless times. But I could never bring myself to do it, not when I wouldn't be the only one affected by my decision.

And the consequences when they'd find me—because undoubtedly, they would—would be irreversible.

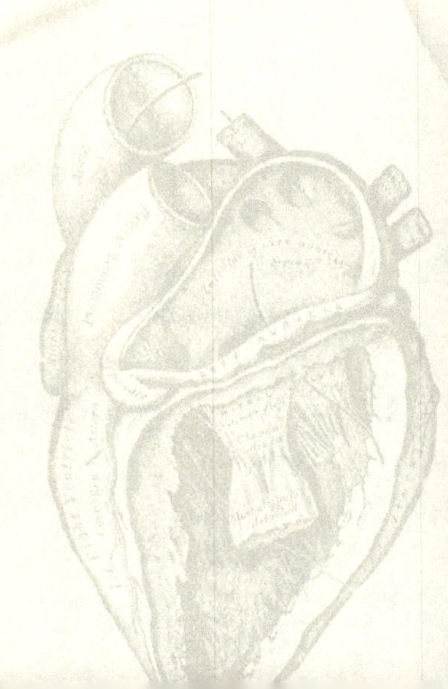

CHAPTER 3

AZARA

"HEY, KBIDA DIALI[5].

It's Mum. Just calling to see what time you think you'll be home. I'm off to the shop to pick up a few bits for dinner since babak[6] is running late, like he always is."

She let out a small laugh, and I felt a small smile pull at my lips at hearing it again.

"*Alright, I have to go. I will see you later tonight. Love you.*"

A tear slipped down my cheek as I pressed the replay button for the third time this morning on the last voicemail she'd left me, just moments before a driver collided with her after running a red light.

This time of the year was always hard, but for some reason, the weight attached to it felt more difficult today.

My mother had passed away fourteen years ago, yet whenever the anniversary of her death loomed closer, my grief felt as fresh as if we had been transported back to that fateful day.

---

5 *Sweetheart (Moroccan darija)*
6 *Your dad (Moroccan darija)*

I'd been so eager to get home and share the news that I'd been accepted into my top medical school. I'd received the letter earlier that day and had gone out to buy a few things to surprise them, so I'd ignored her previous call, telling myself that I would see her soon enough.

But the moment I'd stepped into our home, an eerie atmosphere had cloaked the air, almost suffocating. I'd called out for my father, noting that her car still hadn't been in the driveway, but there hadn't been any response. I'd searched for him in every room until I'd walked into our guest bathroom to find him on the floor, clutching Zayd to his chest so tightly, as if he was terrified he would vanish.

Little did I know that he'd just lost the love of his life.

I'd stood frozen in the doorway, confused as to why my father's face had been so pale, his eyes red-rimmed, when I'd never once in my life seen him cry. I still remembered the sense of disbelief that had washed over me when he'd uttered the words "your mother" and "killed" in the same breath. The words had sliced through my reality, reshaping everything I'd known.

I'd never experienced the loss of someone I loved before and the world around me had felt achingly hollow. Yet in that moment, I'd realized that I couldn't allow the grief to drown me. As I'd watched my father cradling my baby brother, I'd understood that our lives had been irrevocably changed and both of them would need me.

I had never been one to sit in my feelings or allow them to dictate my choices because it always left me feeling powerless of what would happen to me or the outcome of the situation I was faced with.

So I'd always chosen to ignore the initial swell of emotions I felt, shelving them for later, and focused instead on what needed to be done.

I'd only been seventeen at the time, but I'd taken it upon myself to care for both of them. And to this day, I still did.

Shaking myself from the sorrowful memory, I rose from the wooden bench in my kitchen and headed for my bedroom to change. It was Monday and I'd just gotten home from a weekend on-call. I usually relied on my job to keep my mind from drifting to thoughts of her and what December 23rd marked, but I'd gotten unlucky this year and had a fairly quiet weekend.

Instead of heading for a shower, I changed into a pair of high-waisted leggings and a long sleeve top. I needed to clear my head and the most effective way I knew how was to distract myself with something else. Because discussing or acknowledging my feelings seemed too difficult of a task.

I grabbed a fleece mockneck pullover from the entryway closet, pulled it on, and laced up my trainers. The morning air burned my face and seeped through the fabric of my clothes as I stepped out of my flat, but I ignored it.

I started to jog, my feet pounding against the wet pavement in a steady beat. I willed each stride to be an attempt to shake off the lingering shadows of grief, but it failed every time.

Images of my mother at the hospital flooded my mind, her lifeless body in that sterile, sickly white room, the acrid scent of antiseptic ingraining itself in my brain, as the doctors told us they'd done everything they could.

I shook my head, desperate to dispel myself from the haunting recollection. Turning a corner, I entered Regent's Park from its southern end and quickened my pace, occasionally passing other early morning runners. I'd lost track of how long I'd been going and the cold air combined with the biting wind made the fingers feel numb, but I welcomed the distraction as I pushed myself harder.

My heart raced faster, the pounding echoing in my ear, and I could practically hear my blood rushing through my veins as my vision blurred, but I didn't care.

I kept pushing myself, aware that it wasn't the wisest decision since I'd barely eaten after my shift, but I was more focused on forgetting than on what was sensible.

Just as I was about to turn another corner, I suddenly collided with something—*someone.*

I let out a gasp at the force of the impact, and my phone flew out of my hand, clattering against the pavement. Strong hands wrapped around my upper arms as the stranger who'd hit me helped steady me.

My eyes darted to my phone a few feet away, noting the now cracked screen. A sudden rush of anger, fueled by the adrenaline battering against my ribcage, washed over me. I looked up, ready to give them a piece of my mind but my scathing words caught in my throat when our eyes met, thoughts of my broken phone vanishing instantly.

Heat seeped through my shirt from where our bodies connected and pooled into my veins. I wasn't one to be rendered speechless by looks, but the man before me looked as if he'd just stepped off a runway.

A strong jawline framed with light stubble, high cheekbones and captivating full lips that I found myself lingering on longer than I should have. Even his dark, medium-length hair was just the right length at the top to run your hand through and grip tightly while he…

"You should be more careful," the stranger said. He tipped his chin down and although his expression was indifferent, there was a hint of annoyance in his tone.

I blinked once, unsure if I'd heard him right.

"You should be more careful before you run into another completely innocent bystander," he said louder this time, dragging out the last word like I couldn't understand.

His words felt like ice water had been poured over me, snapping me out of my trance. The utter audacity to reprimand me when *he* had been the one who'd ran into me.

I yanked myself free from his embrace. "I beg your pardon," I replied, bewildered by his response.

He took out one of his wireless earbuds as he raised an eyebrow, his expression unfazed. "Just watch where you're going next time," he said curtly before turning on his heel and continuing his run, leaving me standing there, momentarily stunned.

I watched him jog away, irritation bubbling up inside me with each distancing step he took. "Arsehole," I muttered under my breath, rolling my eyes as I bent down to pick up my phone.

The screen was worse than I'd thought. The cracks spiderwebbed across it, rendering it nearly unusable. I attempted a few times to unlock it, but it was useless. I'd have to get it fixed.

Fantastic. This is just what I needed.

My frustration lingered like a stubborn shadow, but I decided to take a deep breath, trying to let it go. There was no point in being angry when there was nothing I could do at this moment to solve my problem.

I straightened up and made my way out of the park, needing to go home and put some distance between me and this ridiculous encounter. Feeling slightly dizzy, I fished out one of the small packs of Skittles I always kept on me and shoved the entirety of the bag in my mouth.

As I walked back home, I kept replaying the incident in my head, picturing the man's nonchalance. Who was that arrogant this early in the morning and when *they* were at fault? He didn't even bother to feign remorse or acknowledge that he'd broken my phone.

My annoyance clung to me as I reached my flat and stepped into the shower. I hated it because why was I letting him get to me from such an insignificant encounter?

"ZIZOU, DID YOU SEE THAT?" my brother shouted from the pitch, his arms raised in triumph after scoring. He was far away from where Hazel and I were seated in the bleachers of Tassili Stadium, but we laughed and clapped in encouragement.

"Yes, I did," I replied, my voice echoing throughout the empty arena, but he'd already turned his attention back to the one-on-one game he was playing with Edward O'Donnell, the renowned goalkeeper for the Atlas FC who was one of my brother's all-time favorite players and my friend Hazel's fiancé.

Speaking of which. "I still can't believe your dad agreed to this," I said, glancing at her.

Hazel and I had been friends since our first year at uni. She knew how difficult the holidays were for us, and had managed to secure us private access to the stadium.

She shrugged, a playful smile on her face. "I'm his only daughter and good luck charm. He can never bring himself to tell me no, even when he tries."

I shook my head and chuckled at her response because she wasn't wrong. Diego Mendoza might be famous for being one of the greatest footballers in the history of the sport—from his incredible dribbling skills and speed to leading Argentina to their first victory in the World Cup in the nineties—but to Hazel, he was the doting father she had wrapped around her finger.

He'd also been the Atlas football club's manager for the past nine years, which was how we found ourselves at their home stadium the

Sunday after Christmas.

As for O'Donnell, well aside from being madly in love with Hazel, he owed her father one—especially after he'd fallen in love with his manager's daughter despite being warned to steer clear.

"We're never leaving here in time for the movie, are we?" Hazel asked, amused.

We'd planned to go see the latest Samia Farès film at our favorite little cinema in the heart of London, but I doubted we'd be able to convince my brother to leave this place.

"Count us lucky if we're out of here before the sun sets."

Zayd let out a jubilant scream as he stole the ball from Edward— or rather, Edward let him—and dashed toward the goal and scored once more. Warmth sprouted in my chest and I couldn't suppress the grin on my face at witnessing how happy my brother was at this. He was a massive fan of both the sport and the team, so this was a dream for him.

"I'm sorry your father couldn't make it today," Hazel said, a sad smile on her lips.

I shifted uncomfortably in my seat, pulling the blanket we'd borrowed from the facility closer to my chest. Hazel didn't mean any harm by bringing my father up, but her observation still stung.

We'd invited him to join us, as he was also a fan, but he'd given me his familiar excuse about being too busy.

Mum's passing had hit him the hardest. Even now, it felt as if a part of my father was gone the moment he'd gotten the news. I didn't think anyone could ever truly heal from losing the love of their life, but I had hoped he might eventually find his way back to even a fraction of who he once was.

Over the years, I'd done my best to shoulder our family and be the anchor, clinging to that hope, but it never seemed to come to reality. It was heartbreaking to see him like this and I wished there was something—*anything*—I could do to bring my dad back.

But instead, he buried himself in work to avoid the painful memories that came with what happened fourteen years ago. I understood his coping mechanism better than anyone because I often did the same. Keeping my focus on my job and becoming the best was a way to forget, but I'd learned to eventually recognize how I felt when I was more in control.

My father, on the other hand, refused to even talk about her. And that weighed heavily on everyone, especially Zayd. He'd been just a baby when she passed, and while I tried my best to share my memories of her, my dad knew her better than anyone.

I just wished he'd share more of her with us.

"You know how he is with work," I said quickly, before changing the subject. "Now, tell me about the wedding."

Hazel's face instantly lit up at the mention. She was always happy to talk about the latest party she was planning, but her excitement radiated off her whenever the topic of her September wedding came up in conversation.

A little over two years ago, Hazel had launched Rosada Events, and quickly became the city's most sought after luxury event planner after she organized Isaiah King's latest birthday party.

King, who was one of England's most eligible bachelors and a beloved Formula One driver, had sung Hazel's praises to anyone in the Paddock who'd listen and ever since, she'd been perpetually booked.

She reached for the seat beside her and pulled out her pink tablet, before facing me. While Hazel shared every detail she'd planned so far for her destination wedding, the boys played for another hour before Zayd finally ran out of energy and collapsed on the pitch, a wide grin plastered across his face.

We'd missed the first screening of the movie, but we'd managed to snag tickets for the last showing of the day. With two hours to spare, Hazel and I walked to the cafe around the corner where Hazel met Eddy for the first time while the boys got cleaned up at the facility.

"God, I'm starving," Hazel announced, her stomach growling as if to provide proof. We both burst out laughing as I held the door open for her.

Inside, the small restaurant, famous for its homemade empanadas and serving traditional *maté,* buzzed with energy. I'd never been here before, but Hazel always raved about it and had been trying to convince Nakia and I to come to the Argentinian spot for one of our monthly get-togethers.

We made our way to the counter, placed our rather large order, then snagged a table at the back to wait for our food. Eddy had just texted Hazel to say that they were on their way when my last name was called up.

I headed to the counter where a lovely older woman named Emilia informed me that our drinks were ready, but the food would be along shortly and be brought to our table.

I picked up the tray with the two beverages in their traditional gourd already prepared, a large thermos with extra hot water, and the soda I'd ordered for my brother, knowing the Argentinian drink would be far too bitter for him.

As I turned to head back, the bell above the front door chimed.

This might be them, I thought to myself, but when I turned to confirm if it was them walking in, my movement was abruptly interrupted when I collided into something.

Searing pain shot across my chest and I struggled to draw in a breath as the herbal tea splashed down the entire front of my blouse since I'd taken off my coat the moment we'd walked in.

"Bloody hell," a voice hissed.

The tray slipped from my fingers, the cups clattering to the floor somewhere near my feet. "*Wili*[7], *wili, wili*," I muttered repeatedly, pulling the silk fabric off my chest to avoid first-degree burns.

"Are you alright?" a strangely familiar voice asked.

What a ridiculous question that was. Scalding herbal tea had just soaked my front, and this stranger was asking if I was okay?

No, I wasn't, dickhead.

I took a deep breath to rein in my emotions. When I finally looked up, the frustration I'd managed to restrain flared again as I recognized the set of eyes staring back at me.

Not him again.

The annoyingly handsome and rude stranger who'd broken my phone after running into me a few days ago was standing in front of me, his mouth morphing into annoyance. I rolled my eyes and scoffed. He had no right to be *anything*. I was the one with tea all over her.

"Are you stalking me?" I asked, irritation boiling beneath my skin. Running into him—quite literally might I add—once could've been a coincidence, but twice was becoming suspicious.

"Stalking you?" he frowned, clearly taken aback by my accusation.

"Yes, stalking me. This is the second time you've run into me. Do you ever watch where you're going?" I snapped.

"Me? That's quite rich, considering *you're* the one not paying attention to where you're going."

My eyes widened. "Excuse me?"

Chivalry was clearly dead and buried seven feet under hell. This was exactly why I didn't like men. They were only good for one thing and it certainly wasn't for keeping their mouth shut.

He crossed his arms over his broad chest, the sleeves of his jacket

---

7 *Oh my god! (Moroccan Darija)*

inching up to reveal a hint of tattoos.

Why do the most attractive men have this uncanny ability to make you want to throttle them?

"I said—"

I snapped out of my thought and interrupted him with a laugh of disbelief. "Oh, I heard you," I said, turning to walk away.

But I paused and instead closed the distance between us, leaning in. Hearing the small hitch of his breath sent a thrill of satisfaction gliding over my skin.

"Just a piece of advice for the next time you plough into another innocent civilian," I whispered. His eyes darted down for a brief second before he locked his gaze with mine again. I noticed the small flush rising in his cheeks, but ignored it as I continued, "Don't be such an arsehole and learn to apologize instead of berating them for something you *clearly* caused."

With that, I turned away only to find a small audience had been watching our exchange, Hazel being one of them. Her eyes were wide as she signed to ask if I was okay. She knew I wasn't keen on confrontation and having an audience to witness it made it all the more uncomfortable.

"Can you believe this guy?" I signed back, still in disbelief.

Hazel had been born deaf so shortly after we met her, Nakia and I had started learning British Sign Language. Although she wore a single cochlear implant, we often used it whenever she needed a break from the sensory overload she experienced from wearing it or in moments like these.

She handed me a few napkins as I approached her. Eddy and Zayd walked through the door just as I began to attempt salvaging the top I'd just bought a few days ago.

They both rushed over to us. "What happened?" they asked in

unison.

I glanced over at them and shook my head. "Nothing, just an accident," I lied, not wanting to recount what just happened and risk a barrage of questions from either of them.

Eddy's skeptical expression clearly suggested he wasn't buying it. He exchanged a glance with Hazel who signed that she'd explain everything to him later.

That's when I remembered the mess that must be all over the floor and moved to tidy it up only to discover that it had already been sorted. I scanned the area to find the small group that had been watching us was also gone.

Even the clumsy stranger was nowhere in sight.

"Are you sure you're alright?" Hazel whispered, concern etched on her face as she passed me more napkins.

"I'll be fine," I insisted as I attempted to dab more of the liquid from my shirt. "I'll be back," I told her before following the signs to the loo.

Once inside the tiny room, I looked at the extent of the damage in the mirror and grimaced at my reflection. There was a large, dark brown stain *directly* over my breasts.

Just brilliant. Things just keep getting better.

With a heavy sigh, I turned on the faucet and removed my top, attempting to rinse the fabric. But all I managed to achieve was a damp mess that seemed to only make the stain stand out even more.

After several minutes of futile effort, I grabbed a handful of paper towels, doing my best to blot at the stain. The blouse was beyond saving, but at least by the time I finished, it was somewhat dry and had faded to a light green.

When I emerged from the toilet, I found all of them seated at the table with a fresh round of drinks and our food spread out before them.

We'd ordered four of each empanada, hoping it would be enough for all of us. But judging by the way Eddy and Zayd had already devoured half of it, we'd likely need to order more.

I slid into the seat next to Zayd, doing my best to push the earlier incident from my mind. I managed to keep it at bay throughout our meal, during the film, and even as I dropped my brother off at home.

But the moment my head hit the pillow that night, the only thing that seemed to occupy my thoughts was the stranger I'd had the misfortuned luck of crossing paths with one too many times.

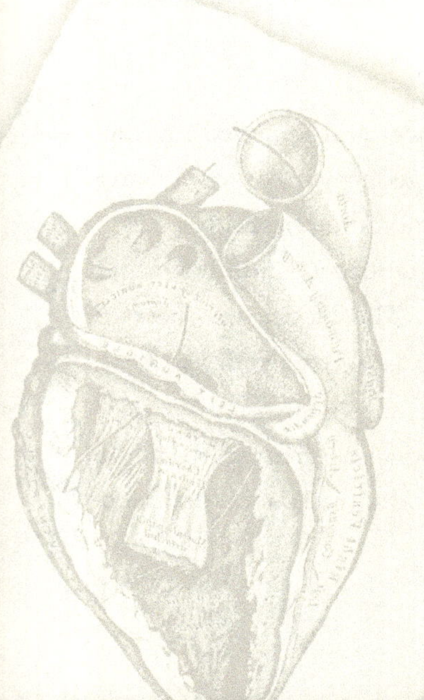

CHAPTER 4

MICHAEL

I WAS IN THE MIDDLE of a deep slumber when the shrill cry of my ringtone reverberated through the stillness of my bedroom. With a groan, I aimlessly reached for my bedside table and fumbled for my mobile.

As I slowly opened my eyes, the harsh glare of the screen made me squint. Who was calling me at this ungodly hour? I wasn't starting my new position as the lead consultant at Amanar until tomorrow so no one else would call me at this time unless…

The moment I saw that the call was from a blocked caller, I jolted upright in bed, clearing my throat before swiping to answer.

"*Neh abeonim*[8]."

"255 Hackney Rd," my father said in greeting before abruptly ending the call.

I loathed these phone calls. It had been months since the last one,

---

8 *"Yes, father" (Korean)*

but I knew it was only a matter of *when* not *if* before I'd be summoned again. A flicker of my rebellious old self resurfaced for a moment and entertained the idea of ignoring the order, but I knew better than to go against my father, let alone the House.

As an Atlas, the House expected three things from you. Ascend. Obey orders given by your elders. And finally, keep your mouth shut.

With a resigned sigh, I got out of bed, headed for the en suite bathroom and took a brisk cold shower to shake off the drowsiness. I had no idea of the extent of the injuries I'd have to deal with so I'd need all the help I could get.

I quickly donned a pair of trousers and a black dress shirt before retrieving the bag I always kept at the ready for calls like these from the back of my closet. Then, after grabbing a coat since the temperatures in London had been drastically cold, I headed toward the lift at the end of the long hallway.

Taking the private lift to my designated underground parking level that each penthouse in the building I lived in came with, I pulled my phone out to check the time—it was 1:30 a.m. Once the doors slid open, I pocketed my phone and strode over to the side wall where different sets of keys hung in a glass compartment.

I wasn't one to flaunt my wealth, and rarely splurged, but cars were the one thing I indulged in. Particularly old classics. My collection included some of the rarest models, but tonight wasn't the time for showing them off. I tapped in the code to unlock the compartment and grabbed the keys to the least conspicuous vehicle I owned. Stepping into the dimly lit room, the scent of polished metal and leather clung in the air as I walked to the other end.

The overhead lights glinted off the sleek lines of my black motorcycle. I rarely used it anymore, but out of all the vehicles I owned, Levi was my favorite. Yes, I'd given him a name. Attack on Titan was one of my favorite manga series and the name seemed fitting.

The roar of the engine hummed to life as I inserted the key and turned the ignition. After strapping the bag to my back, I entered the address my father had given me into the navigation system and made my way out.

The streets were eerily quiet at this hour, the crisp night air wrapping over my body as I sped through the streets of London. I drove as fast as I could, but still kept it within the speed limits to avoid being caught. Last thing I needed was to explain to the authorities where I was going and arrive late to wherever my father was waiting for me.

Veering slightly to the left, I finally merged onto the main road and made my way down Hackney. As I approached the address, I parked a few streets away, not wanting to draw attention. I climbed off my motorcycle and stored my helmet under the seat before heading toward the place.

I'd never been to this area before. Locations changed with every call and given the House owned a significantly large part of the country, it wasn't difficult for them to remain discreet and have access to countless warehouses for their various needs.

The neighborhood was relatively quiet, the only sound being the distant hum of a few late-night citizens. Just as I neared the building, my phone suddenly buzzed with an incoming call. Assuming it was my father, I answered without glancing at my screen.

"I'm a minute away," I informed him in Korean.

Instead of the expected stern reprimand, loud music blared from the other end. Amar's laugh filtered through the line before he quipped, "I hate to disappoint, but it's just me."

I raised a brow, surprised to hear from him. "You realize it's nearly two in the morning."

Amar Belkacem was the second oldest Atlas and the most annoying person I'd ever had the misfortune of having in my life. I loved him like a brother, but he always had an uncanny knack for bothering me at the most inopportune moments.

"Relax, grandpa," he teased as I heard the sound of a door slamming shut before the music grew slightly more dull. "It's the New Year, you too should be out celebrating."

"As much as I'd *love* to indulge you, I just got a call."

"Another late-night booty call," he chuckled.

I arrived at the designated building and glanced around to see if anyone had followed me. If I took any longer, my father would berate me until my ears bled. "Listen, unless this is for an emergency, I need to go before my head ends up delivered on a platter for you and your next in line."

Just as I was about to end the call, his tone shifted, taking on a more serious note. "I might need a favor."

"For heaven's sake, what have you done this time?" I asked with a heavy sigh.

Amar had a talent for landing himself in trouble. We all had strict rules to abide by and although he'd never technically broken any, he seemed to find it exhilarating to toe the line with every single one of them. He acted like this was all a game for his sole entertainment. I couldn't even begin to count the number of times I'd had to get him out of situations that would have had him terminated if any of the Elders found out.

The fact that he was still alive was truly a miracle.

He clucked his tongue. "Why do you always think I've done something?"

"Amar, stop wasting my time," I replied sharply.

"Fine. I need a hundred and fifty thousand pounds."

"What the hell do you need that kind of money for?" I asked, running a hand over my face. The sum didn't faze me, it was just money and we all had it in abundance. But I couldn't help but wonder what he'd done to require that much so quickly.

"I may or may not be at Thorn and just lost a poker game to Marcus."

I pinched the bridge of my nose, trying to quell the surge of frustration. Everyone in the city knew the club's reputation and how Marcus Blackthorn, its owner, was notorious for being a complete scam. He always cheated and wouldn't let you leave the premises until you settled your debts.

"Amar," I warned.

"Yes, yes, I'm aware. Little Marcus is the bad, bad wolf. But the wanker deserved a lesson. I was winning until he began accusing me of cheating. Me. Of cheating. Can you believe this arsehole? He—"

"Amar, get to the point," I interrupted, knowing I'd be here all night listening to him ramble on about how much he hated the man. You wouldn't think so with how often Amar frequented Marcus's establishment.

"Normally, I'd handle it, but if my father sees that much disappearing from the account, he'll ask questions that he won't like the answers to and I'd rather not disappoint him more than I already have," he teased but I noted the slight wavering in his tone that was always there when his father, Nacer, was brought up in conversation.

Amar never openly spoke about his relationship with his parents, but I'd always sensed he'd been hiding something for as long as I'd known him.

"I would resort to more *physical* means, but we all remember what happened the last time I did. If we have a repeat of last year, he'll actually have a coronary this time. And as much as I dislike the man, I'd prefer him to be breathing."

"Why didn't you ask for Sofiane's help? He's the computer whiz."

Sofiane Ouali was four years my junior, making him the youngest and last Atlas.

He worked as a software engineer at his father's multi-billion pound hedge fund company, Atlas Capital. He had a knack for computers and could have easily hacked into any account at the bank to wire the money without a trace. We'd done it countless times before to settle scores with anyone who'd crossed us growing up.

"I hope I'm not hurting your feelings when I say you weren't my first call."

"Just send me the account number, I'll deal with it," I said, not wanting to waste any more time than I already had. "Try to be less reckless next time."

I hung up before he would respond, knowing he'd likely come up with some ridiculous retort. Almost immediately, my phone pinged with a text message from him.

I wired the money to the account he'd provided, using a foreign account I'd set up for emergencies just like these and that wouldn't be traced back to any of us. After the first ten times he'd asked for help, I'd learned it was easier to be prepared.

I received another message from him but I ignored it and turned my phone off to avoid any further interruptions. After tucking it into the pocket of my jacket, I pushed open the heavy black iron gate and made my way up the steps to the front door. I knew the property would already be unlocked so I pushed it open.

I stepped inside and locked the door behind me, a sudden heavy silence wrapping around me like a thick fog. The building seemed to be unoccupied and newly acquired by the unmistakable smell of fresh paint lingering in the air. The walls were bare, and painted a stark white. There were a few light fixtures suspended from the ceiling, though none were turned on.

The moonlight streaming from large windows on the left side as well as the large skylight were the only source of light as I moved down the corridor. At the end of it, a grand, looped steel staircase led to what seemed to be a basement.

I leaned over the banister, peering down, and noticed three doors, a sliver of light spilling from beneath one of them. As I headed down the stairs, hushed voices filtered through that same door.

Taking a deep breath to steady myself before facing whoever was on the other side, I pushed it open. The room that greeted me was steeped in shadows, illuminated only by two flickering surgical lights that cast a pale yellow glow over the walls and the three figures standing before me.

Nacer Belkacem. Abdelrahim Ouali. And my father.

Collectively known as the Elders.

They were the previous generation of Atlases and the ones we were bound to honor with our Ascension.

A flicker of dread brushed against my spine but I quickly pushed it away.

Unless it was a societal event they were required to attend to ascertain their power, they were rarely ever all together in the same room. They showed a united front to the world, but unlike Amar, Sofiane and I, they were not friends.

At least, not anymore.

As boys, we'd often eavesdropped on their arguments behind closed doors, each blaming the other for some accident that had happened years ago. We'd been strictly forbidden from prying into the matter or asking any questions about it.

To this day, all we knew was that the very structure of the House had shifted during their generation, because before us, there were four

Atlas families.

Until one was banished.

"You're late," my father stated, nonchalantly shoving a hand into his pocket. His expression didn't betray any irritation, but I'd observed him long enough to recognize the simmering anger beneath the surface.

It's only been seventeen minutes and I live nearly thirty minutes away, I wanted to say but I kept my mouth shut. My father had little tolerance for defiance, especially in front of company. It would suggest that he was incapable of keeping his son in check to the others. I'd already done enough of that in my early twenties to learn my lesson.

Without a word, all three stepped aside, revealing a black operating table with an unconscious man laying on it. White medical restraints bound both his wrists and ankles, while an IV line was attached to his left arm. He was also connected to a monitor, the faint beep of his heart rate filling the room.

The stranger had blood coating almost his entire body that from where I stood, I couldn't tell where the source of it was.

Amar's father thrust a file toward me, and I took a step forward, taking it from him. "Fix it, and when you're finished, send a text message to the number at the back. The rest will be handled," Belkacem instructed, before they all filed out of the room.

My father brushed past me, whispering in Korean that he expected nothing less than perfection before following after them.

The moment the door clicked shut, the tension in my shoulders dissipated.

I closed my eyes for a brief moment before opening the file and approaching the patient. My eyes scanned over the single sheet of information I had been provided. Thirty-seven year old male with no known allergies and a medical history consisting solely of an appendectomy at the age of twelve.

Most patients brought to me were relatively healthy, though occasionally they'd bring someone with a multitude of complications, expecting me to perform a miracle. I was a God in the operating theater, but I had a skilled team and the latest equipment money could buy.

What I was given here was always the bare minimum. The Elders were lucky I never backed down from a challenge and didn't deliver anything less than perfection, but that didn't always prevent losses.

As usual, there were no names or photographs. I glanced at what remained visible of his face. He appeared familiar, but I couldn't quite place where I'd seen him before.

But it didn't matter who he was.

I made my way to the small table at the back of the room and placed both the file and my bag upon it. After changing into a pair of disposable scrubs, I secured my hair away from my face with a scrub cap, gathered my personal instruments, and got to work.

The next two and half hours passed in a blur as I operated on the stranger. After my assessment, I'd discovered deep lacerations marred his entire torso along with a ruptured spleen that I'd detected with the portable ultrasound I'd brought with me.

After suturing his wounds and removing the damaged organ, I meticulously closed him up to ensure minimal scarring. Satisfied with my work, I tidied the area, discarding any used material along with my used scrubs into the steel container behind the operating table.

I found a small ensuite bathroom attached to the room I'd operated in, hastily washing my hands before changing back into my clothes. By the time I sent the text message to the number Belkacem had instructed me to and left the building, it was already 5:00 a.m.

I had to be at work in less than three hours and had barely gotten any sleep earlier. Rubbing my eyes from fatigue, I mounted my motorcycle and headed home for a quick shower and an extra hour of rest.

It was nearly 8:00 a.m. when I eventually walked through the doors of the hospital. I'd only been here once in the past, filling in for another surgeon who had fallen ill a few months back.

But everyone knew of Amanar General Hospital. It was the pinnacle of medical excellence, and every aspiring doctor dreamed of working here.

I hadn't turned down AGH's offer to train here because I hadn't wanted to; in fact, it had been quite the opposite. I'd always dreamed of being a surgeon here, but when I'd discovered it was my father's top choice and he'd expected me to come to the same decision, everything in me rebelled against the idea.

Everything in me at the time rebelled against *anything* that he wanted.

So, when the time came to accept an offer, I'd chosen the only hospital I knew my father would disapprove of. My decision had been undoubtedly influenced by the satisfaction I felt at vexing my father, but Orion had afforded me the opportunity to carve my own identity away from his shadows and the suffocating feeling of duty I'd felt compelled to when it concerned the House.

For almost a decade, I'd enjoyed that freedom, but unfortunately for me, that time was now coming to an end. I had no idea what my Order would entail and what I'd be expected to perpetrate.

My father hadn't explicitly influenced my decision in accepting the lead consultant position I'd been offered by AGH—he wasn't authorized to—but my intuition told me the assignment I'd be given next month before my thirty-second birthday had everything to do with this place.

Amar, Sofiane and I had all been groomed for a specific field, expected to acquire a particular set of skills that would become valuable to the House. Amar had a gift for arts, Sofiane with computers and I, of course, had the brains. But despite knowing our education would potentially serve us to complete our Ascension, none of us knew to what extent.

Or if they would even be relevant.

So albeit reluctantly, I made my way down the large entrance hall, passing by the security office to collect my new credentials. I then climbed the stairs and made my way to the staff lifts on the other side, swiping my badge to access them and heading over to my new medical director's office.

Adnan Ziani was a renowned vascular surgeon and the current medical director at Amanar General. He'd invented the Ziani method for which he'd received countless awards over the years. Any other doctor in his position would have long retired after years of working, but I'd heard he'd been refusing to do so, stating his love for the job and the desire to stay as long as he'd be capable.

The doors slid open with a soft chime onto the ninth floor, and I stepped out onto the bustling corridor of the surgical ward. Staff was scattered everywhere. Some were typing on computers, while others came in and out of patients' rooms.

A wave of whispers broke from a group of nurses gathered around the nursing station as I walked by, and I aimed a smile toward their curious glances.

I gave them a curt nod in acknowledgment and made my way down the ward toward Ziani's office. Our meeting was just a formality since he'd already given me the position, but we'd never properly met. We'd exchanged a few emails over the years and I'd finally relented to his last offer.

I rounded the corner and stood in front of his office, his nameplate gleaming on the door, before knocking lightly on it.

"Come in," a voice from within called out.

I opened the door and stepped into the room to find him grabbing a folder from a filing cabinet and moving toward his desk. "What's the matter?" he asked without looking up from his papers and running a hand over his black buzzed hair. He wore black trousers with a white dress shirt that were too large on his figure. Like he'd lost weight recently but hadn't changed his wardrobe.

Stress emanated from his posture, but with his job, it was understandable.

"I believe we ought to meet," I said playfully, closing the door behind me and planting my most charming smile on my face.

He finally looked up and smiled warmly when recognition settled in. "Mr. Young, we've been impatiently waiting for you," he said, his empty hand outstretched as he walked toward me. "Your reputation precedes you."

"I hope it's only good things," I teased, grabbing his hand in a firm handshake.

"Yes, indeed. Please, take a seat," he replied, gesturing for me to sit as he settled in his large leather chair. Placing the file he had in hand on his desk, he focused his attention on me as I slipped into the chair in front of him.

"How were your holidays?"

"Good," I replied. I would have asked him about how his went, but the way he eagerly interjected the moment the word "good" had left my mouth told me he probably didn't want to discuss it.

"Well, I'm glad to hear," he said with a little too much enthusiasm. He leaned back in his chair and pushed his black rectangular glasses up with his index finger. "Listen, I won't bore you with formalities. Your work at Orion was impeccable and I know you'll emulate the same here."

I nodded, not feeling the need to add to his statement. I was great at what I did, he'd said it himself.

"I know in our last correspondence I'd said you'd only officially start as of next week so you'd have enough time to get acquainted with the team and the hospital and its policies, but we have an important patient in our private wing," he explained, sliding a folder across the desk.

I took it, my eyes scanning the patient's file as I listened to him explain the case.

"The Prime Minister was admitted this morning for an acute aortic dissection. His surgery is scheduled for later this afternoon and we have our best surgeon on the case, but if you're up for it, we'd love for you to assist."

I could do this surgery in my sleep, but he wasn't asking me because of my competence. Any complications on a member of the government would be bad publicity for the hospital. One decent surgeon was good, but having two ensured a better success rate.

I met his gaze and said without hesitation, "Absolutely. I'd rather be spending my day in the theater than spend it reading hospital policies," I said with amusement in my tone.

"Very well then." He chuckled, standing from his seat. "Let me give you a tour and then I'll have you meet the surgical team you'll be taking charge of."

I stood, following closely behind him. I opened the door for him but before I could move and gesture for him to go first, a body stumbled against mine.

"Good lord," I heard muffled against my chest before delicate hands gripped my shirt to regain balance. My hands had already found her waist, my fingers digging into her sides to help.

"Are you alr—" I started saying, but the words died on my tongue as I came face to face with the woman that had been plaguing my mind from the moment I ran into her.

It can't be.

Her hair was tied up in a bun instead of down in loose curls like the last time I'd seen her at the coffee shop, and she wore green scrubs, a black full-zip fleece jacket over it, instead of a blouse and jeans, but it *was* her.

The girl from the coffee shop and that day I went for a run in Regent's Park.

She had the same dark hair, the same full lips with a defined cupid's bow that made you want to bite it and the same mesmerizing gaze that was currently boring a hole through my face as she glanced up.

The expression that crossed her face was downright murderous when realization sparked in her deep brown eyes.

"You."

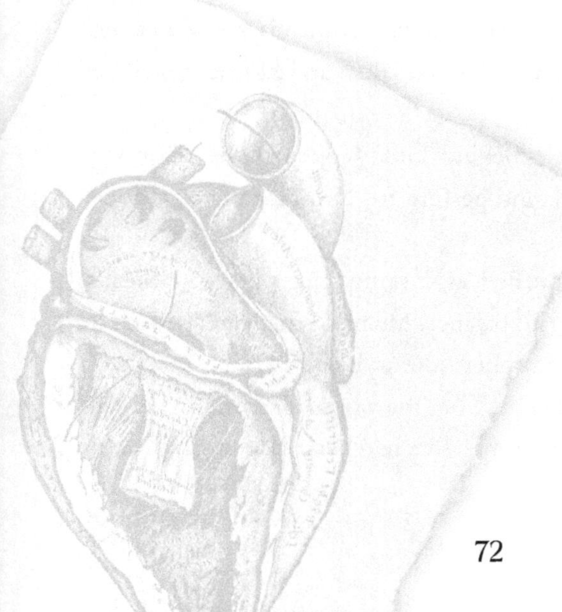

CHAPTER 5

AZARA

I WAS CURSED.

That was the only plausible explanation for crossing paths with this man now *three* times in the span of a couple weeks. Or perhaps I must have committed some terrible transgression in a past life that I'd earned this unfortunate fate.

Breathe, Azara.

I'd managed to spare a few minutes before my ward rounds, so I'd decided to stop by my dad's office for a quick hello and to make sure he'd remembered to eat something before starting his day. He had a habit of forgetting, so I'd made it a part of my routine to come by his office at least once each shift before diving into my work day.

The last thing I had expected was this.

"Have you two met before?" my father asked, jolting me out of my thoughts. I hadn't even noticed he was standing there.

I pushed the stranger—who I had the extreme urge to strangle—

away and created a healthy distance between us before he broke my phone again or somehow materialized a hot drink to spill all over my scrubs.

"No," I replied, at the same time *he* said, "Yes."

My father's brows knitted together in confusion.

"No, we haven't," I insisted, casting a brief threatening glare at the stranger before turning my attention to my father who still looked confused. "I was merely passing by to say hello before rounds."

My dad joined me in the hallway outside of his office and placed a hand over my shoulder, giving it a gentle squeeze. He was rarely affectionate at work, especially in front of others, so this was about as close as he got.

He looked from me to the man who was becoming the bane of my existence. "Dr. Young, this is my daughter Dr. Ziani," he introduced, then shifted his attention back to me. "Azara, this is our new lead consultant in the department."

I knew my father would be meeting this Dr. Young at some point today, but when he'd mentioned I'd be closely working with a new surgeon, the infuriating stranger I'd had the displeasure of already meeting had been the last person I'd ever anticipated.

I can't deny the temptation to look my future coworker up hadn't crossed my mind, but each time I'd opened my search engine, my pride had taken over and I'd swiftly closed it. I didn't want to give it any more energy than I'd needed to.

Now, I was regretting it.

"Seungwon Young, but you can call me Michael. It's a pleasure to meet you," the stranger said with a hint of flirtation lacing his tone as he extended his hand.

I eyed it for a moment; my instinct was to ignore it, but I could feel my father's gaze burning the side of my head, his words from a few weeks ago echoing in my mind.

Be nice, Azara.

With a resigned sigh, I took his hand. I dismissed the jolt of electricity that shot up my spine at the contact and shook his hand briefly before withdrawing it. "Dr. Ziani. Welcome to the team, Dr. Young," I said, ignoring his informality. We weren't friends.

Dr. Young's lips curved into a smirk at my brusqueness.

"Right, well… I should get to work, " I said, and turned on my heel, desperate to escape.

I'd barely taken a step down the corridor when my father called after me, "Azara."

I closed my eyes, cursing under my breath before glancing back over my shoulder

"Yes?"

"Just one moment," he said, nodding at Dr. Young, who was watching me with an unsettling mix of curiosity and amusement. My father closed the small distance I'd managed to create between them and me. "I'll have someone cover your rounds. I think you should show Dr. Young around the facility before you two head to Prime Minister Buxton's room to check on him. Michael will be assisting you with the surgery."

My eyes subtly widened in shock. I didn't even know what to focus on. That I'd have to play tour guide or the fact that another surgeon would be *helping* me perform a surgery.

"With me?" I asked, because surely I must have misheard him. "What do you mean, *with me*?"

"You know how important this case is for the hospital. Dr. Young will be your second pair of hands in the theater," he explained, a stern look on his face that left no room for arguments.

"Do you not trust me?" I asked, slightly stung that he might think

I wouldn't manage on my own or do a good enough job.

I hadn't done this surgery a million times, but I'd done it enough to be confident in my skills. I knew I was one of the best surgeons at Amanar, and my father had never asked someone else to supervise, let alone assist me in surgeries.

He looked taken aback by my question. "I do trust you, Azara, and you're a brilliant surgeon. But I need the hospital to present a united front. He's your new consultant, and until you finish your hours, you'll be reporting to him."

None of his explanations made sense. Amanar was the best hospital in the city; I would venture to say it was the best in the country. Why did my father feel the need for us to show a united front when we already did?

But for now, none of that mattered.

I let out a resigned sigh and gave him a curt nod of understanding.

"Good," he said before I steeled myself and began walking away. When I realized my new boss wasn't following me, I turned back.

"Well, are you coming? I don't have all day," I said curtly, a brow raised.

Dr. Young gave my father a charming smile, telling him they'd talk later before he walked over to me, the smile never leaving his lips.

Which only fueled my annoyance even more.

I subtly rolled my eyes as he came to stand next to me. My gaze roamed up and down his figure, assessing him.

He leaned his body slightly closer to mine. "Like what you see," he said, his voice smooth and slightly teasing.

I took a step back and checked that my father was back in his office. Once I made sure the coast was clear, I glared at who I'd unfortunately have to report to for the next year. He towered over my five foot six, but I didn't let it deter me from what I needed to tell him.

"Listen, I'm not buying or interested in your charming boy next door tactics," I said, waving my hand in front of me. "I don't care that you're technically my boss, I've been at this hospital for a decade and I won't let anyone, let alone you of all people, tell me what to do or how to run this department."

I waited for him to nod in agreement before I had to take him through this tour and how I'd envisioned today's procedure. But instead of giving me the reaction I'd expected, he erased the remaining distance between our bodies and leaned his head down.

"I think you'd like being told what to do," he murmured.

My mind raced with a mix of frustration and disbelief. And unfortunately for me, a hint of arousal. I wanted to ignore what he said or how it sent goosebumps erupting across my entire body, but I wouldn't let him have the upper hand.

So instead, I quickly scanned our surroundings to make sure no one was around before I leaned closer, our lips almost touching.

I locked my gaze with his and whispered, "Wouldn't you like to know?"

Then, I left him standing there, stunned, and set off down the corridor.

"I'M THINKING OF LEAVING EDDY," I heard Hazel say and my head immediately snapped to where she was sitting.

"You're what?" I asked, a mix of shock and worry filling me. Hazel had been with Eddy for three years now and they were getting married next September. They were so in love with each other, it was sickening. So for her to even think about leaving was unfathomable. "What happened? What did he do? Because if he hurt you, I swear—"

"So now you're listening?" Hazel said, her eyes narrowed.

"I *was* listening," I lied, hoping she couldn't tell.

"Yeah?" Nakia asked with a brow raised.

I maintained a neutral expression, sitting straighter and hoping my stance would convey confidence because I had no idea what or who they'd been discussing.

Nakia, Hazel, and I were at Rubis Rouge, our favorite local pub, for one of our girls' nights. We were all busy with our jobs, but we'd always made sure to see each other in person at least once a month. Nakia and Hazel both had more flexible schedules, so they'd often followed mine and since this was my only weekend off in January, we'd decided to jump on the occasion.

And I desperately needed the distraction.

"Then tell us what I just said," Hazel added, crossing her arms over her chest and looking at me with the same skeptical look Nakia was giving me. Or at least, she was trying to.

"Yeah, okay. I wasn't listening," I said, relenting.

"Is this about that hot new doctor?" Hazel said, and I shot her a pointed look.

Nakia glanced back and forth between us, unsure what Hazel was referring to. I'd made the mistake of slipping up and mentioning Michael's name over the phone last night as I'd driven home after my horrible shift with him.

I hadn't told her much before ending the call, but for the little bits I *had* told her, she'd sworn on Blue's life—her frenchie mix she'd rescued a few months ago after seeing it at a shelter and deciding she needed to have it immediately—she wouldn't say anything to Nakia.

Guess that was all in vain now but I should have known better. It wasn't like Hazel was known for her secret-keeping skills.

"What hot doctor? Are you two keeping something from me?"

Hazel held her hands up. "I don't know much either," she said, in her defense. "Our Azara over here pretended her phone died last night when I started asking too many questions."

"Hazel," I muttered under my breath, closing my eyes and groaning in exasperation.

I'd said yes to tonight because this was exactly what I'd needed a distraction from, but I should have known better. Hazel loved anything that was related to love, and Nakia, well, she loved making fun of my predicaments.

"Now, I need you to tell me everything," the latter insisted, waving at our server for another round, before she leaned back into her high chair and crossed one leg over the other, her intertwined manicured fingers resting against her lap.

Why did I say yes to going out tonight?

"Are you guys really teaming up on me?" I said with a hint of mock hurt in my tone, trying to divert the attention away from me.

Hazel's stance softened, and she reached over to place a hand over mine. "No, we would n—" She started, but Nakia interrupted her.

Fuck, it almost worked.

"Hazel, don't fall for her theatrics, she's just distracting us," Nakia said, firm on needing me to confess.

"Me?" I said, clutching my chest. "Why would you accuse me of such—"

She raised her brow, and I sighed heavily, knowing I'd lost this battle the moment Hazel said the words "hot doctor."

"Fine," I finally said, downing the rest of my glass of red Bordeaux.

I then proceed to tell them everything that had happened yesterday. I'd hoped after I'd left Dr. Young in front of my father's office, he'd give up and leave me alone for the rest of the day. That he'd ask my father to just watch the procedure and that he'd operate another day.

Unfortunately for me, as it seemed to be the case every time he and I crossed paths, he'd followed me and asked more questions than necessary through each department I'd shown him.

I'd had to bite my tongue and suppress the urge to roll my eyes after every word he'd said. He'd been even more insufferable when we'd walked in the Prime Minister's private suite, acting like he'd been *his* patient.

And Buxton fell for Dr. Young's charms.

Why was everyone so enamored by this man?

It had taken everything in me not to break my oath in that room. If only a scalped had been nearby, I could have—

"You should fuck him," Nakia said, interrupting my train of thought.

I snapped my gaze toward where she sat across from me. "I'm sorry, I should what? Because surely I misheard you."

"No, you heard me perfectly well. Sleeping with him would solve all of your problems," she explained, like it was a logical proposal.

"I'll be doing no such thing,"

"Why? Hate is a powerful source for great orgasms."

I groaned. "My goal is to avoid him, not spend more time with him."

"I didn't say spend time with him, I said f—"

I reached over the table and placed a hand over her mouth, the rest of her sentence muffled under my palm. "Nakia, *please* stop."

That earned me a laugh from Hazel who was sitting on my right. I shot her a glare and she cleared her throat. "Sorry," she signed.

I rolled my eyes and turned my attention back on Nakia. "I'm going to take my hand away, but before I do, you have to solemnly swear that you will never put the concept of the hot doctor and me fucking him in the same sentence again."

She waited a few minutes before she nodded her head. I slowly withdrew my hand, and regretted it almost instantly, because the moment I did, Nakia said, "So you *do* think he's hot," her eyes sparkling with mischief.

"I did no such thing," I scoffed. "I merely used Hazel's own words."

They both burst out laughing. "Keep telling yourself that."

Aretha Franklin's "Think" first notes boomed through the speakers, distracting Nakia and Hazel as they began belting the notes. I would have joined them since it was one for my favorite songs, but my mind was preoccupied with other things.

I let out a frustrated sigh, but beneath it all, I couldn't help the flood of images of Dr. Young's chiseled face swarming my mind. Aside from the fact that I hated the man, I couldn't deny how gorgeous he was.

Or how his calloused hands felt over my body, the brush of his fingers against my bare skin, my imagination wondering how…

Azara, stop.

That man was an arsehole.

Thinking of him in any other capacity than him being my boss and coworker who I couldn't stand would be strictly prohibited from now.

If only it were that easy.

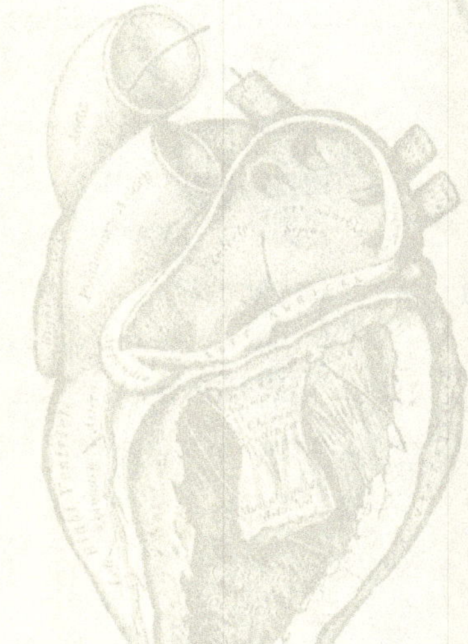

CHAPTER 6

AZARA

"DO WE REALLY HAVE TO go to this," I said from Nakia's living room. I'd been sitting on her three-seater dark emerald green velvet Chesterfield sofa for the last twenty minutes waiting for her to finish getting ready.

We lived only a few minutes away from each other, so once I'd finished my shift at the hospital, I'd driven home for a quick shower before heading here to get ready.

"You've asked me three times already in the span of ten minutes and the answer is still the same," she shouted from her bedroom's ensuite bathroom.

Tonight was *the* event of the season.

There were a dozen high-society events held throughout the year, but the annual masquerade ball at Anzar, the renown private art gallery in London where Nakia worked as the first female chief curator, was the most sought-after invitation.

Anyone who mattered or wanted to matter went to unbelievable lengths to be granted access. It was the perfect place to see, be seen and gather society intel.

I didn't understand it, but since Amanar General was one of the major donors for the event and my father was the medical director, I'd been invited every year. I'd usually been able to use work as an excuse to get away from it, but this year, my father had personally asked me to attend and cleared my schedule so I wouldn't use my usual excuse.

"I know," I replied, letting out a heavy sigh. "I was just checking in case you had a momentary lapse of judgment and agreed to stay home to watch movies and eat our weight in Moroccan takeout."

Her laughter echoed through the apartment. *Guess that was a no.*

While I waited, I scanned her living space for something—*anything*—to do while I waited. My gaze landed on a stack of papers and journals neatly piled on her hand carved coffee table.

I picked up the single-page newspaper that had *The Gilded Truth*'s distinctive logo at the top. The mysterious gossip column had arrived on the doorstep and email inbox of every member of high society that was remotely important two months earlier. It had created a wave of outrage at first, but quickly, those who'd critiqued it the most became addicted and were impatiently waiting for the next issue.

The pattern of delivery was still undetermined but whenever a new gossip sheet dropped, everyone halted whatever it was they were doing to read it. Its issues were a mix of commentary of the city's most influential, social news like tonight's event, scathing insults and the occasional praise—the last one a rare occurrence.

I didn't understand the appeal of wanting to read about a complete stranger tearing someone else's reputation apart.

Except when it was warranted.

There were an abundance of trashier gossip columns, but unlike the others, whoever the newly influential gossip writer was, they'd managed to expose, with frightening accuracy, a few influential parties that were committing some quite unsavory deals to heighten their status.

I was holding the latest edition that had come out a few days prior. It was discussing tonight's events, who hadn't been invited and—

"And you say you don't read *The Gilded Truth*," Nakia said with amusement in her tone, startling me.

I cursed under my breath, my hand clutching my chest from her sudden presence, the column crumpling under the pressure. I looked up to find her standing beneath the door frame that separated her bedroom from the living room.

"I wasn't reading it, simply holding it safe until you finished getting ready," I said defensively, blurting out the first excuse that came to mind.

She gave me an incredulous look and I rolled my eyes, placing the sheet back on her coffee table. I sighed and said, "It's not my fault it takes you forever to get ready. I was bored out of my mind."

"It takes time to look this good," she replied, waving her hands from her head to her toes before giving me a little twirl.

I laughed. "You do indeed look hot."

She wore a stunning olive-green satin gown that flowed to the floor with a long train, the color complementing her brown skin. The halter neckline wrapped around her neck, leaving her shoulders and back bare.

Her long passion twists were secured into a high bun, a few loose tendrils coming out of the large updo. She'd paired her dress with gold jewelry—small hoop earrings, layered necklaces and various sized rings she wore over elbow-length gloves that matched her dress. The delicate black lace masquerade mask that was wrapped around her face made her look like she'd just stepped out of a dark fairytale

The fact she was still single baffled me every day. She was beautiful, talented and extremely intelligent. If I didn't love men so much, I'd have married her myself.

"Well, thank you my dear," she said, giving me a small curtsy.

I stood and glanced over to her kitchen to look at the time. I groaned. "We have to leave or we'll be late," I said, heading toward the large mirror in the foyer.

"Would you relax? It'll be fine if we're a few minutes late," she replied, coming to stand next to me.

Since my hair was already secured in a low messy bun, a few loose curls framing my face, I tied my lace mask that matched hers before reapplying a coat of clear gloss over my brown lip combo. I'd kept my makeup minimal since most of it would be hidden and had borrowed some of Nakia's gold jewelry to complement my dress.

I'd opted for an off-the shoulder dark red gown, inspired by the Victorian era, with a plunging V-shaped backline that revealed my shoulders and spine. The material hugged at my waist, before flaring into a dramatic cascade of folds. It cascaded down to the floor in a sweep of rich velvet, catching the light with a subtle sheen.

Nakia had cinched the structured bodice so tightly at my waist, my breasts were pushed up high, threatening to spill over the neckline. I'd tried to get her to loosen it, but she'd refused under the principle that this was how it was supposed to be worn.

It was the complete opposite of what I'd normally wear, but people attending tonight's festivities to celebrate the New Year didn't dress to blend into the surroundings, they dressed to stand out.

Knowing she wouldn't let go, I'd easily relented.

"Ready?" she asked, looking at our reflection in the mirror.

"Unfortunately," I replied, as I adjusted the pair of sheer black gloves I'd borrowed from her and slipped on my gold strappy heels.

We snapped a quick photo and sent it to Hazel in our group chat who quickly replied with a string of messages, telling us how good we looked, how she missed us and was jealous she couldn't be there with us. We'd planned to all go together, but she was currently in Ireland with Edward to celebrate his parent's thirtieth wedding anniversary.

I grabbed my clutch from the entryway table. It was larger than what I'd like to bring for an event like this, but I needed the space to carry all of my essentials—phone, lip products, a few of my favorite go-to low blood sugar snacks and my diabetes pouch. We'd already eaten a few hours earlier, and I wasn't planning on drinking much, but being unprepared as a diabetic never fared well.

We then swiftly grabbed our coats before stepping out of Nakia's four-bedroom townhouse she'd bought last year when she'd been promoted to chief curator. A discreet black town car was already waiting outside for us. The gallery provided each guest a private chauffeur, limiting the risk of uninvited guests and straddlers showing up.

The driver slid out of the vehicle to open the door for us. I settled into the backseat, Nakia sliding next to me. The sweet older gentleman shut it behind her before moving back into his seat.

We spent the drive to the art gallery in a comfortable silence while Nakia answered emails and dealt with last minute details for tonight's event. While she worked, I turned and stared out of the window, watching the city blur as I prepared myself for a long and arduous night of small talk and thought of how long it would be appropriate before I could get away.

We drove down the busy streets of London toward the southbank until Anzar came into view. The elegant neoclassical building that stretched over three floors and multiple acres was an absolute masterpiece on a normal day, but tonight it was even more magnificent.

Its grand white exterior was illuminated by soft floodlights, and a black carpet covered the wide set of steps leading up to the portico entrance supported by large Corinthian columns.

A line of similar luxury cars to our own lined down the drive, dozens of expressionless guards on duty dressed in identical black suits helping guests out of their vehicles. Ours stopped four cars down from the entrance.

"Is it too late to leave?" I mocked, although I was serious.

"Don't be so dramatic, it'll be fine," Nakia said, rolling her eyes and sliding her mobile into her small black purse.

I glanced over at her. "Easy for you to say, you love these things."

"You're here with me and your dad is coming as well, isn't he?" she asked, placing a reassuring hand on my thigh.

She was well aware of how much I hated overcrowded spaces. I worked in one, but the hospital felt different. It was home and I mostly had control over every aspect. I was at ease there and knew how to navigate it.

Unlike here.

The ballroom would be filled with strangers I knew nothing about, alongside high-ranking society members that I didn't care for. The games they played amongst each other with their veneer of polite niceties weren't something I was used to or wanted to be a part of.

Just hearing Nakia's tales about these events was enough.

On top of it all, people who attended these occasions seemed to scrutinize each guest's every move. I didn't particularly care about others' opinions, but the last thing I wanted was to find myself caught up in the middle of strangers' conversations—or worse, the focus of *The Gilded Truth*'s newest edition.

Because while the identity of the gossiper remained a mystery, I was certain they'd be present tonight.

"Yes, but he'll want to mingle and speak with anyone who could be a potential donor for the hospital, and I have no desire in doing so," I replied with a heavy sigh.

My father was likely already there, making his rounds and persuading the wealthy elite of our society to invest in our facility. We were the best and our present donors were more than generous, but hospitals were perpetually in need of funding.

"I promise it'll be fine. We'll find a quiet corner at the back of the ballroom and observe the mothers attempting to match their eligible daughters with all the suitable bachelors present tonight."

I placed my hand over hers, giving her a firm look. "You better not leave me alone."

She chuckled, her rich laughter filling the car. "I'm technically off-duty. Francesca and Kensington are in charge of tonight," she explained. Nakia had taken care of planning tonight with Hazel's help, but her two assistants were responsible for ensuring everything ran smoothly this evening.

Our car finally rolled forward, and once it came to a halt, one of the valets opened the door for us. Nakia stepped out first, brushing a hand over the silk of her dress, and I followed, stepping onto the plush black carpet rolled out for guests.

The night air buzzed with anticipation and excitement. I'd expected photographers to be present, yet none were in sight. Instead, a steady stream of guests dressed in traditional white tie attire ascended the stairs, their chatter mingling in the crisp evening air.

Each guest presented their black and gold chip-embedded invitation to more stoic-faced guards and once cleared, the large, intricately designed, wooden doors of the gallery were opened to them.

Nerves danced against my skin as we were escorted up toward the grand entrance. A worker collected our coats and belongings before

Nakia offered her arm and I looped mine through hers as she guided us into the entry hall, our heels clicking against the marble floor.

If the outside looked grand, the inside of Anzar was from another dimension. The ceilings stretched impossibly high, adorned with frescoes that depicted mythological gods through various scenes. The soft golden light chandeliers bathed everything in a warm glow, casting long shadows over the poshly dressed guests as they made their way to the second floor.

We joined the flow of guests as we made our way up one of the winding grand staircases. The muffled sound of elegant laughter and the soft clink of glasses mingled with the strains of a string quartet covering contemporary popular music, growing louder as we approached the closed ballroom ahead.

"Let's do this shit," I said in my best American accent, attempting to inject as much enthusiasm into the words as I could.

Nakia stifled a laugh, but she was used to my antics. "Let's."

The grand doors of the ballroom swung open, and I felt as though I'd been transported into the nineteenth century.

Various paintings from the era were displayed around the room while chandeliers, heavy with crystals, hung along the ceiling like sparking crowns, bathing the room in an ethereal glow. At the far end, rich velvet curtains draped the tall windows, with musicians seated in gilded chairs forming a semi-circle in front of them.

A long, dark mahogany bar spanned the full length of the eastern wall, embellished with ornate carvings along its edge and gleaming just as brightly as the rows of fine liquors in antique bottles and vintage wines displayed behind it.

Some guests were on the dance floor, while others mingled in intimate circles around the room. Impeccably dressed servers circulated with trays of flutes brimming with champagne. I swiftly grabbed one, downing its entirety in a single gulp hoping it would help steady my nerves.

Nakia and I spent the next hour chatting with guests and patrons from the gallery. Well, I let her do most of the talking, only chiming in when a question was directed my way. In the midst of our countless and monotonous conversations, my father had briefly greeted us before returning to making his own rounds of the floor.

Once the first hour of the evening had drawn to a close, we'd been sitting at the bar, chatting, when Kensington interrupted us in a state of panic. Her words tumbled out in a frantic rush as she whisked Nakia away to remedy whatever situation they'd found themselves in.

This, unfortunately for me, meant I found myself sitting alone at the bar, clutching yet another flute of champagne and scrutinizing it. I wasn't much of a drinker and the earlier glass had been more than enough for me. But I had nothing better to do to occupy my time, and it helped keep the men at bay from offering to buy me a drink—even though they were all complimentary.

I turned in my seat and scanned the room, spotting a mother hurrying after a fleeing bachelor, her daughter trailing behind. I laughed under my breath at the scene and continued my perusal for something to occupy my mind while waiting for Nakia to return.

I had told her I'd head home when she'd left to solve whatever the issue with her assistant was, but she'd insisted I stay and made me promise to do so until she returned.

My wandering gaze roamed around the room until it caught an unmistakably familiar pair of dark eyes, and the breath stalled in my lungs. Although he wore a mask, I immediately knew who it was by the way the seconds stretched into a tense eternity and tiny sparks of unwelcomed awareness ignited all over my body.

My pulse hammered as he made his way toward me.

I really must be cursed.

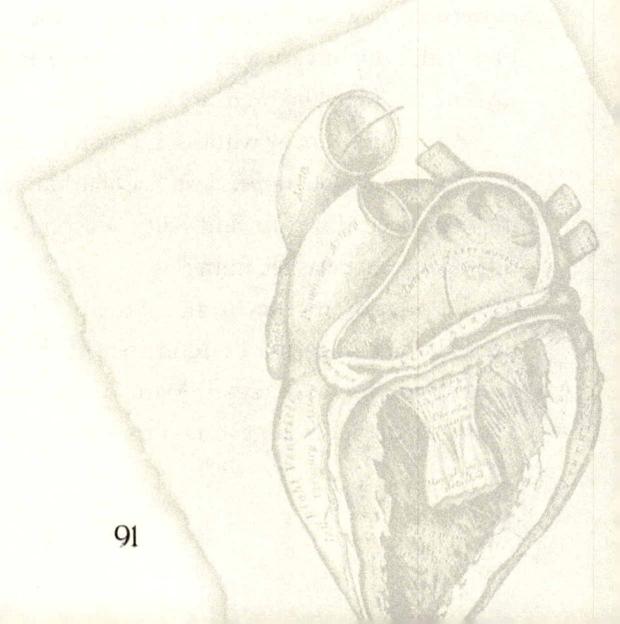

CHAPTER 7

MICHAEL

THIS BALL WAS POSITIVELY BORING.

It was the case more often than not, but if one more mother spent an entire conversation listing her daughter's attributes like she was livestock to be bartered for marriage, or if another business entrepreneur wasted my precious time discussing the "brilliant" ideas they had, I might very well break my oath and have a trail of bodies in my wake as I left the premises of the gallery.

And with so many witnesses, I didn't think I could get away with it.

"Wouldn't you agree, dear?" a high-pitched voice piped up beside me. I glanced down to find Kitty Wilson gazing up at me with wide doe-eyes, her eyelashes fluttering.

I'd been on my way to the gardens for some fresh air and much-needed quiet when the London socialite had sauntered into my path, intercepting me. Her father, Mark Wilson—a private wealth manager at one of the UK's largest multinational banks—had promptly joined us the moment he'd spotted his daughter with me.

I'd tuned out of the conversation the moment he began discussing the stock market, droning on about where I, along with the rest of the Atlases, should be investing, pulling out big words like diversifying portfolios and risk management.

Sofiane's father owned one of the largest hedge-funds in the city, so why on earth would I take advice from a wanna-be, a man who I knew had divested funds from his client's portfolios to stop the bleeding of his own mounting debts?

If it wasn't for the fact that I was representing my father, I would have told him to fuck off and left the conversation. But that type of behavior was unbecoming of an Atlas, so I stayed quiet and endured the torture.

Typically, our fathers would be in attendance, but they were all currently overseas in Korea to deal with Atlas ventures. Besides, as soon as my Ascension would be complete, these social obligations would officially fall upon us.

My gaze roamed the room until I spotted Amar, who was casually leaning against a column with one hand nonchalantly tucked in his pocket, flirting with his latest conquest. We'd barely been here for an hour, and I'd already seen him with three different women, each one enamored by whatever fantasy he was feeding them.

He wore a formal evening tailcoat and black trousers, paired with a crisp white shirt, a black waistcoat and perfectly tied black bow tie.

The very same outfit I, and most men in attendance, were wearing.

He raked a hand through his thick, wavy hair, which fell past his ears and brushed his shoulders, and said something that made the young woman before him double over in laughter, her gloved hand delicately coming to rest on his forearm as she inched closer to him in the process.

I wasn't one to interrupt his escapades, but I couldn't bear to listen to another word from either of the Wilsons. This incessant, vapid chatter made the evening stretch out before me like a dreary nightmare, and all I wanted was to find a semblance of peace.

"Michael?" Kitty's voice grated my ears once more as she placed her yellow-gloved hand on my upper arm. I stifled the urge to recoil at the contact. I had to get away.

It was at that precise moment that my gaze was irresistibly drawn back to my mystery girl who'd captured my attention the moment she'd entered the room. I'd felt pulled to her like a magnetic field, unable to divert my eyes away from her.

Although most of her face was hidden from the black lace mask she wore, there was something about her that was utterly… mesmerizing.

And for some inexplicable reason, I'd wanted to approach her, but she'd been busy roaming the room with her friend by her side the entire night.

Until now.

The House had rules and while I'd occasionally toyed with their limits, I'd never been tempted to cross them. Well, except with…

Don't, my mind chimed in.

The only other person that had the unnerving ability to unsettle me wasn't someone I should be thinking of right now. I'd caught sight of her father when I'd entered the ballroom earlier, but I doubted this was her sort of scene.

All evening, every time I'd watched the mystery woman look increasingly uneasy as she and her friend navigated the crowd, the urge to march over to her and whisk her away somewhere to see if I could *taste* it on her lips grew more ardent.

She sat on a high stool at the bar, staring mindlessly into an untouched flute of champagne. Her slender fingers brushed against the stem, before tapping against the foot. Crossing a leg over her other, she turned slightly, her eyes roaming around the room.

A radiant smile bloomed across her face and I'd never seen anything quite so beautiful, it disarmed me. So beautiful, my body acted before my brain could catch up.

"If you'll excuse me," I said smoothly, offering no further explanation to the Wilsons as I pushed my way through the crowd to make my way toward her. As I closed the distance, our gazes locked and for a fleeting moment, a semblance of recognition flickered before she turned away.

Once at her side, I casually leaned against the polished mahogany bar, propping an elbow on its surface and keeping a reasonable distance between us. Faint familiar notes of musk and vanilla filtered through my senses as my eyes glided over her smooth tanned skin, committing every inch to memory as I followed the elegant line of her neck, lingering at her pulse point before fixing my gaze on her delicate profile.

But before I could utter a word, she glanced over her shoulder and said, "You can find someone else to entertain your advances."

I arched an eyebrow, taken aback by her unexpected and abrupt dismissal. But I wasn't one to give up so easily. "That's rather presumptuous of you to think I was coming here to flirt, considering we've only just met," I teased with a smirk.

"Oh, I know who you are," she replied, her tone frigid, suggesting that knowing me wasn't particularly a good thing. Which was quite the unusual occurrence.

She sounded oddly familiar, though I couldn't quite place it. I had a feeling we'd met before, but it wasn't from the ball's previous years or any other high society event I'd been dragged to since this didn't seem like her scene. And I rarely went out unless it was with Amar or

Sofiane, so perhaps she'd been a former patient?

But all of my patients adored me—I quite literally had saved their life.

So if we had indeed met, I needed to know from where. "Then, dare I say it's rather unfair that you know my name, yet I don't know yours."

"Life isn't always fair," she scoffed, and that's when the pieces fell into place—I recognized exactly who she was.

Azara Ziani.

Her button nose always scrunched up in this adorable way whenever she was irritated with me but didn't want to show it. We'd been working together for a week now, and it was evident she didn't like me, despite her best efforts to be welcoming—most likely compelled to do so by her father given I was her superior.

I wasn't quite sure yet what I'd done to garner such animosity from her. We'd had a couple unfortunate encounters, but I'd apologized— well, for the incident at the coffee shop, the run had clearly been her fault.

The only other conceivable explanation was work. She was a skilled surgeon, but perhaps something about my talent threatened her.

Though I hated to admit it, she unsettled me in ways no one else had, but I enjoyed pushing her buttons and testing how far I could go. She sparked an itch within me to spar with her and win. She always remained professional whenever I did anything to get under her skin, but we weren't at work.

As the faint strains of an orchestral rendition of Lauryn Hill's "Can't Take My Eyes Off Of You" began to play, a crowd started to form on the dance floor and an idea formed in my head.

I straightened, extending my hand to her. "Dance with me."

"Why on earth would I want to do that?" she replied, her gaze resolutely fixed ahead.

"Why not?" I countered, a playful grin tugging at my lips.

"I have no desire to dance, least of all with you," she retorted, disdain evident in her tone. As she attempted to rise from her seat, I gently placed my other hand on the small of her back, causing her steps to falter.

"Just dance with me, 구미호[9]," I insisted. "I promise I won't bite," I added, leaning in slightly until my lips brushed the shell of her ear, lowering my voice so only she could hear me. "Unless you ask me to."

I was being far more persistent than usual, but I would have backed off if she had shown any signs of discomfort. Instead, a wave of goosebumps rippled across her skin and this time, she couldn't hide her reaction beneath her scrubs.

Tension between us crackled like a live wire and after a moment that felt like an eternity, her resolve finally wavered. "One dance, and I'm only indulging you so you'll leave me be," she relented, sliding her hand into mine.

I raised her hand to my lips and kissed the fine silk of her glove. "Of course, if that's what you need to tell yourself."

She shook her head. "I'm already regretting this," she muttered under her breath as I threaded her arm through mine and led us toward the dance floor.

I could feel eyes watching us and murmurs around the room as we navigated through the crowd since they'd never seen me take to the dancefloor at these functions in the past.

Yet, my attention was singularly focused on her.

As we reached the center of the dance floor, I turned to face her, taking her hand in mine while my other one found her waist, drawing her closer.

---

9 *Nine-tailed fox (Korean)*

She rested her free hand hesitantly on my shoulder, her back ramrod straight.

"Just relax," I murmured, guiding her into the rhythm. "Follow my lead."

"I know how to dance," she hissed.

I chuckled softly. "And I didn't say otherwise, but you are undeniably tense," I explained, pulling her closer.

She shot me a look, yet visibly relaxed in my hold as we fell into the familiar steps.

The melody from the orchestra swelled with a violin solo, the intense notes filling the space and seeming to wrap around us. The bustling noise of the gallery faded into a distant hum, and all I could hear was the thundering beat of my heart.

All I could feel was the warmth radiating from her, my skin jolting to life everywhere we were joined despite the fabric separating us.

We were quiet for a few beats until I decided to ask what I'd been wondering since we'd met. "Now that you aren't avoiding me like I'm carrying the plague, I suppose you can tell me why you hate me so much."

Azara inadvertently stepped on my foot before quickly regaining her balance. "I don't know what you're referring to."

I cocked my head to the side before spinning her around. "There is no use in pretending with me, Dr. Ziani," I said once we faced each other again.

"You asked for a dance; talking wasn't part of the deal," she replied, glaring at me.

I spun her around again, dipping her as the notes of the song shifted into something slower, more intimate. The atmosphere around us transformed as I leaned closer, our breaths mingling. If I moved even the slightest inch, my lips would brush against hers.

"What if I wanted to change the conditions?" I whispered, my voice huskier.

I noticed the unmistakable hitch in her breath and the slight widening of her eyes.

It would be so easy to just...

A sudden blaring sound severed the thread that held the moment together. I straightened us to see where it came from.

"Shit," Azara cursed under her breath as she quickly pulled away from me. "I have to go," she blurted out, and then with no further warning, she left.

I stood frozen on the dance floor for a moment before reality sunk back in and I went after her. However, by the time I exited the ballroom, she had already vanished.

An unexpected disappointment washed over me and I decided to head home. As I descended the steps of the winding staircase, I caught sight of something lying on the bottom step. It was only when I reached it that I could discern what it was.

She must have dropped it in a hurry.

I knelt and grasped the delicate piece she'd worn in my hands. My thumb ran over the black lace before I pocketed it and headed home.

AMAR

Where did you disappear to the night of the ball?

AMAR

Leave with your Mystery Girl?

SOFIANE

Mystery Girl? Please tell me you didn't do anything foolish.

ME

That's neither of your business. But nice of you to care about my well-being over two weeks later.

SOFIANE

Do I need to remind you your birthday is coming up.

AMAR

Would you just relax for once? A bit of fun won't break your precious rules.

SOFIANE

They're not my rules.

AMAR

Could've fooled me.

AMAR

Did you take her home?

AMAR

We need all the details

SOFIANE

There is no 'we'. I refuse to be held responsible for anything either of you do.

SOFIANE OUALI HAS LEFT THE CONVERSATION.

AMAR BELKACEM ADDED SOFIANE OUALI TO THE CONVERSATION.

SOFIANE

Just for the record, I never consented to be a part of this group chat.

AMAR

Who are you talking to? You're literally a tech wizard; you could make this conversation vanish if you wanted to.

ME

Stop flooding my phone, I'm at work.

I SILENCED MY PHONE BEFORE shoving it into the pocket of my fleece vest.

If Sofiane had any choice in the matter, he'd never speak to either of us again. He seemed to age exponentially every time Amar recounted one of his *adventures* or when he dragged us for a night out that always ended with us in precarious situations.

I just tagged along because I found it rather entertaining to watch the two bicker, because I knew better than to join in on Amar's antics. Well, not anymore.

"Dr. Young," a soft voice called out as I exited my office, where I'd been catching up on administrative work after Facetiming my grandmother to perform my *Sebae*[10]. Today was the Korean New Year and although I was at work, she'd be really disappointed if I'd missed it .

I'd been at Amanar for nearly a month now, but my predecessor had left so many tasks and issues to resolve that I was still catching up.

I glanced to the right to find Marcella, our department's booking coordinator, making her way down the corridor toward me. I'd met her right after Azara's joyous tour of the facility and she was God sent. We hadn't had someone with that role at Orion, but here she expertly managed the entire cardiothoracic surgical team's schedule, allocating operating rooms and coordinating with the other surgical teams to prevent any overlap and maintain the hospital's efficiency.

"Is everything alright, Marcella?" I asked as she approached, clutching a stack of documents to her chest.

Her usually immaculate gray hair, typically slicked back into a bun,

---

10 *A tradition of bowing to show elders respect during the Lunar New Year (Seollal)*

was disheveled, with a few rebellious flyaways. I'd only recently met the older woman when I officially started performing surgeries, but the retired theater nurse was always put together and she currently looked like she'd been put through hell.

"It will be if you can tell me your schedule for the next two hours is clear," she replied, a note of discouragement creeping into her tone.

I'd finished my surgeries for the day and planned to round on my patients before finally heading home. I was exhausted after being on my feet all day with back to back surgeries, but by the desperate look on her face, that answer wasn't what she was looking for.

Besides, one thing I'd learned the moment I'd first stepped into a hospital was the importance of befriending the nursing staff and having them on your side.

"What can I do for you, Marcella?" I asked with a reassuring smile.

She closed her eyes for a moment, releasing a sigh of relief and muttering gratitude in Spanish under her breath, before meeting my gaze again "Dr. Ziani had a complication," she began.

A sudden—and surprising—panic gripped in my gut. "Is she alright? Where is she?"

Marcella shook her head, bringing a hand up to stop my string of questions. "No, no, she's fine. Her *patient* had a complication."

Immediate relief washed over me.

"She was scheduled to perform a cardioverter-defibrillator implantation in," she glanced at her watch," fifteen minutes, but she's still in surgery. Mr. Alastair has already had his surgery delayed three times already and I would hate to do that to him again."

"Has Dr. Ziani approved of this?" I asked, surprised that she would let me operate on her patient.

I'd never officially met the famous football player since he was Azara's patient, but I'd heard of him through my cousin since they ran in similar circles.

Tobias Alastair, one of the best center-backs in the last decade, had been in and out of different hospitals over the last few days before he was admitted here, where my team finally discovered the reason behind him collapsing on the pitch during his last football game.

Marcella gave me a noncommittal shrug as she rummaged through her papers, retrieving a file. I hadn't had the chance to look over his chart so I grabbed it from her, flipping through the pages and reading his diagnostic tests. "He's headed for Theatre B, and I would be immensely grateful if you took over the case."

I'd operated on many athletes before but operating on someone as important as the darling of the Premier League would bode well for me. And having Marcella on my side would be a nice bonus too.

"For you, Marcella, anything," I replied with a smirk, closing the document.

"I knew I liked you," she said, reaching up to gently tap my cheek. "The patient has already been informed that you'll be performing the surgery. He's being prepped as we speak."

I chuckled softly. "And what if I had said no?"

She shrugged. "I knew you wouldn't want to get on the nurses's bad side. I may be retired, but I still have a bit of sway with them," she said with a knowing look.

I clutched my chest in mock outrage. "You wouldn't."

She huffed out a laugh. "You're lucky you're charming. Now, off you go before you're late," she ordered, gesturing for me to hurry-up and leave.

"Goodbye, Marcella," I said playfully, throwing her a wink as I headed down the corridor toward the lift to the thirteenth floor, where all the operating theaters were.

Once inside the room, I swiftly introduced myself to Alastair and the team I'd be working with, some of them now familiar, before scrubbing in for surgery. I then spent the next forty-five minutes working on him before I moved to the scrub area to unscrub.

I was in the midst of washing my hands when the swing door to the room slammed open. The atmosphere instantly shifted and I turned to find Azara glaring at me.

"What on earth do you think you're doing?" she said breathlessly as if she'd run around the hospital before she got here.

I guess Marcella didn't run the surgeon swap with her before recruiting my help.

Tonight was the first time Azara had actually spoken to me with more than one-worded syllables. She had been avoiding me ever since the night of the ball.

Although we had very similar schedules—which I knew because I was the one who set hers—I hadn't seen much of her over the last two weeks. It was almost like she'd made a deal with Marcella that our scheduled surgeries overlapped, and sent the junior doctors who reported to her to me whenever any information needed to be relayed.

With my birthday coming up and the responsibilities I'd be shouldering once I officially joined the House, I should have been happy that she'd been distant because nothing could ever come out of whatever it was that transpired between us, but I would be a liar if I said I wasn't a little disappointed.

I waved the thought away and shut off the water, grabbing a disposable towel. I propped a hip against the sink next to me to face her as I dried my hands.

"Well, I just performed a flawless ICD implantation and beat my personal best record," I replied nonchalantly with a small grin, knowing she wouldn't like it.

"Excuse me? Did you just say your best record?" Her nose twitched and she tried to keep her tone neutral, but her indignation was clear in her expression.

She appeared to be fresh out of surgery. She wore the mauve scrub cap with cherries drawn in brown on it that I'd noticed she always wore for her surgeries, her surgical loupes still perched on top of her head.

"Yes, it was quite remarkable. It's a shame you couldn't—"

"Patients aren't *records* to beat," she cut in.

A wave of satisfaction washed over me and my smile threatened to stretch wider. This was the first time I'd managed to break her poised calm, and it was quite the sight to see.

"I'm well aware, I just meant..." I started but she interrupted me once again.

"Why did you steal my surgery?"

I frowned at her outlandish accusation. "Steal?"

I tossed the used towel in the trash before crossing my arms over my chest. Her gaze fleeted to my upper body for barely a second before she returned to her glaring. Too caught up in her accusations, she'd inadvertently reduced the distance between us.

She cleared her throat before saying, "Yes, Tobias was *my* patient."

I frowned. There were more important things to think about, but all I could focus on was her calling him by his given name. She *was* his doctor, but did they know each other?

"You had no right to operate on him," she gritted out, pulling me out of my thoughts. She took a step forward and pointed an accusatory finger at me.

Before she could make contact with my body, I wrapped my fingers around her wrist, bringing her hand down, and in the process, erasing the remaining distance between us. We both froze at the same time, prickles of electricity buzzing across my skin where it touched hers.

Our eyes locked on where my hand encircled her wrist. I brought my gaze to her face, to find her still watching where we touched. I focused my attention on her, on how disturbingly close we were, close enough for me to note the faint musky vanilla scent wafting off her skin that I'd been thinking about since the night of the ball.

Close enough to discover the light constellation of dark freckles all over her face.

This wasn't my most brilliant decision, but it was already done.

Might as well lean into it.

"What is it, love?" I willed my heart rate to steady despite her suffocating proximity. "Can't handle a little competition?"

My words broke whatever trance she seemed to be under because her glaring gaze came back full force, threatening to drown me as it collided with mine.

But she hadn't moved.

"This isn't about competition, although you would never win. Everyone here might think you're this," she looked me up and down, "handsome and charming doctor who's a genius in the theater, but I'm not falling for your act."

"Are you sure? Because you just called me charming *and* haven't asked me to let you go."

As if she'd just realized only mere centimeters separated us, she attempted to pull back but my grip tightened around her wrist for a few more seconds before I finally let her go.

She took several steps back as if I'd just burned her, her fingers brushing over the skin where we'd just touched.

My mouth curled into a small grin at the blush creeping over her neck and face. I looked away from the gesture and met her gaze. "Just for your information, I didn't *steal* anything from you. I did you a favor so the word I think you're looking for is thank you."

"Thank you?" Azara cocked an eyebrow as she spat the word.

"Yes, thank you," I repeated, removing my scrub cap and running a hand through my hair. "If it wasn't for my kindness and working overtime to *help* you, Mr. Alistair would be quite unhappy right now."

"I could have done it once I was done with my other patient."

I abandoned my post next to the sink and walked toward her. Her body faltered back when I paused next to her. "Yes, but Marcella was the one who asked me for my help, so I did. Now, if you'll excuse me, I have a date waiting for me at home."

Her posture stiffened at the words date and the earlier flush darkening her cheek reappeared. She had nothing to be jealous of since my date in question was with my bed and leftovers from last night's takeout from UMMA.

But it didn't stop the slow smile spread across my face as I walked out the room without another word.

I was well-aware I was playing with fire, but I found myself not caring.

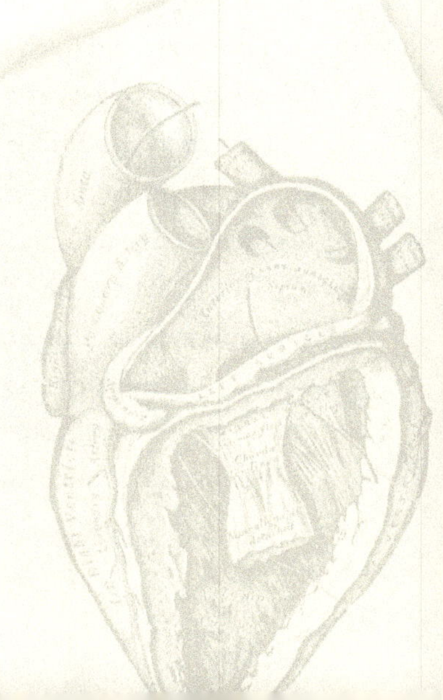

CHAPTER 8

AZARA

"ARE YOU OKAY?" HAZEL AND Nakia asked in unison as they answered my video chat call.

"Ugh, that absolute arsehole," I scoffed, slamming the entrance door to my flat and aiming to toss my keys into the wooden bowl on the entryway table, but missed.

They clattered to the floor with a resounding thump.

Could this day get any worse?

I pinched the bridge of my nose, letting out a heavy sigh before bending down to pick them up, this time successfully throwing them into their designated place.

"I can't believe him," I muttered under my breath, kicking off my shoes and padding further into my flat.

"Um, Z, did we miss something?" Hazel asked and I heard sheets ruffling in the background.

I glanced down at my phone to find their faces staring back, their brows furrowed with concern. I'd nearly forgotten I'd called them.

Nakia appeared to still be at the gallery from the stacks of paintings propped behind her, while Hazel seemed to have already been in bed with the way she quietly closed her bedroom door before settling on her pink couch in her living room and turning on a small lamp.

Closing my eyes for a brief moment, I inhaled deeply, before bringing my phone up. "I know it's late, but if I don't get this off my chest, I might call you in a few days with a body to bury," I explained, tossing my large work tote onto the couch and heading for the kitchen after getting the alert on my phone that my sugar was trending low.

I'd been able to manage throughout the day, but I'd barely eaten because my schedule had been abnormally filled with back-to-back surgeries. The workload itself wasn't an issue, but then my last surgery, which was meant to be a quick and straightforward one, turned into a bloody nightmare—quite literally.

My patient had been stable throughout the operation when his vitals suddenly plummeted. He started bleeding, and it took us far too long to locate the source, only to discover it hadn't been from a mistake on my part.

It'd stemmed from a hidden complication related to the bowel resection he'd had last month. The general surgery team who'd operated on him had used this ridiculous new surgical device from NyxMedica that the hospital had introduced last year, and it failed.

Again.

I couldn't understand why we were still using it, given all the issues many Amanar surgeons had encountered using it.

Thankfully, we'd managed to control the bleeding and save the patient, but he would have a long recovery road ahead of him.

"What happened?" Nakia asked, a hint of mischievousness suddenly flashing in her gaze. Before I could stop her, she added, "And does it have anything to do with the infamous hot doctor you danced with at the ball?"

Hazel's eyes widened as she let out a small gasp. "Danced with? Why has no one told me about this already?"

Why did I choose the most indiscrete people as friends?

I groaned, propping my phone on the small kitchen counter. After throwing my hair into a ponytail, I leaned my hands onto the concrete worktop and said, "Firstly, he is *not* hot. Annoying and unbearable, yes."

They both exchanged knowing looks.

Of course, I was lying but right now, discussing how infuriatingly attractive the bane of my existence was, or how every time he touched me my skin felt like it was alive wasn't what I wanted to focus on.

"I'd like to remind both of you that I called to vent my grievances, not gossip about his charms."

"So you *do* admit he is charming," Nakia teased, trying to hide her smile.

"Goodbye," I groaned, feigning to end the call when she stopped me.

"Alright, alright we apologize. Go on," Nakia encouraged, barely containing her amusement at my situation.

Ignoring the giant smiles on their faces, I launched into a detailed explanation of what transpired earlier—well, mostly everything—all while making myself a quick dinner. Fifteen minutes later, Hazel and Nakia were still quiet as I snuggled up on my sofa with a turkey bowl in hand.

I swiftly opened my app, inputting the values to cover myself for what I was about to eat, before taking a bite, still waiting for them to say something.

Nakia was usually quiet, but Hazel always had something to say.

Too anxious to wait, I prompted, "So? Proper arsehole, isn't he?"

I took a few more bites of my food, waiting for either of them to say anything.

"You want the truth or would you prefer we lie?" Nakia replied, brow raised.

Confused, I shot back, "You've never held back before, so why start now?"

"Okay, but just a fair warning, you might not like what you hear. It was actually a really nice thing he did," Nakia said.

"*Nice*? Have you both not been listening to a word I said?" I asked, outrage creeping into my voice.

How could him undermining me with a patient and taking such an important surgery from me be *nice*? Surgery was in and of itself a cutthroat field. I knew this better than anyone. But I'd been working closely with Atlas FC, Alastair's football club, to make sure he had the best care and he could return to the pitch after his rehabilitation.

Michael could have easily told Marcella that I'd get to it once I was done. But instead, him and his inflated ego took countless hours of hard work for granted.

I shifted my attention to Hazel for reinforcement because clearly Nakia wasn't thinking clearly, but she quickly averted her gaze.

"Oh, we both have," Nakia said, knowing Hazel wouldn't want to hurt my feelings. "I hate that you weren't able to perform the surgery, especially with the hours you've put in to come up with a plan, but *he* doesn't know that. Because I'm assuming you didn't explain that to him and just jumped to conclusions?"

I hated when she was rational.

"You're supposed to be on my side."

"We are, Z, and you know I would *never* give a man the benefit of the doubt under any circumstances, but he probably thought he was doing you a favor. Which he has because if he hadn't, you would probably still be at the hospital right now with an unhappy patient. His approach could have used more," she paused, musing on the right word before saying, "tact, but—"

"He likes you," Hazel chimed in, a glimmer of hope in her eyes.

I shot her a glare. "He doesn't *like* me. He's egocentric and makes it his mission to unnerve me."

"Which means he likes you," Nakia said, her lips fighting a smile.

I sighed, rolling my eyes. "Oh, for goodness' sake, not you too."

They both burst into laughter.

"Admit it," Nakia said, leaning forward, her voice lowering to a conspiratorial whisper. "You've got a bit of a crush on the hot doctor, haven't you?"

"No," I scoffed.

Was he attractive? Sure. Did his proximity cause the signals in my body to go haywire? Unfortunately. But I'd rather endure open-heart surgery without anesthesia than feel more than irritation toward him. Anything else should be inconceivable.

"He's nothing more than insufferable," I reiterated. I didn't know who I was trying to convince more with that statement. "And could we please stop calling him the 'hot doctor'?"

Hazel's face beamed as she propped her chin on her hand, gazing faraway dreamingly. "This is straight out of a romance novel."

Typical Hazel.

I shook my head, placing my half-empty bowl on the coffee table, having lost my appetite, before leaning back against the couch. "I wouldn't call my desire to strangle him in his sleep straight out of a romance *anything.*"

She shrugged, unfazed. "We'll see. Come back to me in a few months, and we'll determine who was right."

Just then, the sound of a door creaking open echoed through the phone, followed by Eddy's voice. "Hazel, *mo cuishle*, it's nearly midnight, what are you—" He halted mid-sentence once he noticed we were on a call.

"Oh, hello, ladies," he said, a faint blush creeping up his freckled fair skin. He was practically naked, wearing only a pair of briefs. Swiftly, he grabbed a tiny pink blanket from next to Hazel and wrapped it around himself, though there wasn't much fabric to work with.

Hazel glanced at him as he perched on the arm of the sofa. She opened her mouth, but I interrupted her before she could utter a word.

"Hazel," I warned, knowing she was about to tell him that I was in love with the 'hot doctor'. Which might I add, wasn't true. I already had these two hounding me; I didn't need a third person in my predicament.

Edward was generally a quiet and reserved lad, but that man loved to gossip, though he would absolutely deny it if asked.

"What?" she asked, glancing back at me with feigned innocence.

I raised a brow. "You know exactly what."

"But it's just Eddy," she protested.

"Yeah, it's just Eddy," he echoed, popping his head next to hers with a cheeky grin. "Besides, she already told me about the hot doctor if that's what you're afraid of."

Oh fuck me.

I groaned and buried my face under my free hand, feeling my cheeks heat and wishing I could vanish somewhere far away from here—somewhere the words 'hot doctor' never existed.

Hazel slapped his arms, glaring at him—well, her version of glaring.

"I liked you far better when you were quiet and shy and trying to impress us to get on Hazel's good side," I said, running my hand down my face.

Nakia shifted off-screen, suppressing a laugh.

He just shrugged. "To my defense, she," he nodded toward his fiancée, "freely offered the information. Anyway, I'll leave you three to it, but don't keep my wife up too late." He placed a small kiss on her temple and stood to leave.

The gesture sent a wave of wistfulness through me. I used to long for that kind of love, someone to share my life with, until my mother's passing doused me with a cold dose of reality. Love was beautiful until it wasn't, and I stopped believing that such a fantasy was worth the inevitable heartbreaking loss

"She's not your wife yet," I scoffed before he disappeared from the screen. "Anything to say in your defense?" I asked, glaring at Hazel.

"I'm sorry?" she replied, her expression turning sheepish.

I shook my head.

"So," Nakia began, and we all turned our attention to her. "What happened next?"

My brows furrowed in confusion. "What?"

"I know you well enough to know you didn't tell us everything. Once you confronted him about your surgery, what happened next?" Nakia pressed with a knowing expression.

I knew that if I mentioned the part where our bodies were so close I could almost taste his heady scent, I would never hear the end of it. It would only fuel this delusional scenario they have about something transpiring.

I shrugged off a shiver at the inconceivable idea.

Keep telling yourself that, my mind mocked.

And keep your thoughts to yourself, I shot back.

Brilliant, now I was having a conversation with my subconscious.

Instead of dwelling on my ridiculous inner monologue, I gave them the safest answer. "He just left before I could get another word out because he had a *date*,"

They exchanged a knowing look before turning their attention back to me

I sighed. "What is it again?"

"Do we sense a hint of… jealousy in your tone,"

I furrowed my brows. "Me? Jealous? Are you mad?"

"Well, you did say the word 'date' with a lot of disdain,"

"Okay, I think it's rather late for you two. I believe a good night's sleep will help bring back some sense into the both of you," I said, bringing the conversation to a close. "So goodnight, I love you both."

Before either of them could respond, I ended the call and tossed my phone aside, the device landing on the far end of the sofa. It pinged with a text message, swiftly followed by another, but I ignored it, knowing it was from either or both of them.

I leaned my head back against the cushion. Grabbing a nearby pillow, I pressed it over my face and let out a scream of frustration into it.

It hadn't even been a month of being forced to work with him, and I was already losing it. I'd always prided myself on my non-confrontational nature and my composure under pressure, but it seemed like he brought out the worst in me.

Just his simple presence got under my skin.

How on earth would I survive however long it would take him to either quit or worse retire? I eventually wouldn't be under his supervision once I finished my training, but I'd still have to work with him.

And why did he have to look like *that*?

My mind unwillingly drifted back to the night of the ball. I'd regretted saying yes to dancing with him the moment I slipped my hand in his; the warmth of his skin seeping through the fabric of my glove and sending an unexpected jolt through me.

I could still recall the way he gently placed his fingers against the small of my back to bring our bodies closer. The way he'd looked at me as we swayed on the dancefloor.

Intensely and completely disarming.

His intoxicating proximity wrapped around me like a fog. I'd almost forgotten where and with whom I was, until the invisible thread that connected us, our lips a breath away from each other, was cleaved in half by the blaring sound of my Omnipod.

I'd never been more grateful to have diabetes then at that moment.

If my expired insulin pump hadn't started obnoxiously beeping, I might have let him—or worse, I might have done it myself.

I groaned, tossing the pillow aside and sitting up straight. My mind was a tangled mess of thoughts, wandering from the pressure of succeeding at work to *him*. With a huff, I stood and trudged to the kitchen, grabbing the bowl I'd abandoned earlier.

I wrapped the leftovers with cling wrap, too lazy to transfer it into a container and wash the dishes. It'd be tomorrow's problem.

I took the stairs and padded to my room, the events of today clouding my thoughts. After brushing my teeth and washing my face, I changed into a large sleeping shirt, foregoing underwear, and I climbed into bed, pulling the weighted duvet over my body, hoping that sleep would smother the feelings that seemed to plague me.

But as soon as my eyes fluttered shut, my mind betrayed me. Again.

Images of him, of us, swirled behind my eyelids—his dimpled smile, the way his eyes sparkled with mischief and desire whenever he taunted me, the feel of his skin against mine.

I could almost feel the warmth of his breath brushing against my lips. Could practically taste him on my tongue.

I was bloody doomed.

I tossed and turned, fighting the onslaught of unwanted flashbacks and the prospects of what ifs assaulting me at every turn. My frustration grew into a headier aching and before I could stop myself, my hand slowly drifted down my body.

Almost teasing as if it knew this was a bad idea in the making.

With featherlight touches, I warily slipped a hand and found myself soaked with my arousal. My mind battled with my body for a brief moment before I closed my eyes, and gave in to the forbidden thoughts for a few reckless minutes.

Maybe this is what I needed. Scratching the itch.

Almost instantly, my breath shallowed into pants as I brought myself closer, snapshots of him fueling the fantasy. His strong arms pinning me down, his deft fingers knowing exactly how to bring me over the edge, the softness of his lips leaving not an inch of my body untouched.

His commanding words, guiding me through every step of what he planned to do with me at his mercy.

A loud moan escaped past my lips.

My skin slicked with sweat as I stroked myself faster before pushing two fingers inside me, the slippery sounds of my pumping in and out intermingling with my sighs.

Suddenly, my orgasm crashed over me with a blinding force, drowning me in a warmth that trickled into every inch of my skin and sent a sensation of lightness floating through me.

I lay there, sweaty and breathless, until the wreck of what I'd just done crashed me back into reality.

This definitely hadn't scratched the itch.

It simply fueled it more.

CHAPTER 9

MICHAEL

MOST PEOPLE EXPECTED A CAKE or maybe even to receive presents for their birthday.

I, on the other hand, waited for when I'd be kidnapped.

It was the day before my birthday and tonight I'd receive my Order—the task I'd have to accomplish to complete my Ascension and officially become part of the House of Atlas.

I'd been conditioned for this moment from the moment I drew my first breath and now that it was almost here, I wanted to simultaneously run far away and get it over with.

But what I did or didn't want, didn't matter.

I'd been born to serve the House and we all had to do as we're told. Amar, Sofiane and I all had to make our fathers proud because even though we were born into this world, we were forced to earn our place.

It was either that or be killed for failing.

Tonight would change my life. For better or worse.

I'd finished my shift earlier and had been home for the last few hours, waiting.

None of us were told anything beforehand. From what our Order would be to when or where I'd be taken from and to. We weren't allowed to visit the House until the eve of our thirty-second birthday. And even then, I wouldn't be privy to its location or given a tour until after my Ascension next year when I turned thirty-three.

I'd tried to keep myself occupied the entire evening, but nothing helped settle my frizzling nerves. I wasn't an anxious person, but the notion of the unknown had always unsettled me.

I prided myself in always being prepared for any situation and although I'd always known this part of my life had to stay a mystery until I'd shown I was worthy, I was never able to make peace with it.

Good thing that would end tonight.

It was almost 10:00 p.m. and I'd just finished rinsing and putting away the dishes I'd used to make dinner, when the lights in my flat all shut down. Almost instantly, a hood was placed over my head and my vision went dark.

I woke up minutes, or maybe even hours later, kneeling and stripped down to only my underwear. They wanted us down to our most vulnerable self and at their mercy. Not that any of us would ever fight to escape our responsibilities.

No matter how much we wanted to.

The smell of fire crackling filled my nose and I breathed heavily into the cloth covering my head. I slightly shifted to relieve some of the soreness in my muscles from being in this position for god knows how long. The fabric was too thick to see through, but by the biting cold from the abrasive concrete floor seeping into my skin and down to my bones and the shackles binding my wrist to my ankles behind me, I must be in some sort of basement.

I stifled the shiver running down my spine because I could *feel* their scrutinizing eyes watching over me. The room was eerily quiet before someone finally spoke.

"Young Seungwon." I heard my name over the pounding headache resounding against my skull. Whoever they'd sent to take me hadn't chosen gentleness in their approach. "You've been summoned to serve the House. Do you wish to accept your Order?"

"Yes, sir," I immediately answered. Any ounce of hesitation would have warranted swift termination. Even if my father was standing just a few feet away from me.

Blood didn't matter in the House, only loyalty did.

A click echoed in the room and my cuffed wrists were released, but I didn't move. I waited for the distorted voice to speak again, to give me direction as to what was expected of me, but it was utterly quiet.

I waited a few more minutes before I shook the iron shackles off. When nothing happened to stop me, I brought my hand up to remove the cloth from over my head.

Still nothing.

I took a deep breath, blinking several times, waiting for my eyes to adjust to the dim lighting. Once they did, I scanned the room I was held in.

Over the years, I'd imagined this moment and what this place would look like a million times, but it was nothing like I'd imagined. Instead of the underground cave and rock walls I'd pictured, the room that greeted me was the complete opposite and oozed wealth.

The flickering glow of candles cast shadows across the stone and elaborate moorish architecture. Tall, arched windows filtered moonlight through stained glass, creating an eerie atmosphere. Geometric patterns lined the walls and a small and rectangular reflective pool in the center captured the faint glimmers from above.

My eyes traveled across the water's surface and landed on the large circular platform, its surface covered in arabesque details, on the other side of the room, where the fire I'd smelled earlier erupted from. Three men—the Elders—stood behind it. They all wore black cloaks and matching ornate masks adorned with intricate gold filigree with the House's emblem weaved into it.

I didn't understand the need to hide their identity since I already knew who each of the men were. The House didn't recruit outside of the three sacred lineages, but I guessed it made them feel superior—as if running the world wasn't enough.

My gaze scanned over their figures and despite the masks concealing their entire face, I could feel their harsh glare on me. One of them— my father, judging by the height since he towered over the rest of the Elders—gave the slightest, almost imperceptible nod toward a dark envelope laid on a wrought-iron stand in front of the altar, its legs surfacing from the water.

I stood, ignoring the dizziness swarming my vision, and walked over the edge of the pool since it was the only way to get to the stand. The frigid water seeped into my bones as I stepped inside. The level of the water kept increasing as I walked across the pool's length until it stopped rising once it reached my knees. I halted in front of the stand, the crackling fire's heat stinging my skin from its proximity.

The Elders still hadn't moved from their position or said a word.

Warily, I reached for the black envelope with a warm brown seal with an Atlas lion engraved in it and the moment I grabbed it, the Elders trickled out of the room through a large wooden door, leaving me alone.

This isn't at all what I expected.

I waited until the last one was out before breaking the seal and pulling the frail paper inside. Written in the middle of the note in bold, black ink was a single sentence.

Become the next medical director
of Amanar General Hospital.

My eyes widened, but I quickly schooled my expression because I knew that even if they'd left the room, they were still watching my every move.

I'd always wondered what these tasks would be and knew they wouldn't be easy, but this was beyond what I'd expected. I was brilliant at my job and climbed ranks faster than any trainee before, but I'd just become a consultant doctor—early might I add, but that's beside the point.

Becoming medical director took years of work, loyalty to the hospital, and most importantly, a vacancy for the role. Adnan Ziani had spent over forty years at AGH and was a well-respected *and* loved surgeon.

How was I supposed to take his job? How was I supposed to convince the board that *I* was better suited than him?

For fuck's sake.

This would be an impossible task, but I never forfeited to a challenge. No matter how hard it was. I wasn't starting now, especially when the only way out of this was death.

My father's legacy and honor depended on it, because although I'd be six feet underground, he'd find a way to haunt me and repeatedly remind me of how I'd failed him.

And more importantly, Amar and Sofiane's lives were also on the line. My failing or refusing to proceed would be followed by their immediate termination and I wouldn't be able to warn them because the House had eyes and ears everywhere.

They'd be dead before I even managed to take my next breath.

I closed my eyes for a brief moment, my breathing threatening to turn heavy but I pushed it away and opened my eyes again. My gaze caught a tiny imprint at the bottom of the page.

Following the instruction, I dropped the piece of paper into the fire and watched it burn, knowing it meant the countdown to my Ascension had officially begun.

365 days.

I had 365 days to complete my Order.

365 days to Ascend and officially become part of the House of Atlas or die.

Before I could walk away or ask what was next, the ceramic floor of the pool gave out from underneath me and I fell into oblivion.

INCESSANT POUDING JOLTED ME OUT of a deep, foggy slumber.

I groaned, struggling to peel open my heavy eyelids. My mind, thick with sleep, fumbled to piece together what was happening or even where I was, but the hammering kept on, unrelenting.

What is with all this noise?

My fingers brushed against familiar Egyptian cotton, confirming I was in my bed, although I couldn't recall how I'd gotten here. But before I could even gather my thoughts, the pounding had ceased and a voice bellowed from the other side of the door.

"I hope you're decent in there." Was the only warning I got before Amar slammed the door to my bedroom open.

I rubbed a hand across my face, hoping to clear the fog that still clung to my senses, and looked over at where he stood through half-closed eyes. He had a giant grin on his face as he marched inside my bedroom uninvited, with Sofiane reluctantly trailing behind him with an apologetic expression on his face.

"What—" I tried to say, my voice thick and sluggish. I cleared my throat and tried again. "What are you doing here?" I finally managed to ask.

The last thing I remembered from last night was burning my Order as instructed and then everything went dark. I must have been drugged, because my head and my body felt like I'd been run over by a train full-speed.

Under normal circumstances, I would have questioned how I'd ended up in my bed completely clothed, but nothing about our lives was normal.

Amar threw himself down onto my bed while Sofiane stood at the edge, his hands clasped behind his back. "It's your birthday," Amar said, as though that explained him barging into my house.

"I know it's my birthday, Amar, but why are you really here?"

Amar opened his mouth to respond, but Sofiane was quicker. "He showed up at my house, demanding I come with, even though I repeatedly told him you weren't allowed to tell us anything."

Amar shot him an exasperated glance over his shoulder, before focusing his attention back on me. "Don't pay him no attention, he doesn't know what he's talking about. You can absolutely tell us what it was like."

We all knew what happened the last time we'd talked about the House amongst ourselves and, frankly, I'd rather not have a repeat situation.

I rubbed my temples, trying to assuage the headache building. "What time is it?" I asked, changing the subject.

Sofiane glimpsed at his watch. "It's 9:07"

I shot upright in bed. "Fuck," I muttered, the fog in my mind suddenly clearing up. "I'm late for work."

Without another word, I scrambled to untangle myself from the covers and rushed past them toward my closet. After quickly changing into the first thing I could find, I made my way back into my bedroom, only to find them still there.

"I have a job to get to, so if you'll excuse me," I said, grabbing my phone that had somehow ended up on the floor.

"But you haven't told us anything," Amar grumbled as I walked out of the bedroom and hurried down the stairs.

Reaching the lift, I scanned my fingerprint and the doors slid open automatically. "You've got five minutes to leave before Mamadou comes up," I called out, not waiting for a reply.

By the time I arrived at AGH, I had just enough time to get a pair of scrubs from the dispensing unit and change. I walked into the scrub room with barely a few minutes to spare, only to find Azara already getting ready.

She gave me a once-over, and let out a deep sigh. "You're late," was all she said as she returned to scrubbing her hands and forearms.

I'd scheduled us for a heart bypass this morning and this was always how she greeted me when she saw me walk in. Maybe it was a waste of resources, but I enjoyed seeing the look on her face when she realized that we'd be stuck together for the next few hours and there was nothing she could do about it.

"Always with the warm welcome, Dr. Ziani," I teased, fastening a surgical mask over my face. I could almost hear her eyes roll as I grabbed a scrub brush pack and moved to the sink to begin the same process when the door to the room opened.

Marcella popped her head in. "Dr. Young, I moved your mitral valve repair for Mr. Gonzalez to 3:30 this afternoon," she announced.

I nodded in understanding, acknowledging the change without needing further elaboration. Marcella never wasted time on pleasantries when it came to delivering any updates she'd made to the schedule so

I'd learned to simply nod and follow along with her plans.

Just as she turned to slip out, she paused, her hand still on the door. "Oh, and happy birthday," she added nonchalantly, before slipping out of the room without giving me a chance to respond.

I blinked, slightly taken aback. I hadn't told anyone it was my birthday, so I had no idea how she'd figured it out. But with Marcella, it was always best not to question how she seemed to know everything.

I turned back to my task, but my focus faltered when I saw Azara staring at me with wide eyes, her previous annoyed expression faltering.

"Wait," she said, her voice lace with surprise. "It's your birthday?"

"Yeah," I replied reluctantly. I didn't like talking about my birthday. I'd stopped celebrating it a long time ago. The day I'd realized that every time I did, it was one year closer to binding myself forever to the House.

The day I'd used to look forward to as a child had been tainted by the prospect of what my life was meant to be.

A shadow of guilt washed over her face, and I watched her gaze slightly soften.

She'd never looked at me that way.

She paused, hesitating for a moment, before drying a hand on her scrubs. Then, to my surprise, she reached into one of her pockets. My brows furrowed in puzzlement while I watched her pull out something from it. My eyes glanced down at her extended hand.

"Happy birthday, Dr. Young," Azara said softly and my eyes flicked up to hers.

My heart lurched against my ribcage as my mind tried to grapple with the mix of emotions I was feeling at the gesture, but I could only focus on the barely-there smile tugging at her lips as she handed me a small pouch of Skittles. I still didn't know why she carried so many wrappers of the candy, but I'd seen her occasionally dump an entire bag in her mouth during a shift.

But none of that mattered because Azara Ziani just smiled at me.

My eyes widened. "Was that a smile, Dr. Ziani?"

Her face immediately morphed back into the one I'd slowly grown accustomed to. She scowled, shoving the packet into my chest. "Just take the bloody Skittles, so we can get to work."

I closed my hand around hers. The simple touch sent a jolt of electricity through me, and when I met her eyes, time seemed to slow.

For the briefest moment, something transpired between us...

But just as quickly, she snatched her hand away, flustered. She muttered something under her breath as she lasered her focus onto scrubbing in again.

I wanted to say something but decided against it.

Instead, I pocketed her gift and got ready for surgery. Again.

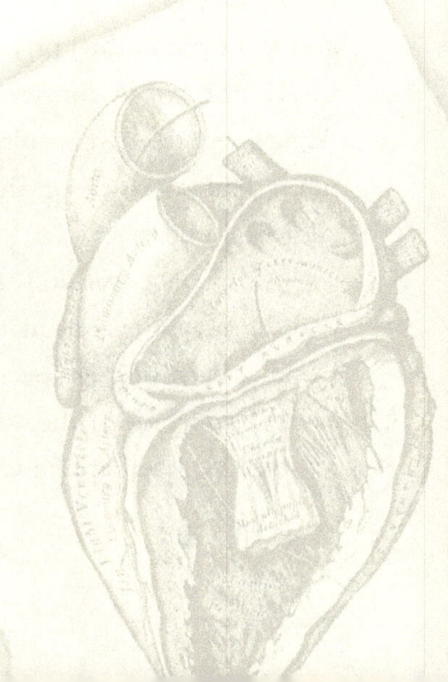

CHAPTER 10

AZARA

AFTER WHAT I NOW REFERRED to as *the incident*, I'd instated a new rule: *Avoid him unless absolutely necessary and never,* ever, *scratch the itch again.*

Even thinking about the notion of doing so was forbidden.

I'd managed to handle the second part of my mantra, but unfortunately for me, rules always seemed to have a knack for rebelling and someone in the universe clearly hated me because I'd kept finding myself thrown in constant proximity with Dr. Young. He'd been the department's lead consultant for the past two months now, and I'd never had to work or share surgical duties so much with another surgeon in the past.

Although I was still technically in training, this was my last year and the previous consultant had always let me go about my own way. Besides, each doctor specialized in different surgeries and we usually each had our side of the ward and stuck to it, but for some godforsaken reasons, I'd been appointed to assist in every single one of Michael's surgeries because of course we had the same area of expertise.

If his sheer presence wasn't enough to deal with, he'd managed to get under my skin every time, like getting on my nerves and seeing how far he could go before I snapped was some sort of game to him.

He had yet to succeed and I'd never let him, despite how many times I'd dreamed of just letting it all out. His arrogance was unbelievable and it took everything in me not to stab him with a scalpel when we were in the operating theater.

Not that I would do it even if I was given the chance—albeit extremely tempting. Cutting didn't faze me, it was literally my job, but it was much different doing it to someone unconscious and that needed it versus injuring someone.

My mobile ringing with my 9:00 a.m. alarm pulled me out of my thoughts. Realizing I'd been lost in my own head for the last two hours, I quickly silenced it and got up, pushing the words Michael Young into the far back of my mind.

If only they could stay there and never resurface. Better yet, if *he* could stay there and never cross my path ever again.

I grabbed a jumper from next to me and walked over to the small closet from my childhood bedroom, pulling out the wrapped box from it.

My brother turned sixteen today, so after my shift yesterday, I'd come to my dad's house and stayed the night so it'd be easier to be here early this morning. Besides, we'd have to leave soon to head to the Tassili Stadium for Zayd's big birthday gift.

Eddy had gotten tickets for today's match—his club was playing against their biggest rival Sufax United—and Zayd would get to go on the pitch before the game while the players went through their warm-ups.

I pocketed my phone in my sweatpants and swiftly left my

childhood bedroom, making my way to Zayd's room on the upper floor of the townhouse.

Although I'd be surprised if he was already awake since he always slept until the early afternoon on weekends, I chanced a peek into the kitchen on my way to make sure he wasn't there.

But instead of finding it empty like I'd presumed, my father was sitting at the head of the dining table, a full tea glass in hand with a small, untouched plate of olive oil mixed with a dollop of what looked like amlou and a basket of bread in front of him.

Although he was usually off on weekends, he still often went into the office to do any administrative work he hadn't tended to during the week. He always needed to work, a trait I'd definitely inherited from him.

For better or worse.

He looked lost in thought, his face filled with worry.

"*Baba*," I said from the open doorway.

He didn't look up.

"*Baba*?" I repeated, louder this time as I stepped into the kitchen.

Startled by my presence, he knocked his glass over, the *atay*[11] spreading across the circular wooden dining table. He cursed in Arabic as I quickly placed Zayd's gift on the counter and grabbed a rag from it, placing it over the streak that had formed before it spilled over the edge and onto the floor.

"I'm sorry," he said, finally looking at me

"It happens to the best of us," I said with a small smile, hoping to lighten the somber atmosphere that surrounded him, but he still had the same faraway look in his eyes than when I'd stumbled on him a few moments ago.

There used to be a lightness to my father's face, a constant joy that

---

11 *Moroccan mint tea*

I hadn't seen in years. He used to laugh everything off and didn't take life too seriously.

The man sitting in front of me, however, looked at the mess he'd just accidentally made like it was just another bad thing to add to the list of unfortunate events that happened in his life.

It pained me to see him like this, knowing there was nothing I could do to help. I'd tried to get him to go to therapy to help with his grief, but he'd just say that everything was fine and he didn't need help. And unfortunately, in our culture, going to therapy wasn't something many people did despite how helpful it could be, much less men.

I finished cleaning up and rinsed the cloth in the sink before wiping the table one more time to avoid it being sticky later. I took the seat closest to him and poured him another glass.

"Here," I said, pushing it toward him.

He muttered a thank you before placing his thumb and index against the bottom of the glass, but not moving to drink it.

Although his expression was more often than not somber, the one he currently sported was weighed with something else. In addition to the usual sadness, he looked conflicted.

I didn't often push for him to talk about his feelings because it just made him put up more walls around him, but the look on his face worried me.

"Is everything alright?" I asked him in Darija as I tore a small piece of the now cold bread and dipped it in the plate. Placing the piece in my mouth, I leaned back in my chair and did my best to hide my concern as I chewed.

His eyes met mine. "Yes, why wouldn't it be."

I flinched at his harsh tone, raising my hands up. "I was just asking."

His gaze filled with remorse. "I'm sorry, *benti*. It's just work."

I didn't believe him, but chose not to push him any further.

"You know it's Zayd's birthday today?" I asked, hoping the answer was anything but what I knew he'd say.

My father wasn't a bad man and I knew how much he loved us both, but over the years, he started forgetting things, anniversaries and birthdays included. Grief came in many forms and was such a tricky thing. Although it hurt when he forgot and I didn't want to blame him for it, it didn't lessen the disappointment I felt every time.

I'd learned to brush it off, but Zayd was still just a kid and deserved better.

I pushed my chair back and stood, resting my palms against the wooden surface.

"I got him a football jersey and a tablet for his art. I signed your name on the card that I attached." Learning to forge his signature when I was younger for school related communications came in handy. He let out a heavy sigh and as he was about to say something, I cut him off. "I'll go upstairs to wake him up and I'm taking him to the game today. Hazel's fiancé got us tickets."

I didn't stay to see what he'd have to say and grabbed Zayd's gift on my way out. As I began climbing the stairs, I chanced one last look toward the kitchen, finding my father with his head in his hands. He looked defeated and I hated that I'd been a part of it, but he needed to do better.

For Zayd. My brother only ever knew our father like this and I could only do so much to shield him from what our dad had become. And most importantly, he needed to do better for himself because he couldn't keep going like this. No one should.

But forcing someone to get help never worked. They needed to be willing.

Pushing my remorse and guilt to the side, I climbed up the stairs and paused in front of Zayd's bedroom, hearing his snores from the other side of the door. I pulled my phone out of my pockets and scrolled through the list of songs on my music app until I found the one I was looking for.

The first notes of a remix of 50 Cent's "In Da Club" that repeated the intro verse of the song played from my phone as I opened his door with the hand holding it and walked inside of my brother's messy room, belting the lyrics and dancing to the beat.

I carried my mother's loss deep in my bones, but had found a way to soothe it with moment's like these. Moments where I could share glimpses of who she was with others, especially my brother.

On every birthday morning, she'd burst into my room with the song playing and a single doughnut from Kareena's Bakery, a small business owned by a sweet older lady in Camden, and a lit candle shoved in it for me to blow.

I'd foregone the doughnut since the bakery had been closed by the time I left work last night, but I'd take him for breakfast before we had to meet Hazel and Nakia at the stadium an hour before kick-off at 3:00 p.m.

Zayd groaned and pulled his black duvet over his head as I approached his bed. I sang louder as I loomed over him despite his pleas to stop. Once the twenty seconds clip was over, I sat at the edge of his bed, placing his gift on top of his cover.

"Do you always have to do that?" he grumbled, his voice groggy, his face still covered with his duvet.

"And deprive you of my beautiful voice?"

He snatched the cover off his head and shot me an annoyed teenager look, but I knew he secretly loved the tradition. "I'd rather—" His cheeky reply died on his tongue when he noticed the large wrapped present at his feet.

He abruptly sat up in bed, his eyes wide and filled with excitement.

I feigned to grab the gift away. "What were you going to say? I mean if you don't—"

"No, no, no," he said in quick succession, pushing the cover off his body. He was wearing a black graphic shirt and gray joggers. He swiftly reached for the gift and placed it on his lap, almost exploding from excitement. "Your voice is the most wonderful thing I've ever heard."

I snorted out a laugh at his response.

"Can I open it?" he asked, his eyes glued to his present.

"It is your birthday after all."

I'd barely finished my sentence when he tore through the wrapping paper Hazel had chosen and meticulously packaged. She'd insisted on doing it, refusing to let my brother be a witness to my horrendous gift wrapping skills. Although I had many talents, apparently that wasn't one of them. Besides, I didn't really understand the point of perfectly wrapping presents when the receiver would just decimate the meticulous work within seconds of receiving it.

Zayd's jaw fell open when he discovered the contents. He immediately reached for the packaged tablet, seeing the well-known brand I'd heard him talk about before.

"You didn't," he noted in disbelief as he removed the wrapping around it and retrieved the device from its box.

My brother had entered a competition recently with other young graphics designers so he could help pay for more professional equipment and expand his portfolio. He'd been using the same old tablet for the last few years and always complained about how slow it was or how it had inaccurate calibration.

Whatever that meant.

So after some research and online videos, I'd figured out the best one to help him continue the latest project he'd been working on.

I chuckled. "Well, you *are* holding it in your hand."

He began turning it on, while rummaging through the other accessories that came with it. He'd never go look further into the box and spend the next few hours playing with it if I didn't redirect him.

"As exciting as seeing you play with your thing, you might want to look at the other gift inside," I suggested, eager to finally reveal our plans for today.

He whipped his head up, glaring. "It is not a *thing*," he deadpanned. "This is—"

I cut him off before he launched into an hour long explanation about the specs of this tablet and how great it was. Not that I didn't want to hear all about it, no matter how boring I'd find it. I loved hearing about his hobbies.

But we'd waste precious time and I was just too impatient to keep this secret any longer.

"Oh dear, tablet. I apologize for calling you a thing," I directed toward the device he was still holding. "Now, just open the rest, pretty please," I finished with a smile.

He let out a sigh, placing his new device aside. "What could be better than—" His sentence was cut short when he pulled out the red and black Atlas football jersey.

"Holy shit, is this a real one?" he asked with a giant smile on his face. He held it up in front of him, turning the shirt over to find the name and number of his favorite player printed on it.

I sure fucking hoped so with the amount I'd spent on it. Why on earth were football jerseys over a hundred quid. For printed fabric. In my opinion, it was pure robbery, but Zayd never owned an authentic one, the fake ones filling his wardrobe all from small stores in Morocco.

"This is actually perfect for later when I watch the game," he went on. "They're playing against Sufax United who's their biggest rival. And their two major players absolutely *hate* each other so it's always so hilarious to see DeMarco feign fouls because he wants the advantage."

He was buzzing with excitement and it put an even bigger smile on my face. "Wouldn't it be so much better to watch it in person?"

He brought the shirt down in one fell swoop, his brows raised. "Well obviously, but tickets have been sold out for months. And they're so expensive, even if I saved up for a whole year, I still wouldn't have enough."

I cocked my head to the side. "First, you never save any money you're given. You spend it so fast, it's like you think it'll disappear if you leave it alone for a few days."

Since our father wanted him to focus on his education and enjoy his free time instead of working, Zayd had been given a monthly allowance to pay for anything he needed, whether it was for school or his hobbies. But my brother always found a way to spend it within the first week the funds hit his account.

He huffed out a laugh. "Fair point."

"Secondly, it's a good thing that your wonderful sister happens to be best friends with one of the team's player's fiancée."

His eyes widened. "You're kidding." He tightly gripped the jersey and abruptly stood on his bed, looking down at me. "If this is a joke, Azara, I will never forgive you."

"We're going to the game."

He began chanting the team's anthem while jumping on his bed, my body bouncing with each hop.

I shook my head, laughing at his reaction. "Alright, settle down before father comes in here."

He plopped on his bed, his bare feet landing on the wooden hardfloor with a loud thump. He then leaped over to where I sat and wrapped his long arms around me, pulling me into a tight side hug.

He repeated the words thank you in quick succession before

pulling away, eagerness radiating off of him. "What are we waiting for, let's go."

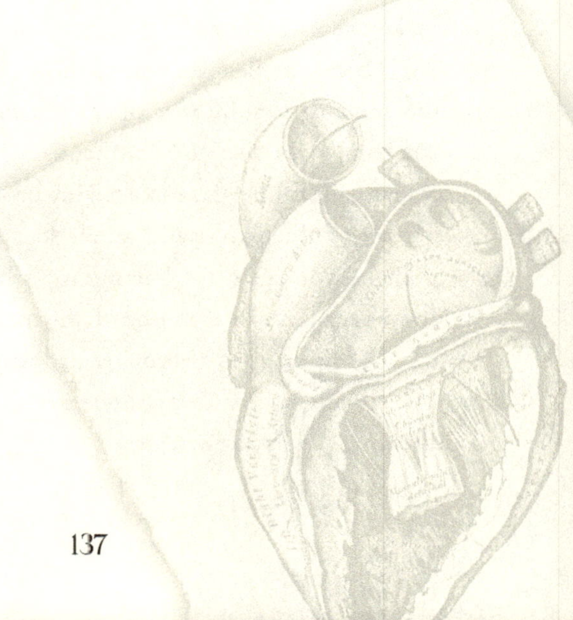

CHAPTER 11

AZARA

AFTER BREAKFAST, I'D DRIVEN THROUGH the absurd traffic to the stadium where the match took place. London roads were almost always busy, but I'd never been to a game before so I hadn't anticipated being stuck in traffic for almost an hour when the trip would normally only take twenty minutes.

We'd barely made it on time to meet with Hazel and Nakia in front of the stadium for the rest of Zayd's birthday surprise. Hazel had quickly handed us our VIP wristbands, while one of the social media coordinators for the Atlas escorted my brother to the pitch so he could meet some of the players and watch their warm-ups.

"Thank you again for helping me with this," I told Hazel as we followed her to our seats in one of the main stands behind the player's benches. The place was already packed with fans in a sea of black and red on our side, with a few scattered ones wearing navy blue shirts—representing the opposite team.

"*No hay de qué*[12]," she replied with a warm smile, placing her hand on my arm.

We sat in our padded seats just as the players filed onto the field for warm-ups, the crowd's excitement reaching an audible crescendo of cheers. My brother came out a few moments later, wearing a branded team jacket and a ball under his armpit.

As if he'd felt us watching him, he turned around and gave me two thumbs-ups, a beaming smile on his face.

"I will never be able to top this next year," I noted with a shake of my head, seeing as my brother was almost bouncing with joy.

She waved me off. "We have plenty of time to think of something," Hazel said and I could already see the plans forming in her head.

"I now understand why people love watching football so much," Nakia sighed as she propped her knuckles under her chin and leaned forward in her seat, pushing her large black sunglasses over her head with her other hand. "I'd pay good money to see that every Saturday."

I tamped down a laugh as I looked at the players. I could understand the appeal of footballers, but I personally didn't subscribe to it. Not only did they have a reputation I'd much rather stay away from, they were too pretty for my personal preferences.

Yeah, you prefer tattooed arsehole surgeons, my brain chimed in.

I groaned internally at the intrusive thought for fear of manifesting his presence. With fate's cruel conspiracy against me, I wouldn't put it past her.

"Why do you think I'm marrying one?" Hazel said as her gaze briefly met Eddy's. His face instantly lit up and he winked at her before returning his attention to his trainer.

"Well played, young one," Nakia said proudly, leaning over me to give her a high five. She'd given the nickname to Hazel even though

---

12 *Don't mention it! (Spanish)*

she was only two years younger than us. "Is it true what they say about them being *remarkable* in bed? I bet their agility comes in handy," she whispered.

I rolled my eyes before casting a nervous glance over my shoulder to see if anyone had heard her. Neither of these two were known for their discretion, and I'd rather not have complaints by the other families before the game even started.

"Could we just please behave for once?" I asked with a sigh, mortified, as I returned my attention to both of them.

Nakia slipped her hands into the pockets of her dark olive leather jacket she'd worn over a white shirt and leaned back in her seat. She crossed one bare leg over the other, flicking her stilettoed foot up and down. I never understood how she could walk in those, but it was her favorite style of heel and she had that particular pair in every color to match her varying outfits.

Nakia was always perfectly dressed no matter the occasion while Hazel and I looked almost underdressed compared to her with our team jerseys and oversized jeans.

"You're the one to talk, Miss 'I want to bone my hot doctor coworker'," she replied with a mischievous smile.

My eyes widened. "I do *not* want to sleep with him nor will I ever," I muttered under my breath.

Nakia arched an eyebrow, incredulity written all over her face. "Keep telling yourself that, love."

They both laughed at my expense while I fought an exasperated sigh. I loved our trio, but I didn't appreciate their recent liking to ganging up on me.

Hazel opened her mouth to say something, but I cut her off.

"And that's my signal to get us some drinks," I said, swiftly getting out of my seat before I was subjected to another round of their matchmaking. The last person I wanted to think or discuss was my unbearable boss.

I walked up the steps we'd come down from and headed inside the hospitality room where a plethora of men in business attire and club colors stood around the room, chatting. On the far right from where I'd entered, a group of a few women, who appeared to be partners of the players, sat on a long red leather sofa with children either sitting on their lap or next to them.

I tossed them a small smile as I made my way through the small crowd. I'd almost made it to the large bar at the back of the room where an array of foods and beverages were offered when I heard the sound of a familiar voice.

Just as I thought my imagination had been playing tricks on me, the older gentleman that had been in front of me moved and I got a front-row view of the last person I'd planned to see here today.

You've got to be kidding me.

Dr. Young stood by the left side of the bar with two other men.

The one who stood to his right was slightly taller than him and had a warm, olive complexion. He had medium-length wavy brown hair that was slightly tousled and a thick, well-groomed beard. He wore black trousers and a dark blazer over a black shirt with a low neck that highlighted his broad shoulders and muscular frame.

Charisma emanated off of him just like it did Michael, with their effortless charming smiles and dimples.

On the other hand, the other man appeared quieter, his fingers tightly holding a green glass water bottle in his right hand. He was slightly angled away from me, but just from his profile, I could tell he was just as attractive as who I assumed were his friends by their ease with each other.

He had short, dark curly hair that was neatly styled and facial hair that was trimmed into a light stubble. He paired his dark, loose-fitting trousers with a textured white shirt with three-quarter length sleeves that complimented his medium skin tone.

I'd planned to turn back and pretend like I'd never seen him, but of course Young turned his attention toward where I stood the moment my legs caught up with my brain.

Our gazes locked and I muttered a curse under my breath, trying to figure out my next move.

You know what? Screw this.

I tore my gaze away and closed the remaining distance to the bar, Michael and his friends standing a few inches down from where I was. I could feel his eyes on me, but ignored it. The bartender was preoccupied with another patron, but briefly looked my way and gestured that he'd be with me soon.

I tapped my fingertips against the wooden surface as I waited, when I felt someone come up behind me. I closed my eyes, trying to tamp down my bubbling annoyance, before looking over my shoulder to tell him to fuck off.

Only the person behind me wasn't Dr. Young. Instead, standing almost a foot taller to my five foot six, was Tobias Alastair, the Atlas FC's famous center-back.

"Oh, hi," I said, surprised to see him. "I didn't expect to see you here."

He'd usually be on the pitch, warming-up with his teammates, but since it'd be a while before he could play again, he probably came to support his team during one of their biggest matches of the season.

I wasn't in charge of his case anymore, but the cardiology team at the AGH were coordinating with the rehabilitation center where he'd been for the last several weeks to monitor his progress. Although I hadn't operated on him—courtesy of Dr. Young—I'd been told that he worked hard and his chances of playing again were looking promising.

"I could say the same to you, Dr. Ziani."

"Please, Azara is fine," I amended. Since we weren't at the hospital and he was technically no longer my patient, it felt weird to have him call me anything but by my forename.

"Well, Azara, it's nice to see you here," he said with a cheeky smile. He came to stand next to me, leaning a hand against the edge of the bar and bringing him an inch closer.

I shifted to keep facing him and unwillingly caught a glance in Michael's direction, only to notice he was still looking at me. But this time, something I'd never seen there before flashed in his gaze, sending an unsettling spark of electricity dancing over my skin.

I shook it off and brought my attention back to the footballer in front of me. Aside from the fact that he was a former patient and not my usual type, the man was undoubtedly beautiful.

Tobias had that effortlessly rugged look, like he'd just rolled out of bed but somehow still managed to appear like he'd put in time and effort. His light brown curly hair framed his face, drawing attention to his chiseled features, and the light stubble dusting his jaw emphasized the fullness of his lips.

He leaned to rest his chin on his hand, his fingers splayed gently against his cheek. "So, what brings you here? Are you here by yourself?" he asked, locking his deep-set eyes on me.

Before I could get a word out, Dr. Young's presence joined us.

Ya rab[13].

Couldn't I get just one day of peace? I already had to tolerate him pretty much every day at work and when I wasn't at the hospital, I was mentally preparing myself to have to deal with his inflated ego the next time I had to be.

---

13 *Good lord (Arabic)*

My autobiographical memory had been a blessing for the most part of my life—especially throughout medical school—but ever since Dr. Young stepped into my path, it seemed to be nothing but a fucking curse.

I didn't really hate people and normally easily let go of things that bothered me, but with him, it always seemed like an impossible feat. No matter how many times I'd tried to forget and move past it, a memory of his infuriating behavior sparked in my mind.

"I was looking for you," Michael said, interrupting our conversation.

Looking for me?

I was preparing to call out his nonsense when he rested a hand on the bar behind me, his body brushing against my back from the movement. He was so close that I could feel the warmth of his body and get the faint scent of his intoxicating cologne.

The words died in my throat as he spoke again, his eyes only on me.

"I appreciate you keeping her company." His usual smile was gracing his lips, but there was a bite to his tone, like he was trying to effectively dismiss Tobias.

I sputtered out a laugh because there was no way I'd heard that right.

Tobias didn't seem fazed by Michael's behavior. "Dr. Young, it's nice to see you again," he said, extending his hand. "Thank you again for accepting to step in for Dr. Ziani and do my surgery."

Michael looked at Tobias's outstretched hand for a brief moment, before shaking it and slipping on his charming doctor act.

"It was my pleasure. I've heard your rehabilitation is going well, and hopefully you'll thank me for getting you back on the pitch when you win your next *Ballon D'Or*," Michael said with an easy smile, but I could see it wasn't entirely sincere.

From working with him so often and having nothing better to do, I'd started studying him to understand why people seemed to love him so much and always fell for his charms. I despised the man, but even I could admit that he was really good with patients, even when he didn't mean it.

Tobias's gaze flitted to mine. "I never got to see you after my surgery, but I'm immensely grateful for your help and the plan you'd come up with. I do apologize if my impatience to get the surgery done caused any scheduling issues for you."

He briefly looked over at Michael, who was still standing too close for my comfort, before Tobias's gaze landed back on mine. This time it was shadowed with guilt.

"I know you were meant to do it, but I was really restless with the delays and the press breathing down my neck. Dr. Young must have reassured me a dozen times that you'd be out of surgery momentarily and I could discuss my anxiety with you, but I just wanted to give the journalists some good news, so they'd stop harassing my family for updates."

I'd heard everything Tobias had said but my brain couldn't help but latch onto the part where he'd mentioned Michael had wanted to wait for me before proceeding with the surgery.

I realized at that moment that I'd been wrong about his intentions. He hadn't maliciously taken the surgery from under me like I'd assumed.

Tobias ran a hand through his hair, bringing my attention back to him. "I also needed my coaches to know that I was okay. They say the team is behind me, but this sport is fiercely competitive. Any news is better than none."

I quickly placed a hand over his forearm, feeling the need to reassure him. I felt Michael's body stiffen behind me, but ignored it, my imagination clearly playing tricks on me.

"Hey, that's alright. My primary concern was for you to get the best care and Dr. Young is just as qualified as I am. You were in good hands," I told Tobias with a soft smile.

The compliment almost burned my esophagus coming out, but I tamped it down. Patients came first, and Young was talented. Not as much as me, but enough that I trusted him not to fuck it up.

"Alright, well, I should get back to see the boys before the game," he said with a small smile. "I hope you both enjoy the entertainment. These Sufax boys are quite the actors," he added with a playful laugh as he walked away.

I wanted to plead with him and ask him to stay so I wouldn't have to suffer the fate of being alone with Michael, but he was already gone before I could do anything.

I spun around to face him and immediately regretted it because it only brought our bodies even closer. I took a step back, although it wasn't nearly enough.

"What are you doing here?"

"Same as you. To watch some football."

I glared at him. "Don't play coy. You know what I meant." I didn't have the patience nor the desire to play his usual games. I just wanted to be left alone. "Why did you interrupt us?"

He raised a brow in surprise. "I didn't know I was interrupting anything."

"I don't… That's not the point. You were being rude."

"I'd beg to differ. I was nothing but charming, Azara," he said with his signature smile but the tension in his shoulders betrayed him.

He'd always called me Dr. Ziani. It was the first time he'd said my name, and I hated how I liked how it sounded leaving his lips.

I shook the ridiculous thought away. "Well, go be charming elsewhere,"

He inched closer, invading my space even further. "Ah, so you do believe I'm charming."

I rolled my eyes. "I didn't say that," I replied curtly, looking away and hoping to get the attention of anyone behind the bar so they'd come to my rescue.

"Can I get you anything?"

I glanced at him sideways. "The drinks are complimentary."

"Doesn't mean I can't be a gentleman and get you one," he replied, the ghost of a smile touching his lips.

Of course, this interaction would amuse him.

"Could you just, *please*, leave me alone. We're not at work, and therefore there's absolutely no need for you to speak to me."

"What if I wanted to?" he asked, just as one of the staff came to take our orders.

Once the young lady walked away, I stared up at him. "For heaven's sake, Dr. Young." I shot him a glare and raised my hands, tempted to just...

Ugh.

Instead of doing as I'd asked, he stepped closer, my fingertips grazing the skin of his neck. "I dare you. I know you want to."

Does he mean...

My lips parted at his insinuation. "You want me to choke you?"

"If it'll make you feel better. Have at it. I've never tried it, but the thought of your pretty fingers around my throat sounds quite enticing," he murmured the last words, the soft vibration of his words brushing against my chest.

My eyes grew wide as warmth irrationally washed over me at his words, at the image he'd unwillingly created in my mind. One of me riding him while doing exactly what he'd just insinuated. I'd never be able to get rid of it.

Fuck me.

I met his gaze, finding a look I'd seen there once before. At the night of the masquerade ball. Which was the last time I'd almost made a grave mistake.

I stepped back, snuffing away the curiosity swarming in my head.

"Stop doing that," I said, hating how breathless I sounded.

A charged silence crackled between us before he spoke again.

"Doing what?"

Looking at me like that.

I didn't bother responding and just headed back to my seat.

The drinks I'd ordered long forgotten.

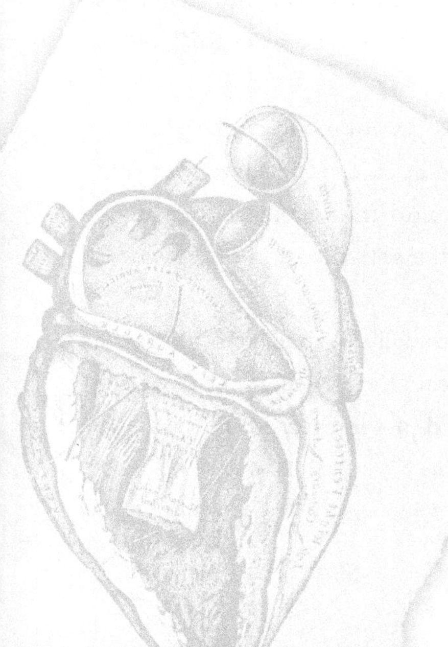

CHAPTER 12

MICHAEL

"WOULD YOU JUST RELAX? ONE fun night out won't kill you," Amar said to Sofiane, tossing an arm around his shoulders as we entered Rubis Rouge, the famous pub downtown.

It was a Saturday night and the evening after a highly anticipated game, which meant the place was packed. Dev, the owner, streamed the games every weekend on the large screens that plastered the back wall of the property, so a sea of red and blue alike were scattered around the room.

"I'm relaxed. I just don't adhere to your type of *fun* nights," Sofiane retorted, clearly counting the minutes until he'd get to go home by the way he was playing with his ring.

We both were, but where I just preferred the comfort of my home, Sofiane craved it after a day like this. He had social anxiety, and easily got overwhelmed when we were crowded with so many people, especially when Amar was around.

Amar was the outgoing one in our group. While I could turn it on when needed, he carried most conversations and *loved* meeting—and charming—new people. There wasn't a room Amar entered where people didn't love him and craved to get an ounce of his attention.

He meant well, and he didn't know about Sofiane's anxiety, which the latter made me swear never to tell Amar about. Sofiane didn't want to hurt his feelings and promised that if it ever became too much, he'd let me know one way or another so I could bail him out.

Neither of us usually went to football games, but Amar's father had gotten us tickets for today's match and we couldn't find it in ourselves to tell him no. If I thought my father was scary, Nacer Belkacem was frightening.

The Algerian business tycoon and philanthropist had founded and owned the Tassili hotel chain, a multinational hospitality company, which was the global hotel of the Atlas FC amongst several other sports organizations.

The Atlas FC had won 4-1 against Sufax so Amar had made Sofiane and I go celebrate their victory. I hated going out, but I'd only accepted because I needed to keep an eye on them and Sofiane would have never forgiven me if I'd left him alone with Amar.

Well at least that's what I was telling myself.

I definitely hadn't said yes to coming here tonight in the hopes that I'd see her because I'd overheard Azara and her friends mention the pub's name. We'd been seated two rows behind them at the game and my attention was on her the entire time.

Throughout, I'd replayed our conversation in my mind, the cheers of the crowd barely piercing through long enough to divert my attention to anything else.

When I saw her in the hospitality lounge, I'd know better than to approach her, but the moment I'd seen Tobias come up to her, I'd acted before thinking.

I might have glazed over this type of reckless behavior before I'd gotten my task, but now that my initiation was officially underway, I shouldn't, *couldn't*, let any distractions in.

And yet, I couldn't help myself when it came to her.

She obliterated every shred of common sense I had.

"Nonsense, you just need to spend more time with me," Amar replied with a boisterous laugh. "Tell him, Michael."

The sound of my name pulled me out of my reverie.

Sofiane gave me an imploring look that said, *get us out of here.* I wish we could, but I knew Amar wouldn't let us off that easily. So I did the next best thing I could think of.

Buy us some alone time.

"Why don't Sofiane and I find us a table, while you go get us drinks," I proposed to Amar, knowing all too well he'd be more than happy too. He loved chatting with the bartenders and anyone who'd be willing to listen to him talk.

"That's a great idea," he replied, squeezing Sofiane's shoulder.

Thank you, Sofiane mouthed as Amar walked away toward the bar.

I gave him a curt nod as I spotted a vacant high-table. We swiftly made our way toward it and each took a seat. I remained quiet, wishing to give him a few moments of reprieve, but he surprised me when he spoke up.

"So, how's your research going?" he asked, twirling the matching ring we all wore. Most would think he was asking me about work, but I knew exactly what he was referring to.

My Order.

I propped a hand under my chin. "It's not there yet, but we're making progress."

"That's good. Let me know if you ever need—"

"You know we can't," I said, cutting him off.

"How would they know?"

"Do I need to remind you of your fifteenth birthday?"

The instant dread that took over his features was answer enough.

We weren't allowed to discuss the House and anything related to it amongst each other until each of us completed our Ascension. Amar and I had snuck Sofiane out for his fifteenth birthday and we'd gone to my favorite place at the time—where I'd used to escape my father and the responsibilities I'd felt burdened with.

We were a few beers in and daring. The moment we uttered the name of the House, a man (who we now knew was their Fixer) had all of a sudden shown up and taken us without a word to our fathers.

To this day, we still hadn't figured out how they'd found out, but after meeting the wrath of all three of our fathers together that night, we'd decided it was best not to break that rule ever again.

So, we'd come up with ways to broach the subject that didn't have the mysterious and quiet stranger who'd shown up that first and last time we'd spoken about the House without being permitted to.

Amar came back a few minutes later with our drinks.

"So what are you two gossiping about?" he said, taking the seat between us and dropping their pints and my soda in the middle of the table. I was in charge of taking them home and at my age, hangovers weren't as fun as they'd used to be.

"Sofiane's fifteenth birthday," I said, grabbing the bottle of Coke and taking a sip.

A haunted look flashed through Amar's eyes at the mention of that night, before it quickly disappeared. "Ah, yes. Such a memorable night," he said with a laugh, but I could tell from his tone he was deflecting.

After that night we hadn't seen or heard from him for almost an entire week, until he'd suddenly shown up to our weekly Saturday football games. We'd tried asking him what happened, but he'd just brushed it off as being busy studying for finals even though I knew he'd already finished his.

I shot him a quizzical look over the rim of my bottle before placing it on the table. "I wouldn't call being locked in a dark room with you two for an entire night while drunk, then taken home and constantly getting lectured over the following weeks about how much of a disappointment we were for risking the House, on top of being grounded for weeks 'memorable'. My father still even brings it up."

Amar rubbed the small scar above his right eyebrow with his thumb before taking a large swig of his beer. "Count yourself lucky that's all you got," he said nonchalantly, but before I could ask what he meant, he changed the subject. "Alright, birthday boy, which one?" he asked him, placing a hand on Sofiane's shoulder.

"I turned twenty-eight two weeks ago so technically I'm no longer a birthday boy and what do you mean 'which one'?"

"Well, which one is more your type?" Amar clarified, nudging his head forward.

We both looked to the side to realize what he was referring to. A group of women wearing bridesmaid sashes and one wearing all white were blatantly staring at us.

Amar shot them his signature smile, his deep left dimple making its appearance, as he waggled his fingers at them. A few of them waved back before they all giggled to each other behind their hands.

I turned my attention away, my mind already occupied with images of luscious dark hair and eyes that you couldn't look away from, even when you tried.

Sofiane's gaze briefly flitted to the group of women again before he returned his attention to Amar. "I'm okay," he replied, hoping Amar would drop it. But we both knew Amar didn't give up so easily.

"Oh, come on, Sousou. Have a little fun for once," Amar pleaded as he leaned closer to him and gave Sofiane puppy dog eyes.

Sofiane shrugged him off. "Firstly, I've told you to stop calling me that. Secondly, not if it means…"

"Yes, yes. All members of the House must remain virgins until A—"

Sofiane's eyes widened as he brought his hand over Amar's mouth, effectively stopping him from saying rule IV of the Book of Aman. One of the things we were strictly prohibited from ever saying out loud. Much less in a public space.

We'd all been reckless with the rules before—except Sofiane—and pushed their limits, but this was deliberately irresponsible, even for Amar.

We were introduced to the Code on our thirteenth birthday after we debuted society at the annual masquerade ball and were responsible for memorizing it *and* abiding by it until we took our last breath.

No one except the Atlases were allowed to know of its existence.

"You have a death wish. Did my fifteenth birthday teach you nothing?"

Amar visibly stiffened at Sofiane's comment before he shrugged him off, and stood from his seat. "Suit yourself," he said before finishing his pint in two large swigs and placing it back down on the table with a large thunk.

He moved to leave but Sofiane placed a hand on his forearm to stop him.

"Do you have no care for consequences?" he asked, concerned.

We were used to Amar doing whatever he wanted, but he'd been different recently. He was next in line after me and still had two years before he got his Order.

Only if you complete yours.

"I *do* fucking care, " Amar replied with a bite, and the sharpness in his tone took us both by surprise. He never raised his voice, swore, nor spoke to anyone, much less Sofiane, with anything but softness. Realizing it, he shot us a laconic smile. "But there's always ways to bend the rules without breaking them," he added before making his way through the crowd toward the group of women.

They all gathered around him and laughter boomed from them at whatever he was telling them. He'd slipped back into his charming persona like what just transpired here never even happened.

I looked over to Sofiane, a guilty expression covering his features. "Did I say something?"

I shook my head. "You did nothing wrong, mate. He's just been on edge," I lied, using the only thing I could think of and hoping it'd be enough to reassure him.

I could tell he didn't believe me but he'd dropped it.

We didn't talk again about my 'research' or Amar's sudden shift in behavior for the next hour, instead choosing safer conversations like our work or the next societal event we were required to attend at the end of next month that was honoring his father's philanthropic work.

It was almost ten at night when we'd decided to call it. I was walking toward where Amar stood in the corner, cozying up with one of the bridesmaids, when a flash of familiar dark curly hair caught my attention.

Against my better judgment, I followed it as it rushed through the crowd and walked out of the pub. By the time I stepped out after her, there was no one outside. My imagination must be playing tricks on me.

Get it together, Michael.

I stood there for a moment, to see if I hadn't imagined her, before walking back inside.

"Everything alright?" Sofiane asked, grabbing his coat from the back of his seat. "I saw you going outside."

"Yeah, I just thought I saw someone," I replied absentmindedly, grabbing my own jacket. "Wanna call it a night?"

Amar had decided to stay back so Sofiane and I headed to my car parked on the other side of the street. Once we were inside, a flitting reflection of someone watching us appeared in my rearview mirror but when I adjusted it, it was gone.

You've been thinking about her so much, you're now imagining her.

I shook the thought away and placed my car in drive, navigating toward Mayfair where Sofiane lived. It wasn't really his scene, but it was the closest to his work and he hated commuting or driving.

After dropping him off at his place, I checked on Amar's location to see he was still at the bar before I made my way toward my flat. Once home, I quickly showered and heated up leftovers from last night.

I settled on my couch to eat and scrutinized my wall that had been transformed into something straight out of a thriller movie, hoping it would be enough of a distraction from thinking about Azara.

Not that my current leads would help with any of it.

After a few hours of wondering how the hell I would become the new medical director of AGH, I'd gotten to work. I'd spent the last six weeks working on leads and finally had settled on the two weakest links on the board of directors after using some hacking tricks Sofiane had taught me over the years.

Julian Hayes, AGH's consultant and divisional director of emergency medicine, and none other than Adnan Ziani, the father of the woman I couldn't stop thinking about no matter how hard I tried to.

Some of the other members also had secrets I could hold against them, but a cheating scandal rarely hurt anyone. People could always apologize to their spouses and promise to never do it again.

I needed something substantial, something that could ruin someone's life in a way that it can never be taken back, and these two were the ones who had the most to lose.

Besides that, Dr. Hayes and Dr. Ziani had the most power on the board. Their opinions were highly valued and the most consequential. Something I'd determined from looking at previous board voting results.

When it came to Dr. Hayes, I'd overheard the nurses gossip about his excessive flirting with patients. At first, I thought it was harmless because I knew many doctors who did the same, myself included when it came to more shy patients so they'd feel more at ease.

But I'd never crossed a line or been inappropriate.

Unlike Julian.

I'd started paying more attention whenever I was in A&E for consults and that's when I noticed that his flirty behavior was more than what a doctor-patient relationship should be.

He was pushy and I'd eventually even discovered that he'd abused his power and had slept with more than one patient. I'd even found inappropriate pictures on his Cloud storage that clearly were taken without their subject's knowledge.

I could use the information to my advantage, but there was more than him at stake. I didn't want to expose the patients involved against their consent.

I would figure out a way to and he'd get what was coming for him, but for now, I'd have to focus on my last option.

Adnan Ziani.

He wasn't as easy to solve.

The man was practically a saint.

But in every saint, there was a sinner.
Now, I just had to figure out his blight.

158

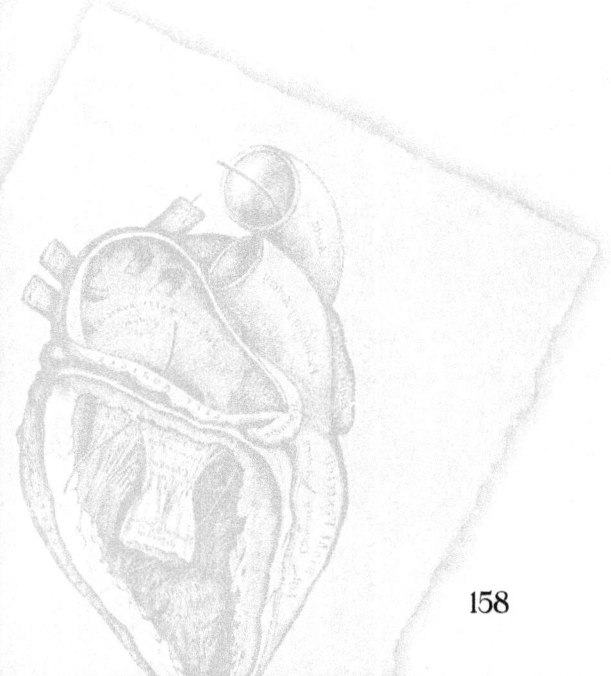

CHAPTER 13

MICHAEL

"COULD YOU WIPE THAT SMILE off your face?" Azara scoffed as I held the door open with my back to let her into the scrub room after our final surgery of the day.

We'd just spent the last five hours repairing an aortic aneurysm, and she'd argued against every one of my directives, as she always did when we operated together. Which, admittedly, happened quite often over the last four months of being here—solely because I had a say in the matter.

If it had been any other surgeon, I'd have them out of my theater without a second thought, but with Azara, I enjoyed every second of it. She often had great alternatives to my old-school methods because even though we were only about a year apart, we'd been surgically trained from two different mentors.

Besides, I'd be lying if our bickering didn't turn me on.

"But I was right," I said, finishing washing my hands and leaning against the sink where she was doing the same.

She turned the water off and dried off her hands before facing me with the glare I'd grown accustomed to. The one she specifically reserved for me.

She was remarkably charming and polite to everyone we worked with, but the moment I entered her orbit, the scowl she currently pinned me with became a permanent fixture on her face.

At first, she'd tried to hide it, and maintain her nice facade, but it didn't last long. Unless, of course, her father was around—then she put in extra work to be cordial toward me.

"You merely made a suggestion that didn't turn out terrible," she said, not conceding an inch.

I raised an eyebrow, amused. "So I was right," I repeated, peeling off my surgical hat.

Her eyes narrowed before she crossed her arms. "You're insufferable, you know that?"

I couldn't help but laugh at that. "You wouldn't like me any other way," I replied, intently watching her reaction.

Her expression faltered for a brief moment, but I caught it regardless. And she couldn't hide the blush creeping up her tanned skin. "Yeah, keep telling yourself that," she said, her tone half-annoyed, half-flustered, as she rested her hands behind her against the edge of the sink.

I took a step closer, closing the space between us, despite knowing that I shouldn't risk it. That I *should* maintain the professional boundary that was supposed to exist between us.

But when had that ever stopped me before when it came to her.

"You like a challenge, Azara." I paused, placing my hands on either side of her, my fingers barely grazing hers. I expected her to push me away, to even hit me for being this close to her but she didn't move.

In fact, I would bet that her body shifted closer toward mine. My gaze roamed over her features before meeting her gaze head-on. "You like *me* keeping you on your toes, *gumiho*," I said, barely recognizing my voice.

Just like she kept me on mine. Not that I'd ever complain about that.

The silence that followed stretched for a moment, thickening with weeks of unsaid words. A hint of molten fire flashed in her gaze, but it didn't erase the stubborn tilt to her chin.

"You're doing it again," she said, ignoring my latest statement.

"You'll need to be more precise," I replied, leaning down.

Her head slightly tilted to maintain my gaze. "You keep looking at me like that," she explained, her voice barely above a whisper.

I moved my face closer to hers, just enough our lips nearly touched. I brought a hand up, gently brushing my knuckles along the edge of her cheekbone before bringing it back down.

"What if I like looking at you like that?"

Her small gasp feathered against my lips, and I could practically taste her. Desire simmered in my blood at the thought. It had been four months of this constant back and forth. Four months of torturous days and nights where I'd imagined her lips tangling with mine.

More times than I'd like to admit and I could make those dreams a reality.

All I had to do was obliterate the last inch separating us.

"Someone could walk in, Dr. Young," she whispered, still not moving away.

"What if they did?" I paused, my gaze flitting between her eyes and lips. "And I think we're far past you calling me Dr. Young."

Just the thought of hearing my name with that silky voice of hers, passing through those alluring lips of hers, was sending goosebumps skittering across my skin.

"Calling you anything else would be inappropriate."

"Say my name, Azara."

With every word we spoke, our lips brushed and the temptation to just fucking kiss her was so potent, I found myself leaning forward to bridge the gap when the double-acting doors bursted open.

Azara immediately pushed my body away, just as Marcella's voice filled the room.

"Mr. Young, we need you in Theater D." She finally looked up from her tablet, and pushed her red reading glasses up her nose, her scrutinizing gaze flitting back and forth between Azara and I. "Am I interrupting something?"

"No," Azara blurted out, her demeanor bleeding guilt. "You were interrupting absolutely nothing."

Marcella raised a brow, the look she gave both of us, knowing. We definitely would have escaped any suspicions if Azara hadn't been so blatantly obvious. For someone who was unyielding during surgery, she folded like a house of cards under social pressure.

"If you say so," she told Azara, brushing it off, before turning her attention to me. "You're needed in Theater D. The two idiots scheduled to operate have been arguing for the last twenty minutes over whether or not to use the NyxMedica stapler. I would have gone to Mr. Ziani, but for some reason, I can't find him, and you're the most senior surgeon."

My brows furrowed at the mention of NyxMedica. The corporation owned by billionaire Arthur Nyx had made waves when it was founded a few years ago. Although from the outside, his company looked like it was thriving, the engineer was well-known to be a fraud. His company should have been seized a long time ago but the amount of money he had was the best shield anyone in our society could ask for.

People always did stupid things for money.

"I'll be right with you," I told Marcella, attempting to gently dismiss her and hoping she got the message.

She looked between the both of us. "Oh, right. I'll wait for you there. Don't be long," she said before turning on her heels.

As soon as she exited the room, I pinched the bridge of my nose, trying to contain my laughter. And failing.

Azara smacked my chest. "This isn't funny," she reprimanded, but when I looked up I found a smirk tugging at the corner of her lips.

"You have to admit it is," I noted.

She shook her head, but didn't say anything. She'd inadvertently bridged the distance between us, leaving her within reach again. But even though all my senses pulled me toward her, I knew I couldn't actually cross that line.

No matter how much I *really* wanted to.

"I should go," I said, but my statement came out more like a question.

"Yeah, you should before the idiots kill someone."

I chuckled. "I'll go do that," I agreed as I walked toward the exit.

I paused, a hand on the door as I glanced at her one last time. I brought my free hand up, my thumb gliding over my lower lip where I could still feel the tiniest brush of her lips against mine.

"I'll see you tomorrow, Dr. Ziani," I finally said before pushing the door open and heading down the corridor.

Marcella was waiting for me outside the operating room just like she'd said. She gave me a knowing look after what she'd *almost* walked into, but I ignored it and pushed past the doors, her short frame following right behind.

I found the two idiots still at it, going back and forth with their arguments on whether or not to use the device. I listened to them for a few seconds before intervening and cutting their conversation short.

I didn't like dictating how another surgeon should operate, but when the potential risks were too high and these two were wasting everyone's time, I'd made the decision for them and ruled against it.

Marcella and I had tried paging the older Ziani again before going in since he was the one who had a say in determining which surgical devices were used by his staff, but both his personal cell and pager went unanswered.

Which I found rather peculiar.

I'd only known him for a little over four months now, but he'd always made himself available, even when he wasn't at the hospital.

As I walked to the doctor's lounge fifteen minutes later, I briefly stopped by Theater A to see if she was still there, only to find it empty. Something close to disappointment brushed against my breast bone but I waved it off and headed out of the surgical area.

I finally climbed into the lift, but once the doors closed, one thing kept bothering me. On top of his unresponsiveness, I couldn't understand how a reputable and diligent doctor like Ziani would allow the use of any device from NyxMedica.

The company's high-tech new surgical devices were promoted as avant-garde and aiming to improve efficiency during surgery, but all I'd ever heard from colleagues about the products was the opposite.

I knew the company had funded a part of AGH's new surgical wing, and some of the devices had been previously used by some of the team, but I wasn't aware the board was still allowing its general surgeons to do so after the leaked report that came out a few weeks ago showing how many complications had actually arisen from the use of the company's products.

It contradicted every other report the company had issued in the past, especially from that fucking surgical stapler. The mortality rates attached to that device alone were too high.

Not that Nyx took any responsibility for it and instead blamed his manufacturer for not doing their due diligence and following his successfully proven prototype. And of course, the public and officials believed him.

The hospital had a reputation to uphold, so why would Ziani risk it?

As I made the short walk from the hospital to my flat, there was only one plausible answer that came to mind.

People always did stupid things for money.

I'D SPENT THE NEXT FEW weeks focusing my attention on collecting any information I could find on Ziani, no matter how minute it seemed.

Since I couldn't ask for Sofiane's help, I'd put to use all the tricks he'd taught me over the years and dug through Adnan's bank account, and phone logs as far back as I could. I went over every bit of information with a fine-tooth comb, trying to spot anything that would indicate something unusual.

I'd already tapped each of the board members' phones during the few days following my birthday, but I had yet to find anything on his. He received solicitors' calls like everyone else did, but nothing seemed out of the ordinary.

Ziani's routine was simple.

Work. Home. And more work.

Azara had come over a few times for dinner, but she only stayed for an hour or two before leaving and heading back to her flat which was not too far from her childhood home.

I even followed him during my spare time (which wasn't much), and unluckily for me, the only places he went to were the hospital and the townhouse he lived in with his teenage son, Zayd. Occasionally, he made trips to the pharmacy or the grocery store, but only if Azara hadn't already gone for them.

Which I'd noticed she did a lot—taking care of them even though she worked just as much as I did.

May was nearly drawing to an end, and each lead I'd pursued had so far frustratingly hit a dead end. I had eight months left before it'd be too late, and yet I'd barely made much progress. Finding my entry point to the board was one thing, but actually claiming a seat was an entirely different order.

My computer suddenly pinged with the ringtone I'd set for when Ziani received a call. I paused, halting my task of cutting the cucumbers for my *bibim-guksu* and switching off the heat on my boiling pot of water. I then walked into my living room, which currently looked like an inspector's office in the middle of solving a crime.

It was a quarter past ten on a Friday night so I couldn't help but wonder who'd be calling him at this hour. I brought up the app only to find out the incoming call was from another solicitor. I almost dismissed it and returned to my cooking, when the number caught my eye.

I'd seen it before.

Solicitors rarely called from the same number so I pressed the button to listen in on the conversation and quickly hit record before pulling Ziani's previous call logs to confirm I hadn't imagined it.

The line was quiet at first, until a voice I'd heard before—one that had been splashed across headlines countless times—filtered through the speaker.

"Why aren't you answering my calls?" the voice snapped, sharp with frustration.

My brows furrowed as I searched my brain for explanations as to why Arthur Nyx would be calling Ziani's personal cell, and at this hour of all times. My confusion deepened as I refocused on the conversation.

The sound of a door clicking shut came through before Ziani responded, his voice laced with irritation. "Need I remind you, I'm the medical director of an incredibly busy hospital. Besides, you're only meant to call me at the times we agreed on."

Ziani's voice sounded completely different from the golden retriever man I'd gotten to know over the past few months.

Nyx's reply came swiftly. "Need I remind you that I'm responsible for putting you there," he gritted out as a door slammed in the background.

"*I* put myself there," Ziani growled, every word steeped in resentment.

"Do you forget that *my* money is a large contributor to where you and your family are?" His response was almost casual, but Nyx's words were laced with an unmistakable threat.

The line was quiet for a moment, crackling slightly, until Adnan exhaled and spoke again. "What is it that you want?" he asked, clearly wanting the conversation to be over.

"Someone is leaking false information about my devices."

Ziani let out a huff. "False isn't the word I'd use," he muttered, his tone thick with disdain. "But how is that my problem?"

"We both know what's at stake here, Adnan. Find a way to fix it, or you won't like the consequences."

The line went dead before Ziani could respond.

Forty seconds. That was how long the call lasted.

I stopped the recording and sat there, their words hanging in the air. My mind reeled with the onslaught of information. I'd expected to eventually find something on Ziani and use it against him, but a connection to Arthur Nyx was the last thing I would have imagined.

When I looked through Ziani's phone logs again, the number only appeared one other time, lasting just as long. So, instead of focusing on the incoming caller, I looked at the length of his calls over the last year.

Only to discover that someone had called Ziani and stayed on the phone with him for exactly forty seconds every three months for the last three years of records I could access.

I made a list of all the numbers and imputed them into another encrypted app that would trace who'd made them, or at least *where* they'd been made from. After a few minutes of processing, a message popped up on my screen with the lead I'd been after.

NyxMedica's head office.

This piece of information wasn't damning enough, but it was a solid lead. Now, I just needed to uncover the true nature of Arthur and Adnan's connection. So, after quickly finishing dinner, I grabbed my bowl of cold spicy noodles and moved back to my sofa to get to work.

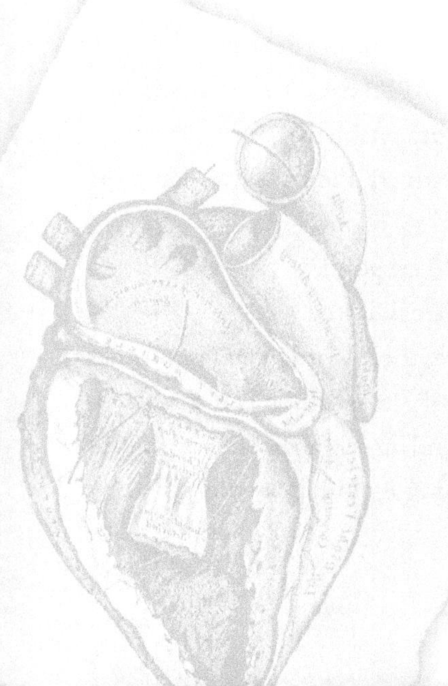

CHAPTER 14

MICHAEL

I GLANCED AT MY WATCH to find that it was nearly the end of his shift.

I had about a minute before Adnan Ziani stepped into his office to find me sitting in the dark at his desk, legs crossed and casually propped up on the hard surface, completely unaware of what awaited him.

Just as I'd anticipated, the wooden door creaked open. Without missing a beat, I reached over and flicked on the small lamp standing next to his computer. The small bulb flared to life, basking the room with a sickly yellow glow.

Ziani recoiled at the sudden light, a hand instinctively flying to his chest. He looked up, his gaze finding mine. When he realized who I was, he exhaled a small sigh of relief before confusion took its place on his features.

"What are you doing in my office?" he asked, with a strained smile.

The kind that didn't reach his eyes like it usually did.

I swung my legs off the desk and slowly stood, my knuckles pressing onto the cool wooden surface as I leaned forward, fixing him with an unwavering gaze. "I'm so glad you asked, Adnan."

He was clearly caught off guard by my use of his first name, his eyes widening just a fraction. Although we had a good professional rapport, I'd never referred to him as anything other than Mr. Ziani. But I didn't really have time for pleasantries, it was easier to set the tone straight away.

It had been a while since I'd had to blackmail anyone, since I'd stopped doing it the day I'd finished medical school. But I hadn't forgotten how satisfying it was to watch someone act completely clueless when they were anything but innocent. To watch them scramble their way out of a trap they'd set for themselves.

After being unsuccessful in finding information on his private computer at home, I'd turned my attention to the next place he spent the majority of his time.

Here.

Only to find that the evidence I'd been searching for had been right in front of me all along.

I'd spent the past month after the call between Nyx and Ziani combing through every file at the hospital that involved the use of NyxMedica's devices. I read countless operative reports, clinical notes, and progress notes from the nurses, comparing the events and trying to find discrepancies.

Anything that might stand out.

At first, it seemed like there wasn't anything that could be useful to me, until I came across one operative note that unraveled everything I'd found after.

Adnan shifted his weight, pushing his glasses up and rubbing his eyes together, before looking at me again. "It's late," he said, forcing another smile. "I really think it'd be best if you went home," he added, hoping that would effectively dismiss me.

"Sure, I'll go home, right after we have our little chat. Why don't you take a seat?"

He readjusted his glasses back in place, clearly rattled by my sudden lack of diplomacy. "As I recall, this happens to be my office," he said, attempting to reclaim some semblance of authority, but it didn't erase the flicker of doubt in his voice.

"Not for long," I said, gesturing at the seat in front of his desk. "Now, take a seat. I think you'll really want to hear what I have to say."

I settled in his seat again, leaning back and propping my arm against the armrest. There was a long, tense moment where he stood, his fingers fidgeting with his glasses as he weighed his options. I kept my gaze fixated on him, waiting, until eventually he sat down across from me, sinking into one of the leather chairs with a resigned sigh.

"What's so important that you're practically holding me hostage?" he asked, his collected demeanor cracking, his irritation creeping in despite his best attempt to stay composed.

Instead of answering, I reached over and rotated his computer screen toward him.

"What's this?" he asked as he leaned forward and pushed his glasses up his nose, squinting to get a better look. As his eyes skimmed over the screen, I watched his pupils contract ever so slightly when he realized what it was, but he quickly schooled his features back.

Just not quickly enough for it to go unnoticed by me.

"Patients records," I said, coolly.

His face twitched slightly, the blood increasingly draining from his features. "I don't understand why you're showing me confidential information," he stammered, a hint of desperation creeping into his voice, betraying him.

I held his gaze, unwavering. "I think we can both do each other a favor and stop pretending by dragging this charade of yours out."

An unnerving silence cloaked the room as he wrung his fingers together. I could hear the cogs turning in his mind, desperately trying to formulate some viable excuse to get himself out of this.

But before he could speak, I cut him off. It was rather late, as he'd pointed out a few minutes ago, and I had no intention of wasting any more time.

"Since you're still struggling to come up with a lie, let me save you the trouble," I said, my voice cold and deliberate. "I know you've been falsifying reports for NyxMedica so they wouldn't lose their UKCA mark. They've been paying you handsomely in exchange for this hospital to push and endorse their devices."

I paused and watched him squirm as I braced myself against the desk. "You've been altering patients' records by adding the use of NyxMedica's devices into procedures when it wasn't the case to improve their success rate, overriding access logs and making sure your name never appeared in any of the notes once you'd made your 'adjustments'."

He looked at me, eyes wide in shock, clearly not having expected for me to have unearthed all of this.

From what I'd gathered on him, Adnan Ziani was a typical sixty-three year old man who'd come from a regular background and had worked as a doctor for most of his life. And surprisingly, for a while, he'd done an impressive job of covering his tracks.

Initially, despite the discrepancies between the reports, I couldn't find anything that directly linked him to the changes. Until I'd slipped into his office during an on call shift and logged onto his computer.

Although he'd managed to stay under the radar, he was still an ordinary man because when his desktop lit up, I'd found a draft of a patient's note he was in the middle of editing.

From there, I'd installed a surveillance chip I'd acquired from the dark web. It recorded every time he accessed files under another doctor's name and made changes to already approved notes. It also turned on his webcam to capture him doing it.

I'd collected enough over the last week to use for blackmail. And I knew he'd confess to every other time as well once I came head to head with him.

"This," I said, holding up a small USB key, "contains every altered patient file you've meddled with."

Ziani's mouth opened as if to speak, but no words came out so I continued.

"While this," I paused, grabbing a manila folder I'd stored to the side and placed it in front of him, "has all of the statements for the bank account you opened in your son's name."

His brows furrowed, and I could see him trying to process how I could have uncovered that.

I'd run a thorough check on Ziani's finances, but couldn't find large sum deposits or glaring red flags that would indicate the money he'd received in exchange for this scheme they were running.

That's when I dug further and began investigating his family—his sixteen year old son, Zayd, and his thirty-one year old daughter, and the woman I still hadn't managed to get out of my head, Azara.

Nothing on her end came out of the ordinary, which didn't surprise me. I'd been wrong about him, but I knew she had nothing to do with her father's deceit.

At least I'd hoped so.

Although nothing came up for his daughter, I'd come across a second bank account for his son where weekly deposits from

NyxMedica were made and they'd dated as far back as when he was a toddler. Which was quite odd since Ziani's teenage son clearly wasn't an employee of the company, and certainly not when he was child.

Despite the curiosity, I hadn't cared to dig into why he'd been receiving money from Arthur for so long. My only focus was on if it tied to this hospital and how it could benefit me getting what I wanted. The rest wasn't important.

Adnan's face grew ashen as the weight of what I'd just confronted him with sank in. I could practically see the shift in him, the realization that his entire web of lies was about to come crashing down, washing over him.

"Since there's no point in you denying any of this, here are your options. You'll either resign as medical director and from your position on AGH's board, or this all becomes public."

I leaned forward, locking eyes with him.

"The choice is yours."

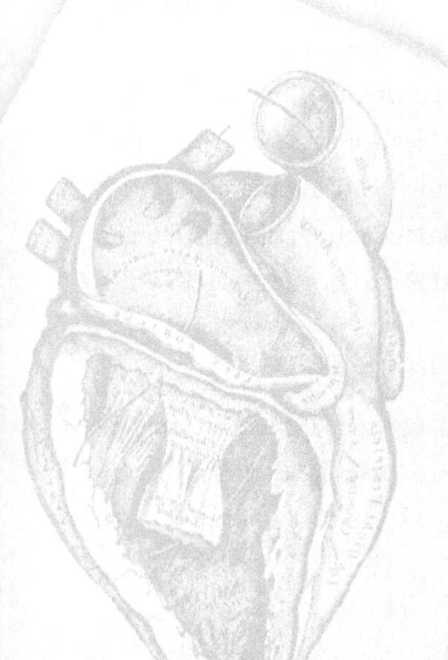

CHAPTER 15

AZARA

I HAD NEVER DREADED GOING to work the way I did nowadays.

I'd been working with Dr. Young for a little over five months now and not a single day went by that my mind didn't dream up different scenarios on how to get rid of someone for good while also inflicting him with the most pain.

I wasn't a violent person by nature, but it was the only way I could quiet the *other* images swarming my thoughts any chance they got. The fact that we were in constant proximity, practically joined at the hip every day, and that his flirtations hadn't ceased from the moment we met surely didn't help with that.

Let's not forget the almost kiss before Marcella walked in on you both, my mind reminded me.

Shut up.

Brilliant, I was talking to myself again.

I shoved my feet into my clogs, slammed my locker door shut and made my way to the ward, hoping the busy day ahead of me would keep my mind preoccupied. And fortunately for me, I had no surgeries scheduled with Michael until tomorrow.

Just six more months. Six more months before I'd finally complete my surgical training and I'd no longer have to operate with a senior surgeon. Which meant no more operating with him.

A small, subtle wave of disappointment joined the usual relief I felt when I thought about finally accomplishing what I'd spent the last seven years training toward.

Shaking my head at the absurdity, I stepped off the lift and onto the surgical floor, heading for the nursing station. Since I was early, the floor was quieter than usual and there were only a few overnight nurses present, busy charting.

I didn't recognize any of them, but when they looked up, I smiled and waved good morning. However, when our eyes met, their expressions faltered and their responses were short before they focused back on their task, effectively ignoring me.

That's odd.

I ignored it and went on with my day, blaming it on the early hour.

But then it kept happening everywhere I went.

During my morning rounds on the ward.

When I grabbed a latte from the cafeteria.

As I walked into my first surgery of the day.

People, even the ones I'd always gotten along with, were distant and avoiding me everywhere I went. I started wondering if I'd done something wrong, but ended up convincing myself that my mind was playing tricks on me from an exhausting week and I had a packed schedule of back to back surgeries and didn't have time to ruminate or second-guess myself.

By the time I finished my third surgery of the day, it was just past two in the afternoon. I had about an hour free before my next procedure, so I decided to head to my father's office for lunch, passing by the cafeteria to grab us something to eat since I was almost certain he hadn't eaten all day.

Always too caught in his work to think about feeding himself.

Not that I was much better, but with my diabetes, I'd tried to do my best to at least eat enough to avoid a hypoglycemic episode. The only person that knew about my diagnosis aside from my father was Marcella, our surgical coordinator, and I intended to keep it that way.

I wasn't ashamed of it at all, but whenever someone discovered I had an autoimmune disease, they started acting differently and treating me like I was fragile.

Which I hated.

My pancreas just didn't work like everyone else's, I wasn't dying or contagious.

Only a few people were roaming around the halls as I made my way toward my father's office. There was an unusual heaviness in the air, but with the day I'd had, I ignored it again.

I needed for this day to be over already.

When I reached his office, I knocked once with my free hand, before cracking the door open and coming inside.

"Hey, I thought we could have lunch…" My words trailed off when I looked up to find the room empty.

I knew I hadn't gotten his schedule wrong because we were in the middle of the week. He should be here.

I walked further into the eerily quiet room and rounded his desk, placing the sandwiches and waters down on it. I then grabbed his planner to see if maybe he was in a meeting that I hadn't known about, but when I flipped it to today's page, I found his schedule clear.

My brows furrowed as my eyes roamed around the room. It looked like he hadn't even been in yet. Confused, I pulled out my phone from my scrub's pocket and texted him.

ME

Hey, baba. I'm in your office for lunch, finek[14]?

I hit send and waited for the two check marks to appear beneath the message, confirming it had been delivered. But it didn't happen. I followed up with another text message, thinking the first one might just still be processing.

ME

Baba? Wach nta flkhadma[15]? Are you okay? Did you get another one of your colds?

I knew we were in June, but for some reason this man always got sick when the temperature changed often like it had over the last two weeks and he never prepared for it.

I watched my screen intently, yet still nothing. My messages not only went unanswered—which never happened, my father always replied almost instantly to my texts—but they weren't even being delivered.

A knot settled in my stomach as a wave of panic creeped in.

No.

I took a deep breath and shoved the paranoid feelings away, knowing I was being ridiculous for letting myself jump to the worst conclusion.

My father was fine. He had to be.

Opting for the rational route, I headed two floors down where the operating theaters were. It was one of the few areas in the hospital

---

14 *Where are you? (Moroccan darija)*
15 *Are you at work? (Moroccan drija)*

where phone service was spotty and the only other place I could think of where my father could be.

He often went there to either check on other surgeons or perform a surgery himself. Although most medical directors stopped operating after taking on the role because of the busy schedule and all the responsibilities that came with it, my father refused to give it up. So he still occasionally took on cases to stay connected with his first love—operating.

I stopped by the large whiteboard where all scheduled surgeries were displayed, and searched for his name. After my third time scanning every single slot on the board and not finding his name, the dread I'd felt earlier surged again and this time, I couldn't ignore it.

My heart pounded in my chest as the worst case scenarios flooded my mind.

Where is my father?

This was so unlike him to disappear and not answer my messages. After my mum died, we'd made it a point to never miss a text or phone call and if we did, we immediately called to reassure the other.

I checked my phone again, thinking I might have missed his reply but there were no new notifications.

God, please let him be okay.

I tried to control the fear gnawing at my insides, but it was no use as I darted from theater to theater, checking each one and hoping I'd just missed his name on the board.

Still no signs of him.

I was about to break down in the middle of the hallway, when I finally saw Lucia coming out of one of the small resting rooms. She'd been my father's assistant for almost a decade, so if someone knew where he was, it'd be her. She was heading for the lifts on the opposite side from where I stood.

"Lucia," I called out her name, my voice shaking.

She glanced over her shoulder as I hurried toward her. The moment her eyes met mine, the color drained from her face and her features sported an expression I'd grown woefully familiar with over the last several hours.

I was about to lose it. Why the fuck was everyone looking at me like that today?

"Oh, Dr. Ziani," she stuttered, her voice cracking as she shifted her weight.

"Hi, I'm sorry to bother you, but have you seen my father?" I asked, my nerves on edge.

"Your father, oh, he…" Her eyes darted away from mine, her fingers fidgeting with the papers in her hands as she tried to finish her sentence.

Dread pooled down my spine at her aversion. "Lucia," I said, my voice tight. "Where's my dad?"

An unsettling silence suffocated the space between us as I waited for her answer. Her gaze flickered nervously as people passed us by, curious glances shot our way before they scurried away.

I swear if no one tells me what's going on…

"Lucia, could you please look at me?" I asked, barely recognizing the hopelessness in my voice. After a long pause, she finally did, her eyes filled with sorrow. "Listen, everyone's been acting strange today, and now you're doing the same. So please just tell me what's going on?"

Lucia shifted on her feet, biting her lip. She gave me an apologetic look before delivering the staggering news. One I'd never anticipated in a million years.

"Your father resigned from Amanar earlier today."

MY FINGERS GRIPPED THE STEERING wheel of my car tightly, my knuckles turning white as I turned onto my father's street. I headed down the road, faster than the limit permitted, and sharply pulled in front of my family's townhouse.

After what Lucia confessed, I'd tried calling him so he could deny her inconceivable claims, but the line went straight to voicemail.

Every single time.

I still had a few other surgeries on my schedule, and I'd already been late to my next one, having completely lost track of time searching for my missing father.

I'd had to push away the fact that my dad, who adored his work and had dedicated over half of his life to it, had resigned without even telling me. It was a bitter pill to swallow, but I couldn't focus on any of it when I had patients counting on me.

So I did what any doctor would have done. I'd compartmentalized my personal feelings, had taken a steadying breath and had gotten back to work.

But as soon as I'd finished my last surgery, I'd grabbed my car keys from my locker and drove straight here, still in my hospital scrubs and cap, the scent of antiseptic clinging to me. I'd even forgotten to grab my bag which had my wallet.

Thankfully, I'd managed to make it here without getting arrested, though I was sure I'd broken a few speed limits along the way. The evening was well on its way when I threw the car in park and bolted out of it.

I marched up to the front door and knocked. When no one answered, I knocked a few more times, louder this time, the sharp sound reverberating in the quiet street.

"*Wa nari*[16]," I heard my fathers voice curse behind the door, his footsteps shuffling closer. "I'm coming. There's no need to knock this loud," he groaned, his voice thick with frustration before the door creaked open.

"If you're selling—" He cut himself off, his eyes widening when he noticed I was the impromptu visitor.

He hastily pulled his lounge robe tighter around his round belly. "Azara," he stammered, pushing the frame of his glasses up his nose, "*benti*, what are you doing here?"

I stood frozen in the doorway, shell shock at his disheveled appearance. His hair was a mess and his usually neatly groomed salt-and-pepper stubble had grown wild from the last time I'd seen him. I'd had the last four days off and hadn't seen him since last week.

What the hell is going on?

My father was always put together. The only time I'd ever seen him like this was right after Mum died.

"I could ask you the same thing," I said, brushing past him to step inside. "What are you doing at home on a weekday?"

The door clicked shut behind me. My father sighed heavily as I stopped in the middle of the living room. "Well," he paused, clearly looking for an excuse. "I wasn't feeling well, so I..."

I whipped around, cutting him off. "You resigned," I said, sharply, not mincing my words. I'd never raised my voice against my father, but I hated being lied to. Let alone by my own father.

He pointed his finger at me, a scolding expression on his face. "Watch your tone when you speak to me," he said, berating me.

"I will, once you tell me what's going on. I've spent all day garnering people's pity while I had no clue what was happening, until

---

16 *Oh my days (Moroccan darija)*

Lucia blindsided me with the news that you'd quit your job."

He sat down heavily in one of the armchairs facing me, his shoulders slumping as he exhaled a frustrated breath. "I was going to tell you," he declared, his tone apologetic.

I didn't move, standing stiffly in front of him. The hope I'd been holding on to withered with his admission because it cemented that these weren't just rumors.

My father really had resigned from his post.

My earlier confusion only grew further and mixed with a sudden and unwelcomed indignation. "Really? When exactly? When were you going to tell me? You just… quit. When did you even start thinking of doing so? We could have discussed it, or at least you could have warned me. "

He shook his head slowly, pinching the bridge of his nose in exasperation at my onslaught of questions. "It was my decision to make, Azara. I don't have to tell you everything." His tone grew unexpectedly harsher with each word.

The weight of his words felt like a cold, jarring wave. My father and I had shared everything for as long as I could remember. Yes, our relationship had changed after my mother passed, but he'd never shut me out like this before. We'd always been a team.

At least I'd thought so.

A feeling of abandonment started to creep in, a heavy knot tightening in my chest and my frustration slowly simmered into worry. "What's going on, *baba*?" My voice dimmed as I asked a question I dreaded most. There was only one other reason I could think of that would make him leave so abruptly. "Are you sick?"

I'd already lost a parent, I didn't think I could bear losing another.

His brows furrowed in confusion. "What? No, I'm completely fine."

Nothing was adding up. On my way here, I'd tried to come up with reasons as to why he'd leave but none of them made sense. He *loved* AGH, he'd dedicated so many years of his life to the place, so why on earth was he quitting? He always said he'd keep working there until he physically couldn't anymore.

My shoulders fell, feeling utterly defeated. "Then why? Why are you leaving?"

"Because I decided to."

"But this doesn't make sense, you love the place. You said you'd never retire, that you'd—"

His chair scraped abruptly against the floor as he stood, his face suddenly hardening with an emotion I couldn't quite place. "Because I made my decision, Azara. End of discussion," he spewed with an anger I'd never seen from him before.

My face fell, the sting of his demeanor cutting through me. My father had never yelled at me before, not even when times were hard. He'd always removed himself from the situation and came back later to finish whatever conversation we were having when he was calmer.

"*Baba…*" my voice faltered, unsure of what even to say with the mix of emotions battling inside me.

He didn't respond. Instead, his eyes flicked to the clock on the wall. "Your brother will be home any minute now. You should leave before he sees you," he said, clearly dismissing me.

I wanted to push him to talk to me, to make him tell me what was really going on. I wanted him to open up and share whatever it was that had driven him to make such a drastic decision. But I knew, deep down, that if I kept pushing, it would only drive him further away.

I tightly gripped the keys in my hand as my mind reeled with this new reality. I watched him for a moment. His tired eyes—eyes I hadn't seen like that since Mum passed away—almost looked right through me.

I'd never seen my father look so… defeated. So lost.

Eventually, I nodded slowly and made my way toward the front door. But just before I left, I paused in front of him. When I looked up at him, he averted his gaze. I ignored the blooming pain in my chest from the rejection and stood on my tiptoes, brushing a soft kiss against his stubbled cheek.

"I wish you'd talked to me," I said, my voice barely above a whisper. And with that, I left.

I got into my car, and mindlessly drove home, my thoughts in disarray with the thousand questions left unanswered. I knew my dad wasn't telling me the full truth. There had to be more to this, something deeper than what he was letting on because he wouldn't just leave his beloved job so suddenly without a good reason.

He'd always been so protective over his career and the thought of retiring was nowhere near his plans the last time we'd spoken about it. The last time I'd even suggested he work less, he'd become our medical director.

So the idea of him walking away from all of it without a valid explanation was absolute nonsense.

But I would find out the reason behind my father's resignation.

No matter how long it took.

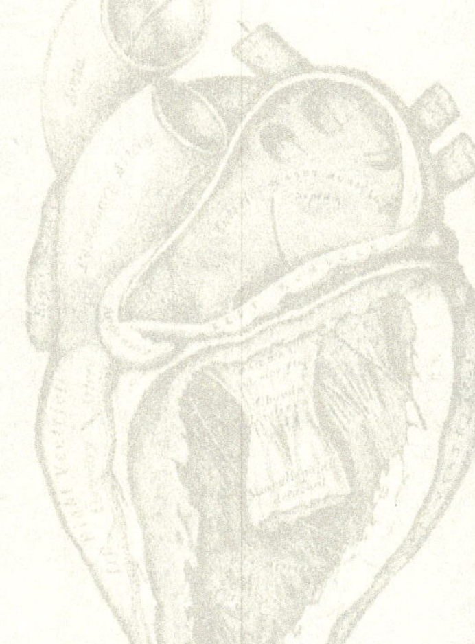

CHAPTER 16

MICHAEL

"YOU'RE LATE, MATE," ISAIAH CALLED out as I stepped out of my sleek red Atlas V8 that I'd parked into the narrow entrance of Azel. I spotted him leaning casually against a stone pillar near the entrance, his arms folded against his chest.

"*And* you're driving the competition," he chastised with a shake of his head in disapproval, though the grin on his face betrayed him.

I left the driver's side door open, handing my keys to the valet on duty tonight. I shot him a wink in thanks before turning my attention to my known-for-dramatics cousin.

"It's good to see you too," I replied with a smirk, striding toward him. "Besides, I'm right on time. You're just always bloody early to everything. As for the car, if my memory serves me right, it was a handover gift after *you* made the most controversial move of your career."

My cousin had previously been with Atlas Racing for six years where he'd won his first World Championship at the age of twenty-three, before he'd made the decision to race for their fiercest rival, Matrix Motorsports.

The sudden swap had made the headlines for weeks, the move seen as a huge betrayal to the team that had given him his first break into the elite sport. But I knew why he'd made the decision and it wasn't for the money. He had enough of that already.

"Yeah, don't remind me," he muttered, rolling his eyes at the memory of that time. "I still have nightmares of the media days following the leak," he added as we were escorted into the club.

While Azel seemed modest from the outside, the interior was an entirely different story. Isaiah and I had made it a tradition to come here every year before his home race at Silverstone, and yet, every time I walked through the grand oak doors, this place was still just as impressive as the first time I'd seen it.

I'd grown up surrounded by wealth so little could take me aback. I'd seen countless luxurious real estate properties, just my parent's house giving most of them a run for its money, but Azel still managed to do exactly that every time I visited.

The exclusive social club had been founded in the early 1900s by a group of England's richest and most noble families. Although Azel hadn't changed much over the years in that it remained exclusive for the world's richest and most powerful, it had now expanded into every major city across the globe.

And more importantly, it allowed people who looked like me to become members after the Atlases acquired its ownership a little over fifty years ago. The House had always made it a mission to say fuck you to white supremacy and owning Azel was one of the many ways they'd done that since its inception.

"You know we barely ever see each other, you could have made an effort," Isaiah remarked, giving me a onceover, as we approached the imposing solid bronze bar that stood as the centerpiece of the lounge.

Isaiah lived in Monaco whenever he wasn't racing, so he rarely came home anymore. The only times I did see him were at the annual King family's gathering in August that was mandatory—that was if he even graced us with his presence, not that I blamed him, his father was a lot—or for our yearly drinks before the madness of his home race started.

I raise an eyebrow at him. "I'm in a suit on a Monday evening. What more do you want?" I said, taking the plush leather chair next to him. I normally only wore suits for events, but Azel didn't allow any member to walk through those doors without the appropriate attire.

The bartender immediately came over to take our orders before he moved to prepare our drinks as I looked around the quiet room. Although we were in the middle of summer, the place was emptier than usual which I very much welcomed after the whirlwind these last few weeks have been.

"Yeah, but you still look like you haven't slept in weeks," he said, huffing out a laugh.

Because I barely have.

Being a surgeon already limited my sleep schedule, but ever since my birthday, I'd spent practically every free waking hour working on my Order.

It had already been a week since the first part of my plan was brought into motion. It wasn't long after I'd given Adnan the ultimatum that he'd handed in his immediate resignation from AGH.

As I'd suspected, when Nyx learned that Ziani had resigned from AGH, Arthur had come barging at his door the same night and I'd had the perfect view when it happened. Equipped with both photographs and audio, I'd paid another visit to Ziani and it hadn't been difficult to remind him what was at stake.

The hospital had desperately tried to offer him anything he'd want to stay, but like the reasonable man I knew he'd be after my last visit, he'd insisted that he was happy finally retiring from a place where he'd spent the last four decades.

I would be lying if I said I hadn't felt a slight tinge of remorse from forcing Ziani's hand, but I had a job to do and he'd sealed his own faith the day he'd dishonored the oath we'd vowed to cause no harm to people.

As for Arthur Nyx, let's just say he wouldn't dare go against my wishes. Not after I'd welcome him into his office last week with enough evidence of his fraudulent activities to put him in jail.

The bartender returned and we each grabbed our drinks—a whisky for me and a bourbon for Isaiah.

"I could say the same about you," I replied, redirecting the conversation and taking a drink from my glass.

Isaiah didn't know anything about the House and I could use work as an excuse, but I'd seen myself in a mirror before coming here. My lying skills were excellent, but he was the closest thing I had to a brother and I hated doing it to him.

So diversion seemed like the better option.

"I mean, I am in the middle of a triple header," he deadpanned, but I could tell something was on his mind.

"That's fair. You do have a big race coming up," I said, leaning forward slightly, trying to nudge the conversation to where I knew it was going.

Isaiah wasn't big on sharing, but I knew these rare get-togethers were the only time he could let go of the persona he put on for everyone else.

He shrugged, though I could still see the tension in his shoulder.

"It's just another race, right?" he said, but I didn't know who he was trying to convince more.

Myself or him.

"Right," I replied. "Your family's all coming, yeah?"

He tossed back his drink, his face wincing from the alcohol, before he gestured to the bartender for another one.

"Mum is, but Dad is still unsure whether or not he'll be able to make it," he said, giving me a stiff smile. His refill came a few seconds later and he took a long sip of his drink, his eyes shifting briefly to the side, avoiding mine. "Something about an important business meeting, but you know how it is with him. Every meeting is extremely important," he muttered.

To say my uncle James hadn't taken my cousin's team change well would be an understatement. Where I had a strained relationship with my father, Isaiah had a tumultuous one with his.

Although his father was—used to be—his biggest supporter, he'd also been his harshest critic. My uncle abided by a strict and uncompromising mentorship to push his son to success. He firmly believed that it was necessary for Isaiah to thrive in the competitive world of motorsports.

I could still remember quite vividly one day where Isaiah had finished second in a karting championship and my uncle had stormed in the room right before the podium ceremony, furious at his son's ranking.

"Only wankers are content with a second position and I won't have one carrying my name and legacy."

The smile that had previously been on my cousin's face had completely shattered and he'd spent the entire drive home berating himself for not doing well enough although he'd only finished second by a point off.

I wasn't fond of his father, but he was my mother's only brother and unfortunately my family. I'd tried to intervene once and that led to him leaving both Isaiah and I at a gas station in the middle of winter when we were twelve to walk back home for daring to go against his criticism.

James had barely even made it to Formula One—only competing for three seasons before he'd been replaced for his lack of results— while Isaiah was light years more talented than he ever was.

I never understood why some parents just seemed to hate being parents. What was the point of having children if it was to make them feel like shit for no valid reason.

Not that there should ever be a reason to treat your children the way I'd seen Isaiah's father treat him.

I'd never given much thought about having kids, because no matter what my feelings about it were, I'd be obligated to provide an heir for the Atlas's legacy to carry on. Although if it was up to me, I didn't know if I'd even want to bring children into the fucked up world we lived in.

"Fuck him."

He glanced at me sideways as he let out a derisive laugh. "I wish it were that easy."

Yeah, if only it were that easy, I also thought to myself, thinking of my own.

"Alright, enough about family, how's the new teammate?" I asked, hoping to lighten the mood.

He groaned at that. Well, I clearly touched another sore spot.

Cynara Cruz, the first ever female driver in Formula One, had become my cousin's teammate right after their summer break last year. It was rare for F1 drivers to be replaced in the middle of the season, but she'd wowed the entire motorsport crowd with her incredibly raw talent.

"I guess it's going as well as it's portrayed in the media."

He looked at me, like he was debating whether or not to say anything. Then, he exhaled in frustration, running a hand through his dark hair, styled in a similar fashion as mine.

"She's fucking impossible, mate. At first, I thought it was cute, but now we have to work and do all these media things together and she's always so… angry at me. I mean for fuck's sake, I should be the one who's angry. She crashed into my car three times already this year and of course, she keeps blaming it on me not leaving her enough space."

He clenched his jaw and rubbed the back of his neck.

"And she's got this way of…"

"Making things complicated," I finished for him because I knew the feeling all too well.

My mind instantly conjured the image of a lethally beautiful doctor who I had to work with every day while simultaneously ignoring the pull I felt toward her.

"Yeah, definitely complicated," Isaiah said, lost in his own thoughts.

"Alright, let's stop these drab talks," I proposed, needing to stop myself because otherwise I'd spend the rest of the night thinking about *her*. "Tell me about this new film."

We launched into conversations about his latest project he'd been a part of. Isaiah was approached by a renowned director a few weeks ago about being part of this new movie where Hollywood would meet Formula One. He'd been brought on board as a producer and key advisor for the project.

Isaiah explained how everything was going and where they were heading, informing me that they'd be filming this weekend for it, but I was only paying half attention, because my mind wouldn't stop going back to thoughts of her.

"WANNA MAKE A RUN FOR it?" I asked Isaiah, my voice breaking through the silence of his driver's room. He'd been staring at a blank spot on the wall for the last fifteen minutes without saying a word.

He jerked his head in my direction, blinking at me. "What?"

"Wanna make a run for it?" I repeated, raising an eyebrow. "I could probably come up with a medical reason to get you out of the race," I suggested, only half-joking. I wasn't exactly known for being the greatest at cheering people up, so this was the best I could do, but it worked. At least, a little.

He shook head, a reluctant laugh escaping him. "I'm fine. Fifty-two laps to the finish line and it'll be over," he said, sounding more resigned than relieved.

Today was Isaiah's most anticipated event of the entire race calendar. Not only for him, but for his fans who'd packed the stands.

Which was why I'd taken the entire weekend off to be here for him—just like I did every year. I wasn't the type to take time off, but I'd always made sure I wasn't scheduled to work during his home race because I knew this was the hardest one for him.

Isaiah always felt like he had to prove himself even more when it came to racing at home, understandably, and not winning wasn't something he wanted to experience in his own backyard.

Especially when his father had decided to show up.

The tension in the garage had been palpable from the moment James had stepped into the room wearing his son's old Atlas Racing merchandise. Everyone in the garage gave him looks, but no one dared to say anything as he strolled past them.

My uncle had mostly kept to himself, standing stoically beside my aunt in the viewing area, and muttering curses under his breath every once in a while when Isaiah made a marginally small mistake.

I opened my mouth to reply, but a knock on his door came from someone in his team to alert him that the pre-race National Anthem would be starting in ten minutes. Without missing a beat, Isaiah frantically shot up from his seat. He bolted for the door and exited his room in a hurry, running straight into someone.

I watched as he managed to catch Cynara, and righted her, preventing them from both tumbling to the ground.

He opened his mouth to apologize, but she was already pushing him off. "Watch where you're going," she hissed, glaring at him, before promptly storming off.

Isaiah glanced at me over his shoulder. "See what I mean?" he grumbled, shaking his head.

I couldn't help but laugh as I followed him back to the garage.

A voice over the loud speakers announced the impending anthem just as we made it back. "Bloody hell, I better get going before they fine me. I'll see you after the race," he called out over his shoulder, already breaking into a sprint toward the grid.

I had about fifteen minutes or so before the race started, so I decided to use the spare time and pop over to the neighboring garage to see Amar, who was attending the race as one of Atlas Racing's guests.

The House was ingrained in many facets of our society, and Formula One was just another of its many ventures. Amar's grandfather had purchased a significant stake of a previous team that had been in dire need of financial endorsement after its former owner filed for bankruptcy.

Something tells me it wasn't a coincidence.

Once inside, I spotted Amar straight away. The British national anthem had just come to an end, and he was deep in conversation with what looked like a couple. At least, that's what I assumed given how the man had his arm possessively around his partner's waist.

At first, I couldn't quite make out who they were, both of them slightly turned away from me since I was entering the garage from the back, but as I drew closer, I instantly recognized who it was.

Edward O'Donnell and Hazel Mendoza—one of the world's finest goalkeepers and his manager's daughter turned fiancée. Who also happened to be Azara's best friend. Something I'd discovered while looking into her for research purposes, of course.

My eyes instantly flickered around the red and gold garage, searching for her, but disappointment set in when I realized she wasn't there.

"Michael," Amar called out, once he caught my gaze.

I closed the remaining distance between us, offering a smile as I came to stand beside him and the couple. "Hey, man. Just thought I'd stop by and see you before you guys lose today's race."

Amar shook his head, gripping my shoulder. "Cocky as ever," he said with a grin before turning to the other two guests. "Hazel, this is Michael—someone I'm very unfortunate to have in my life. And Eddy, well… you two have already met."

I huffed out a laugh at the dig before shifting my focus to the couple. "Good to see you again, Edward," I said, giving him a clasped handshake in greeting. I then turned to Hazel, holding out my hand before pressing a brief kiss to her knuckles. "Michael Young. It's a pleasure to finally meet you properly, Hazel. Eddy never shuts up about you."

I hadn't spent a ton of time with the football player, but every time we'd met with him before a game or spent time at an event, he'd always found a way to bring her up in conversations.

Hazel briefly glanced at her fiancé, a faint blush coloring both of their fair complexions, before she focused her attention back on me, a flicker of curiosity in her hazel eyes.

"Young?" she asked, raising a brow. "You wouldn't happen to work at Amanar General, would you?"

I blinked, caught off guard by her question. "Er, I do, actually. I'm a surgical consultant there."

Hazel's smile widened, her eyes now gleaming with a quiet amusement, as if she was privy to something I didn't know. "Cardiothoracic?" she asked, her tone suggesting she already knew the answer, and it only deepened my confusion.

This was our first time meeting, and although I didn't remember the name of every patient I'd operated on, I did remember their faces. The only time I'd ever seen hers was through digital pictures.

"Yes, that's my specialty," I confirmed warily as her fiancé glanced down at her with the same puzzlement I was feeling.

"So you're the hot doctor," she remarked under her breath, but I still managed to hear her.

"Sorry?" I said, unsure if I'd heard her correctly.

"Oh, nothing," she said lightly, waving me off, but the mischievous grin she had clearly stated differently.

I would have pressed for more answers, but the drivers had started their formation lap so I brushed her comment to the side, knowing I had to head back before the race started.

"Alright, well, that's my signal to head back, but I'll see you all at the podium ceremony, when you come to cheer my cousin for breaking another record," I teased before quickly saying goodbye and heading back to Matrix Motorsports garage.

Throughout the entire race, as I watched my cousin lead by a significant margin, my curiosity kept going back to the peculiar conversation I'd just had.

Even when Isaiah won his eleventh consecutive race, the only thing that occupied my thoughts was what Hazel meant by 'hot doctor', and if it had anything to do with Azara.

CHAPTER 17

AZARA

TODAY WAS QUITE LITERALLY FROM hell.

And I didn't mean in a metaphorical sense.

My day started with a lovely flat tire as I was on my way to work and I'd barely managed to make it to the hospital on time. Then emergency surgeries kept piling up, and I'd barely had time to breathe, let alone eat, stuffing myself with packs of skittles in between operations.

And, of course, to top it all off, the sweltering heat we were currently being imprisoned with in London was clinging to my skin, making it feel like you were encased in a sauna all day.

Like did it have to be so bloody hot? And where was a breeze or the A/C when you needed it? I'd lived here my entire life and I still hadn't grown accustomed to the unbearable heat.

I was already well past my breaking point when I slipped into my favorite supply closet to get a moment of reprieve. I'd discovered the sanctuary on my first day as a junior doctor after a registrar yelled at me for a mistake that was entirely *his* fault.

I'd always advocated for myself because men tended to look down on female doctors, especially ones that wanted to become surgeons, but with the new environment, it being my very first day and needing to prove that I belonged here on my own merit and not because of my father, I'd remained quiet.

I'd managed to keep it together until he'd released us for lunch and I'd beelined for anywhere that wasn't public. I'd been looking for the toilets when I'd stumbled on this spare storage room on the short-stay surgical floor where they stored CPR dolls.

It had been the perfect escape and I'd been using it ever since whenever I needed a break from the chaos outside of these doors.

Which was exactly what I needed right now.

I hung my head back against the cool wall behind me and let out a deep breath. I'd just finished my fifth surgery of the day and my shift was almost over.

One more surgery and I'd be free to go home.

I closed my eyes for a brief moment, taking a few, long steadying breaths. It was rare that my work got to me, but this past month had been one unrelenting wave of trials after the other, all triggered by my father quitting, and I truly felt like I was drowning.

I'd tried stopping by on multiple occasions, but he'd been more dismissive and distant with each of my visits. He barely left the house, spending his entire days locked in his home office as per my brother, and still wouldn't tell me the real reason behind his sudden decision.

Because clearly it wasn't because he *wanted* to like he'd been arduous in having me believe. Just one look at him immediately revealed that. He was miserable with his new reality.

I'd initially thought that maybe the board had forced him out, but with the frequency at which I'd been accosted by a different member at least once a day since my father's resignation to ask if he would be willing to return, confirmed that my theory was wrong.

They still hadn't even filled his position because they'd been holding out hope—like I was—that my father would come to his senses and come back.

A beeping sound pulled me from my thoughts. I sighed and shifted to grab my phone. An alert from my glucose monitor flashed on the screen.

Ugh, not again.

I reached for the inside pocket of my long-sleeve fleece jacket for another small packet of skittles only to find nothing but empty wrappers.

This is just great.

I'd already plowed through my entire emergency stash and didn't have anything nearby. The cafeteria was a floor down so I decided to head there to grab a juice and a protein bar. I made my way there, but just as I stepped out of the closet, I heard a voice call out my name.

I closed my eyes and let out a long, exasperated groan when I registered who it was. The urge to just abandon my composure, scream and melt into the ground was growing stronger by the second. I'd managed to be out of his sight the entire day because I didn't need another thing to add to my list of grievances today.

Guess the world really hated me right now.

With a resigned sigh, I faced the way his voice had come from.

"Hey," Michael said, jogging up toward me with that annoying smile of his.

Keeping convincing yourself it's annoying, my brain managed to quip before I brushed it off. The last thing I needed was to argue with myself over this.

"What is it you want?" I asked when he halted in front of me. My phone rang again with another alert as my sugar dipped lower, but I quickly silenced it.

"Can't I just say hello?"

I'd roll my eyes if I wasn't so tired. With a sigh, I turned on my heels to leave but he grabbed my elbow to stop me. I immediately shrugged him off and turned to face him again.

"Look, I have somewhere to be," I said, my patience already worn thin. He was wasting my time, and I needed to get to the cafeteria before my alarm went off again. "I don't have time for your little act, so either tell me what it is you want or let me go."

"Someone's in a bad mood," he observed, shoving his hands in his scrubs.

I didn't bother acknowledging his stupid response. I started to walk away again.

"Okay, okay," he said with a surprisingly sincere smile as he came to stand in front of me, effectively blocking my path. "I'm sorry, that was a stupid thing to say. You have a tendency to make me do that." He'd muttered that last part to himself and realizing his slip up, he immediately changed the subject. "The hospital's COO wants to see us in his office."

My eyes narrowed with caution. "What for? And why is it just you and I?" I asked, surprised, because the hospital's administration never really talked to us, let alone summoned us for impromptu meetings.

"Yes, and I have no idea. I got an email from him just a few minutes ago. I was about to send you a message, but thought it'd be faster to just come find you since we have to be there," he paused, glancing down at his watch, "now."

I wanted to ask how he knew I was here, but I brushed it off when my mind only latched on when this meeting was supposedly happening.

My eyebrows shot up. "Now?"

"I know your shift is ending, but their email sounded quite… pressing."

Fuck me.

I should tell him I'd meet him there so I'd have time to get my blood sugar in check, but the urgency in his tone had me following him to the nineteenth floor where David Thompson's office was located.

Once there, Thompson's assistant told us he was already expecting us in his office. Michael opened the door and gestured for me to go first. I quickly rubbed my eyes and swallowed before stepping into the glass-walled office.

"Dr. Young, Azara," Thompson greeted us with a wide smile as he got up from his chair, his blond hair neatly combed back. He'd been the hospital's COO long before I started here but I'd only met the old man a handful of times. "Please, do come in and have a seat."

I controlled the stifling urge to scoff at him for not addressing me properly. If I wasn't so exhausted from the day I'd just had, I would have corrected him, but it wasn't really a battle I wanted to take on right this moment. The quicker I could get out of here, the better.

I cast a quick glance toward Michael as Thompson came to embrace him. For the briefest moment, I swore I could have seen a flicker of annoyance—one that matched mine—but it was gone almost instantly as he plastered his usual charm on like a second skin.

The familiarity between the two was a bit unnerving, but not surprising. People might believe hospitals would be an exception, but Boys' Club was just as prevalent here as it was in every other industry.

I focused my attention back on the COO as I gave him a firm handshake before settling into one of the plush and luxurious suede chairs. My eyes briefly scanned the room, taking in the sleek and high-end decor. Thompson's office looked straight out of a catalog and probably cost more than what I earned yearly.

The place had drastically changed from the first and only time I'd been here with my father when we presented solutions to help run the surgical department more smoothly.

I supposed this is where all our budget cuts went.

"Thank you both for coming," he said as he sat back down into his oversized chair. "I know you're both terribly busy, so I'll get straight to the point." He leaned slightly forward, his arms resting against the glass surface of his desk, and pinned us with a serious expression.

"As you know," Thompson continued, "the medical director's position has been vacant ever since your father—" he paused briefly, casting a fleeting, almost pitying look in my direction, "—resigned."

I swallowed thickly against the lump in my throat at the mention of my father and focused my attention on the COO, impatiently waiting to know why we'd been called into his office.

"We've been looking for a suitable replacement, but, so far, we haven't had any luck. It's been rather difficult to find someone, especially since it would mean the candidate would get a seat on the board as well."

He paused, his gaze shifting between the two of us, before he spoke up again. "I made a proposal to the rest of the board last week and they've just given me their approval to move forward."

This man said he would get straight to the point, yet still had to say anything that we hadn't already known. *Just get on with it.*

"I'm still not quite sure what this has to do with us," Michael interjected, seeming as eager to find out as I was.

Thompson's smile faltered, a flash of displeasure crossing his face, though he recovered quickly. "Yes, I understand," Thompson said, but I could tell he hadn't appreciated Michael's interruption from the way his smile wasn't quite reaching his eyes now. "I was getting there."

Michael gave him a short nod, as if to tell him to go on.

"As I was saying," Thompson continued, leaning back in his chair with an almost theatrical sigh, "I've made a proposal to the board and it was to consider you both for candidates."

I blinked at him, my mind struggling to catch up with what he'd just said. Becoming a medical director took years of work to accomplish. Michael had *just* been appointed as a consultant and I still had a few months of training before I'd join him. Of course that was the ultimate goal later down my career path, but being given the opportunity at this point in our careers was unheard of.

"I'm sorry. What?" Michael echoed my thoughts, equally taken aback by the revelation.

"Both of you have shown tremendous talent and commitment to this hospital," Thompson started to explain, his voice heavy with intent. "However, we couldn't agree on who was best suited for the job. So, the board has agreed with my decision to put both of you up for the role. We'll keep evaluating you until the new year and come to a vote at the end of that period. Whichever one of you shows the most promise will be appointed to the position."

I was stunned into silence for a solid ten seconds before I asked, "So you're… pitting us against each other for the role?"

"Consider it more like a friendly little competition," Thompson said as though this was a lighthearted game rather than a job that could shape a doctor's career.

Five months? A competition? I stared at him in disbelief as the realization of what he'd said slowly filtered through.

Working in healthcare was an arduous job in and of itself, but doing it in horrible working conditions made it almost impossible. You constantly found yourself battling between doing what you loved and quitting because we were often overstretched, overworked and underpaid for our labor.

This was a once in a lifetime opportunity and I'd always dreamed of following in my father's footsteps. He'd done so much for the hospital and I'd always wanted to do even half of what he'd accomplished.

So I'd kept my head down and worked tirelessly to make my mark, proving that I was one of the best surgeons here—if not *the* best.

Which led me to my next point.

"Why is Dr. Young even considered? He just started here," I said flatly, unable to stop myself. Because truly, what had Dr. Young done for this hospital. He'd been here for less than a year while I'd poured blood, sweat and tears into this facility.

Both men seemed a little surprised at my reaction, but Thompson was the one who spoke. "Yes, but his work here and his years at Orion make him just as qualified. Besides, a broader pool of candidates is much preferable. You wouldn't want to get the job by default."

I kept my face neutral and breathed calmly through my nose before I replied, "It wouldn't be by default. I've been here for almost a decade."

"The vote will take place right before the holidays and we'll let you know our decision on January 5th once we're back in the office," Thompson said, ignoring my last comment.

I wanted to say more, but knew it would be pointless. I let out a slow, centering breath, when Michael finally broke his silence.

"So, what exactly does this 'evaluation' consist of?" he asked, his demeanor not revealing how he felt.

Thompson leaned forward again. "Over the next few months, we'll keep monitoring your performances like we've been doing since you started working here. The decision will be taken based on your skills in the theater *and* your role in leadership of course. We expect initiative."

That should be easy. I'd been leading teaching sessions and workshops for younger doctors the moment I finished my foundational years.

"Anything else we should be aware of?" I asked, knowing to question anything that seemed to be this easy.

"May the best man win," he said, before winking. "Or woman in your case."

I gave him a tight smile. "Great. Thank you for letting us know. I have a valve repair to get to very soon," I said stiffly before getting up from my seat and letting myself out.

I probably shouldn't leave both men alone, but I wanted my shift to be over and entertaining Thompson any longer wasn't on my list of priorities.

All I cared about was the upcoming vote. We were in almost mid-August, which meant I had four months to complete my training hours and prove to AGH's board that I was the right choice.

I waited for the elevators to come when I heard Michael come out of Thompson's office. They seemed to be exchanging pleasantries which I did my best to ignore. The steel doors finally opened and I stepped inside the cabin.

I watched the two of them shake hands in goodbyes, when suddenly Michael firmly pulled our COO closer to his body. Just as the doors were about to close, I heard Michael's voice again, however this time his tone had changed and carried a threatening note.

"Oh and by the way, it's *Dr.* Ziani. Next time you'll refer to her as such," he said, his voice low enough that I almost didn't hear it.

The lift doors slid shut before I could fully process what I had just overheard. My brows furrowed as I stood there, staring at the closed doors.

Surely I'd misheard him.

Yes, I must have. I was tired and delirious from the day I'd had and the weather.

I shook my head, dismissing it. I stepped out onto the surgical ward when my pager bleeped, notifying me that my surgery was canceled and pushed to tomorrow morning. There had been a medical emergency on another patient and the theater that had been booked for my surgery was needed.

After quickly checking on my patient, I changed, grabbed my things and headed out. I felt like I was forgetting something, but I pushed it aside, eager to get home.

Gosh I couldn't wait to jump in bed and sleep.

As I headed for the parking lot at the back, my muscles protested with each movement, but I ignored it and walked down the stairs to reach where my car was parked. Once in it, I'd be able to go home, eat and rest.

But every move felt heavier than the next.

My phone rang with a notification, but as I reached to get a hold of it, I felt my steps falter. I reached out to grab onto the railing, steadying myself.

I shook my head from the sudden dizzy spell and reached for my phone again. I glanced down to see what it was, but the letters on the screen started to blur together.

Footsteps sounded from behind me and I heard someone call my name. The familiar voice sounded far-off so I moved to turn around to see who it was, but dark spots danced in front of my vision.

Panic lit the voice when whoever it was said my name again, much closer this time. The vision of a blurred face appeared in front of me just as strong arms wrapped around my body.

I heard them ask me something, but couldn't quite make out what they were asking me. Throughout the brain fog, I'd finally realized my mistake, but before I could tell whoever it was helping me that my blood sugar was incredibly low, my head slumped against their chest before the darkness that had danced at the corner of my vision pulled me under.

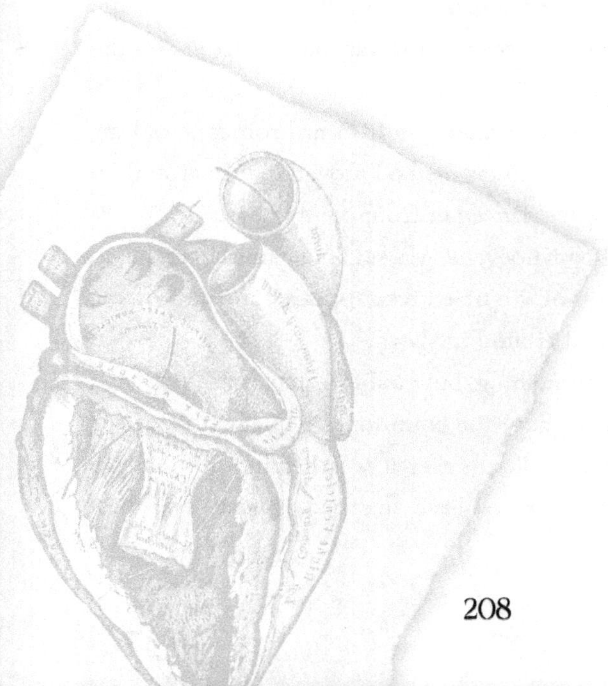

CHAPTER 18

MICHAEL

I'D FELT FEAR BEFORE, BUT nothing quite like this.

When I set my mind to look for her after our meeting with David Thompson, finding Azara on the edge of passing out had been the last thing I'd imagined.

She was in my arms, her head still slumped against my chest, as my doorman pulled the door to my building open. I could have taken her inside Amanar General, but my place was just across from the hospital and seemed like the best choice.

At least that was what I'd told myself when I carried her here.

"Is everything okay, Mr. Young?" Mamadou asked, his eyes wide in concern as he swiped his card to call the lift to my penthouse.

"It will be." I really hoped it would be. I didn't know why she'd fainted, yet, but I just had to get to my flat and I'd be able to figure it out. Maybe this was a stupid idea, maybe I should have just taken her to the hospital.

I was suddenly starting to regret my decision, but immediately shook the thought away as the doors to the elevator opened up.

"Would you please call the hospital and let them know that I had an emergency? Tell them to either push my surgeries to tomorrow or ask Dr. Ahmad to cover for me," I asked Mamadou, right before I stepped inside the cabin.

"Of course, sir," he replied as he pressed the button to my floor, bypassing the need for my fingerprint. The second the doors opened, I rushed into my living room—which thankfully no longer had any of my research on her father plastered over the walls—and gently laid her down on my couch.

I got to my knees at her side and pushed the panic I'd felt when her body slumped into my arms as far away as I could. My eyes roamed over her in a quick assessment. Her face was paler than usual and her skin was clammy to the touch. Instantly, a fact I'd found while I'd gathered intel on her popped into my mind.

She's diabetic.

I swiftly grabbed her phone that was already unlocked. I found the app I was looking for and found that her sugar was scarily low.

A thousand curse words assailed my brain, but instead of berating myself for not taking her to the hospital, I grabbed her tote, praying that she had an emergency bag on her, and pulled out a few items—wallet, keys, empty Skittle wrappers, lancets—until I found what I was looking for.

Grabbing the glucagon pen, I pulled her shirt up and injected it into her abdomen. I then safely placed her on her side and briefly left to grab what I needed for when she woke up.

Once I got what I needed from my kitchen, I came back to sit on the floor by her side, half a cup of different types of juices since I didn't know what she liked, three glucose tablets I'd found in her emergency kit dissolving in a cup of water since it'd be easier for her to take, and a few snacks that were high in carbs and protein.

I reached for her phone and watched her glucose readings like a hawk as it slowly climbed up, counting down every second of the fifteen minutes, praying and begging whoever was up there to have her wake up.

I ran a hand through my hair, shaking my head. I should call the hospital. This was the dumbest decision I'd ever made. I was a doctor for God's sake. I should know better.

Her body stirred next to me but I was in the middle of cursing myself under my breath in Korean to notice right away.

"Michael?" she asked in a whisper, and it immediately had me on high alert. It was also the first time she'd called me by my name and I didn't think it ever sounded better than coming out of her lips.

Michael, now's not the time.

I turned my head to find Azara slowly regaining consciousness.

"Hey, *gumiho*," I said, instant relief flooding my bloodstream at seeing her wake up. Before I could stop myself, I reached for the loose strands of her curly hair that had fallen and pushed them back and away from her face.

I skimmed her cheek with my thumb, but dropped my hand down when her eyes fluttered open, letting it rest in a safer position on her arm.

"What happened?" she asked puzzled, her eyes scanning the room we were in.

"We're at my place. You had a hypoglycemic episode," I explained, softly.

She blinked a few times, the information slowly registering.

"Can you sit up for me?" I asked,

Her eyes narrowed slightly, but she nodded in response. She moved to do it herself, but I quickly shifted to my knees to help. Once she was sitting upright, I asked, "Apple, orange, or pineapple?"

She glanced at me quizzically. "What?"

"What do you prefer?"

A hint of surprise filled her features, before she scolded them back into something more familiar to what I'd grown accustomed to over the last few months.

"Orange is fine," she replied, moving to grab one of the cups, but I beat her to it.

I picked up the cup with the orange juice in it. "Drink," I ordered softly, carefully bringing it to her lips.

"I'm not a child, I can do it myself," she retorted, reaching for the cup.

I pushed her hand down and held it on top of her thigh. "I know. Drink," I repeated, more firmly this time.

She rolled her eyes, but did as told and a small wave of unexpected satisfaction rippled through me. She parted her lips and I brought it closer, resting it on her bottom lip and tilting ever so lightly to let her drink at her pace.

I watched her intently, my gaze glued to the slender column of her neck as it bobbed with each swallow. Unwarranted images filled my mind, but I immediately cursed myself.

Get a grip Michael.

I pushed the thoughts away because it was highly inappropriate to imagine her throat doing the same under very different circumstances.

Once she was done, I pulled the glass away from her lips and a small drop of orange juice trickled past her lips. I caught it with the pad of my thumb just before it trickled down her chin. Then, almost instinctively, I brought my finger to my mouth and sucked on the droplet, quietly relishing the sweetness and wondering if it came from her or the liquid.

Shaking the thought off, I looked over to her to ask how she felt, only to find her gaze zeroed in on my lips. I knew our bodies were close given our positioning, but the distance became more striking at this moment.

Her tongue snaked out the tiniest bit, licking at that same spot.

My eyes trailed up to meet hers and I watched as she swallowed thickly before slowly meeting my gaze. Something that closely resembled desire swarmed across her irises, but it was just as quickly gone.

She cleared her throat and said, "Right, well I should get going."

As if she'd snapped the cord of whatever trance we were briefly in, I shook my head and said, "No."

Her brows furrowed. "What?"

Realizing how my reply might have come across, I added, "Yet." I reached for her phone on the coffee table to show her the screen that displayed her sugar was still below the safe zone. "We need to monitor it again."

"I can do it myself," she said, echoing her earlier words.

"I know, but I'd feel much more comfortable if you did it here. You know, so I can make sure you don't faint again on your way home."

I didn't want her to think that I didn't think she was capable of caring for herself, but I wouldn't let her leave mere minutes after she'd regained consciousness.

"Doctor's order," I added with a smile, hoping to infuse a little bit of humor into the moment as I moved from the floor and perched myself onto the coffee table.

I knew she didn't have any allergies, so I grabbed one of the protein bars I'd brought from my kitchen and handed it to her. "Eat."

She eyed the bar for a moment, before accepting it with a resigned sigh. "Fine," she muttered before leaning against the back cushion and started eating.

We sat in silence for a while, waiting for the next fifteen minutes to pass. But after the second minute lapsed, I broke the silence. "Does this happen often?" I asked, opting for a safe question. "The fainting, I mean."

"No," she replied without looking at me.

I waited for her to offer more, but she kept her attention focused on the timer.

Well… okay then.

The silence wasn't necessarily uncomfortable, but I found myself wanting to talk to her. So I tried again. "How long have you been diabetic?"

She shot me a sharp look with a raised brow. "What is this? An interrogation?"

I wanted to laugh at her witty remark, amused that even a hypoglycemic episode didn't dull her hatred toward me, but I wouldn't put it past her to hit me if I did.

"I just want to know more about you," I replied sincerely, surprising both her and myself at my answer.

Her features softened and she let out a long sigh before replying, "I was diagnosed with Type 1 diabetes when I was seventeen," she said her voice quieter now, "right before I started medical school."

"That must have been a lot."

"It was," she replied, the hint of a sorrowful look flitting across her face.

Since I'd poured hours over learning everything about her and her family that the internet could give me access to, I knew that was around the same time she'd lost her mother. I wanted to say something, but that would be careless since we'd never talked—*really* talked—before so there was no reason for me to be aware of that information.

"Did your Dexcom malfunction or something?" I asked, steering the conversation away before I outed myself. "I'm surprised you didn't get an alert."

"I did," she replied with another sigh before answering the puzzlement that she must have read on my face. "I always have small packs of Skittles with me, but I'd already gone through them. I was on my way to the cafeteria when you stopped me."

I felt a wave of guilt wash over me. "Shit, this is my fault," I muttered. If I'd known, I wouldn't have pressed her to come with me. I should have paid more attention. I should have noticed the signs, I'm a doctor for…

"Hey," she said, placing a hand on my arm and pulling me back. "It's fine. It wasn't your fault." She shook her head. "I'm the one who should have done a better job at listening to my body," she admitted.

I met her gaze, and she withdrew her hand, standing up abruptly. "I–I should go," she said, quickly moving to leave. But in her haste, she miscalculated her steps, and tripped on my foot, stumbling forward.

She almost fell face down on the carpet, but I caught her just in time.

I steadied her and she looked down at me, her gaze flitting between my eyes and where my fingers gripped her waist. My heart increasingly thumped in my chest as my brain scrambled on what to do next.

Logically, it would be to let her go, but logic didn't seem to be common for me these days. I met her gaze again and before I did something stupid like pull her down on my lap and kiss her, I forced myself to opt for reason.

"Maybe we should go to the hospital," I suggested, my voice hoarse.

Even though she'd woken up and said she was fine, I'd much rather have her see a practitioner or we could ask for labs without having to go through the proper channels if she didn't want others to know.

My comment snapped her back from wherever she'd seemed to be. "No, I'm fine," she replied, shrugging my hands off her body and putting a reasonable distance between us.

"But—"

"I said I'm fine," she repeated, more firm this time, as she pulled her curly hair into a bun on top of her head using the elastic band on her wrist. She stopped mid-way, then looked at me with a sigh. "Could I use your washroom before I leave?"

"Yeah, third door down on your left," I replied, gesturing toward the hallway where it was.

Without a word, she stepped out of the living room and headed for where I'd shown her. When the bathroom door finally closed shut, I sat there for a moment before the reason I'd come looking for her dawned on me.

I'd planned to use her distraught from the meeting to my advantage and get a hold of her mobile, but then I'd found her outside on the verge of passing out.

Everything was swept away by the panic of seeing her in that state.

Shaking the memory away, I swiftly grabbed her phone that she'd left behind and hurried to my kitchen table where my laptop was. Once unlocked, I plugged her phone in and transferred her data into a private folder.

While I waited for it to be downloaded, I opened the encrypted program Sofiane had installed on my computer ages ago and installed a virtual chip into her server so I could track her whereabouts and listen in to her conversations.

After her father had officially been taken care of, all that had been left for me to do was to convince the board that I was the best candidate for the new open position. With Adnan planting a seed into the board member's ear—since I knew they trusted him—I'd planned for the rest to be straightforward.

But I should have anticipated that this wouldn't be so easily wielded in my favor.

I knew the only other person that could potentially be a hindrance to me swiftly taking the position was Azara. I had no doubt she'd be equally fit for it. She was an excellent surgeon and the beloved daughter of our previous medical director, but she had yet to finish her training so the idea she'd be considered hadn't felt like something to be worried about.

I'd grown complacent, a mistake I wouldn't—couldn't—make again.

I was prepared to do whatever it took to complete my Order. And although a part of me recoiled at the thought of burying her, I needed to adhere to 'by any means necessary'.

And what better way to do so than to keep your 'enemies' closer.

At least, that's what I convinced myself was the best plan.

Nothing to do with wanting to be near her, of course.

I wanted to feel wrong about invading her privacy, but I didn't care. I had six months left before my Ascension, and with my father's disappointment that I hadn't accomplished it already breathing down my neck, this job had to be mine, and if it meant taking her out, then she'd have to be collateral damage.

The transfer was ninety-seven percent done when I heard the bathroom door creak open.

Fuck.

The door clicked shut behind her, and her footsteps came closer as I watched the progress bar move, but it wasn't fast enough. I was a good fucking liar, but what kind of excuse would be plausible enough for me to explain why her phone was plugged into my computer.

I jumped out of my seat the moment right before she walked back into the living room. In one fluid motion, I leaned my forearm against the wall, intercepting her.

She stopped short, her eyes flicking up to meet mine, startled. "Michael, wh-what are you doing?"

I hadn't thought this far.

"Let me drive you home," I suggested. I knew she'd say no, but it was the only thing I could think of that wouldn't sound suspicious.

"I can get myself there," she replied, trying to sidestep me.

I shifted my position, placing both hands firmly on either side of the hallway, effectively boxing her in. "Yes," I said, "but I think it'll be safer if I do it."

She frowned, clearly growing irritated. "Move," she said curtly, trying to move past me again, but I stepped in front of her once more.

"I could do that, but not until you let me. What if something happens?" This data transfer better ought to be done by the time I let her go.

Her eyes narrowed, lips pressing together in annoyance before she said, "Listen, I'm tired and don't have time for this. So either move or I'll move you."

I couldn't stop the faint smile that tugged at the corner of my lips. "I'd like to see you try," I goaded her, stepping just a fraction closer to her.

Taking me by surprise, she placed her hands on my chest with a deliberate, almost playful touch. Then, her fingers trailed down the front of my scrub top, the movement sending a ripple of warmth down my spine.

"Michael," she said, her voice dropping to a low, almost husky tone.

My pulse quickened, and I could feel a flush creeping up my neck, my thoughts scrambling to catch up. My brain knew what she was doing, but my body seemed to be lagging behind, caught off guard by the sudden intimacy of her gesture.

And how much I wished there wasn't fabric separating us.

Before I could get my brain and body to corroborate with each other, she used my brief moment of distraction to give herself just enough room to slide past me.

Whatever trance she'd put me in abruptly snapped in half when her touch disappeared. I wasted no time, dashing to the dining table to grab her phone, seizing the opportunity where her attention was diverted as she headed where she'd left her purse on the large sectional sofa. I tucked it behind my back, carefully keeping it out of her line of sight as she turned to face me.

"Goodbye," she said, making her way toward the entryway. She slipped on her trainers, then summoned the private lift which arrived almost immediately. The doors opened and she hurried inside the cabin, but as the doors began to close, I quickly erased the distance and shot a hand out, halting the elevator doors with a swift motion.

Her lips parted in exasperation, but before she could speak, I interrupted her.

"You left this behind," I said casually, holding her phone out toward her with a nonchalant smile.

She gave me an exasperated look before taking it from my hand. I then leaned in, scanned my fingerprint, and pressed the button for the ground floor before stepping back.

"Azara," I said in goodbye, giving her an amused smirk.

"Michael," she replied, shaking her head.

The elevator doors slid shut, leaving my name hanging in the air between us. I'd never tire of her saying it.

Shaking my head, I pulled my phone out of my back pocket to watch her live location as she headed for the hospital parking lot. Once she'd made it, I headed down to my parking garage. Sliding into my most inconspicuous car, I kept a safe distance between her vehicle and mine as I followed her home.

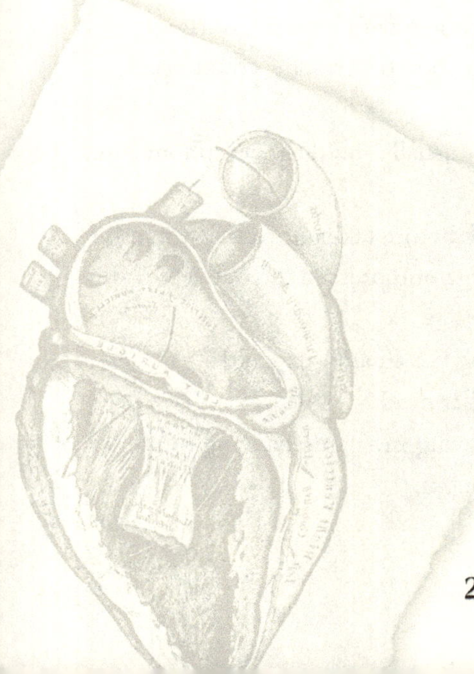

CHAPTER 19

AZARA

I KNEW THIS WAS A terrible idea the moment I'd downloaded that bloody dating app at Hazel's wedding two weeks ago.

"Like I said, it's a really big opportunity they've entrusted in me and I'm looking forward to showing them what I'm capable of," Craig, my date, finished, ending his fifteen minute monologue with a smile and looking straight at me.

Craig had brought me to Alessandro's, a renowned fine-dining Italian restaurant in Mayfair. I would have much preferred something more casual for a first date, but the man I'd matched with last night had insisted on coming here.

Although the company was questionable, the place was quite beautiful and reminded me of the month I'd spent in Italy after my second year of medical school.

"That sounds great," I replied with as much enthusiasm as I could muster after taking another sip from my water.

I'd barely said a word once we were seated at our table before he took over and just kept on yapping. I'd tried to add into the conversation earlier in our date, but had quickly given up, because with men with egos like his, there was no point in even trying.

"Yes, I'm committed to making important changes in the company, and hopefully make partner by the time I'm thirty-five," he droned on.

Tearing my hair out strand by strand would have been less painful than the last hour I'd just wasted listening to this man talk. But, I shot him a fake smile, not wanting to say anything that would set him off onto another endless monologue.

I hadn't been on a date in a very long time and this was exactly why.

For some puzzling reason, men seemed to always think that women either wanted to hear them talk about themselves all night, be mansplained basic concepts even a child would understand or worse, thought we wanted to go home and have sex with them after they'd treated us to a nice dinner.

I glanced at my phone on the table and subtly tapped a finger on my screen to check the time, praying that it was almost time for me to see myself out of this date. It was only 5:00 p.m., and I'd given myself until 6:30 p.m. to leave if I was to make it to my overnight shift on time.

Conveniently, he'd chosen a restaurant that was only a ten-minute Tube ride from AGH. I'd dropped my things at the hospital before meeting him here so I wouldn't have to carry my things or need to go home before heading to work.

"Do you have somewhere to be?" Craig grumbled, startling me out of my thoughts.

I focused my attention back to him. "Sorry?"

He leaned slightly back into his chairs, his fingers drumming along the table. "You keep checking your phone, so I was wondering if you had somewhere else to be," he said, his tone oozing with annoyance that I wasn't hanging on to his every word.

And here I thought he wasn't paying attention to anything but himself.

"No," I paused. "I mean technically, yes I do, but not right away. I just have work this evening," I explained, waiting for his very predictable reaction by the way his eyes widened at my words.

"You're working after our date?" he asked, almost outraged that I'd dare have other plans after this.

If we were being technical, I hadn't been scheduled to come into work tonight since this was my weekend off, but I knew the moment I'd said yes to this date that I'd need something to make me forget if this proved to be a disaster.

At least this proved that my gut was never wrong.

Except for Michael, my mind chimed in and I groaned.

He was the very reason I was subjecting myself to this date with Craig. It had been just over a month since my diabetes had placed me in a rather peculiar situation, one that ended with me at Michael's flat.

Of all places I'd thought I'd end up waking up at, his living room had been the last place on my list. I'd expected him to bring me to the hospital, but instead I'd learned that he'd carried me all the way from Amanar's parking lot to his apartment.

Something I'd learned courtesy of his doorman that had seemed relieved to see me well and awake when I'd left Michael's apartment complex.

For the rest of that day, while I drove home, made myself dinner and then laid in bed, my thoughts were entirely consumed by that fact. I didn't trust many people with my disease, but Michael had been unbelievably… kind and attentive.

Still overbearing and infuriating, sure, but what he'd done for me had made my reasons for hating him less, well, hateful.

I'd spent that night wide awake, just thinking about how he wasn't just the boss I couldn't stand, but the person who'd carried me all the way to his home, somehow knowing I'd prefer the privacy, treated my low blood sugar, stayed with me until I regained consciousness and didn't make me feel like an object of pity when I told him I was diabetic.

So to deflect whatever weird feeling my body was going through every time I thought about him or saw him at work, I'd made the grave mistake of downloading a dating app after years of refusing to do so and said yes to the first match I'd made that didn't look like a serial killer.

"I am," I finally answered Craig, and without disappointment, he proved my hypothesis about his reaction to that fact correct.

His green eyes hardened. "What kind of job has you going into the office on a Friday evening?"

His voice was a note louder than before, attracting the eyes of other customers in our direction. I gave them a small, apologetic smile, before turning my attention back to him. In any other circumstance, I would have just excused myself and left, but Davide, the poor kid who had been assigned to work our table had had to endure my date's lack of mannerism the entire night and I wanted to make sure he'd be tipped well before leaving.

"I'm a cardiothoracic surgeon," I said calmly, not surprised that Craig had forgotten what I did for a living. I wasn't one to flaunt my job, but the disdain that flashed across his face from my response sent a thrill of satisfaction through me.

At least one thing about this date would be.

Before he could say anything, we were thankfully interrupted by our server. "Would you like to look at the desert menu?" Davide asked with a forced, professional smile.

"No, we'll get the check," Craig responded curtly, and I'd never been happier for a date to end.

After taking care of the bill because who the fuck asked to split the bill on a first date, I'd hailed for a taxi to drive me to Amanar because I was too exhausted to deal with the evening rush hour of the Underground.

I got to the hospital with plenty of time to spare despite the traffic we'd been stuck in. I walked through the giant glass sliding front door of AGH and headed for the elevators on the left, my heels clicking against the vinyl floors and echoing in the quiet evening lobby.

A few of my colleagues shot me surprised looks, but I just smiled and pretended my attire was a normal occurrence. I rarely wore dresses or even dressed-up coming to work since I'd just change into scrubs, work all day and go home right after.

I lived and breathed surgery and occasionally went out with the girls. The last time I'd worn a dress was for the masquerade ball and it wasn't a time I'd like to reminisce on.

I pressed the button to call the lift. While I waited for what I knew would be a moment, I reached inside my shoulder bag to grab my phone and check if I had any important emails or urgent tasks to complete before I began my shift.

I had a few emails about miscellaneous meetings that I ignored, and continued scrolling to see if the surgical program director had given me an answer to my proposition.

It'd already been a little over a month since Thompson had announced to Michael and I that we would be competing for the medical director position.

As much as I hated admitting it, Michael and I were pretty matched in our surgical skills, and we'd even both done the specialty run-through program, on top of finishing it earlier than most surgeons. I'd even thought my years of loyalty and dedication to this hospital would give me an advantage, but according to our COO, that didn't matter.

Which was absurd if you asked my opinion.

So the only thing that I *could* do to set myself apart from Michael was to come up with an idea that would benefit the hospital and help run it more efficiently.

I'd been volunteering to hold teaching sessions for medical students and junior doctors over the last few years whenever I had time, but AGH didn't have any permanent teaching programs in place.

We learned a ton in school, but theory wasn't always practice. Frankly, I'd learned most of everything I knew now while working in clinical settings because things were vastly different with real patients and real situations, especially when our bloody textbooks weren't diverse and inclusive in their teachings.

I'd sent a proposal earlier this week, but still hadn't received any sort of response.

The lift doors slid open with a soft *ding* just as I finished typing a reply to another email. Without looking up, I stepped forward when the sound of someone sharply sucking in a breath made my steps falter.

I paused, my skin already prickling, as if my body knew exactly who it was before I dared to glance up. And sure enough, when I did, my gaze met an all too familiar one.

For fuck's sake. No matter what I did, I could not stop seeing him. He was bloody everywhere. I couldn't go just *one* day without crossing paths with him.

Michael stood there in the otherwise empty cabin, leaning against the railing of the back wall with his hands casually shoved in the pockets of his navy scrubs. His hair was slightly tousled from what I could only assume was a long shift—Fridays here were always like that.

"Are you getting in?" he asked cockily as his dark eyes slowly roamed over my figure, taking in my sleek black satin dress with lace detailing that I'd paired with strappy black sandals.

An expression I'd never seen there before flickered across his features as his gaze locked with mine again, sending warmth rippling through my body and igniting that weird fluttering sensation around my stomach.

My lips parted to say a reply, but then I remembered that I was supposed to be ignoring him. That was the whole reason behind my attire and the ridiculous date I'd just suffered through.

I briefly considered waiting for the next lift, but it would take ages to get here because despite the hundreds of thousands of pounds this place received every year, investing in faster elevators wasn't quite on their top priority list.

Shaking whatever virus my body must be developing, I squared my shoulders and finally stepped inside, deliberately keeping as much distance between us as possible. I pressed the button for my floor and kept my gaze firmly fixed ahead. I watched the doors slide shut, and suddenly, the soft hum of the elevator felt deafening.

The warmth of Michael's gaze burned between my bare shoulder blades, and the foreign fluttering from earlier multiplied uncontrollably. I cursed myself inwardly and silently willed the lift to hurry, so I could get away before he said anything that would force me to acknowledge him.

Unfortunately, luck was never on my side when it came to Dr. Young.

"Bit overdressed for surgery, don't you think?"

I didn't look at him. *Don't engage him*, I told myself. *Don't eng—*

I felt him step closer. "Ignoring me, Dr. Ziani?"

I closed my eyes for a brief moment, bracing myself before

reluctantly responding. "Not ignoring you, just didn't think your comment was worth a response," I said, my eyes fixed on the illuminated floor number.

He laughed softly under his breath, warm and deep, and I could feel him moving even closer. "Can you blame me for wondering why you look so breathtakingly beautiful?" His voice dropped on the last word, and I gripped my phone tighter.

I'd been called beautiful before, but coming from him felt… more.

I could almost feel his eyes trailing over my bare back and I hated that my body was reacting to it. This was ridiculous. Why did it always do that when he was near? Couldn't my body, just once, do as I asked it and ignore his presence?

"That's none of your business, Michael," I said, attempting to sound indifferent but even I could hear the faint waver in my voice.

"Oh, it's Michael now?" he teased with that infuriating lilt that always seemed to make my pulse spike. The front of his top grazed against my bare spine, my skin tingling at the friction

Why were these elevators so damn slow?

"Quite unlike you to let me have the last word," he said, amusement threading through his voice.

"Aren't you supposed to be home by now?" I snapped, risking a glance at him over my shoulder. The previous distance between us was now gone. He was wearing his stupid, smug grin and I had to crane my neck to meet his gaze.

"I could say the same thing about you," he said smoothly, "but let me guess—bad date?" The corner of his mouth lifted in a knowing smirk, though his smile looked a little strained. Or maybe I was imagining it.

Not that it should fucking matter what his smile looked like.

"What?" I said, feigning ignorance.

He leaned his back against the wall next to me, crossing his ankles and folding his arms across his chest. "The reason you're working on a Friday night, wearing that dress."

"Not that it's any of your concern, but it was a *great* date," I lied, refusing to give him the satisfaction as I faced forward.

"Great, right," he repeated, dragging out the word and knowing it would get under my skin, but I ignored it. He was quiet for a moment before he added, "He's really a fool, then." His voice had dropped to a murmur, almost as if the words were meant more for himself than for me.

Against my better judgment, I glanced at him again. "What?"

His eyes flicked down my body, then back up to meet mine. "I don't think I would have been able to let you go after seeing you wearing that."

His presence suddenly sucked all the air out of my lungs and I swallowed thickly, when the elevator finally came to a halt. I didn't wait for the doors to fully open before bolting out of there.

"See you later, *gumiho*," I heard him call after me.

My heart was still hammering by the time I reached the surgeon's lounge and only when I walked inside did I realize that I'd been holding my breath this entire time.

After I'd washed my face clean of makeup and changed into my scrubs, I caught up on finishing writing up my cases and checked the referral system for any emergencies that might require my attention since I had almost two hours to kill before my shift started.

When 7:00 p.m. rolled around, I treaded the familiar path to the surgical ward. I wouldn't have much to do tonight unless there was an emergency but it was a better distraction than staying at home and thinking about *him*.

Despite the disastrous afternoon I'd had, I found myself looking forward to settling into my work routine. I'd finally have the chance to shut everything else off and focus on others. That was one of the things I loved the most about being a physician.

However, my promising mood evaporated the moment I stepped onto the ward and saw Michael leaning casually against a corner wall. He'd changed into a knitted jumper that left nothing to the imagination of his upper muscular frame, the navy fabric molding every inch. Even his pair of dark trousers made him look even better.

As if that was even possible.

I groaned in exasperation. What had I done to deserve such treatment from fate?

He was in the middle of a lively conversation with a tall, leggy brunette dressed in an outfit that probably cost twice more than my monthly salary.

What was he still doing here? His shift had been over ages ago. Way before I was even scheduled to start. Trust me, I'd checked before accepting the overtime.

Her back was turned to me, but as soon as I heard her laugh, I recognized who it was. Michelle Thompson. One of the consultant plastic surgeons here, who also happened to be David Thompson's wife and another member on the board.

I'd only had to work with her once a couple of years ago, but it had been one too many. Her reputation for looking down on anyone who wasn't in her field and her hate for interdisciplinary cooperation was well-known amongst AGH's staff. It was either her way or she wouldn't help.

Young and her were huddled a few feet away from where I stood at the ward's front desk, far too close to each other.

I rolled my eyes and moved behind the station to find out which nurses had been assigned to my patients in the previous shift so I could get a quick update on how they were doing.

I'd been trying to focus on what Marissa was saying about Mr. Casas for the last few minutes, but Michelle was laughing so obnoxiously loud, I couldn't concentrate. I glanced over at them again, their bodies now even closer and her manicured hand resting on his forearm.

We were in a hospital, not a bloody pub.

And she was married, did he have no shame? Besides, since when have they known each other? She barely operated anymore so this couldn't be an exchange about a patient.

It definitely wasn't looking that way to begin with from the scene in front of me.

"Dr. Ziani?" I heard Marissa say.

"Yes?" I replied absentmindedly, my gaze still fixed on the utterly inappropriate exchange.

"I asked if you could write the exit prescription for Casas so it can be ready for his discharge?" Marissa asked, her voice firmer this time.

My gaze snapped back on her to find her looking at me with puzzlement. "Yes, sorry. I'll do that after I see him tonight."

"Great, thank you," she said, before going back to writing her progress note since her shift would be ending soon.

Before starting my rounds, I swiftly logged into a computer to claim it as mine and to have it ready when I needed it before heading to see my first patient. And unfortunately for me, I had to pass them to get to the hospital room.

I kept my gaze firmly ahead, doing my best to appear unfazed. They were exchanging goodbyes and I caught the last part of their conversation just as I walked past them.

"You have *nothing* to worry about," Michelle said, with resolute confidence in her tone.

I hadn't been able to hear their conversation this entire time and kept wondering what they could even be talking about that would warrant such camaraderie. But just as I was about to walk into one of my patient's rooms, my hand froze on the panel when the way she'd said those words dawned on me.

You have nothing to worry about.

She couldn't be referring to…

I was being paranoid. He wouldn't try to win votes that way. *Right?*

I should have pushed the door open and stepped into the room. But—

He had his back to me when I glanced over at them again just in time to find her placing a kiss to his cheek before waving her fingers in a goodbye and walking toward the ward's exit.

When she was out of sight, Michael briefly looked over at me with a smug smile on his face before walking toward the hallway that housed both my father's office and his own a few doors down.

The bastard.

He was probably taunting me and I should let it go and get to work, but my feet grew a mind of their own and before I could stop myself, I stalked after him.

And once I caught up to him in a few strides, I grabbed his wrist, and pushed us inside the first room I saw.

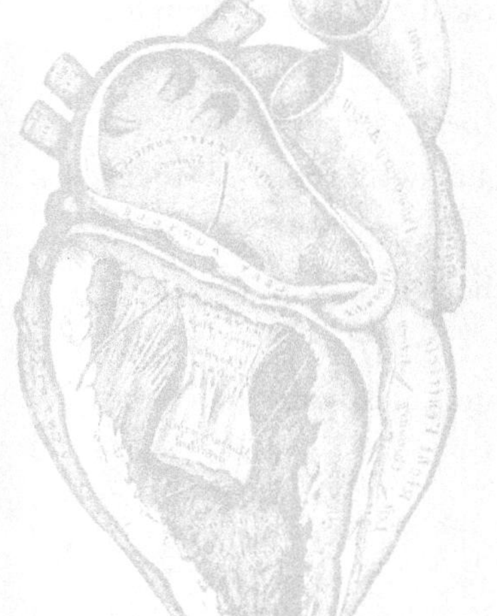

CHAPTER 20

MICHAEL

"WHAT DO YOU THINK YOU'RE doing?" Azara snapped, her tone accusatory. She slammed the door shut after we were both inside and whirled around to face me. She stared up at me like she was about to murder me.

"What am *I* doing?" I asked with a perplexed raised brow. "You're the one who took me hostage into your father's old office."

She slightly jerked back, her fingers slipping from my wrist, her touch lingering, as she took in our surroundings. Realization of where we were washed over her features, but she quickly brushed it off and narrowed her eyes at me.

She inhaled a sharp breath, as if she was trying to reign in her frustration. "Answer the fucking question."

I shoved a hand in my trouser's pocket and replied, "I'll need you to be a bit more precise."

She gave a dark, brittle laugh. "Of course, you'd play the innocence card,"

"Darling, I can assure you there's nothing innocent about me. But I can't plead guilty if I have no clue what you're accusing me of."

"Ms. Thompson." She'd said the name with such venom in her tone, it took me by surprise. She usually reserved her abhorrence for me. Before my thoughts could conjure what the COO's wife had done to her, Azara's voice brought me back.

"Why were you talking to her?"

I frowned at her question. "Didn't know it was a crime to talk to other doctors."

"This is just a game to you, isn't it?" She brought her finger to her temples, shaking her head. "You know exactly what you were doing. There was nothing professional about that conversation. If you think you can win the position by charming your way up, you're sorely mistaken."

Her brown eyes found mine again. Her frustration was clear in them, but there was something else there. Something much more potent than just her annoyance at me talking to Michelle or her assumption that I was in fact trying to warm the board member up to me.

I needed all the votes I could get, sue me.

I took a moment to take her in. Her posture was stiff and a flush darkened her tanned skin. She always looked beautiful, but something about her in scrubs seemed to be a weakness of mine.

Especially when she was furious at me.

My lips curled up in a perverted satisfaction. "Azara… are you perhaps jealous?"

She scoffed in disbelief. "Are you serious? From everything I just said, that's what you came to the conclusion of?"

I took a step toward her. "You are, aren't you?"

"This is ridiculous," she argued, taking a step back, but she already had her back to the door so there wasn't much space where she could escape to. "This is just like you. You're just finding twisted excuses to dispute the validity of what I just said."

I'd only been meaning to rattle her, but the way she was combatively answering everything but what I'd asked, made me think that I was correct in my assumption.

"And you're avoiding my question," I fired back, taking another step forward.

She craned her neck and glared at me. "Do you ever just stop fucking talking?"

The animosity she held against me should have deterred me, but it only fueled the burning desire I'd been harboring for what felt like ages.

"Are you offering to keep my mouth busy in other ways?"

I was well-aware I was playing with fire with what I was implying with my question. But I was tired of fighting her, fighting whatever had been brewing between us over the last eight months.

The air around us stilled. Her lack of response to my question should have brought reason back into my mind, but I ignored it. My pulse beat with a frantic rhythm as I advanced into her space.

"What are you doing?" she asked. Her tone was hesitant but she wasn't doing anything to get away or stop me.

"I'm closing the distance between us," I whispered, my breath fanning across her skin. My hand slowly trailed up her arm, the pads of my fingertips lighting on fire everywhere my skin connected with her.

Azara faltered, but her tone still carried an undercurrent of bite to it. "Why?"

This was leading to a path of self-destruction, and it was confusing the hell out of me, but once again, I found myself not caring for the consequences. Not even a little bit.

The persona I'd spent years building to be ready for my Ascension disintegrated into dust when it came to her. I loved that she fought me and I wondered if it would translate into what I was about to do.

My palm reached the nape of her neck. "Because I'm about to kiss you."

Her eyes widened. "God, you're so full of yourself. I knew the moment I saw you that you were trouble. You're so bloody infuriating, it makes me want to—"

I didn't let her finish.

With no hesitation, I shoved my hand into her wavy brown hair and kissed her, taking everything I'd been dreaming of taking the moment she yelled at me for running into her at the park.

There was a split second where the only response she gave was a shocked gasp but then any resistance simply melted away and her body softened against mine, a soft sigh slipping past her lips.

I roped an arm around her waist and pinned her harder against the door, using the opportunity to deepen the kiss. I slid my tongue inside and leisurely explored her mouth.

She fisted her hand in my shirt, tugging me closer, and met every stroke of mine with her own. Nothing about the way we devoured each other was gentle.

She was fucking addicting and I willed time to never end so I could go on forever. I wanted to curse myself for waiting this long to discover what she tasted like, but her small whimpers mingled with my own dissipated any other thoughts but one.

More.

I wanted—no *needed*—more. Of this. Of her.

She sank her teeth into my bottom lip and I groaned when a faint copper taste flooded my taste buds to mix with her. If I was already this addicted to just the taste of kissing her, god what would it be like to taste *all* of her?

Images of my head between her legs, my mouth spending countless hours discovering every singular inch of her body crashed in waves. But before I let myself drown in them, I broke away from her, and a disgruntled whimper fell from her lips as her head fell back against the door.

I know.

My heartbeat was erratically beating against my chest, my hand still buried in her hair as I slowly peeled my eyes open. I took in her face, commemorating it to memory because I knew that I'd never get a chance to have her like this again and stored it into my little library of moments of her that I'd been keeping tucked away at the far back of my brain.

Where it was safe to dream of her.

Fuck me she was beautiful with all her flushed skin and puffy lips.

All of it because of *me.*

It was taking everything in me not to slam my lips to hers again and take even more than I already had. But my stupid sense of duty had reared its head back up and I knew that I didn't have enough willpower left to stop myself again if I succumbed to my need for her.

 Our kiss was short-lived, and yet I knew there was no going back. This memory would be engraved in my brain forever and nothing could ever top it. Because whatever she'd made me feel over the past few months—feelings that I'd done my best to ignore— exploded in technicolors the moment my lips met hers.

She still had her eyes closed when she asked breathlessly, her chest heavily rising and falling. "Why did you do that?" Her eyes slowly peeled open and her lust-filled gaze finally met mine.

"Because you infuriate me just as much," I rasped before slipping out of the office and leaving her behind before I let all of my inhibitions go and did way more than just kiss her again.

After coming back to my senses—at least some of them—I got the hell out of the hospital, completely forgoing passing by the doctor's lounge and grabbing my things before I headed home.

By the time I got to my flat, completely soaked from the battering rain outside, I was still trying to catch my breath after what just happened.

I'd given myself one very simple rule when she came into my life. Stay the hell away.

Clearly, I wasn't a great listener because how could I stay away now that I knew what she tasted like.

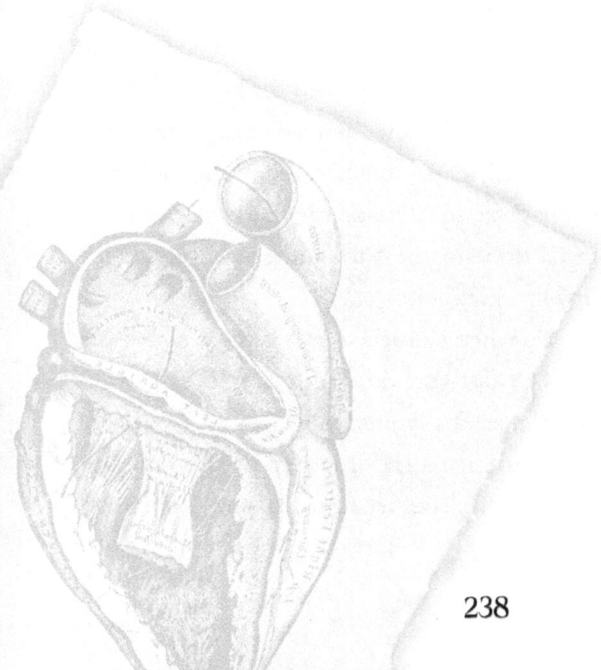

CHAPTER 21

AZARA

THE ONLY WAY I COULD describe the kiss was…

Electrifying.

Every one of my senses buzzed in the aftermath. Something that I'd never experienced. I'd been kissed before, but none that even came close to how maddening Michael's lips against mine felt like. I'd never been kissed with so much passion. One that consumed every one of my senses and all I'd wanted to do was drown more into it.

It was hot and wild, and desire was still coursing through my veins long after he'd left. I could still feel the phantom tingling at the back of my skull from how hard he gripped my hair. I could still feel the press of his body against mine.

It was hard to breathe, think or honestly do anything. My mind was spiraling a mile a minute because what the hell had just happened. How could I just go back to normal after what felt like a delirious experience that would be hard to forget?

"Why did you do that?"

"Because you infuriate me just as much."

His response should have snuffed out whatever he'd made me feel into oblivion, but it only made it burn even brighter. It lit it aflame in a way that I didn't even know how to extinguish.

I didn't know how long I'd just stood there, reliving every second of what probably was only a mere few minutes until reality came crashing back like a tidal wave.

What the fuck had I done?

Michael Young had just kissed me. And worst, I'd kissed him back.

Groaning, my head fell back in a loud thump against the wooden panel of the door behind me. This wasn't supposed to happen. Kissing my annoying coworker should have never happened.

I raked a hand through my hair while I checked the time on my phone. Fuck. It was already almost an hour into my shift and I'd yet to do any actual work because I was too busy kissing someone I definitely had no business kissing.

But why did I want it to happen again?

I shook the unexpected thought away. This was absurd. It was just a kiss. It didn't mean anything and I clearly was under the weather, hence why my skin was still peppered with goosebumps.

That was a plausible excuse. Or at least that's what I was trying to convince myself of. Because the only thing I was allowed to feel around Michael was irritation.

I was an expert at pretending. I'd practically done it my entire life.

What was one more lie to myself?

I *REALLY* SHOULDN'T BE HERE.

Standing in front of his flat was one of the worst decisions I'd ever made and I'd dare say I'd already hit my quota of bad decisions for the day. Rationally, I knew the smartest thing to do was to walk back to guest lifts and head out.

I prided myself for always being a sensible person, yet I couldn't bring myself to walk away. That part of me I'd always known to rely on always seemed to dissipate into irrationality whenever he was involved.

Go home, Azara, I tried telling myself, but even I knew it was a wasted effort.

After I'd made a quick pit stop in the small bathroom in my father's office to fix my hair—it had looked like I'd battled someone—and had attempted to make myself look less frazzled, I threw myself head first into my job.

And it worked.

For a while.

But after a small moment of weakness where I'd let the memory of him kissing me with such passion break through the brittle barrier I'd erected, it was all I could think about.

No matter how hard I'd tried *not* to.

It didn't help that work was rather slow, which is how I found myself at his doorstep at two in the morning. The plan had been simple. Go home, and rest until one of the junior doctors paged me for help or an emergency, but my body had apparently sprouted a mind of its own and threw reason away for the second time tonight.

I knocked. Once. Twice.

I didn't even know why I was even here in the first place. What was I hoping for? What would I even say if he answered his door?

A small shiver ran down my spine and I crossed my arms over my chest, hoping the flimsy knit jumper I'd thrown over the dress I'd worn earlier for my date would help.

But it did nothing to help stave off the nerves skittering across my skin.

God this was stupid and I should know better, but there was this craving that I couldn't seem to get rid of. It had been simmering for months and the contact of his lips against mine seemed to have unleashed it with a force even the most strong-willed person couldn't combat against.

This irritating ache lingered throughout the night until it slithered its way up my chest and lodged itself there, unmoving.

I'd never experienced anything like it. The feeling was so foreign and unnatural to my nature that the only thing I could think of was how to get rid of it. The only thing I *needed* was how to fix it.

Because I couldn't go on like this.

Whatever he'd inflicted me with, I needed to rid myself of.

My myriad of thoughts came to a screeching halt when the door finally creaked open. "Azara?" Michael said, slightly stunned by my presence. He stared at me then rubbed a hand over his face and blinked like he couldn't conjure me being here. "What are you doing here?"

My heart was pounding so hard inside my chest, I could hear my pulse battering in my eardrums as my eyes fell to his bare chest and torso, momentarily distracted by the tight cords and deep ridges of his muscles.

Holy fuck.

I knew Michael was attractive—as much as I'd tried to ignore it—but *this* wasn't what I was expecting. His joggers hung low, and I glimpsed at a dark dusting of hair that disappeared into his waistband that left my mouth watering at the sight.

It left almost nothing to the imagination and countless intricate tattoos covered the expense of his arms and the upper part of his chest. That on top of his messy bed hair and this heady scent wafting off him was a lethal combination.

I heard him say something, but I was too enthralled in my own thoughts to make out what he asked. My breathing turned shallow when my gaze landed on his lips, the sight of them lulling me into the memory of his lips against mine.

And how much I wanted the phantom sensation that had lingered to become reality again. The small whispers of a warning blared inside my head, but before I could come up with a list of reasons why I shouldn't do what I did next, I closed the distance between us, threw my arms around his neck, and captured his mouth with my lips.

The butterflies I'd done my best to keep at bay exploded in my stomach, my heart fluttering out of control. The world around us disappeared once again, just like it had the first time he'd kissed me.

All of my thoughts sharpened to only focus on the possessiveness in his response to my kiss. His movements held no hesitation. He wrapped an arm around my back while the other moved to lift me up, my legs wrapping around his waist as we stumbled backward.

I heard the dim thud of a door slamming shut before the weight of his body pressed down on me, trapping me between him and a hard surface at my back. He slanted his face over mine, his tongue dipping past my lips. His kiss turned aggressive and the moan emanating from his throat vibrated into mine, making me dizzy with want.

My strappy heels dug against his back as he rolled his hips up and I felt his growing erection brush against my core, fueling my urgency for him even more. His skin was hot under my roaming hands and I needed to feel it against mine. As if he'd read my mind, his hands gripped the hem of my jumper.

"Off. Now," he groaned over my lips. He continued kissing me, only briefly breaking away to swiftly pull the fabric over my head.

Michael kissed along the edge of my jaw and I gripped his hair, pulling him closer. His mouth burned a path down my chest, his teeth nipping along the way and there was something so erotic about the idea of him marking me.

"Michael…" my words trailed off as he rolled his hips up again.

He pulled his mouth away. An involuntary whimper of protest escaped me and I opened my eyes to find him already looking at me. His irises were drowned with dark desire as he spoke.

"Where do you want me?" His voice, pitched low and deep, danced across my skin, leaving goosebumps in its wake.

There was an endless list of where I wanted him, but only one held more urgency.

I gripped the hair on the nape of his neck. "On your knees."

He slowly set me down on my feet, his hands firmly holding me steady by the waist. "With pleasure, *gumiho*," he whispered against my chest as he lightly trailed kisses over my dress until he hovered against my front.

"What do you need?" he breathed, looking up at me. His hands skimmed down to my hips, his fingers gripping over every inch like he was memorizing the feel of my body as I watched him lower himself to the ground.

He gripped the hem of my dress and with an excruciating slowness lifted it up to my midriff as his warm breath hit the inside of my thigh.

I glanced at him down on his knees before me and it sparked a foreign sensation inside my chest at watching him like this. His eyes shimmered with reverence as he paused for a moment and pried my knees apart to settle himself between them.

"Kiss me," I commanded in a whisper.

"Where? If I aim to please you, I'll need you to be a bit more precise." He smiled, slow and lazy, satisfied with his torment.

I was heavily panting as he snaked his tongue up, my skin tingling in its wake. I let out a low moan when he bit the inside of my thigh before soothing it with his tongue and moving further up.

"You liked that, didn't you?"

I hummed and squirmed against the sensation of his mouth almost exactly where I craved it, so I braced my hands on his head, my fingers snaking into his lush hair.

Emboldened by his possessive touch, I brought his face closer to the apex of my thighs. "Here."

My heavy eyes fell shut when Michael brushed his nose against my covered pussy.

"*Fuck.*" I heard him curse under his breath. "Is this where you want me, Azara?" he asked, his words muffled. The vibration sent a thrill of anticipation up my spine as I moaned the only word I could string together.

"Yes."

The word was barely past my lips when I felt his fingers slide ever so slowly down inside the material of my thong. He pulled it from my pussy just enough to where I could feel his knuckles graze my cunt.

"Such a pretty pussy, Azara," he rasped, his voice dripping with need, before he dragged his tongue up my slit in one long lick. My grip on his head tightened as he pulled away. "You're dripping just for me aren't you, *gumiho.*"

Frustration licked my veins at his baiting. I looked down to find him already peering up at me, the fabric of my dress hiding the bottom of his face.

I pushed his head harder into me, slowly twisting my hips to get him back where he needed to be. "Michael, stop fucking around and just—"

The words died in my throat as he wrapped his lips around my clit and sucked it into his mouth. He then pushed two fingers up inside of me and I gasped at the sudden intrusion.

"*Fuck,*" I hissed under my breath at hearing the wet sound of my arousal against his fingers as they fucked me relentlessly.

He slightly tilted his head back, our gazes locked, as he began rhythmically pumping them in and out. A string of moans rippled out of my throat at the pleasure tingling down my spine as he licked and sucked everywhere he could. Every swipe of his tongue was deliberate, bringing me teetering over the edge.

It only took a few more drags of his tongue over my sensitive clit before my orgasm crashed over me like a tidal wave. I felt Michael hum against me as he continued licking the remnants of my orgasm.

His fingers glistened when he withdrew them. I watched him through hooded eyes as he shoved them into his mouth and the sight almost brought me down to my own knees.

Michael shuddered and satisfied rumbles reverberated from his chest as he stood. The gentle brush of his lips feathered across mine, and the remnants of my own taste flooded my senses.

"Better than I imagined," he whispered before sucking my bottom lip between his teeth.

I felt drunk on him, the fumes of his scent mixed with my own so intoxicating, I could barely conjure enough words to respond other than with a deep sigh. His tongue circled my parted lips and I caught it with my own, wanting to know what I tasted like in his mouth.

I tore my lips from him and dragged them down his neck as his hands ran over my ass, exploring, but there was nothing gentle or tentative about it. He dragged a hand to my thigh, down the back of my leg, before bringing it to his waist and notching himself between my legs.

The fire that had slowly begun to subside from the high I'd felt between my thighs reignited with a passion when Michael grinded his cock against me.

A strangled sound between a moan and a whimper drowned out everything else around us.

"I need you," I muttered against his skin before bringing my lips to him again, "inside me."

"Anything you want," he replied urgently in between kisses. "It's all yours."

His words snapped whatever self-control I was still holding on to and my hands hungrily reached for the elastic band of his joggers. Michael's forehead dropped against mine and I felt him whimper against my lips travel to between my legs the moment my hand wrapped around his cock and I squeezed.

"Michael," I moaned breathlessly, at the feel of him scorching under my palm, imagining what that would feel like inside. Our breaths mingled in the small space between our parted lips as I tugged on it, once, twice. I watched in fascination as the engorged tip of his cock slipped past the band of his joggers, a drop of precum leaking on my hand.

I wanted him inside me like I wanted my next breath, and I moved my other hand to shove his pants down his firm ass, but before I could pull all of him out, the sharp sound of a ringtone sounded from afar.

Mindless with greedy arousal, I ignored whatever it was and watched his cock spring free. And *oh god*, it was beautiful. It was the perfect amount of thick and long, and I could feel my cunt begging to be filled with it.

"*Fuck*," Michael groaned against my lips as I ran my thumb over his tip, tugging on his length once more. "What are you doing to me?"

His words only managed to heighten my arousal. "I could ask you the same," I whispered, my voice hoarse. I hadn't intended to say that, but the words were out of my mouth before I could think twice about them.

His fingers dug into my thigh while his other hand yanked something off my body with one sharp tug, but I was too far gone to realize that he'd ripped my underwear off.

I maneuvered him to rest against me and shifted to slowly allow him to stretch me open when the shrill ringtone from earlier sounded again, the familiarity of it momentarily snapping me out of the haze.

My pager.

"Shit," I cursed, letting him go and pushing him away. I stood on shaking legs as I looked around for my bag that was nowhere to be found. Where the fuck was it? It rang again, but the sound was more muffled the further into his apartment I went.

Groaning, I swung his front door open only to find my bag's content scattered across the cream marbled floor. I snatched the small blue phone, answering before it rang again.

"This is Dr..." I started, momentarily forgetting my name. I cleared my throat. "Dr. Ziani," I finally managed to say. I tried my best to listen to the doctor on the other end of the line while frantically shoving everything that had spilled out back into my bag. Once she finished giving me a quick rundown on the patient and his condition, I quickly laid out for her next steps while the team waited for my arrival.

I swiftly hung up and threw in the work phone amongst everything else. I stood up and expected to be faced with Michael's disappointment of my dismissal but when I whirled around to face him, he had a giant grin plastered on his face.

A rumble of laughter sounded from his throat and it tugged at the corners of my lips, but I shook it off.

"Why are you laughing?" I asked, as he closed the distance between us. His renewed proximity sent a thrill down my spine but I forced myself to remember that I had to leave.

He grabbed the thin strap of my dress that had fallen to the side and hauled it into place before his lips grazed a small kiss to my exposed collarbone. "Just never thought I'd see the day where I got Dr. Ziani so flustered, she almost forgot her own name."

I huffed at his implication despite the truth behind it. Before I could come up with a reply, he kneeled on one knee before me.

"I really have to go…" My words trailed off when he placed my free hand on his shoulder. I was about to ask what he was doing when his fingers grazed my right calf and he began undoing the leather straps.

An unfamiliar warmth spread through my chest. I watched as he removed my heel, then the other before pulling socks on my feet and placing them in a pair of Crocs that were at least twice my feet size. The gentleness in his touch was such a jarring contrast from just a few minutes ago that I didn't know how to react.

"Arms up, love," he ordered gently before getting back on his feet. I normally would have questioned him, but in this moment, I just did exactly as told.

I felt a butter soft fabric, much warmer than what I'd worn to come here, being tugged down around me, the fabric almost reaching my knees. A woodsy scent mixed with Michael's body odor enveloped me and I found myself wanting to bury my nose in it for hours.

Michael's finger pushed the stray hairs that had clung to my face from the static and tucked them behind my ear. "It's cold outside," he explained.

I tilted my head to look at him. "Thank you," I managed to say through the small knot that had formed in my throat. "I should go," I added, hesitantly.

"Yeah," he replied, taking a step back and shoving his hands in his pockets.

I didn't want to leave despite knowing I really had to.

I was so fucked.

I briefly hesitated for a moment before placing a small kiss to his lips and making my first sound decision in the past twenty-four hours.

I left.

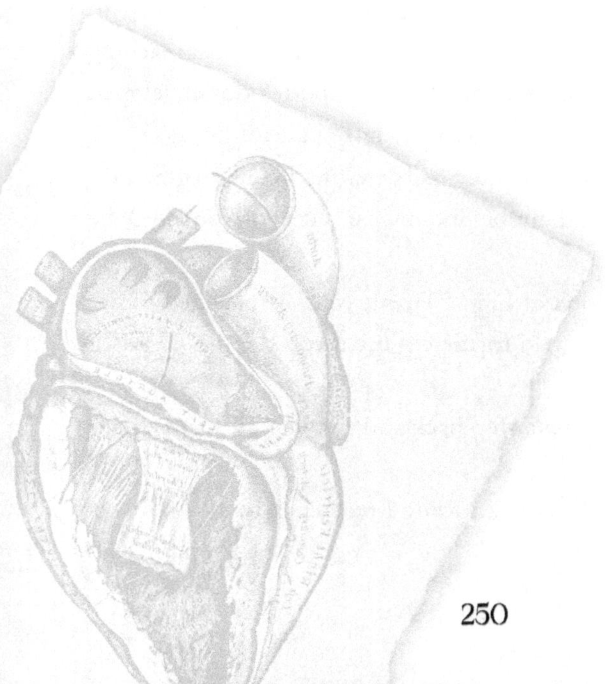

CHAPTER 22

MICHAEL

I'D LOST MY FUCKING MIND.

That was the only plausible reason I could come up with to explain why I'd just almost broken one of the most sacred rules as an Atlas less than five months short of my Ascension.

The worst part was that I hadn't even *attempted* to stop her.

The right thing to do would have been to walk away. Hell, maybe even pretend I wasn't home when I found out it was her knocking at my guest door. I'd been tossing and turning for hours, unable to sleep. Unable to rid my mind of her body writhing beneath me as I kissed her like I'd needed it for survival.

I'd thought keeping her closer would bring *me* closer to completing my Order. But unlike her father, Azara was untainted by greed. I'd turned every stone to find anything to leverage over her, only to come up empty-handed at every turn.

So I'd promised myself when I'd come home that I would iron-clad my self-control when it came to her and keep things strictly professional. No more forcing our schedules to align, or ending up in isolated rooms with just the two of us.

And I was usually excellent at controlling myself.

Excellent at smothering that incessant obsession I had with her that seemed to follow me around constantly.

And yet, when she showed up at my doorstep, and slammed her lips to mine, I'd simply lost my fucking mind. The desire for the imminent picture of her cunt swallowing the head of my cock had been so potent, any restraints I'd ever had had completely vanished.

I'd toyed with the line in the past but I'd never been *this* close. If it hadn't been for her DECT phone interrupting us, I would have let her do whatever she'd wanted with me.

Whatever she was willing to give me, I was desperate for.

Desperate for it like I'd never craved anything more in my life before.

And *fuck* she tasted good. She'd tasted like *mine*.

If Azara had plagued my thoughts before, what had just transpired between us made her a permanent fixture in my mind and there was no eradicating her from there. The impression of her taste still lingered hours after she was gone and my cock was still painfully throbbing, in dire need of release that I didn't indulge it in because I didn't need more reasons to think about her.

She'd already been all I could think about as I'd followed her to work to make sure she got there safely—it was almost three in the morning when she'd left my place—and while I'd taken my second cold shower of the night.

Dawn had barely just broken the horizon when I walked back into my bedroom, a towel wrapped around my waist. I briefly glanced at the clock on my dresser to find out it was almost 5:00 a.m. and I'd just spent the last two hours under a glacial stream trying to dim any trace of her.

Not that it helped whatsoever.

I only had a few hours ahead of me before I'd have to get on with my day so I padded toward my walk-in closet to get changed and get a few hours of sleep when black lace flashed in my periphery.

I shook my head. *Ignore it, Michael.*

I knew better than to march over to my dresser where I'd left it earlier, but against my better judgment, I did the exact opposite of what I'd promised myself and unfortunately for me, the moment my palm closed around the fabric, I couldn't resist. It was a shit idea, but right now the only thought that drowned everything else was the need for relief.

With one swift move, the previously fastened towel around my waist pooled at my feet. My skin instantly buzzed with memories of how Azara had felt under me, and the moment the fabric was wrapped around my cock, my earlier burning desire for her came crashing down over me.

Releasing a harsh breath, I closed my eyes and palmed the edge of the mahogany surface. Visions of her, mouth parted and her moans in my ears drowned out everything around me as I stroked my cock once.

Twice.

A minute of indulgence wouldn't hurt.

Just one minute and surely it would get her out of my system.

But it didn't.

This wasn't the end.

And I had no idea what the fuck to do about it.

AFTER A FEW HOURS OF restless sleep, I'd begrudgingly dragged myself out of bed and got myself ready to meet my sister.

Every fiber of my being wanted to cancel our plans, but Alice was leaving tomorrow for Scotland to start her autumn term on Monday, and I hadn't seen her in weeks. She'd spent the entire summer in Korea with our grandmother, as she did every other year, and I'd specifically taken this weekend off to be able to see her before she left.

Once I was dressed, I headed down to the lobby and found Mamadou waiting for me with a car ready, just as I'd requested last night when I came home from work. I could have easily taken one of my vehicles, but it was a Saturday afternoon and I didn't want to deal with the headache of driving into the city.

He greeted me with a curt nod, and a suggestive look in his eyes as he held the door open for me, but I ignored it and climbed inside.

The lingering shame from my indulgence earlier this morning still clung to my skin, and I really didn't need any reminders that my willpower had failed me. Again.

It wasn't as if Mamadou was privy to my personal life or the rules I had to abide by, but the mere thought that he might suspect what I'd been up to last night made me want to bash my head into a wall.

Despite the torrential rain that fell the moment I stepped outside of my flat, traffic was surprisingly light and I made it to Azure with a few minutes to spare. Alice and I usually met at UMMA, but she'd insisted on coming here instead because she was craving their tarte tatin.

As soon as I walked into the renowned French bistro, the maitre d' immediately recognized me since our family was well-known to the establishment. She grabbed my coat and umbrella, passing them to another staff member, before leading me to our usual reserved table, where my sister was already waiting.

"You look like absolute shit," my sister said in greeting as she got up from her seat. Her brown hair was styled in her signature bob, her smooth olive skin tone a few shades darker than when I'd last seen her, making her hazel eyes that she'd gotten from our mother stand out even more.

"Jesus, what a way to say hello to your brother," I replied, wrapping my arm around her shoulder to pull her into a hug and planting a kiss on top of her head.

Alice pulled back slightly, her eyes scanning my face. "You know what I mean, you look like you've been up all night."

If only she knew. My sister and I were close, but I wasn't about to tell her the reason why I'd barely slept last night. So instead, I shrugged, and tried to play it off as I slid into the seat across from her. "Just a late night at work."

She raised an eyebrow, clearly unconvinced. I knew she wouldn't easily let it go, it was in her nature to be inquisitive, but before she could drill me with a plethora of questions, our assigned waiter came over and I was grateful for the brief distraction.

"So, how is *halmeoni*[17] doing?" I asked after we placed our orders, switching subjects. The faster I gave my sister something to talk about, the easier it would be for me to stay under the radar.

I'd only talked to her briefly over the phone since our family always kept her busy with a million things. Especially our grandmother. Despite her being almost ninety years old, there was no pause button when my sister visited.

Ever since our grandfather died a few years back, she took advantage of every moment with Alice. Our grandmother loved feeding Alice, claiming we didn't eat "good enough" back in England, spent hours gardening in the giant backyard our *halabeojji*[18] had built for her, and

---

17 *Grandmother (Korean)*
18 *Grandfather (Korean)*

dragged Alice around the city to meet our family. Which seemed to multiply every year even though most weren't actually blood-related.

But as per my grandmother, everyone was family and it would be disrespectful not to visit. It was often tiring, but whatever she wanted, we indulged her in.

We were her only grandchildren and since Alice was a bonus one, she actually was treated as such.

I, on the other hand, got the Atlas treatment. Whenever I'd visited, it had been to learn how to effectively carry the Young's legacy. My sister didn't have to bother with the burden. I'd used to envy her, envy how much freedom she had to be whomever she wanted to be.

But after years of resenting my name, I'd learned to accept it because whether I liked my fate or not didn't matter.

Alice began recounting all the details about her summer abroad as she devoured her main course while I picked at my plate, distracted. I usually inhaled the braised lamb risotto, but after taking a bite, everything tasted like cardboard.

And as much as I kept trying to listen to my sister, my thoughts kept drifting back to one person.

Why couldn't I get her out of my head?

I'd never had an issue forgetting about a girl before. As a matter of fact, I never thought about a girl more than a few hours before she was long forgotten. My dating history wasn't extensive with the whole no-relationship and no-sex rule I had to abide by, but I wasn't totally innocent.

So what was it about Azara that I couldn't scrub my mind of.

You know exactly why.

Before I could think too much about what that meant, I heard my name being called. I looked up to find Alice studying me with a hint of suspicion.

"Sorry, what were you saying?"

"What's going on with you?" she asked, pointing her fork at me. "You're acting strange."

"It's just been a long week at work," I replied, but even I could hear the lies in my tone.

Although my sister and I had a twelve year age gap, she knew me better than most and could read me like an open-book. I was excellent at deceiving everyone else, but it seemed my sister was the only person immune to it.

"Don't bullshit me," she deadpanned. "Did something happen with Dad?"

I wished. At least then I'd know how to react to my predicament.

Only members of the House knew about it. Everyone else was just a means to an end. A clog in the machine to keep illusions and guarantee the Atlases remained intact.

My sister obviously knew about my strained relationship with my father, but only thought it was because I was his only son and responsibilities fell on my shoulders. Not because me successfully carrying out his legacy in the House was the only way to guarantee my survival.

On one hand I could lie to her and pretend I'd had another disagreement with my father. We clashed so often, it wouldn't be completely out of character. But part of me wanted to just be an older brother and talk to my little sister about my life.

"It's not Father," I finally offered.

"Okay?" she said reluctantly. "Then what is it?"

What could I even say?

Hey, there's this girl I think I like but I can't be with her because I'm a member of a notorious secret society that controls our country. I also can't date anyone—emotionally or physically—until I Ascend into the House and they've been vetted by the Elders which Father is part of or I'll be terminated (i.e. killed).

I tossed back my drink, hoping to buy myself a few minutes

This was a fucking bad idea. I should've just lied and told Alice I'd had another fight with our father. That would have been much easier than trying to tell her… what?… that I had a crush on my coworker? That I was so infatuated by her, she'd been all I could think about for almost a year.

That her presence was so intoxicating I'd almost broken an oath I'd kept for almost twenty years.

My empty tumbler landed on the clothed table with a soft thud. Our server, who had been standing a few feets away, glanced at our table and hurriedly moved toward us to refill my drink, but I gestured for him to stop.

I met my sister's gaze and she interrupted me before I could even say anything. "Is this about a girl?" she asked, her eyes widening.

My silence must have been confirmation enough because her silverware clattered against her plate and her hand came up to flick my forearm.

"It is, isn't it?" she shouted before realizing that people were looking at us. "Michael, spill now. My brother is in love with a girl and didn't even tell me," she added, her tone more hushed this time.

My brows knitted at her insinuation. "Wait, what? No. I mean, yes it is about a girl, but I'm not in *love* with her."

Azara made me feel a lot of things, things I'd never felt before but I wasn't in love with her. That would be ridiculous. I meant I barely really knew her and falling in love with her—or anyone—would be a much bigger complication than I was currently facing.

Alice cocked her head to the side, unconvinced. Yet, instead of arguing on the matter, she pushed her plate to the side, and rested her elbows on the table, propping her chin against her hands and settling on what she was really after.

"Tell me about her," she said, excitement gleaming in her eyes.

I leaned against the back of my chair, hesitating. What should I say or where should I even start? My sister and I talked about almost everything, but I'd never shared about a girl before. Hell, I'd never wanted to because no one had ever consumed my attention the way Azara did.

"Her name's Azara," I finally said, settling on an easy answer.

"Okay, go on," Alice prompted.

"We work together and she's a stunningly brilliant surgeon, and, I, we…" I brushed my fingers against my brow, stumbling over my words.

Clearly, I wasn't very good at this. Logically, it wasn't that I was struggling to find things to say about her because I could spend hours describing Azara and how magnificent she was, but I wasn't the most gifted at talking about feelings, especially when it came to mine.

I'd spent the first part of my life doing exactly as I was told and following a strict set of rules. Then, for a few years while I was in medical school, I did the exact opposite. But those years still weren't really mine. I might have thought that I was finally doing something for me, doing what *I* wanted for a change but in reality, I was simply going against everything I'd been forced to abide by in order to anger my father and what I'd been born into.

My decisions were still dictated by someone else.

Which meant I'd never really let myself feel anything because I couldn't afford attaching myself to anything or anyone. What was the point anyway when I'd have to abandon it for my duty?

"Wait, is this the mystery girl from the masquerade ball?" my sister asked, pulling me from my thoughts.

I opened my mouth to answer her question, when what she'd just said registered. I narrowed my eyes at her knowing smile. "How do you know about that?"

I realized the answer to my question the moment she replied, "Amar."

I was going to kill him. Why couldn't he just mind his bloody business for once?

"Why is Amar texting you about my love life? Actually, scratch that. Why is he even texting you in the first place?"

A thousand thoughts raced through my mind. Did he...

Alice raised both hands in mock surrender. "Ew. Hold on. I know exactly where your mind just went, and it's not like that. Now, don't get me wrong, Amar's *fit*, but I don't do the whole 'brooding artist' thing." She shuddered exaggeratedly, as if repulsed by the very thought.

My face contorted in repulsion. "You calling him hot just negated everything you said after that."

She rolled her eyes at me. "Anyway. You weren't answering his messages the night of the masquerade, so he reached out to make sure you were alright after you'd taken off so abruptly."

After Azara had practically fled the ballroom, I couldn't bring myself to engage in more idle chatter when all I could think of was the feel of her under my fingertips.

I shook the fleeting memory away, and raised a brow in mock offense. "So, instead of ensuring my safety, you two had a gossiping session?"

Alice scoffed, clearly unfazed. "Oh, stop being so melodramatic. You share your location with me, remember? Amar was proper surprised when I called to tell him you were at your flat. When I asked him why, he told me about this mystery girl.."

"You're a pain in my arse, you know that?" Both of them were. My sister was one thing, but I'd deal with Amar and his blabbering mouth later.

"Please. You'd be utterly lost without me in your life." She had a point. "Now, let's go back to this Azara business. Tell me *everything*."

I gave her a quick rundown of the last few months with Azara—leaving out this morning's incident, of course.

"That's lovely and all, but you haven't mentioned anything that doesn't revolve around the hospital. Well, except the time where you helped with her hypoglycemia, which, by the way, was very sweet of you. Didn't think you had it in you to care for more than yourself," she teased.

I raised a brow. "Should I start listing all the times I've had to look after you?"

Our parents traveled a lot, and had often left her in my care. Alice hadn't been rebellious or bratty by any means, but her scattered nature and tendency to spontaneously jump head on into new hobbies sure kept me on my toes.

I still remember the time she begged me to enroll her into woodworking lessons after seeing a single picture of a bed frame on the web and decided she must have it. I told her we could buy it or commission it from an *actual* professional—our family had more money than would ever be necessary in a lifetime—but she'd insisted that *she* had to make it.

And whatever my sister wanted, she got. Even to this day.

"*Yes*, but I'm your little sister. That's in your job description."

Another fair point.

I shrugged. "I haven't really seen her outside of work."

That was a lie, but the intricacies of Azara and I's unusual relationship wasn't a confession I was about to make.

"Are you telling me you've never taken her on a date?" Alice asked, outraged. "Young Seungwon, please tell me you've taken her somewhere, *anywhere.*"

"It's complicated," I tried to say but the words had barely left my mouth when she interrupted me.

"Complicated? Michael, what do you mean?" She was trying to keep her tone composed, but I'd evidently touched a nerve. "You clearly like this girl, what's stopping you from pursuing her?"

"There are many reasons," I started, trying to think of normal excuses people used since mine were far from it. "I'm her boss," I finally said, thinking it was a sound reason before Alice gave me a look.

"Many people date their bosses. Besides, it's not like you have actual power over her faith as a surgeon. You just do the scheduling."

"Way to diminish what I do."

"You know what I mean," she said, brushing me off with her hand.

I tried to think of another lie, but after rummaging my brain for one, I finally settled on a truth.

I averted my gaze away. "I just can't, Alice."

There was a moment of silence before she finally spoke again.

"Is this about the arranged marriage?"

My brows cinched as I met her gaze again. "What?

"I overheard you and Dad talk in his office at Christmas two years ago," she said quietly.

I knew exactly what she was referring to despite how much I'd prefer not to. My visits to my father's office were never for leisure. They were always to discuss one thing.

My duty as his heir.

Being tied to the House by blood and allegiance wasn't the only thing we were responsible for, carrying its legacy was just as important.

If not more.

My father had always been a step ahead when it came to my future and continuing the Young's lineage was no exception. Which meant that after I was officially sworn into the House of Atlas, I'd need a wife and of course, the choice ultimately wouldn't be mine.

Like everything else in my life seemed to be.

Arranged marriages weren't uncommon in our society, and a mandatory requirement for an Atlas. Our wives were to be thoroughly vetted by the Elders before we were appointed one.

It wasn't like I was oblivious to the fact, but I'd done my best to ignore that aspect of being an Atlas. I'd spent my entire life alone and would have much preferred continuing doing so.

It was just much easier that way.

I'd never pictured white picket fences or sharing my life with someone. Least of all having to keep up this veil of deceit with one more person.

"I know your relationship with Dad is different, but I'm sure he would understand," Alice said when I remained silent. Her hand came to rest over my own and I met her gaze again.

Her eyes were filled with hope and I wished I could harbor the same.

Could Azara be different?

Yes, my subconscious answered unbidden.

Despite the short time we'd spent together, there was something about her that buried itself in me and refused to let go. The feeling was so foreign to me and I had other more pressing things to focus my attention on, but at every turn, there she was.

I'd never looked forward to much in the past. Although I loved my job, I dreaded most days. The constant pressure of delivering and having lives at stake at my fingertips became daunting over the years despite the thrill when everything worked perfectly.

Which was unfortunately not always the case.

Yet since I started at Amanar, I started looking forward to going in because I knew *she'd* be there. That I'd get to see her, even if it was just in passing.

She radiated this aura and whatever this thing between us was, it was more than just physical attraction. A part of me wanted to explore it and see where it could lead, but I couldn't afford it.

Because then what would happen next?

"It's complicated."

"I think you're the one making it complicated. You need to start putting what you want first. You have this tendency to always follow whatever Dad says and as much as I love him, he doesn't have to dictate every aspect of your life."

If only it was that easy.

I moved to change the subject because how could I explain that when every aspect of your life was planned before you were even born. But Alice held her hand up when I opened my mouth. My sister knew me too well, and sometimes it played against me.

"Before you switch gears, just hear me out. What if you tried? What if you explored this thing with her and saw where it led? What do you have to lose?"

The answers to her question were so loaded, I didn't even know where to begin.

"Just give it some thoughts, yeah?" She squeezed my hand once. "You deserve to be happy, Michael," she added, giving me a small smile.

"Yeah," I replied quietly after a moment.

Although we both knew it wasn't sincere, she didn't press me further about Azara. I spent the remaining hour of our lunch listening to her talk, occasionally humming and nodding her along, but I barely registered much of what she said.

When Albert showed up an hour later to bring her home, we both said our goodbyes and I warned her to message me when she landed in Scotland. She'd be taking our family's private jet this time at my father's insistence, but it still made me feel better when she was the one notifying me of her arrival.

Albert offered to drop me off, but it was out of the way and Alice still needed to pack before her early flight tomorrow morning. It was her most dreaded task and she always waited until the last possible minute before doing it.

Once they left, I debated whether to call another car, but my mind was still whirling from the conversation with my sister. Instead I made my way toward the nearest station, hoping the chaos of a busy concorde would quiet my thoughts.

Rain was still falling in fat, heavy drops but I welcomed the rhythmic pelting against my skin despite the frigid temperature. But that only worked for a while. The moment I stepped inside the carriage, my sister's words kept playing on a loop in my head the entire way home.

What if you tried?

What if you explored this thing with her and saw where it led?

What do you have to lose?

Just everything.

CHAPTER 23

AZARA

"I KISSED HIM."

I did rather more than that, but saying I'd nearly had sex with the man I could barely tolerate just a few months ago didn't quite slip off the tongue as easily.

Nakia's dark brows shot up, her words faltering into a stunned silence. She'd been going on about the latest issue of *The Gilded Truth* where it had come to the author's attention that the beloved Prince Anthony, the heir apparent to the British throne and who'd just gotten engaged to his long-term girlfriend, had kept a secret bank account to funnel hush money to his mistress who was currently with child.

The repetitive mention of the scandalous secret affair combined with the fact that I'd spent the past week replaying the images on a loop since I didn't have work to distract me made it impossible to keep a lid on my own Pandora's box. I'd been holding onto it for a little over two weeks now and if I went any second longer, I would burst.

"You did what?" Nakia said, blinking repeatedly as if she couldn't believe me.

"I kissed the hot doctor," I repeated, louder this time and using the nickname they'd given Michael so I wouldn't have to say it again.

Her eyes widened even further and shame crept up my neck. My hands came up to cover my face, mortified by my confession.

The sound of something clattering on the floor snapped our attention to where it came from. Hazel stood in the middle of the modern kitchen with her mouth hung open. She'd been making brownies and her whisk was now laying on the floor, the front of her silk pajama top covered in the chocolate batter.

All three of us were over at Nakia's place for our monthly get-together. Hazel had just come back from Belize, where she had been for the last three weeks on her honeymoon, so we'd opted to stay in instead of our usual night out. She'd insisted on making it a themed-night, hence the over the top sleeper sets we were each wearing.

"When was this?" she said, abandoning her task and rushing to take a seat in the vacant velvet high chair next to me.

"Two weeks ago," I grumbled into my palms.

She slapped my arm. "And you're just telling us *now*?"

"Oi," I yelped, grabbing the spot where she'd struck me. "You didn't have to hit me. And I am telling you *now*," I said, emphasizing the last word by mimicking her offended tone.

I could have texted them about it since we messaged each other almost daily in our group chat, but I'd deleted the thread each time. I'd even debated telling them at all, since I'd spent the last two weeks convincing myself that what happened between Michael and I didn't mean anything.

That it was just a silly indiscretion, and come daylight, I'd come to my senses and realize it could—*should*—never happen again.

But why, even after successfully avoiding him as much as possible since that night, could I still remember it so vividly.

How naturally his lips moved against mine?

How my body ignited under his touch?

How his reverence made me crave more?

"We'll talk about how blasphemous it is that you've kept this secret from us for so long later, but for now we need details," Nakia said, cutting through my reverie.

"Yes, you traitor. Come on, spill it," Hazel chimed in.

Brilliant. I was getting attacked from both sides.

I really didn't want to dish out the particulars of my poor decision-making, but seeing as I was the one who'd brought it up, I knew if I didn't give them a play by play, they'd never let me off the hook.

So, I let out a deep sigh and relayed what had happened that night, keeping the intimate bits to myself. Some things were better left unsaid. Admitting I'd kissed him was embarrassing enough as it was. Not because I hadn't enjoyed it, but because it'd happened not only once, but twice.

And if my pager hadn't gone off with an emergency, I can't pretend that more wouldn't have happened.

"Oh, this is absolutely perfect," Hazel said, clapping her hand excitedly.

"You mean this is my worst nightmare," I retorted.

"No, this was meant to be," she said, her face practically glowing.

Of course she would think that. Hazel believed in cosmic love and firmly believed that transcendental connections existed. I always found her outlook charming. Not so much when it was aimed at me.

I pinned her with a spare-me-from-your-woo-woo-nonsense look, as I scrambled for a rebuttal to squander her hopes. She just ignored me, her eyes flicking past me.

"You owe me," Hazel boasted, her grin widening.

Nakia groaned beside me, and when I glanced over at her, she had a rueful expression on her face. "Does it really count if he kissed her first?"

Hazel shrugged. "Then you should've been more specific from the start."

"Fine. I'll wire you the money tonight," Nakia replied with a dramatic sigh.

I sat there, watching the interaction with stunned disbelief, my gaze bouncing between the two of them. Until it clicked.

"Hold on, did you two bet against me?"

"Well, I wouldn't exactly phrase it that way." Nakia glanced at me with mock innocence while Hazel also chimed in at the same time.

"We totally did."

I was on my feet a second later. "I can't believe this," I said, my eyes wide. "Aren't best mates supposed to be on your side?"

"Wasn't aware they were sides," Hazel quipped, "And of course we *are* on yours, but even you can't deny that this was bound to happen."

"Which, as we've established, *did* happen," Nakia added.

I scoffed and perched myself on the back edge of the sofa, folding my arms across my chest. I opened my mouth to counter her ridiculous notion, but no words came out.

Instead, I collapsed backward in a soft thud onto the cushions with a frustrated groan. "Great, the two people I trust the most, conspiring behind my back."

I lay there upside down, arms flung wide to either side, legs dangling in the air as I stared at the cornice plaster ceiling that reminded me of the architecture back home.

I wonder how difficult it was to find someone to...

"Why are you lying upside down?" Hazel's voice cut through my wandering thoughts, her tone full of amusement.

"Desperate times call for desperate measures," I muttered.

Alright, it was a bit dramatic but laying like this always seemed to help me think. That was how I did most of my studying when I was in school. When I was younger, I'd convinced myself the more blood flowed to my brain, the better it would absorb the information.

There was no scientific foundation to my theory, but it made sense to me. And hey, it worked. I'd been top of my class and had become a cardiothoracic surgeon.

Maybe it'd help with this too.

"If it makes you feel better, it *was* just a snog," I heard Nakia offer. "What?" she added in a hushed tone and I'd bet Hazel was giving her a disapproving stare.

Oh, but it was far more than just a simple kiss.

The moment my lips met Michael's, I knew I was in trouble. Over the last two weeks, I'd constructed a belief that the earlier incident wasn't as good as I remembered because surely what transpired between us couldn't have been that good.

What a lie?

I should be repulsed by the thought of him. He was the embodiment of everything I hated, so why did the mere thought of him send fire coursing through my veins.

Somehow, over the course of these past months and the compulsory time we'd had to spend together, the abhorrence had unexpectedly dulled.

God, what was wrong with me?

I could hear the sound of their footsteps approaching before they both lowered themselves to the ground, sitting on either side of me. Hazel's delighted grin remained intact, clearly enjoying every second of this. Nakia, on the other hand, looked almost concerned, but I knew she was equally relishing this.

Nakia chuckled softly. "Never seen you so bothered about a man," she remarked, leaning against the cushion to my right, resting her face against her fist.

"I am not *bothered*," I countered, but we all knew it was a blatant lie.

I'd never had boy problems before. I'd been too busy with studying and then it was clinical rotations and then it was residency. I had no time for anything else, let alone men. I'd never even given one more than a few hours of my attention because it was really all I had.

It had always been about getting a fix and scurrying away.

To me, men were a headache that I didn't want to deal with.

And for years, it had worked perfectly for me.

Why did this one have to mess it all up?

Both gave me pointed looks and as much as I'd like to keep my head in the sand, and ignore whatever these wings flapping things that erupt in my stomach every time I merely thought about Michael, even I knew it was pointless.

I flipped over and planted my face into the plush fabric with a deep, exasperated groan. "What do I do?" I mumbled, my voice muffled by the cushion.

Nakia was the first to respond. "What do *you* want to do?"

I moved my head to the side just enough to peer up at her. "If I knew, I wouldn't be asking the question, now would I?"

She shook her head at my attitude. "You're overthinking this too much. It's not like you have to marry the guy. You should just fuck him and get it over with."

"*Nakia*," I hissed as I sat up, sitting cross-legged. "Can you stop suggesting I sleep with the man."

"What? I'm just saying. Don't act like a prude. You've had sex before. *Casual* sex. Why should this be any different?"

She rolled her eyes and turned her attention to Hazel.

"If only she would have listened to me the last time, we wouldn't be having this conversation".

"You know I'm right here."

"Stop baiting her," Hazel reprimanded her.

"Listen, I wouldn't have quite put it like that, but whatever," she said.

"You know when Eddy and I started, it was—"

"We know," Nakia and I groaned simultaneously.

If we didn't interrupt her, she'd go off forever about her sex life with her now husband and we'd unfortunately heard about it one too many times.

"Well, excuse me for wanting to be helpful." Hazel feigned offense, folding her arms against her chest, while Nakia shook her head.

"All we're saying is, you kissed him. What's crossing a few more bases?"

I might have done that already, but I wasn't about to tell them. Fragments of that night flashed in my mind, but I hurriedly pushed them away. Although that didn't stop the warmth creeping up my body at the memories of that night.

"Azara Ziani," Nakia gasped, a knowing spark in her eyes.

Oh shit. So much for keeping that part to myself.

My millisecond hesitation sold me out and unfortunately for me, Nakia and I had been attached to the hip since birth. She practically knew me better than I knew myself.

Her mouth hung wide open before she said, "You didn't just kiss him, did you?"

"What are you talking about?" Hazel asked, clueless as to what Nakia had figured out. Her gaze bounced back and forth between us for a moment.

She let out a loud gasp when she finally caught on, slapping my knee in the process. "You've been holding out on us! You had sex with the hot doctor. Please tell me it was good. Listen, I may be married, but I just know by the looks of him he—"

"*Hazel.*" Her tendency to ramble was adorable but I needed to stop her before she started describing fictitious events in great, explicit detail. "It was… more than kissing, but we didn't sleep together."

"You're telling me you showed up at your boss's house—your *hot* boss's house—in the middle of the night, the same boss you spent months butting heads with and didn't have sex?"

I sighed, the same disappointment I'd felt that night right before I'd knocked some sense into myself rearing its head again. "Work called right before anything more happened."

"You idiot. You were still on-call?"

Before I could respond, Hazel hushed Nakia with a flick of her hand. "Oh, stop it. Let's focus on the important part. Was it good?

It was better than that.

I'd had partners before, but I always needed to do extra work to get myself there. With Michael, I barely could walk straight afterward and I hadn't lifted a finger or had him inside me.

"Yeah," I confessed quietly.

"*Really* good?" They both asked.

"The best," I said with a heavy sigh. "But it can't happen again."

"Why not?"

My feelings or whatever it was I felt toward Micahel were complicated. And complications weren't something I welcomed in my life.

I already had enough as it was.

My father still wasn't talking to me and avoiding me whenever I came over to see Zayd, I had to complete my training by next month and let's not forget that I was still competing against Michael for the role of a lifetime.

Any sort of intertwinement would only bring more complications into my life.

No matter how freeing that night had been. It had been the first time in weeks that my brain hadn't been running miles per hour.

"You're overthinking it too much," Nakia said and Hazel nodded in agreement.

"Understatement of the century."

Nakia's brow dipped as she examined me for a moment before she got to her feet. "Come on, get up," she ordered, motioning for me to stand.

I looked at her confused. "What?"

She pushed her thousand dollar coffee table forward, creating an empty space in front of where I sat on the sofa. "You heard me, get up." She swiftly moved to grab her phone from the kitchen island before returning to the living room and placing her phone on the table behind her.

A few seconds later, the first few notes of a song I knew all too well started playing around the living room.

"Not this again," I grumbled as Hazel got to her feet next to my other annoying friend.

Nakia rolled her eyes. "I know you love it. Now, stop pretending you don't and get your arse up," she ordered, clapping her hands to the rhythm of the music as she moved from side to side.

Our parents were from the same village in Morocco and this song was played at every wedding or family function we attended. We often were bored with how long they were, but whenever this song came up, we ran to the floor and danced with the other women.

As for Hazel, she'd been around us long enough, she was an

honorary Moroccan.

"You're really gonna make me do this?" I cocked my head to the side as I watched my friends move their shoulders up and down and leaning closer as if to taunt me.

Nakia just nodded in response as the song neared the hook.

With a groan, I reluctantly got up.

"Come on, let me see those shoulders," Nakia prompted, bumping hers into mine as the notes of the *Reggada* song sped faster and faster. When I indulged her with a small move, she added, "That's it, that's more like it. Dance it out."

I shook my head and let out a laugh as we danced around her living room. Even Shrif, her grumpy cat, who rarely came out when people were over, made an appearance and threaded through our legs as we laughed and swayed our hearts out.

And for a moment, I forgot all about Michael and everything else that had been plaguing my mind for the last several months. But as soon as we plopped down on the couch, sweaty from all the dancing we'd just done, everything came crashing back.

I might have been able to avoid Michael until now, but I couldn't do that forever. I was scheduled to return to work on Monday and was already dreading it.

That night had clearly been a mistake. I should let it be just that, forget and move on.

Then why was I thinking about when the next time would be?

CHAPTER 24

MICHAEL

I GOT OUT OF MY last surgery of the day with only one goal in mind.

I fastened my watch on my wrist and checked for the time. I knew she had a scheduled surgery coming up, but I didn't require much time for what I needed to do.

I headed for the nurse's station, and when Azara wasn't there, I looked in another few places where I knew she liked to be in between surgeries with no luck.

Fuck. Did she get pulled into another surgery or decide to head to the theater early?

I'd almost given up when the familiar sight of her dark brown curly hair pulled into a claw clip flashed farther down the corridor right as she turned the corner to most likely head for the stock closet.

I beelined in her direction.

She'd been avoiding me for the last two weeks and I was over it. After my lunch with my sister, I'd spent hours going back and forth on what to do. I'd initially opted to just let it go and focus my attention on what was important.

But as the days went by, I started to question what that was. I'd been laser focused my whole life and for the first time in… ever… what I wanted, what I really wanted didn't seem so clear anymore.

Besides, would it be so bad to temporarily let go of some of the pressure I'd been carrying and let myself…

I don't know? Feel?

There were only a few steps separating us and I quickly snuffed out the distance as she walked into the room. I followed right behind her and locked the door.

She immediately whipped around, a box of gauze in hand and aimed right at my head. "Who's…" Her words died in her throat when she noticed who she was about to attack.

"Out of all of the things you could grab to hurt someone, you grabbed the least damage-inflicting thing?" I teased with a brow raised.

Instead of lowering the box down, she did the opposite of what I thought she would. She swung at me with it. "You scared the shit out of me, Michael. What is wrong with you?"

I brought my hands in front of me, protecting from her second hit. "Alright, alright," I said with a laugh. "Didn't know you were so skittish?"

Azara shook her head and groaned, turning away from me to grab a few supplies. "I won't even entertain you." Once she'd gathered everything she needed, she faced me again. When I made no indication of stepping out of her path, she said, "Move out of the way."

Instead of doing so, I shoved my hands in my pockets and leaned against the locked door.

She let out an annoyed sigh. "Michael, I have a patient to see before heading to surgery, move."

I loved getting a rise out of her. She fell for it so easily every time.

I was on a mission and I wasn't leaving this narrow closet until I got what I'd tracked her down for. "I'll move if you answer a question first."

"Oh bite me," she groaned, moving to shoulder me out of her way with no success.

I took the opportunity of having her close to lean down, her intoxicating scent filling my senses. "I mean, only if you ask nicely," I said suggestively, my voice dropping low.

"Please," she scoffed, but she hadn't moved.

"I remember you liking it."

She lifted her head up and met my gaze, a blooming blaze taking over her irises. Time stood still until she snapped herself out of it, shaking her head and taking a few steps back.

"Fine. Ask away," she said, waving her hand to hurry me up.

I instantly missed her proximity, but there was no time to dwell on it.

"Why have you been avoiding me?"

I knew the answer already, but wanted to hear her say it. Hear her confirm that I wasn't alone in feeling whatever this was. Her body unquestionably told me that night, but I needed her to voice it.

"I haven't been avoiding you," she quickly replied. Too quickly.

I cocked my head to the side. "We both know that's a lie."

Azara pinched the bridge of her nose with her free hand before meeting my gaze. She shot me a pointed look, but I'd studied her so much since I'd first met her that I knew what was really hiding beneath it.

"This is ridiculous. Let me out."

"Not until you answer me." I took a step toward her. She didn't move.

She glared at me. "*Michael*, don't make me hit you."

I took another step and she craned her neck back, not breaking her gaze from mine. "Oh yeah? What if I like it when you fight me?"

My answer caught her by surprise, because although she was still glaring at me, the tiniest tremor ran all over her body. Her mouth opened a few times to reply, but every time she came short.

My gaze trailed over her face and fell to her lips, the memory of them pressed against mine, of her tongue tangling with mine as she let out the sweetest of moans.

If I was a better man, I wouldn't have rewatched the surveillance footage from the camera that recorded that night. But I wasn't a better man and although finally getting to taste her was cemented in my brain, video evidence didn't hurt.

When my eyes met hers again, long gone was the resistance and there she was.

The same woman that showed up at my doorstep in the middle of the night to take exactly what she wanted.

And I'd be an obliging participant. Every. Single. Time.

But good things came to those who waited.

So instead of kissing her right at that moment, just like I'd imagined on multiple occasions over the last two weeks, I reached for her back pocket.

The sweetest gasp fell from her lips and I couldn't wait to drink it in later tonight. It pained me to do it, but I took a step back and she finally realized my intentions.

"That's my phone," she gasped, eyes wide in stupor.

"I'm well aware," I countered, turning the device to scan her face so it would unlock. I already had her personal number memorized, but pretending I didn't was less conspicuous. I pulled up her contacts and entered my information before sending myself a text message.

She shook her head as if she was still catching up to what I was doing. "Wh-what are you doing?"

"You needed my number," I explained, a smile tugging at the corner of my lips at her dumbfounded expression. Before she could respond, I removed the distance between us again and leaned down, my lips brushing against the shell of her ear. "You still haven't answered my question, but I'll get my answer tonight. See you later, *gumiho*."

I didn't know if she would actually come and there was a chance she'd just ignore my offer and go home. But for once, I'd hold to hope. Even if it was just a sliver.

My lips trailed from her ear to her cheek where I pressed a feather-light kiss, before unlocking the door and heading home.

This should be interesting.

AZARA

WHAT THE FUCK JUST HAPPENED?

One minute I was grabbing what I needed to remove a chest drain from one of my recent partial lobectomy patients and the next I'd found myself ambushed and essentially locked in with Michael.

His heady scent still permeated the air and I still felt the remaining tingling sensation that erupted along where his lips had touched my skin. It reminded me of when those same lips were somewhere *very* different.

What did he mean by 'see you later'? And what had he needed my phone for?

For a brief moment, I'd thought he'd left with it, but when I patted my hand to my back pocket, I realized it was back in its place. I didn't know how he'd managed to slip it back there without me noticing. But truthfully, my awareness had only latched onto being face to face with him for the first time since I'd shown up at his doorstep.

I grabbed and unlocked it, the screen opening to a brand new thread with one single text message. He'd sent himself a text message from my phone, but it was directed at me.

ME

Come over after your shift.

Surprise filled me at his proposition and I didn't know what to think of it. Before I could wrap my head around it, three dots at the bottom of the screen popped up. Sudden anxiety filled me at the sight until my phone whirred with a new message

It was the pin of a location with a text attached to it.

MICHAEL

In case you forgot. Mamadou already knows to let you in.

It was the address to his penthouse.

Very presumptuous of him to think I'd already agreed, but it was up to par for his stupidly charming and charismatic personality. Something I'd unfortunately grown to find slightly endearing. But I'd never tell him that, his ego was inflated enough.

I didn't need to add more to its size.

I rolled my eyes and pocketed my phone before heading out of the closet I'd been in for far too long and heading to my patient's room.

Today had been my first day back after being off, and I'd managed to evade him all day by diving into work. I'd even looked at the surgery schedule board and made changes to theaters so I wouldn't accidentally cross his path. I'd almost succeeded, with my shift being almost over, but of course my luck wouldn't have it another way.

It had only been two weeks since I'd last seen him yet every one of my nerve endings instantly lit up in his presence. I'd thought a lot about my conversation with Nakia and Hazel and spent the rest of my weekend mulling over what I should do.

I agreed that there was nothing wrong with meaningless and casual sex, but I knew that with Michael, it could never be truly meaningless. No matter how much I hated to admit it.

So I'd settled on the smartest, easiest solution to the problem.

Avoidance.

I'd have to see him every day, but once I got the medical director role—which I *would* get—I wouldn't have to work so closely with him and there you go.

Problem solved, right?

So I'd armored myself to face this head on and focus on work.

Like I'd spent my entire life doing.

Could I benefit from letting myself out of this box I'd confined myself in? Sure.

But stepping out of the comfort of the walls you'd erected to protect yourself from getting hurt was utterly terrifying. I might not have experienced heartbreak like most people had, but I'd witnessed and had been subjected to the repercussions so much that it had sobered me from ever wanting to be on the receiving end.

The potential for heartbreak was everywhere the safety of my confines wasn't, and I'd rather stray away from falling for someone now than regret it later.

And that would have been a no brainer in the past. The thought of venturing past what I'd always known had always been met with resistance.

The answer was always that it wasn't worth it.

Then why was it that with Michael the answer wasn't as straightforward.

I *could* stop overanalyzing and overthinking every single aspect of everything for once, but what if what I feared would happen ended up happening?

What would I do then?

What if it didn't?

"Dr. Ziani?" I heard a familiar voice say, snapping me out of my thoughts. I glanced over at the source to find AJ, one of the junior surgeons who'd been under my supervision for this past year, staring at me from under his surgical loupes.

"Shall we proceed?" he asked quietly, almost uncomfortably.

I must have drifted off because he rarely chimed in anything. Not because I didn't encourage it, but it was just in his nature to work quietly and wait for my directions, to which he'd perform beautifully for someone at his level.

My gaze moved around the room to find my entire team watching me, waiting for my command to begin the repair. I cleared my throat and unfolded my hands, extending one to receive what I needed to make the incision.

"Yes, let's." I replied before pushing everything out of my mind. My brain quieted—something that only happened in the confines of these four walls—and I let my hands fall into a routine I knew as well as breathing.

Three hours later, I stepped out of the theater and the thoughts I'd been able to quiet for the last few hours started creeping back in only for my steps to lead me to the only other place where my brain had been able to shut off.

To the same place they did two weeks ago.

As the lift ascended to the top floor, my mind battled with indecision but when the doors opened to reveal Michael already waiting on the other side, all of my reasons for why I'd settled on avoidance suddenly became murky.

"You came."

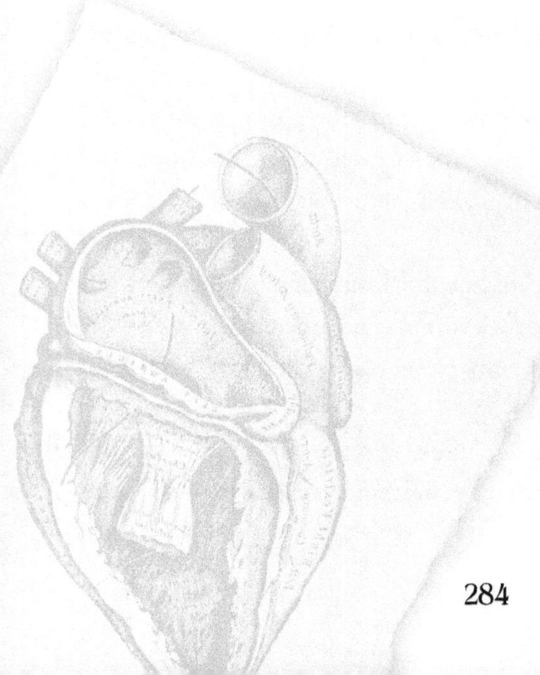

CHAPTER 25

MICHAEL

I WAS ALMOST DONE WITH getting everything ready when I received an alert from Mamadou to inform me that my guest was on her way up.

I gave my place a quick once over before I wiped my hands on a small tea towel before throwing it over my shoulder and walking over to the entryway to greet her.

Seconds seemed to stretch to hours and I wiped my moist hands on the sides of my trousers.

It's just a dinner date, I reminded myself.

Albeit I'd never been on a first date, I knew how to host people. Surely, this wouldn't be any different, right?

But I'd learned early on that when it came to Azara, nothing was ever *just*.

This *was* different in every way.

The lift doors slid open to reveal the only person that seemed to occupy my mind these days. It was like she'd reached into my brain and planted herself there, unwavering.

Azara stood there, her silhouette framed by the soft glow of the lights above her.

Her beauty was truly unmatched.

Her curls draped loosely over her shoulder and she'd changed into a pair of dark washed jeans and a brown cardigan that matched her flats. I'd seen her outside of her scrubs in the past, but the casual nature of her outfit sent a new warmth through my body.

I relished in seeing her so… relaxed in my own space.

But it made what I'd been denying myself for quite some time more apparent.

I was growing to like her.

And I was hoping tonight would… I wasn't sure what I expected tonight would attain, I just knew I wanted to experience her outside of work.

"You came."

She tucked part of her hair behind her right ear. "I did," she said quietly, and I hated the uncertainty in her tone. She didn't seem uncomfortable, but it was almost as if she was unsure that coming over was the right choice.

She stood perfectly still, her gaze lingering in the space between us. Uneasiness started creeping up my spine, hoping I hadn't scared her off by asking her to come over.

The doors began to close, and my hand shot up, firmly stopping them from doing so.

I slipped on a half-smile to hopefully ease whatever she was feeling. "Are you coming in, or do I need to carry you?" I asked, referring to the only other time she'd been here.

My quiet invitation hung in the air between us as my gaze held hers.

Her feet remained rooted in the spot for a moment longer, before she took a small breath and took a few steps forward, until she stood right in front of me.

"Hi," she said, looking up at me.

My smile grew wider. "Hi."

I could easily grab her face in my hands and kiss her, but I knew that we'd never make it past the entryway. I might be playing with fire by inviting her over, but I couldn't break my oath.

Even as tempting as Azara was.

Keep telling yourself that, that voice in my head muttered.

I took a small step back, not enough to put real distance between us because I liked having her close, but just enough to gesture for her to venture farther inside.

After she slipped off her shoes, I placed a hand on the small of her back, finding the warmth of her body strangely comforting beneath my fingers. I guided her down the hallway and into the large lower living space.

Her eyes slightly widened when her gaze trailed to the open-plan kitchen that connected to the private terrace, which overlooked the city. "You're cooking?" she asked, her tone full of surprise as if the idea of me doing so was unimaginable.

My hand dropped from her back when she moved closer to the island counter to look over what I'd made. I'd debated on what to make for hours, until I'd finally landed on *Bibimbap* since I found out after some research that it was diabetic friendly. I didn't want her to overthink about eating. I'd also grown up eating it all the time and needed something comforting so I could find some semblance of it during the night.

I'd never been the nervous type, but since I'd come up with it, the idea of tonight had been looming over my head. You'd think my life was depending on it. In any other scenario, I wouldn't have cared, but I was coming to learn that with Azara, I *did* care about what she thought.

"I can make something different, if you—"

She whipped around to interrupt me. "No, I just meant…" Her words trailed off when a faint blush creeped across her face. She hastily shook her head and cleared her throat before adding, "Never mind. This looks amazing."

She faced away from me again and approached the kitchen island to find the various bowls with all the ingredients I needed. I'd already marinated the vegetables and beef so that I'd only be left to cook them when she arrived.

I didn't want anything to get cold by the time she made it and it'd give me something to distract myself with while she took up space with her presence.

My brows furrowed for a moment, wondering why she was acting embarrassed, when it dawned on me why my cooking dinner for us had taken her aback. I hadn't really told her about my reason behind inviting her over.

She must have thought…

A smile pulled at the corner of my lips as I quietly closed the distance, until my front was flushed to her back. A sweet gasp escaped her lips when I brought mine close to her ear.

"I could spread *you* open on the counter if you preferred," I murmured, my voice dropping, before pulling away and walking into the kitchen.

The idea was all-consumingly tempting, but we'd never make it to dinner and knowing her, she probably hadn't eaten much all day.

I looked over to where she was still rooted in place, the previous faint flush that had decorated her cheeks much darker now.

There were many facets of Azara I found fascinating, but this one had to be my favorite. She was always so assertive and opinionated, that seeing her speechless and embarrassed was quite a sight.

My mind wandered to images of other places she could blush so easily but I pushed them away before I came back on my words and abandoned my original plans.

"Wanna take a seat?" I said, pointing at the chairs on the island opposite me with my chin.

She startled, realizing I was speaking to her, and cleared her throat. "Oh, yeah. Sure." Heading for one of the cushioned high chairs, Azara took a seat, placing her work tote bag on the one next to hers and sinking her chin into her open palm.

I stifled a chuckle and grabbed some of the bowls that contained the sliced vegetables to bring them over to the stove which thankfully still gave me a view of her. I resumed cooking while I watched her from the corner of my eye silently take me in, as if she was appraising me.

I didn't mind being the object of her scrutiny but I wondered what was going on in that pretty head of hers. I refrained from asking, wanting to see if she would make the first move. After a few moments of stillness, the only sound coming from the sizzling pans, she finally spoke up.

"Are you planning on poisoning me?"

My brows furrowed for a moment before a sound I hadn't heard in a long time escaped me. I burst out laughing at her insinuation as I leaned against the counter behind me. I tilted my head to the side with a small smile, and crossed my arms over my chest.

"Don't you think if I'd wanted to poison you, it would be much more efficient to do so at the hospital than at my own place?"

"Fair enough." She shrugged. "Still had to ask."

I huffed out a small laugh and returned my attention to the stove, stirring the vegetables and meat in their respective pans. I was about to ask if she wanted a drink when she started making conversation.

"Where did you learn how to cook?"

I briefly glanced over at her, finding her gazing at me with a curious expression. "My grandmother," I replied, memories of the various moments I spent in the kitchen with her coming to mind.

When we lived in Korea, my parents were often busy, so I'd spent the majority of my time with her. She'd always sit me on the kitchen counter while she cooked, telling me fragments of her life, and when I was old enough to help, she put me to work.

"I grew up in Korea and she always said that a man should stop being lazy and know how to cook. So I would help her in the kitchen whenever she made food for our family."

I never shared personal details about my life with anyone, but I found myself compelled to tell her. My grandmother was blunt and one of the rare people that treated me as me, despite her knowing what I was meant to be.

She hadn't been supposed to be privy to the House, but she'd been too smart and had figured it out within the first few years of her marriage to my grandfather. She'd eventually been sworn to secrecy and became the first and only woman to be a part of the Atlas.

She wasn't a member, but she was held to the same standard.

"I like her," Azara said with a small smile on her face.

I couldn't help but smile myself. She rarely ever smiled when I was around and it was a good thing, because Azara Ziani smiling was dangerously addicting.

My eyes flit up to hers. "She would like you too," I replied without thinking. It wasn't a lie, my grandmother would adore Azara, but it wasn't something I was supposed to say.

This was nothing more than a casual dinner.

Turning off the stove, I washed my hands, before wiping them dry on the cloth draped over my shoulder. I then grabbed the large dish from the counter, it already had the spinach and soybean sprouts side dishes I'd prepared earlier, and plated the sautéed and seasoned vegetables as well as the marinated meat.

Everything else had already been set up on the island, so I placed the large plate onto the centre so it'd be easier to serve ourselves.

"Do you do this often?" Azara asked as I rummaged through a drawer for clean utensils.

"Do what?"

When I made my way to her, she was gesturing at the set up with a sweep of her hand. "This."

I titled my head, raising a brow. "Cook?"

"You know what I mean," she replied, grabbing the two spoons from my hands. Our fingers brushed during the exchange, and she hastily snatched her hand away.

"I'm afraid I don't." I knew exactly what she was implying, but I enjoyed her unease far too much to make it easy on her.

She waited a beat before rolling her eyes. "Never mind." She grabbed one of the shallow bowls and looked at me for instructions. "What's the best way to eat this?" she asked, changing the subject.

I grabbed the bowl from her hand and said, "Let me."

I quickly dished up hers, asking what she'd like while showing how I'd usually plate up mine. I'd made some modifications to the dish to avoid Azara's sugar spiking later on or for her to feel like she couldn't enjoy the meal because she had to manage her portion.

Once I was done with plating hers, I made my own bowl before leaving it on the counter and went to grab a small pan and the carton of eggs from the built-in fridge.

I fired up the stove once more and turned to ask her, "Would you like a fried egg on your bowl?" When she hesitated, I added, "It's much better with it, but you can try mine first, and if you like it, I'll whip one up for you."

Once the egg was cooked, I crossed to the other side of the island and took the empty seat next to Azara. I could have offered for us to sit at the giant dining table behind us, but she'd be too far from me.

I reached for the small bowl, drizzled the sauce I'd whisked over my dish, broke the yolk, and mixed it all together before scooping up a bite and shifting my body sideways so I could face her better.

"Here, try it," I ordered, holding the spoon up to her.

Her eyes flickered between my eyes and the spoon. She reached for it, but I moved her hand away with my free hand. "Let me," I gently ordered, my voice low.

Realizing that I was intending to feed her, she dropped her hand onto her thigh, and bit into her bottom lip, contemplating what to do.

After what felt like an eternity, she hesitantly nodded and said, "Okay."

With a small smirk fixed on my face, I leaned closer, and she met me halfway. Our eyes stayed glued to each other, her gaze turning heated when the spoon touched her lips.

For a moment, neither of us moved. The silence between us was so thick, it was almost palpable. Heat spread across my skin and my heart rate began furiously pounding in my chest as her mouth slightly opened up and I pushed past it, feeding her.

With her eyes still fixed on mine, Azara leaned back and almost imperceptibly shifted in her seat. Her thumb swiped over her bottom lip to catch a small drop of the sauce before she pushed it in her mouth, licking it clean.

A vision of me forcing something different between her soft, full lips flashed in my mind unbidden. Just the idea of her mouth, licking, sucking, *swallowing* me, sent goosebumps filtering across my skin.

"Mmm," she said, as she swallowed her food. "That's actually delicious."

When I brought my attention back to her, she was watching me with a glint in her eyes telling me she knew exactly where my mind had just gone.

I might have been the one who'd initiated it, but she knew exactly what she was doing. I placed the empty spoon against my tongue and licked it, the faint remnant of her taste mixed with the rice dish flooding my palate.

I hummed. "You're right. Fucking exquisite."

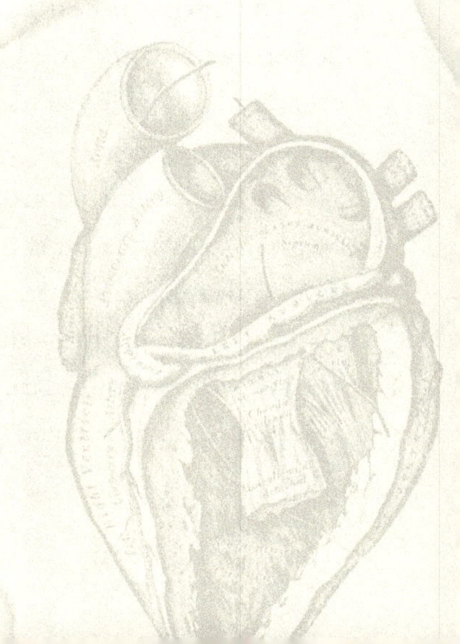

CHAPTER 26

AZARA

I SINCERELY WAS STARTING TO question my aptitude to make sound decisions because why did I keep putting myself in situations like these when it came to Michael Young.

I had no idea what he had planned when he'd asked me to come over, but a home-cooked dinner date hadn't been anywhere on that list.

The intention he'd put behind decorating the place with candles, flowers, and all the food he'd prepared, was more than anyone had ever done for me. Even the most luxurious dates I'd been on had never been this… intimate.

He also seemed almost nervous, something I'd never witnessed before. Almost like he'd been anxious to see my reaction and it was quite endearing to see this normally quite confident man unsettled.

And that I might be the reason behind it.

He wore a loose dark grey polo shirt, his strong arms revealing the intricate tattoos inked over all over his sleeves that made me want to trace every single design with my tongue. And the matching dark trousers molded his thick thighs and bum so deliciously, all I could think about was how he'd felt under my touch the last time I'd visited.

Watching someone cook shouldn't be this alluring, but as I'd come to realize, I'd barely been able to keep my eyes away from him as he moved around his kitchen so effortlessly.

Except when I shot a text to our group chat for help, and of course, both Nakia and Hazel encouraged—more like threatened—me to stay put. I was hoping they'd offer to fake an emergency so I'd have to leave, but they were of no help.

For people who'd never met him, they were surprisingly rooting in his favor.

Michael made quick work at the stove, before returning to his seat beside me, his thigh brushing against my knee as he did. I tried to focus on mixing up my bowl, but his presence was becoming too distracting.

Like that was anything new, but there was a perfectly reasonable *large* dining table just behind us and several other seats around the island, yet he'd chosen this one.

I could spread you open on the counter if you preferred

I shifted in my seat, pulling my phone from my bag, in an attempt to briefly put some distance between us. But it was pointless. He was still far too close as I did quick-math and imputed the values in my phone so I could get enough insulin to cover me.

I knew he'd made changes to the original recipe and swapped a few ingredients for my benefit. The thoughtful gesture sent an all too familiar warmth spreading through my entire body and made those stupid fluttering creatures in my stomach take flight. I tried not to overthink it and brushed it off as him simply being a good doctor and wanting to make sure I wouldn't have another episode where he'd have to take care of me.

Yeah, keep telling yourself that.

I pushed away the annoying chirping voice in my head, tucked my phone away, ignoring the countless notifications from the girls asking for an update, and began eating. We sat in silence for a few moments, but the heated tension from earlier only deepened with each passing minute in his close proximity.

I glanced at him, only to find him already watching me. I tried to ignore the expression in his gaze, but it only reminded me that he'd had the same exact look the last time I was here and he'd sent heat scorching through my veins

Hoping to diffuse the atmosphere, I blurted out the first thing that came to mind. "You know, when you asked me to come over, I wasn't expecting a dinner date."

I didn't tell him that I'd expected us to be standing here, with much less clothing.

He was quiet for a moment, when I watched a smile transform his previously stern face. "So this is a date?" he asks, his tone teasing.

I mentally groaned, chastising myself. I hadn't realized I'd referred to tonight as a date. "Sorry, I didn't…" I let out a nervous laugh. "I shouldn't have assumed."

I took a large bite, hoping to buy me some time and more importantly, get me to shut up.

"And you know, I'm quite offended that you think I'm only good for my body," he added with a raised brow.

I almost choked on my food, grabbing the water nearby to help. I downed half the glass, my cheeks flaming red. This was just perfect, another fucking embarrassment to add to the list. Maybe silence was a better option, why didn't I just keep my mouth shut?

"No," I sputtered, hoping to dig myself out of this even though it seemed to be a lost cause. "Ah, shit. I'm sorry. I didn't—"

"Azara, stop apologizing," he said with a soft laugh as he grabbed my chin between two fingers and turned my face so I would meet his gaze. "I'm just messing with you."

"You're fucking impossible," I said, but my voice faltered as his thumb lightly brushed over my jaw. The revering touch sent a shiver running down my spine.

"I might be, but I like the idea that you also think of this as a date."

I opened my mouth to respond, but the words caught in my throat from his proximity. His heady musky scent inhibited my senses and the intensity of his gaze only left me with one thought.

I wanted to kiss him.

Badly.

I'd never had this visceral need for someone before and although it was so foreign to me, I wanted to bask in it as long as I could. I didn't know what this thing between us was, but I was tired of fighting against it and using logic to make the best decisions.

Because when it came to Michael Young, logic seemed to be the last thing on my mind. And by the way he was looking at me in this moment, I could tell he was thinking the same.

Before I could press my lips against his, like I'd longed for over the last two weeks—despite strongly denying it to myself—he pulled back and dropped his hand, my skin suddenly cold at the loss of his touch.

He clapped his hands together once. "Alright, let's get things cleaned up. I have something to show you."

"What is it?"

"Patience, *gumiho*. You'll have to wait and see," he said with a wink before grabbing our plates and heading to the sink.

I offered to do the dishes since he'd cooked, but Michael insisted on doing it himself and told me to relax. So while he cleaned and put the leftovers away, curiosity got the best of me and I took the liberty to explore the ground floor of his flat.

I noticed a staircase that seemed to lead to an upper level when I came in, but not trusting myself to end up in his bedroom by accident, I chose the safe option and stayed close.

I trailed over to the living room connected to the dining room by a large arched wall. The space was so meticulously decorated, it seemed to be coming straight out of a museum. Every item was perfectly placed and almost seemed untouched.

But if you paid close attention, there were signs of the place being lived in—the reading glasses tucked in the corner of the large sectional sofa where an indent was present, or the cup marks on the dark oak coffee table.

I moved over to the bookcase on the wall near the giant floor to ceiling windows. The drapes were drawn, but I'd bet the view was breathtaking. I'd always wanted to see the city from high up, but a place like this was way out of my budget.

We made decent money as surgeons—well when we weren't trainees anymore— but definitely not enough to afford a penthouse. I'd heard the Youngs were extremely well-off from the gossip mill at the hospital, but I didn't know they had *this* kind of money.

The rows were mostly filled with various medical textbooks or classic novels, my eyes widening when I realized some of them were first edition.

How much money did this man have?

My gaze roamed over the titles when suddenly the books turned into thinner spines and I noticed he had a massive collection of what seemed to be graphic novels. Out of all the types of books I'd expected to see on these shelves, these weren't an option I'd even considered.

As I perused the titles, my fingers slowly trailing over the spines, I was slowly coming to realize that the man I'd grown accustomed to at work wasn't exactly how I'd made him out to be.

There were also a few bits and bobs as well as picture frames decorating the wooden shelves. One in particular captured my attention so I picked it up to get a closer look at it. The photograph was of Michael and another woman, embracing each other on a beach.

She looked like an almost identical younger version of Michael, only with hazel eyes and a smile that made you want to be friends with her instantly.

"That's my baby sister, Alice," Michael offered, startling me. My heart rate pounded against my chest at him finding me. I hadn't even heard him come in.

I turned around to face him, gearing myself to apologize for invading his space, but the soft smile on his lips indicated that he didn't seem to mind.

"Although don't tell her I called her that, she hates when I call her a baby," he added as he headed toward me.

I didn't know much about Michael outside of the hospital but his small concession about his personal life made me want to know more about him and everything that made him.

"How old is she?" I asked, hoping he wouldn't find my question intrusive.

"She turns nineteen next month, which feels even crazy to say because I still remember the day my parents brought her home. She was just a tiny newborn and now she's off to uni and that makes me feel extremely old," he said with a fond laugh.

I understood that all too well. I wasn't one to share, but his ease at telling me about himself, made me want to do the same. "I feel the same with my brother. He's already sixteen and I don't know how time flew by so fast," I shared, my voice growing quiet.

The thought brought a sorrowful feeling squeezing around my

ribcage from how it was when he was a toddler, but no matter how difficult the years after that were, he was the only thing motivating me to keep me going.

My mother's death alone had been hard, but taking care of my brother practically all alone, had been even harder. I loved Zayd like he was my own, but I would be lying if I said I hadn't thought of just quitting a few times. My dad was physically present and provided for us financially and made sure we didn't need for anything, but my brother had reminded him too much of my mother.

Every time he'd pick him up, he'd become even more of a shell of himself and ask for me to take Zayd away because he had some work emergency to deal with.

My father had gotten better at it over the years—not for my lack of trying—but those first few years were… a lot.

"Azara?" Michael asked as his hand came to rest against my forearm. I hadn't noticed that he must've replied to what I'd said and it remained unanswered.

I opened my mouth to give an excuse about why I'd grown quiet, but he beat me to it. I expected for him to push for answers as to why, but instead, he simply extended his hand and said, "Come with me."

I looked at his outstretched hand and back to him. "Where are you taking me?"

"You don't like to be surprised do you?" he asked, with a small laugh.

I lifted my shoulder in a shrug. "Not really. I like being in control."

Michael pinned me with a dark gaze as he shoved his other hand in his pocket. "Oh, I'm well aware you like to be in control, *gumiho*."

I averted my gaze and preoccupied myself by placing the frame back where I'd found it, hoping it'd buy me time to get my body in check and appear completely unfazed by his comment. Although what he'd said and the *way* he'd said it made fire drip through my veins.

And that nickname. I'd been curious about what it meant since the masquerade ball and had wanted to ask him so many times, but a part of me liked the mystery of not knowing. It made every time he said it seem like *more*.

I steadied my breathing before turning to face him again. He still had his hand extended so I finally placed my hand in his, his deft fingers wrapping over it before he tugged me to wherever this surprise was.

Michael guided me out of the living room, past the kitchen and down a small hallway until the helical staircase came into view. Never once did he let my hand go and there was an unpredicted calmness that settled over me with the simple gesture.

We slowly climbed the wooden stairs and once we reached the upper floor, he abruptly stopped and faced me. I stopped in my tracks and peered up at him.

"Close your eyes for me," he told me with a soft smile.

"Why?"

He shook his head with a chuckle. "Just do what I tell you," he softly ordered and with the tone he used, I'd probably do just about anything he asked.

I rolled my eyes. "Fine," I huffed out before doing as told.

Michael let go of my hand before I felt his body shift behind me, his front dangerously close to my back. He grabbed me by the waist right before his breath fanned across the shell of my ear and I let out a small gasp.

"Don't open those pretty eyes of yours until I tell you so, yeah?" he whispered in my ear and a shiver slithered through my entire body.

I swallowed thickly and nodded, knowing that if I used words, they'd come out strained and I'd rather him not know the extent of the effect he had on me.

"Good," he rasped before pressing a feathered kiss there and pulling back. We walked for a few more steps before he stopped. I had the urge to steal a peek, but the strange satisfaction of pleasing him was stronger.

I waited patiently, the anticipation of what he was up to coursing through my veins. Michael let go of my waist, but didn't move to step away from me, his body still pressed against mine.

"You can open them."

I opened my eyes immediately, and let out a gasp at the sight in front of me. Whatever I'd imagined was behind the drapes downstairs, was nothing compared to the view in front of me.

A breathtaking panoramic view of London's skyline was laid out in front of us. Growing up in London, you quickly forgot what it offered since everything just became normal, but seeing it from this viewpoint gave me a new appreciation for the city I'd spent the majority of my life in.

"Want to see it from outside?" Michael proposed, and I paused admiring the view to glance at him over my shoulder.

"Can we?"

"Of course. Anything you want," he said, his hand finding my back.

He reached for a small bench and grabbed a blanket, draping it over my shoulders, before he slid open the doors of the large terrace. We stepped outside, the frigid air wrapping around us and I was grateful for his mindfulness.

I tugged it closer around my body as I neared the edge, Michael following right behind. If I thought the view was beautiful from the inside, it was even better now.

"This is…"

"Beautiful," he finished, and I shifted my gaze to find Michael leaning casually against the glass edge, watching... me. Despite his perfectly chiseled features, there was a softness that graced his expression whenever his attention was on me, and I never wanted him to look away.

"Yeah," I whispered.

We didn't move. Didn't say a word. Didn't shift our gaze from one another.

Instead, I watched the man whom I'd hated being in the presence of for the major part of the year transform before my eyes. There was something so strangely comforting about his presence. The way he made me feel at ease, almost like all my worries that were hanging over my head didn't have to be shouldered alone, and I didn't think I'd ever been given that before.

Sure my girlfriends provided me a sense of security and comfort, but this was different and I found myself craving more of it. Not just him and what had transpired between us two weeks ago, but just time with him.

I'd been on date and hung out with men, but none had made me feel this way.

"To answer you earlier, question." He paused, and I held my breath as I waited for him to continue. "No, I've never done this. You're the only one."

CHAPTER 27

AZARA

"DO YOU SEE HER?" HAZEL asked once we stepped inside the giant exhibit hall.

My eyes scanned the packed room of guests dressed in elegant gowns and tailored tuxedos, but there was no sign of our friend. I glanced at the time on my phone and saw that it was a little after 7:00 p.m. "She should already be here."

We were at Nakia's opening night for her first official exhibition at Anzar as a chief curator. She'd been working on it for over a year now and tonight was her big night. Hazel and I had gotten ready at my place before we took a cab to come here to celebrate the event.

"Has she texted you?" Hazel asked, checking her own phone for news.

I pulled up our group chat thread but the last text from her was when we'd messaged her that we were on our way when we got into the uber. Which was twenty minutes ago.

Nakia was never late to anything, especially when it came to her job. It took her years to get the position she had more than deserved, but we all knew how men were when it came to women in power.

They hated it.

A server passing by stopped next to us to offer canapés and both Hazel and I grabbed a napkin and stacked a few of the artichoke phyllo cups. We hadn't had a chance to eat before leaving because I'd finished work later than I'd anticipated and she'd been stuck in traffic because of some film festival that had been in town for the week.

I was about to tell Hazel that I hadn't gotten any news from Nakia when both of our phones pinged with a text message from tonight's guest of honor, letting us know that she was running late and that she'd explain later.

We each sent her a text back to let us know if she needed us to do anything before we roamed around the room, checking out the pieces Nakia had carefully curated.

Each piece had been uniquely created for this new collection and evoked how music spoke through the human body. Some pieces were modest while others more provocative, which wasn't something these old money guests were used to based on the hushed chatter we'd passed by.

The theme she'd chosen was unlike anything the renowned-gallery had ever held a collection for before, but it embodied who Nakia was perfectly.

She wanted people to be brought out of their comfort zones when looking at art and that was exactly why she'd fallen in love with it. I still remembered the first time we'd been forced to visit a museum for a school assignment. We'd been fourteen at the time and after she'd laid eyes on the first painting, I'd had to drag her out of there before security kicked us out in light of closing hours.

It'd been almost another twenty minutes of walking around with no sign of Nakia when Hazel abruptly stopped, an expression on her face I couldn't decipher.

It was somewhere between shock, admiration and a bit turned on.

Don't ask how I knew that last one.

"What's wrong?" I asked, my brows furrowed as my eyes slid to where she was looking, transfixed.

"Are you not seeing this?"

I titled my head and examined the large painting in front of us. It was the one we'd heard people gossip about the most, but aside from the abstract strokes of various shades of oranges, browns and yellows, I didn't really understand what she was seeing.

I looked over at Hazel, and the confusion must have been apparent on my face because she rolled her eyes and grabbed my chin. Then she proceeded to maneuver my head this and that way as she pointed to the center of the piece.

"Look closer,"

I let out a sigh and tried to focus, narrowing my eyes to attempt to see what was so magical about this piece when I finally saw it.

The art piece featured a couple I hadn't seen initially and the more I studied it, the more the image became clear. The male subject seemed to be on his knees, while the woman was splayed on a table with a paintbrush in hand, her back arched as he…

Holy shit.

"That's…"

"Fucking hot," a familiar voice behind us said, startling us with the sudden intrusion. Hazel dropped my chin as we both whipped around to find Nakia standing behind us.

She wore a brown floor length slinky textured jersey dress with a bardot neckline and rope halter neck tie. It had ruching through the body creating a dramatic silhouette and molding all of the soft curves of her body. She'd paired her outfit with her grandmother's beloved chunky gold earrings she wore at every key moment, and her favorite stack of matching bangles.

Nakia was the perfect depiction of elegance and sophistication.

"You're here," Hazel and I exclaimed as we each embraced her in a tight hug.

"Fucking finally," she groaned, tucking her clutch and phone under her armpit. She snatched a champagne coupe from a passing tray and knocked it back in one go.

"Wanna talk about it?" I asked, watching her place the empty champagne flute on another tray.

"Remember the new artist I'd discovered at the indie artist street festival back in September?" Hazel and I both nodded in response.

Nakia had stumbled on this piece, and instantly fell head over heels in love with it. Something about a fresh outlook while using modern techniques, but I'd honestly lost track of her explanation after she used too many foreign words.

All I remembered was that the painter, who went by the name *Anti*, had opted to remain anonymous and she'd made it her mission to get in contact with them so she could commission more of his pieces. Both to add to the gallery's collection and her personal one.

"I'd been tracking them down for months after I got a hold of this one," she said, gesturing to the canva behind us. That's when I realized that this was the famous piece she'd sent us a photo of when she'd first spotted it back in September. This was actually what had sparked her concept for tonight. "I'd finally made some progress when my lead hit a dead end."

Hazel opened her mouth to respond, but Nakia groaned and added, "And to top it off, the gallery owner has been an absolute arse about this collection."

Her phone buzzed with a text, and she grabbed it, her brows furrowing as she read the message before looking up again. "I have to run, but I'll catch you two later, yeah?"

Before either of us could reply, she quickly kissed both of our cheeks and melted into the crowd. Once she was gone, Hazel and I found an empty high table, and I leaned against it.

"These heels are killing me," I sighed, shifting from side to side to ease some of the pressure. "I don't know how you wear them everyday?"

I spent countless hours on my feet at the hospital, but this was a different kind of torture. I loved a good pair of heels for a night out, but I wished whoever had invented them had put a little more thought into comfort.

Whoever came up with 'beauty was pain' needed a rearranging.

Hazel and I filled each other on our last week as we ate and drank, watching the crowd. It had really picked up compared to when we arrived.

Hazel's phone buzzed in her purse, and when she pulled it out, a picture of her and her husband on the beach flashed on the screen. She silenced the call and started typing to tell him we were still at the gallery, but before she could hit send, he called again.

Eddy never called when she was out unless it was an emergency.

Hazel answered on the first ring, and panic took over her features. "¡Ay, qué boludo![19] Why on earth did you do that?" she scolded him. She listened for a moment before replying, "I told you not to—just, don't move. I'll be right here."

She hung up, quickly ordered a cab and looked at me with an apologetic expression. "I've got to go. My *husband* has been working

---

19 *Oh, you idiot! (Spanish)*

on his 'secret wedding gift,' even though I already know what it is, and he's just managed to injure himself trying to install shelves in my new office."

"Is he alright?" I fought off a smile. Eddy had a tendency of starting projects and although it was very sweet of him, let's just say he should just stick to football.

She waved it off. "He'll be just fine. His ego's probably more bruised than anything." Placing a hand over mine, she added, "Will you be okay on your own?"

I placed my free hand over hers, gently giving it a reassuring squeeze. "I'll be fine. Go and save your man before he does some real damage."

Hazel gave me a soft smile as she hugged me goodbye. "Alright, love. I'll see you next week?"

I watched her disappear into the throng, her heels clicking on the marble floor.

I glanced at the crowd once again, trying to spot any familiar faces, but most were strangers. My eyes landed on the feature painting in Nakia's collection, finding a young couple standing in front of it.

The woman stood slightly in front of him and he wrapped his left arm around her front, his other hand coming up to brush her dark hair to the side. He leaned down to murmur something in her ear before he placed a kiss at the junction between her shoulder and neck.

The right thing to do would have been to look away, but my gaze didn't falter as he trailed his fingers up and down her exposed back as her eyes were locked on the painting while his were on her the entire time.

A meddling idea abruptly popped into my head to message Michael and see what he was up to. We'd exchanged a few messages on our personal numbers since our date last week, but they'd all been work related. I'd been too afraid to shatter the remaining wall of protection I had when it came to him despite the way his words from that night were still echoing in my mind.

I've never done this.

You're the only one.

We'd stayed on the terrace, just basking in the quiet air and the weight of his words before I went home. Everything in me had screamed to stay longer, but I knew I had to get out of there. Besides, I'd had an early shift the next day and if I hadn't left, I doubt we would have gotten much sleep.

Quickly dismissing the thought, I moved to explore more of the art that Hazel and I hadn't had a chance to see when I spotted some of the board members and well-known donors of the hospital amongst them.

I wasn't very fond of sparking conversations, but I hadn't taken the chance to speak to anyone and affirm my candidacy. There were less than three months before the final decision was made and I'd been so busy with finishing my training, and finalizing the details of my teaching program after they'd finally given me the green light to implement it.

I let out a sigh and knocked back the rest of the champagne I'd been nursing for the entire night. I smoothed a hand down my dress before making my way toward their group.

I squared my shoulders despite the nerves prickling my veins the closer I got. I didn't mind the bureaucracy that came with this position, I just hated the people around it. What I cared about was the medicine, not how to deepen my own pockets to the detriment of others.

The sound of laughter got louder as I approached them. I apologized to a few people blocking my path and when they parted, I understood why.

clutch on a nearby chair right before he grabbed my face and crashed his lips against mine while I wrapped my arms around his neck.

He kissed me like it had been on his mind all day.

He savored me like this was the first and last time he'd get to have me.

He devoured me like I was a necessity for his next breath.

This kiss was nothing like the others we'd exchanged.

It was raw.

Vicious.

Passionate.

His fingers tangled at the back of my head and he tilted it up, before tightening his grip on the strands of my hair. The sharp pain elicited a gasp from me and he used the opening to slip his tongue past my lips, thrusting it inside my mouth and tangling it with mine.

We battled for domination and it fueled my need for more.

I moaned against his lips as he walked me backward, until my ass crashed against a hard object. Michael's fingers untangled from my hair and grabbed the back of my thighs before I found myself lifted up from the ground and set down onto whatever I'd collided with.

His hands gripped everywhere he could as I slid my hands under his collar and down his strong shoulders to remove his jacket. Once it was off, I brought my hands down his front, tugging at the buttons of his white shirt to feel his smooth skin under my touch.

I'd only gotten to undoing the second one when he pushed my hands away and yanked the neck of my dress down. Suddenly, his mouth wasn't on mine anymore and he went straight to attacking my chest with his mouth where he alternated between biting and sucking the top of my breasts.

"*Michael*," I whimpered at his assault as my hands found his shoulders.

I shouldn't be surprised he was here. After all, this was much more his element than mine, but I still hadn't expected for him to be here.

As if he sensed my presence, Michael's eyes met mine as I closed the remaining distance to the group of gentlemen gathered in a semi-circle around him, from which some I'd either already met a few times over the years or at least knew of them.

"Dr. Ziani," Michael greeted, his voice smooth with an intimate undercurrent that sent warmth traveling down my spine. His gaze slid over my body, gliding on every curve that the dress I wore highlighted.

I'd opted for a cowl-neck floor length dress in a bold zebra print that had been in the back of my closet for too long, but with the way Michael was looking at me, I'd wear only that for the rest of my life.

I hadn't seen him since our dinner date and I'd been replaying the events of the night on a loop ever since.

"Dr. Young," I replied, giving him a polite smile and hoping my voice didn't betray my bravado. I averted my gaze and greeted everyone else because I knew if I focused my attention on him for too long, I'd get lost and not accomplish what I'd set out to do.

But his gaze never left me as we all fell into easy chatter, discussing the exhibition—which I had to control my urge to roll my eyes at some of their comments. We'd finally broached the subject of work when the director of finance, James Kay, aimed his next words to Michael.

"What are your thoughts on having her as your competition?" he asked

Michael looked taken aback by the sudden shift in conversation. "My what?"

"Well, you know," James continued with a derisive chuckle, clearly oblivious to the sudden loaded shift in the air around us. "Do you believe she's even up to the task?"

The fact that he'd all but ignored my presence from the moment

I'd accosted them wasn't at all surprising, I'd had to get used to it, but my body tensed from his line of questioning.

Why were women so easily locked down upon? We could be the most qualified person in the room, with a list of credentials to prove it, yet little boys in the likes of James Kay still felt comfortable belittling women who were far more intelligent and capable than they could ever hope to be.

I was just about to speak up for myself when Michael beat me to it.

"That's a rather stupid question to ask, don't you think?" he replied, his tone cold.

James must severely lack in self-preservation skills because instead of clocking Michael's reaction, he chose to add fuel to the fire.

"I mean, you must know her father's reputation." I watched Michael's jaw tighten so hard, I feared he would break a molar by the intense pressure he was exerting to not throw his fist into a board member's face. Kay must not notice that either when he added, "The only reason she's even being considered for the role is—"

Michael shoved his fisted hands in his pockets and took an almost imperceptible menacing step into Kay's space, but it was enough to make him flinch.

"I suggest you listen to my next words very carefully because I won't waste my breath on repeating myself for someone like *you*." Michael's tone dripped with more venom with each word.

"Dr. Ziani is remarkably talented and her merit comes from her own doing. Not her father's. Anyone at Amanar can see *and* attest to such. Every junior doctor she has training under her is one of the best we have. Even consultants praise her work and the teaching sessions she voluntarily offers to anyone in the department. I've had the *immense* privilege of performing surgeries by her side and she's the best I've ever encountered, consultants included. Questioning her ability as a surgeon or future medical director, let alone talk about her father's career in light of her own qualifications is absurd. You're merely an accountant, so the next time you dare even think about discussing a *surgeon*'s abilities, you might want to think about doing so a few more times before more stupid words leave your mouth."

Michael nonchalantly glanced at the luxurious watch on his wrist. "Now, if you'll excuse us," he said dismissively before walking away, but not without coming straight toward me.

I'd barely registered his last words when the next thing I knew, his large hand enveloped mine before he pulled me away from them and out of the wing where Nakia's exhibition was being held.

A million thoughts and questions warred in my mind, but I didn't dare interrupt his determined pace with how tightly his grip was holding my hand. He wasn't hurting me, more like making sure I was following wherever he was leading us to.

Michael didn't stop until we stepped inside what looked like an office. Once he locked the door, he turned to face me, his features pulled into a scowling expression.

"What are you doing here?" he asked harshly.

"My *best friend* is the curator of this exhibition. The question should be more: What are *you* doing here? " I replied, my irritation bleeding through my voice. I knew his attitude wasn't directed at me, but it didn't tamper the annoyance I felt at being on the receiving end.

Michael let out a deep sigh before his apologetic gaze met my eyes. "I'm sorry, I didn't mean to be rude. I've met arseholes before, but I'd never wanted to punch one this bad. The sheer audacity to even *question* you."

He looked away and muttered to himself in Korean as he unfastened the single button of his suit jacket with one hand before running it through his hair. I'd tried not to pay attention to how he looked earlier, how well-fitted the black suit he was wearing molded to his body.

But now that we were away from prying eyes, that it was just us in this office, I couldn't help but slowly take him in.

He looked... *hot*.

When my eyes moved back to his face, his gaze was already fixed on mine. The previous anger that had been brewing there was long gone only to be replaced by a heated look that sent goosebumps dancing across my skin.

We hadn't exchanged more than a chaste kiss last week right before I left and it'd left me craving for more. Every time we'd crossed paths at the hospital, I'd fought the urge to drag him into an empty room and relieve some of the tension that'd been brewing since I'd showed up at his place in the middle of the night.

I'd had to settle for my hand and vibrator to try and sate this hunger he'd created inside me, but nothing had worked. It'd only made the desire more ardent.

And the way he was watching what I did next on a bated breath only brought it back to the surface tenfold, sending warmth pooling low in my core.

"Why did you say that?" I asked, my voice coming out breathy.

"What do you mean?"

"What you said back there? Why did you say it?"

Neither of us moved.

Only the sound of our shallow breathing filled the charged air as we both waited for his answer.

Only a second passed before he finally answered, but it snapped the last thread we'd both been holding onto.

"Because it's the truth."

He deliberately closed the few steps separating us and tossed my

"I've dreamt about tasting these and it's even better than I imagined," he groaned against my skin before he bit a mark into the side of my breast.

The image of him branding me set whatever inhibitions I had left free.

My mouth opened to a string of unintelligible words as he sucked a nipple into his mouth, sighing and groaning as he cupped my chest to bring it closer to his face. He moved from one breast to the other, teasing, and I was on fire everywhere.

I'd never felt like this before. To want to be claimed. To want to surrender myself to someone to do whatever they wanted with me and all I had to say was yes.

I needed more.

I needed him.

Now.

I yanked his face up to mine and kissed him with everything I could muster. "Michael," I moaned against his lips before going back to kissing him, almost forgetting why I'd said his name. "I need you," I said, coming up for breath, but the words died on his lips as he brought my lips back to his.

My legs wrapped around his waist to bring him closer and my hips shifted, seeking any kind of friction. I felt his erection exactly where I wanted and I grinded against it, but before I could feel the sweet pleasure of his cock brush against my pussy despite the layers separating us, he pulled back.

I heard a whine resound in the room, tangling with our heavy breathing, only to realize the sound had come from me.

I opened my mouth to complain when Michael spoke up. "Azara, baby. I know you're greedy for my cock, but you'll have to be patient."

His words washed over me and I was ready with a rebuttal when he stepped away from between my legs, his hand going to his thick shaft trapped under his trousers.

His gaze captured mine and I'd seen many expressions in them before, but this one set my skin ablaze like it never had. His eyes pinned with so much pure desire, all I could do was drown in them.

"I want to see you touch yourself first, and only when you give me an orgasm, will I let you get my cock."

There was a note of desperation in his tone and it smothered my previous protest only to refuel with something even more potent. I didn't know whose office we were in, but I scooted back on the desk he'd sat me on, pushing whatever behind me to the floor, the objects clattering to the floor, so I'd have enough space for what I intended to do next.

"Then if you get to watch, I want to do the same."

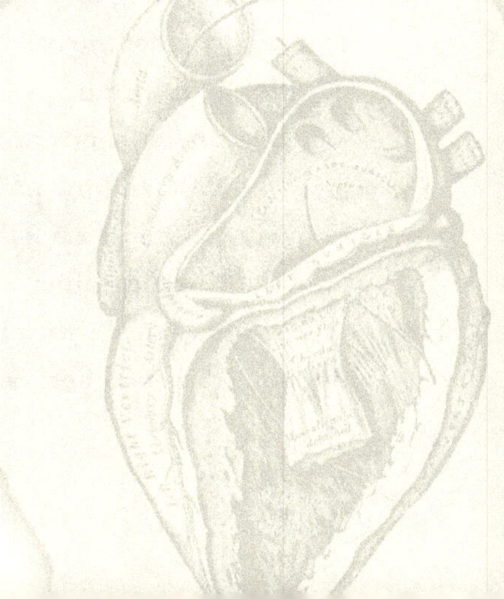

CHAPTER 28

MICHAEL

"SIT."

Her order came without hesitation and I'd never been more turned on. She pointed to one of the guest chairs with the toe of her heel.

I didn't need to be told twice.

"Good boy," she praised with a smirk lifting one side of her smeared red lips when I moved it right in front of her and took a seat.

I'd been thinking of doing sinful things to her mouth the moment I'd spotted her enter the ballroom, but she was in control and I'd bank the idea for another time.

She placed her hands on either side of her hips, clenching at the edge of the desk and my pulse hummed with need as I watched her prop each of her legs on either side of me on the chair arms and I leaned back into the leather.

Then with a snail's pace brought her dress up her legs and thighs until it pooled around her waist, enough to expose the thin white lace covering her pussy.

Fuck. Me.

Her fingers inched up her thigh and closer to where I needed her. "Thinking of going back on your proposition?"

My heady gaze lifted to find hers, a glint of dark satisfaction dancing in her eyes.

I'd abandon and say yes to everything she asked me, but I shook my head, trying to remind myself why I'd made the suggestion. Although that voice of reason was slowly fading into nothingness the more time I spent with this beautiful woman who had defied everything I'd ever been told to believe.

"Then, I need you to take your cock out and show me how much you want me."

I knew Azara wasn't shy when it came to intimacy, but seeing her so bold almost made me come in my pants.

I was completely at her mercy and I'd never felt more powerful.

I made a quick haste of unfastening my belt and trousers before I slipped a hand under my boxers to relieve some of the pressure. I palmed my dick and watched Azara's gaze darken.

"I said take it out," she commanded, her tone urgent. Her fingers traced over her covered pussy before stopping at the edge of her waistband. "Or I won't give you what you want."

God, where was she all my life?

"I like it when you're bossy," I murmured as I took my cock out and her eyes widened when they flicked to my growing erection.

"*Fuck*, you're so big," she groaned as I fucked my fist in long, languid strokes.

Keeping my eyes on her, I shifted my hips forward just enough to not disrupt her position and said, "Spit on it."

Understanding what I wanted her to do, she pushed herself closer and tilted her head forward. Lining her mouth directly above my cock, she let a long spool of spit fall on the tip.

An electric current fired every nerve in my body at the sight and my eyes fluttered shut as I leaned back again and smeared it over my erection.

My head fell backward and I let out a low groan as I pumped my cock into a squeezing fist, imagining I was fucking her mouth.

I opened my eyes and found her watching with fascination.

After another beat of her merely staring at me pumping my cock, up and down, up and down, she finally slipped her fingers under the waistband of her white laced panties and dragged her fingers down her cunt, teasing.

"Look at you touching yourself for my pleasure," I rasped, running a thumb over the head as she started playing with her clit. "I bet that perfect cunt of yours is so fucking wet, isn't she? She's *so* greedy for me to stretch her."

"Yes," she whimpered.

My heartbeat raced as I listened to her breath catch when she pushed a finger in her entrance and the sight almost made me come undone. I would give anything to know what her walls squeezing me felt like, how perfectly I'd fit inside her because she was made for me.

"I want to see you," I said, as she pushed two fingers past her entrance. "I want to see you prepare your pussy for my cock to take it. You want to do that for me, Azara, don't you?"

"Michael, I want *you* to do it," she moaned as she pulled her fingers out.

"No, Azara. You have to be good for me. Otherwise, you won't get rewarded."

"Okay," she said with a low moan as she pulled her fingers out of her panties. I could see her fingers coated with her arousal. My mouth watered and I licked my lips, remembering how intoxicating she tasted.

The sudden anticipation of seeing her bare again played with the edges of my sanity when she lifted her hips to slide her underwear down her legs. Before she tossed them to the side, I grabbed the pair and pocketed it to take home since I'd ruined the last pair.

She propped her feet back in their previous position, spreading her legs farther for me and the moment her perfect pussy came into view, I was completely lost and brought down to my knees at the sight of her pushing those two fingers back inside.

"You're doing such a good job for me, but you need to add another finger."

"I can't," she whined, unabashedly riding her fingers with her thumb moving to circle her clit. Her soft moans were the most beautiful sound and I never wanted her to stop.

An inferno flared in my gut, the air suddenly too thin, and all I could think of was getting there with her. "Oh, love," I started, stroking my cock at a much slower pace to emphasize my next words. "You see how big it is. So do as you're told."

I felt lightheaded as I watched her drag her fingers in and out before she added another finger and I watched her stretch her pussy just for me.

"That's it, Azara. I bet you feel *so fucking good*." I picked up speed and fucked my fist in matching rhythm to her fingering herself, her orgasm teetering over the same edge as me.

She might be following my orders, but I was the one desperate for her.

So fucking desperate.

"*Yes,*" she whispered, her voice aching with need to match my own. Azara threw her head back and I began to hear her tell-tale sign of her nearing the end so I fell to my knees, not wanting her pleasure to be wasted and eager to savor her once again.

"I want to taste you." The words had barely left my lips when I latched my mouth to her hot cunt. I let out a long moan against her wet pussy, the smell of her arousal so heedy, I needed it to be bottled.

A whimper fell from her lips and she halted her movement from the sudden contact, but I firmly gripped her wrist with my free hand to keep it in place and bit down on her clit, unable to form words.

She understood exactly what I asked of her which sent a gnawing satisfaction to explode in my chest as we fucked her cunt while I did the same with my cock. I sucked hard and watched her through hooded eyes as she fell apart for me.

"*Michael,*" she shouted, her body falling slack on the desk and I pulled her fingers out just in time to catch her release on my tongue. I lapped at her through the waves of her orgasm while I fucked my fist faster until my balls tightened and I found my own orgasm, the feel of hot cum landing on my hand.

"So. Fucking. Perfect," I said as I pulled away from her. She laid there, spread open for me and sated *because* of me. A depraved idea sprouted in my mind. I should have been a better man, but I'd never claimed to be one.

So still spiraling in her orbit, I gave into the debauchery.

I brought my hand up and spread the thick white cum all over her and pushed some of it inside her cunt, spreading it around her walls. *Needing* her to have a piece of me living inside her.

Since I couldn't come inside her, this was the closest I'd probably ever get.

She moaned, looking down to find me admiring between her thighs. "Michael, wh-what are you doing?"

"I want to know what we taste like together."

I leaned down again, taking one long languid lick, and my eyes almost rolled to the back of my head at the taste. Before I knew it, I edged her to another orgasm, unable to help myself.

After cleaning her up with my tongue, I stood and kissed her, getting lost in her again. I didn't know how long we made out for, but eventually, when the insatiable beautiful creature she was reached for my cock, I pulled away.

I looked at my watch, noticing it was almost midnight. The exhibition had long ended, but being an Atlas occasionally had its perks, and they came in handy in times like this.

"As much as I would want nothing more than to take you up on your offer, it's rather late, love. The gallery is about to close."

We'd be able to stay however long we wanted, but I couldn't tell her that. My resolve had wavered enough and I'd already crossed too many lines, this last one I really couldn't risk.

Her eyes widened at my words. "What?" She grabbed my arm to bring my wrist to her face, noticing that the last chime to midnight neared. "Oh my god, we have work tomorrow."

I grasped her chin between the two fingers I'd used to spread my pleasure in between her legs. "You just came all over my mouth, *twice*, and you're thinking about work? It never stopped you before."

She shied away from me, but I forced her gaze to stay on mine. "Didn't take you for being shy, Azara." I placed a quick kiss on her lips. "Let's get you home."

"I liked this dress, you know," she said, sliding down from the desk.

I'd been so lost in the intensity of my earlier passion for her that I'd ripped the front of her dress. I wished I'd had the chance to completely undress her, but I knew that if I ever did that and had her completely displayed and layed out in front of me to worship, there would be no way I'd be able to restrain myself.

The fraying edges of whatever I had remaining were already barely holding on.

"I like it better this way, but I'll buy you a new one," I told her, grabbing my discarded jacket from the floor. "I'll buy you as many as you want if you let me ruin every single one of them," I added, draping it over her shoulders so she could use it to cover herself as we made our way out.

I barely recognized myself. I never lost control or gave in to my desires.

But there was no way I'd ever let her go.

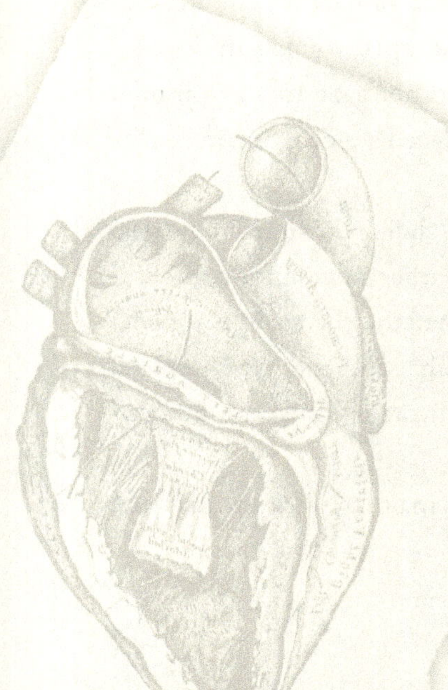

CHAPTER 29

MICHAEL

"MICHAEL, WHAT ARE WE DOING here?" Azara asked, her voice tinged with a mix of curiosity and a mild exasperation as I pulled her into her favorite closet and shut the door behind us.

I placed my hands behind me and leaned against the door. "Can't I simply want to see you?"

"You've seen me all day," she huffed, crossing her arms over her chest, but I saw the ghost of the smile she was fighting to hold back.

I pushed myself off the door and closed the gap between us. I lifted her gently as her gaze met mine. "True. But I haven't been able to do this," I murmured, before pressing my lips to hers. I hadn't kissed her since the night of the exhibit, and I missed it. It hadn't even been a week, yet I felt like an addict counting down the hours to his next fix.

It was only meant to be a swift kiss, but as it always was with her, the moment our lips met, nothing else existed. My mind always went somewhere where time, space and common sense disappeared and it was just us left.

Us and everything she was making me feel that I'd been ignoring. I knew it was stupid to dream of what-ifs and maybes, but whenever I was with her, dreaming didn't seem as foolish.

I hadn't seen much of her since that night at the gallery and I needed her all to myself, even if it was just for a few minutes. Although the hospital only needed one senior surgeon on call this weekend, I'd made sure we were both scheduled so I'd have an excuse to spend more time with her.

Things had settled for the evening and it was almost one in the morning which meant we deserved a break.

"We should stop. We're at work," she said softly against my lips, but made no move to pull away.

"Hasn't stopped us before," I replied with a smirk before kissing her once more. But I quickly reminded myself why I'd taken her here. Reluctantly, I broke the kiss, my hands trailing down her arms that had found their place around my neck. If I didn't stop myself, we'd never get to the good part, even though this would be tough to beat.

"You're right, we should stop," I sighed. "But you have to promise to give me the next twenty minutes of your undivided attention,"

She leaned back slightly, eyeing me with a raised brow. "What for? Besides, what if there's an emergency?"

There wouldn't be, I'd made sure of it.

"Then we'll dutifully do our jobs," I replied, pressing a chaste kiss to her lips.

"Fine," she grumbled, unhooking her arms from around my neck before she stepped back. "So, what did you have in mind?"

I quickly moved two boxes of extra supplies and arranged them so we'd be facing each other. I then retrieved the coffee thermos and cups I'd hidden on the shelf at the back. It was almost one in the morning and we'd had a busy start of our shift, and figured we could both use the fuel.

Once we were both seated, I explained my idea.

Her brows dipped. "So you want to play rock, paper, scissors?"

The game was just a pretext for what I wanted. More of her.

I chuckled. "A version of it, yes. It's called 가위바위보[20]. I used to play it back with my cousins back home, but I'm changing the rules a little."

She rolled her eyes. "Of course you are. What happens when you lose?"

"Every time I *win*, I get a kiss and an answer to a question."

"That seems a bit one-sided, but I'll play along," she said, crossing her right leg over her left and resting her hands on her knee. "What do I get if I win?"

I shrugged. "Anything you want."

I'd give her anything she wanted, if she ever asked me. I'd do anything.

With anyone else, I'd resent someone having this much power over me, but with Azara, I wanted to give it to her.

I poured coffee into two styrofoam cups and handed her one, all while explaining the rules and taught her how to enunciate the words for the game. It was adorable how hard she was trying to make sure she wasn't mispronouncing them, and she picked it up easily.

I gave her a mock demonstration round before we dove into it. I won the first round, and asked her about her favorite color.

"That's your first question?" she teased, leaning forward and planting a kiss to my cheek instead of my lips. "It's red, but I thought you'd be a bit more original and make it more interesting," she taunted before taking a sip of her coffee.

---

20 *Korean rock paper scissors*

I pulled her face toward mine with one hand before she moved away, pressing my lips firmly against hers. "And you're cheating."

"It's not cheating if you weren't precise in your stipulations," she pointed out. "You just said and I quote, 'Every time I win, I get a kiss and answer a question'."

I shook my head with a grin. "It would take you to find a loophole."

"You should know better by now."

I laughed. "Alright, then, when I win, I want you to kiss me on my *lips*."

She shrugged, a sly smile on her face. "That's too bad, really. I had much more… creative plans for where I'd kiss you, but suit yourself,"

I opened my mouth to change the rules back, but she tsked. "You've already changed the rules twice, Michael Young. Besides, I'm not planning on letting you win again."

And she didn't for the next four rounds. For someone who'd never played before, she was absolutely destroying me. Unluckily for me, she'd chosen to stick to the original consequence and flicked my forehead everytime she won. I rarely ever lost as a kid, and I'd forgotten how painful it was.

We laughed, talked, and got to know each other as time seemed to fly by. From our favorite desserts (*bingsu*[21] for me and *sfouf*[22] for her), to her favorite memory (the last birthday she'd spent with her mom) and why we'd chosen surgery and medicine which we had very similar reasons for.

The conversation was easy. Fun. Like we'd done this a million times before.

And as I watched her laugh, her eyes crinkle with joy every time she beat me, something inside me shifted. I realized that if I wasn't more careful, I could easily fall in love with Azara Ziani.

21 *Milk-based Korean shaved ice dessert*
22 *Moroccan treat*

That I would jump in head first if it wasn't for all the obstacles in my way.

If I wasn't holding a legacy that stretched back a hundred years on my shoulders, one that had been built to give people like us a rightful place when the world we live in was built against us, I would give it all up in a heartbeat.

Because even the possibility of being with her was more than worth it.

She was more than worth it.

But I had to remind myself once again that there was more than me and what *I* wanted at stake. It was three families who'd given up everything so we could have a better life.

And as much as I wanted this, her, *us*, this would have to end. I couldn't afford being greedy after all of this was over, but for now, I'd give in until it was time for me to say goodbye.

Azara had just answered my latest question and leaned in to give me another kiss when a knock at the door interrupted us.

My intern's voice came through the other side. "Dr. Young, I know you said not to bother you—"

I checked my watch. Only ten minutes had passed from when we started, yet it felt like we'd been here for hours.

"Then why are you bothering me, Freddy?" I asked, hoping he'd take the hint and give me the next ten minutes like I'd carefully planned for.

The young trainee doctor cleared his throat and his discomfort could be felt from across the steel door. "I'm terribly sorry, Dr. Young, but we've got a 47-year-old male patient with a history of hypertension coming in from Orion with a confirmed aortic dissection and I couldn't find Dr. Ziani."

You couldn't find her because she's with me.

I hung my head back in disappointment that my time with Azara was cut short, before quickly formulating a plan. "Call the team and make them prepare Theater E," I ordered, before telling him to collect all the information I'd need before heading in.

"Yes, sir," he replied, but he didn't move.

"I'll meet you there, Freddy. Now, go."

"Right, y-yes, sir," he stammered, before I finally heard his footsteps retreat.

I turned back to Azara, only to find her laughing. "What's so funny?"

"You really have to stop terrorizing these kids or they'll quit and we need all the staff we can get," she teased with a smile on her face.

"I was *nice* to him. If you think that was terrorizing, you should have spent a day with my consultant at Orion. That woman was a proper nightmare."

Just the thought of Professor Guerrero sent a chill down my spine. She'd been an amazing teacher, but the simple thought of making a mistake and enduring her wrath scared me. And I wasn't someone who scared easily.

"I'll make it up to you," I told Azara, pressing a lingering kiss to her lips. I grabbed the two empty coffee cups from the floor and the half-full thermos before standing up.

Azara followed suit, pushing the boxes aside. "You can make it up to me by letting me join the surgery."

I was hoping she'd say that.

I gripped the front of her scrub top and tugged her close. She let out a surprised yelp as my lips brushed against hers again. "Deal."

CHAPTER 30

MICHAEL

I'D MADE MY FAIR SHARE of impulsive decisions in the past.

Covering my body in tattoos just to spite my father.

Stealing one of his collectible cars to take part in a street race—without a license—that ended in me wrecking it because the other arsehole had been a sore loser.

Almost breaking my oath. Multiple times.

The list went on.

I'd managed to stay on track after my last impulsive decision almost cost me medical school, but ever since Azara Ziani came into my life, my recklessness had come charging back with a vengeance.

But lately, I wasn't concerned with the consequences that this would bring, despite knowing they'd catch up to me eventually. But having her meet my sister? That was definitely something I should've avoided.

Not because I didn't want to. I did. I really did.

But there were so many things that could go wrong from me exposing her to my world. Atlases weren't supposed to be seen out with a woman and we had a reputation to uphold. Flirting at events was frowned upon and one thing, but any form of dating, unless it was the woman assigned as our One, carried repercussions.

I hadn't had the press breathing down my neck since I'd stopped messing about in uni, but that didn't mean the rumor mill wouldn't start running.

I could care less of what anyone in the circles we ran in had to say, but if my father got a hold of this...

I pushed away the possibilities of what he'd do if he found out. For now, I wanted to focus on the time I had left with her, however long that might be, and make the most of it.

I'd deal with everything else later.

"If she starts grilling you, feel free to ignore her," I told Azara, taking her hand in mine, as we approached UMMA, the late November cold air wrapping around us.

I'd never really liked physical touch, but with Azara, I always wanted to have a part of me connected to her. There was something settling about her touch and I'd found myself craving it more often than I'd care to admit.

It was Alice's nineteenth birthday, and we were meeting her to celebrate. We usually did lunch for her birthday every year, but since Azara and I were scheduled to work an overnight shift, we'd opted for an early dinner.

And the last time I'd spoken over the phone to my little sister who wasn't so little anymore, she'd insisted I bring *the woman that had captured my attention* to this year's celebration.

Her words, not mine. Although she wasn't wrong.

I'd like to say I protested against the idea but she'd barely finished asking and I'd already agreed to it.

"I don't have to come," she offered.

I looked over at her expecting to find her mocking me, but instead I spotted something I'd never seen there. Hesitance. Azara avoided my gaze, like she wasn't sure she was welcome and I hated that she thought I didn't want her here.

She averted my gaze. "We have work in a few hours anyway, so I could just—"

I abruptly halted and interrupted her. "No," I said, facing her. I lifted my free hand to her jaw and brushed a finger over her cheekbone before tucking a stray curl behind her ear. "I want you there."

We hadn't had the opportunity to see each other much outside of the hospital over the last month since we'd both been so busy with work and each of us was still focused on getting the promotion, but we'd stolen moments here and there when no one was looking.

I'd missed having her to myself, but with the deadline for the new medical director position looming over our heads as well as my Ascension, I needed to be more careful. Even though over the last month of seeing each other, I'd never felt more at ease with my life than I did with her in it.

Through the stolen kisses, working by her side in surgery or even the occasional late night chats in the closet when we were both on call, she'd opened my eyes that there was more to life than just work and duty.

That happiness existed in the small moments. That in those small moments, I'd fallen for her even though I'd done my hardest not to.

But how did I even stand a chance when it came to her?

Since I'd been with Azara, I felt safe.

Something I hadn't felt in a long time. Not since I was a kid.

She was everything I didn't know I needed and over the course of these last few weeks, I'd let myself imagine what it would be like if I hadn't been born an Atlas.

But I knew it was wrong to want more out of this, and that it *would* end.

Whether I wanted it to or not.

"Okay," she said with a small smile. I brushed my thumb over her dimple and kissed the corner of her mouth, her skin cold against my lips. "But *I* will be asking her for all the embarrassing stories from when you were younger. You can't be this perfect and not have some skeletons."

Although there was no way for her to know about my past and it was only meant as a light hearted joke, it didn't stop the cold shiver slithering through my body at her words. The innocence of her words only made the guilt I'd been ignoring for lying to her resurface and weigh on my shoulders.

But as I did with everything else, I buried it in the back of my mind and redirected the attention elsewhere. I raised a brow, the corner of my lips lifting. "So you think I'm perfect?"

She swatted my chest with the hand I'd been holding, a blush blooming on her cheeks. "That is not what I said."

My laughter boomed in the empty streets as I slung my arm over her shoulder, tucking her to my side as we continued walking. "Azara Ziani thinks I'm perfect. Who would have thought?"

She groaned and pushed the beanie that had fallen over her eyes up but didn't protest. We walked another five minutes before we got to the popular family restaurant.

I moved to open the door when Azara spoke again. "Just so we're on the same page, who should I say I am to you?"

"She already knows," I simply said and her face softened. I tried not to read too much into what her reaction meant and opened the door for her, leading her inside with my hand resting on her lower back.

UMMA was Alice and I's favorite Korean spot in the city. We'd been looking for somewhere to eat a few years ago and had walked by this place.

From the outside, it looked almost run-down, but when you stepped inside it was a completely new world. From the long neon signage running along the middle of the exposed ceiling, to the raw concrete walls painted blue or even the deep red communal booth seatings combined with wooden accents, it reminded us of a trendier version of spots back home

And the food was to die for.

My sister was seated at our regular table that faced the open kitchen, but had her head down, typing on her computer. She still technically had almost a month left of school, but since she only had papers to submit for her finals, she'd decided to come home and spend the rest of her semester here.

As if she could sense us approaching, she peered up from her screen and her entire face lit up when she spotted us. "Finally you're both here," she exclaimed, jumping up to her feet as we made our way to the back of the place.

Alice went straight for Azara, her arms wide open, but stopped short before she smothered Azara in a hug. "Are you a hugger? Please tell me you are, but if not that's completely fine."

Azara opened her arms with a laugh. "Hugs are good," she said and the words had barely left her lips that my sister pulled her into a tight hug. "I'm Azara, it's a pleasure to meet you," she added, her voice coming out strained with the strength my sister was wrapping her arms around her.

Alice was over a foot shorter than me but her grip put people much taller and bulkier to shame. My sister slightly pulled back, the giant smile on her face never leaving as she said, "I know exactly who you are. I'm Alice, and it's *my* pleasure to meet you. Michael talks about you constantly and he's *never* done that."

"Alice," I admonished, but she'd barely even acknowledged my presence since we came in. I had occasionally talked about Azara to my sister after the lunch we'd had, but I didn't need her to know that.

"I hope it was all good things." Azara briefly looked at me, a foreign glint in her eye, before she turned her attention back to Alice.

"Do I just not exist or?" I asked, chiming in with a raised brow.

They both laughed at my expense before my sister finally acknowledged me.

"Unfortunately for us, you can't be ignored," Alice teased, rolling her eyes as she moved to hug me.

I raised a brow. "Unfortunately?" I pulled her face tightly against my chest and scruffed a hand over her head to teach her a lesson.

"Michael, stop," she protested in a hushed tone since the restaurant was packed with customers. "Let me go."

I did it once more before I released her.

Alice slapped my chest once when she managed to put some distance between us. "Gosh, I hate you," she said with a scowl as she put away her computer and took her seat, while Azara and I settled in the booth opposite to her. My sister propped her phone on the glass water bottle and fixed her hair. "I have places to be later and you've destroyed hours of methodical work to get this bob to sit perfectly."

I peered over to my right to find Azara watching Alice with amusement. "Wanna be next?" I asked, resting my arm on the back panel.

"I think I'll pass," she said, the smile never leaving her lips.

I liked seeing her like this. Smiling and carefree.

She was always quite serious at work—which was incredibly

attractive—but this felt like a side only those close to her got the privilege to see and it just added itself to the list of things I lo—liked about her.

"So tell me everything about you," Alice began once she'd finished fixing up her hair. Eventually, the two of them fell into easy chatter like they'd been old friends as we waited for our orders which we'd placed on our phones and the sight made my heart soar.

Having two people I thought highly of getting along wasn't necessarily something I'd ever thought about and I should be happy at how well it was going, but now that I was witnessing it, it made me crave what I knew I couldn't have even more.

My life had been decided for me before I was even born and although it took a few years to come to terms with it, I'd accepted it.

I had a duty and I was content in fulfilling it.

I never desired for more, never even wished for it.

I had a narrow path to walk on and it had been fine.

Until now.

Until I met Azara Ziani and she completely changed the trajectory I'd been faithfully on.

I remained mostly quiet the entirety of our dinner, only occasionally chiming in when they directed their attention to me and when the staff brought the lemon cake I'd ordered—Alice's favorite—joining in to sign happy birthday.

But for the most part, my mind was completely scattered and torn in two different directions, unsure of what path to take anymore.

When I was given my Order, I'd envisioned all the possible hindrances that could arise in the process of completing it.

Azara had simply been a part of executing that plan.

Getting close to her only had one purpose.

Distracting her while I got exactly what I wanted. The medical director position.

What I hadn't accounted for was how hard it'd be to let her go.

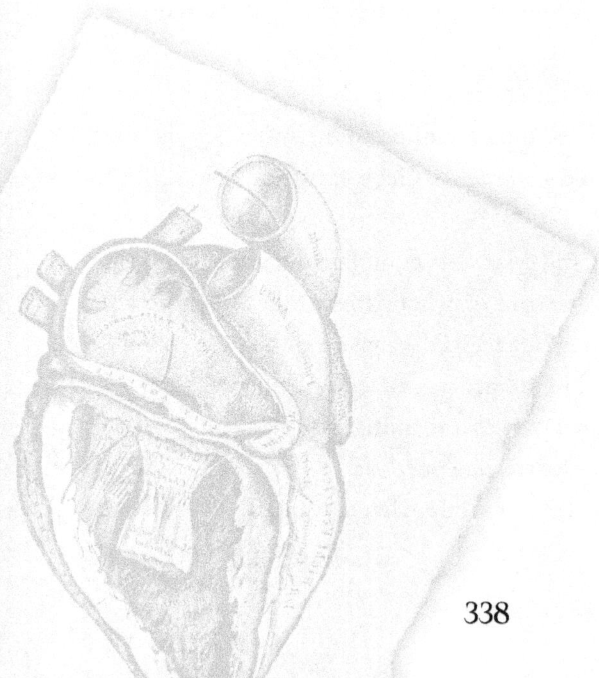

CHAPTER 31

MICHAEL

AFTER DINNER WITH MY SISTER, where Alice and Azara exchanged numbers to set up a time where they could grab brunch, we hopped on the Tube and made our way to Amanar while Alice left in the opposite direction to meet her friends from boarding school.

They were grabbing drinks at a local pub before she'd head home to celebrate the rest of her birthday with our parents. They always stayed up until midnight struck and ate her favorite food while watching her favorite movies.

As soon as we arrived, Azara and I split and I dove straight into work. She took charge of the ward while I locked myself away in an office room. We were working an overnight shift, which meant that unless there was an emergency, we wouldn't be operating.

Which only made my whirling thoughts worse.

I desperately needed to lose myself in the familiar rhythmic cadence that came with being in the operating theater, but instead, I'd been glued to a screen for the past three hours, going through referrals and answering calls from emergency departments across the trust.

My sister had called me, probably to talk about how much she'd loved Azara, but I'd ignored it and told myself I'd call her tomorrow when my thoughts weren't in such a mess.

I'd tried to push everything to the side and focus on the job because people counted on me. But nothing seemed to work. Diving into a case only distracted me for a few moments, but the minute it was done, the rampant thoughts came flooding back with a debilitating force.

I closed my eyes and leaned my head back in my chair. If I thought screaming was in any way therapeutic and I wasn't in a hospital, I'd certainly do it. Instead, I let out a frustrated groan and pushed myself up from my seat.

I had to occupy my mind in any way before my mind drove me mad. Azara meeting my sister shouldn't have been this disconcerting, but it had put things into perspective. Things I'd been ignoring for far too long and if I wasn't careful, I'd be met with irreparable consequences.

After locking my computer, I grabbed my DECT phone from the charging stand, and decided to head for the closet, hoping the space would offer me some of the solace it had provided me in the past.

Or maybe you're hoping she's there, my mind suddenly chimed in, unsolicited.

I shook the thought away, but just as I neared the lifts, I caught sight of Azara at the nurse's station. Despite the whirlwind that had been consuming my mind since dinner earlier, seeing her eased some of the overwhelming weight I'd been carrying—like it always did.

I headed in her direction instead, hoping to bask in the quiet serenity only she'd ever managed to bring me. But as soon as she spotted me, she rushed over like she'd been looking for me.

Except the look on her face wasn't the one I'd become privy to since things had changed between us. It wasn't even the scowl she'd constantly worn when we first started working together.

Her face was drained of color and her features were drawn tight with worry. My stomach lurched at the sight and I closed the narrow distance between us, my hands instinctively reaching out to examine her.

"Azara, what's wrong? Did something happen to you?" I fired each question as my hands roamed over her body for any sign of injury. "Is it your sugar? I have a drawer in my office full of things for you if you forgot like last t—"

She placed her hands over mine to still them. "I'm fine," she said, and relief should have washed over me, but the look in her eyes combined with the uncertainty in her voice betrayed her. She hesitated for just a moment, before speaking again.

"Alice is here."

I frowned, confused. "What about Alice?"

Why would my sister be here this late? She rarely ever visited—she hated the smell of hospitals—and it was almost 11:00 p.m. She should already be home by now.

Besides, Albert was meant to pick her up from the pub, but perhaps he'd had an emergency and he couldn't. Though, if that were the case, my father would have gone instead even if he hadn't driven himself anywhere in years.

But my sister did hate inconveniencing our father, and might have come here in the hope that I could take her home or sort something out for her. I could probably easily slip out and have Azara cover for me, while I drove my sister home. It was late at night and I'd be back within the hour.

"Michael, baby," Azara's voice cut through my thoughts, firm and commanding.

She'd never called me that. *Baby.*

But I knew it was only to get my attention. To soften the blow I knew was coming. As I focused on her, I knew her next words would reveal the only real and plausible reason why Alice was here. Why Azara looked so frazzled trying to find me.

But it just couldn't be.

My little sister couldn't…

"There's been an accident. Alice is in Trauma 3."

"Alice? Trauma 3?" I repeated, my voice barely above a whisper. The air around us felt thick and taking a breath became laborious.

We only used Trauma 3 for critical cases. For when a patient came into the emergency unconscious and required resuscitation.

Someone spoke to me and a familiar hand squeezed mine, but their words were a muffled noise my brain couldn't process, and for a moment everything around me faded to a blur.

But that only lasted for a fleeting second before the world around me sharpened.

I wasn't standing on the surgical ward anymore. Instead, I stared through a glass door as doctors, nurses and respiratory therapists swarmed my sister's motionless body.

"Michael, you can't—" someone called after me, but I'd already slammed the button to open the sliding door and marched inside the room, ignoring everything but the desperate need to reach Alice.

"What happened?" I demanded, my breath ragged in my chest. My throat was closing up as I asked my next question. "What's her status?"

I was trying to remain composed and use the years of training to keep myself collected, but the sound of machines humming and beeping, their rhythmic noise usually calming, now only sent cold dread down my spine.

The team stayed focused on working on bringing her back, but one of the nurses turned and realized who I was. She walked over to me, gently ushering me out. "Dr. Young, you can't be here," she said firmly.

"Like hell I can't," I shot back, my voice biting. "That's my sister. I need to know what's going on."

"Family members aren't allowed in here," she replied, standing her ground.

Rationally, I knew she was right. I'd said the same thing to patients' family members in the past. But an irrational anger replaced the despair I felt at not being able to get my sister back.

This was all my fault. I should have answered her call earlier, maybe she wouldn't be in this position if I'd just answered her bloody call. She might have needed me and I was too busy thinking about Azara and myself when my sister was laying somewhere unconscious and not breathing.

I needed to fix it.

I needed to bring her back.

Before I could respond, a hand softly touched my arm and I instinctively jerked it away, whipping around to face who it was, but my vision was blurry with unshed tears. The simmering rage dulled momentarily when her unmistakable voice reached my ears.

"Michael." She grabbed my hand and tried to pull me out of the room, but I stayed frozen in place. "You need to let them work, I'll get all the information you need. Just please, come with me."

My pulse drummed louder in my ears as I struggled to draw in a breath. *Fuck.*

"I have to do something," I muttered, my voice barely audible. "I need to help her. I can't just stand here and—"

Azara's hands cupped my cheeks and I inhaled sharply. "And the best way you can help her is by letting them do their job. Just like you always do yours."

Her words were calm, measured, but, in that moment, nothing about this situation felt like that. I felt as though everything was slipping between my fingers like quick sand and it was all my fault.

I glanced back at the team, still working around Alice, and stood there for what felt like an eternity when someone called out, "Sinus rhythm."

Then, the room tumbled into a different kind of chaos.

I closed my eyes and hung my head back. It didn't mean Alice was out of the woods, but I'd never been more relieved to hear those two words.

Azara tugged at my hand again and this time, I followed her out without objecting and the moment we were out of the trauma room, I slumped against the wall and sank to the linoleum floor.

The doctor that had led her code stood above me, but I couldn't find it in me to stand. So I just gave him a curt nod to give me his report. "Your sister is stable and is expected to make a full recovery, but she did sustain critical injuries that we'll need to monitor over the next few days."

He didn't wait for a response and I watched as they rolled Alice out to bring her to the intensive care unit, the doctor following behind.

I'd find enough strength to go upstairs and stay by her side but I just needed a minute. I rested my head against the cool wall, the weight of everything that just happened pressing down on me.

What the fuck just happened?

How did she even get here?

Before countless questions spiraled in my mind, Azara sat next to me, wrapped her arms around me and pulled my head down until it rested against her chest. I let out a shuddering exhale as I sunk into her.

"Baby," she whispered softly, her voice laced with a tenderness that nearly broke me. "She'll be okay. I'm right here."

The previous tightness that had been suffocating my ribcage, slowly loosened as Azara rubbed circles on my back with one hand as the other brushed my hair back.

I wouldn't be able to tell you the last time I'd shed a tear, but as we sat there, the woman I was falling in love with holding me in her arms, a stream of quiet tears fell down my cheeks. My sister was everything to me, she was the light in our family, and the mere thought of having almost lost her crashed down over me.

"You're okay," Azara said quietly as she pulled my face toward her, cupping it between her hands. She kissed each side of my temples before making me meet her gaze. "She's stable. She'll make a full recovery," she repeated the doctor's words and for some reason, coming from her, I believed them.

She wouldn't lie to me.

Not like I was.

But I didn't have enough time to relish in her earnestness when a voice shouting echoed down the corridor. I instantly stiffened and my stomach lurched at the unmistakable voice of my father.

"Where is my daughter?" he shouted. "If you don't let me pass, I will have all of your jobs before you can even blink. Now, *show* me where my daughter is."

The sound of his oxfords grew louder with each passing second, and I moved to put some distance between Azara and I, but it was already too late.

I watched him round the corner, his cold gaze catching sight of me, and his expression darkened as he approached us. I closed my eyes for a brief moment, bracing myself from impact, before getting to my feet.

"Seungwon." His voice was a low growl, each syllable laced with authority. The same tone he always adopted just before berating me for how much I'd disappointed him. "Where is your sister? These incompetents keep telling me I can't come back here when I am her *father*. Tell me what happened."

I opened my mouth to respond, but nothing came out. I was so emotionally spent from the past few minutes that my mind struggled to keep up with all these conflicting jarring emotions.

Now is not the time to lose your words, I reprimanded myself. And the worst part was that, beyond what the doctor had relayed, I had no bloody idea what actually fucking happened.

"Your daughter was involved in a pedestrian traffic collision. A young woman witnessed the accident and immediately called the paramedics. The police are still searching for the perpetrator, but your daughter is stable and has just been transferred to the intensive care unit for monitoring," Azara explained, and my father aimed his ire on her.

"And who are you?" His tone was biting, and it took every ounce of willpower not to punch my father for talking to her that way. I would come to her defense, but I knew Azara could handle it herself. I'd deal with my father privately afterward.

"I'm Dr. Ziani," she said, unflinching. "I was in the emergency room for a consult when your daughter was brought in."

If my father had connected the dots on who she was, there was no flicker of recognition that flashed in his expression. "Seungwon, a word?" he said in Korean, pointedly disregarding Azara.

If I thought he was angry before, him dismissing Azara so callously made it clear I'd only seen a fraction of his fury.

Picking up on the unspoken cue, Azara subtly brushed her little finger against mine in a quiet gesture of support, before stepping way, leaving us alone.

I steeled myself, placing my hands behind my back as I faced my father squarely. I'd already shown him too much vulnerability by being found sitting on the floor and comforted by Azara. If I gave him any more ammunition, I'd never get out of this conversation alive.

For what felt like the longest thirty seconds, my father simply stared at me, the look in his eyes hardening with each passing second. I wasn't sure which topic he'd settled on first, but I steeled myself mentally, determined not to stumble over my words again.

Once had been more than enough.

"How did this happen?"

"I don't know," I answered honestly, keeping my voice steady. It wasn't the response I wanted to give, nor the one he wanted to hear, but there was one thing my father valued more than our oath, it was honesty. "But I'll handle it."

I'd find the coward who put my sister in the hospital and deal with him myself. I'd never been very fond of violence, but whoever came for people I love would have to answer for their crimes.

"And Seungwon," my father started, casually shoving his hands in his pockets, but there was nothing casual or warm about his tone.

My dad had slipped on his role as an Elder. It was clear I was no longer speaking to the man who'd raised me outside of the House, but his next words sent a glacial current through my veins.

"You know better than to embarrass me *or* our family name. You know the rules, and I'd prefer not to have to implement the consequences if you fail. Don't forget what's at stake and," he paused, glancing over his shoulder to where Azara stood with other doctors. "Get rid of it before it becomes a distraction that'll make you meet your end."

My father had never explicitly threatened me before. Never even talked about the House so publicly and after weeks of my loyalty shifting to a differing priority, I knew that I'd fooled myself for too long.

That if I didn't do exactly as I was told, the consequences would be even worse than I could begin to imagine. So I was left with only one answer.

"Understood."

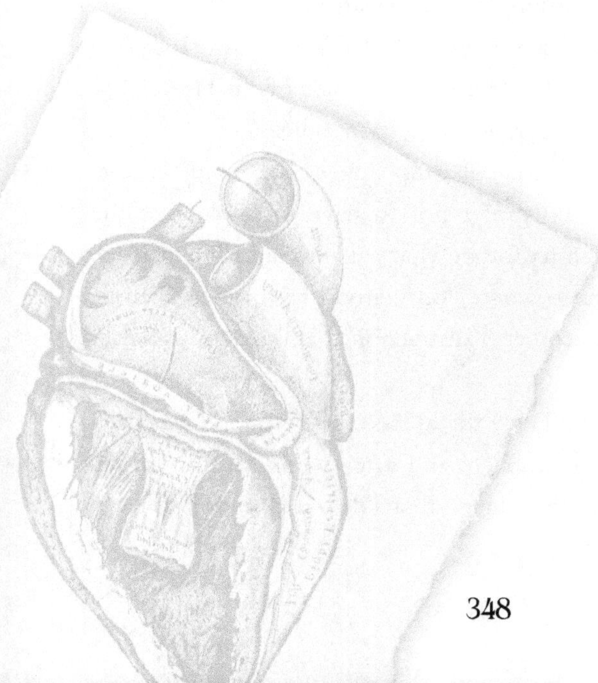

CHAPTER 32

AZARA

ME

How's Alice?

ME

Let me know if you or your family need anything.

ME

Hey, I haven't seen you at work in a few days,
are you okay?

ME

Hey, I heard Alice was being discharged.

ME

Michael?

MY LIFE HAD ALWAYS REVOLVED around two things: Looking after my family and my work.

I didn't mind it. It was predictable. Safe.

Yet ever since the night of Nakia's exhibition—which had been a total success though I'd missed most of it—I'd found myself longing for a life that I'd never dreamed of before.

I thought I'd been happy with the trajectory my life was taking. I had the job I'd always wanted, I was on the path of getting the promotion of a lifetime and although my dad still remained somewhat distant, I felt like he was slowly coming around and was at least answering my calls when I reached out now.

But over these past two months, I'd realized that my life could be, I didn't know… more? I'd spent my entire adulthood putting other people's needs first, but when it was just Michael and me, he made me feel like what *I* wanted mattered.

That it wasn't selfish to need things for yourself.

He'd unwillingly opened my eyes to new possibilities and now, I coveted for more of it.

It had been a little over a week since I'd last properly talked to Michael. I'd sent him messages, but he either didn't respond or only offered one-worded answers.

After Alice's accident, he'd taken a few days off and spent them glued to her side. One evening, when the ward had quieted down, I'd made my way downstairs to see him only to find him fast asleep in the chair next to her. It was the first time his features weren't locked in a constant state of worry like I'd seen every time I caught a glimpse of him when I passed by the ward Alice had been transferred to.

Instead, I'd stayed there for a few moments, watching him for a while before returning to work.

It was still hard for me to wrap my head around how just a few hours before the accident, we were with her. I'd tried not to dwell on it too much because it opened up old wounds that I preferred keeping at bay until it was that time of the year.

Especially when I'd instantly fallen in love with Alice the moment I met her. She'd surprisingly reminded me a lot of her brother. I used to think Michael was arrogant and entitled, but the more I'd gotten to know him, the more I discovered how selfless and caring he actually was.

I saw it with the way he acted with his sister. And I saw it in the tender way he treated me. Now, he still had a way of driving me to madness, but beneath the exasperation, I'd discovered that I cared more about him than I'd let myself believe.

The bitter December air whipped around me as I stepped out of the hospital, the chill biting at my cheeks. It was a little past eight in the morning, and I'd just finished my third night shift this week. I'd been working more to keep my mind occupied, but it wasn't really working.

I fumbled for my phone in the pocket of my jacket, the same disappointment that had been my companion over the last few days resurfacing when I found my latest message to Michael still unanswered.

Logically, I knew there were more important things on his mind. His sister had just been in a terrible accident, and it was selfish of me to expect him to be responsive.

But I couldn't shake the feeling that ever since his father found us that night, he was pulling away. He wasn't mine, and he didn't technically owe me anything, but even knowing that, a knot tightened in my chest.

He might not be yours but for a fleeting moment, it felt like he had been.

Before I could think better of it, I found myself making my way to his flat, stopping at the small coffee shop on the corner to grab three cups of coffee, giving myself a perfectly reasonable excuse to show up unannounced.

In the lobby, I handed one of the paper cups to his doorman, who let me use the guest lifts. I didn't want him to announce my presence to Michael just yet. It gave me the time—albeit little—to reconsider knocking on his door while I ascended to the fifty-first floor.

But once upstairs, I followed through and walked down the narrow corridor toward his front door, nerves prickling beneath my skin. I raised my hand to knock, but the door unexpectedly swung open.

Michael nearly collided with me, but he looked up from his phone just in time.

So his phone wasn't dead.

I ignored the faint sting of disappointment in my chest at knowing he'd probably seen my messages but had chosen to ignore them. My focus was quickly brought back to him when I heard his voice again for the first time in what felt like ages.

"Azara," Michael said, clearly surprised to see me here. His eyes briefly drifted to the cups in my hands before meeting mine. "What are you doing here?"

I frowned at his greeting. He seemed rushed, and I should have called or texted before showing up. "I—sorry, I didn't realize… you're leaving. I shouldn't have come," I stammered, inwardly cursing myself for thinking this was a good idea.

"It's not… I just, I wasn't expecting you," he explained, running an awkward hand through his hair.

I stood there, unsure what to do with myself. I waited for him to invite me in, but my chest deflated when I realized he wasn't going to. Silence stretched between us, and unlike the usual ease that had grown between us over the last few months, an uncomfortable tension weighed around us and I didn't know how to interpret it.

It was like the past weeks hadn't existed and we were back to being strangers. Only this time, it wasn't annoyance I felt toward him, it was hurt.

I awkwardly shifted the cups between my hands. "I should have texted you, but I thought…" I hesitated, breaking the silence. "Well, you didn't really answer any of my messages. I just wanted to make sure you were okay. But I suppose you've got better things to do."

Something soft flickered in his eyes for a moment, before it was quickly replaced by the same detachment I'd seen him in just minutes before.

"I don't need…" He stopped himself mid-sentence but I could hear the insinuation in his words. "I'm fine," he said instead, his tone almost bitter.

I couldn't tell if that bitterness was aimed at me or the situation he'd found himself in, but his words stung more than I cared to admit.

Part of me wanted to press him to tell me what was wrong, but I didn't have the energy to fight after trying for so long without any response.

I'd never been one to give up, but I couldn't force him to confide in me.

Not when he'd made it clear my presence wasn't wanted.

"Clearly. I'll leave you to it then," I said, handing him one of the paper cups. The moment he took it, I turned to leave.

I'd barely taken a few steps when his free hand closed around my wrist.

"Wait," he said quietly.

I briefly shut my eyes before turning to face him. "What is it, Michael?" I asked, my voice coming out sharper than I'd meant to.

The weight of his gaze softened again, almost filling with remorse, but I must have imagined it because it was gone just as quickly. He opened his mouth to speak, but no words came out.

But he didn't need to say anything, his silence spoke loud enough.

"That's what I thought," I muttered, pulling my wrist out of his grip.

This was why I never let myself get too close to people.

This was why I never let myself feel anything for anyone.

Because it always led to one thing.

Disappointment.

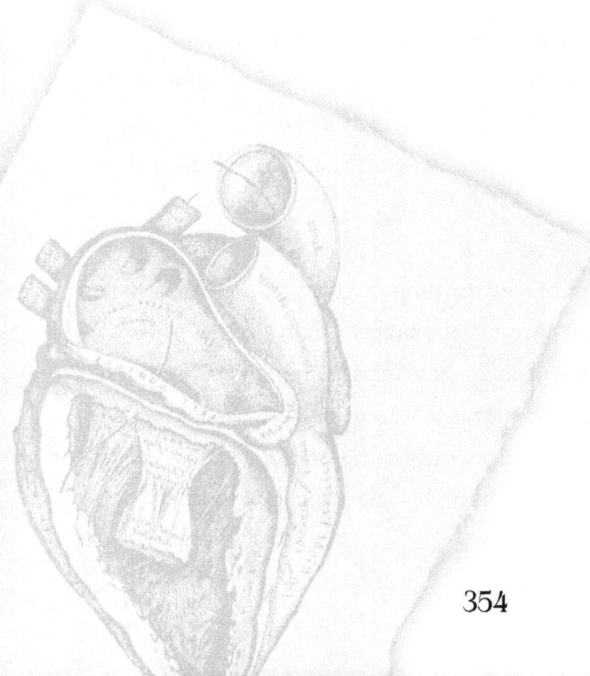

CHAPTER 33

MICHAEL

WHEN I TOLD MY FATHER I had it handled, I never anticipated it would take me three bloody weeks of sleepless nights to finally unearth the bastard who'd hurt my sister.

I parked my motorbike on the deserted side street behind the Thorn, located just a few blocks from where my sister's accident had occurred. Despite how strenuous it was to find the culprit, he hadn't exactly gone to great lengths to cover his tracks.

I pulled my helmet off, and stationed myself at the end of the narrow street, waiting for Walker Simons to emerge from his favorite hiding spot. My phone suddenly buzzed in my pocket and I pulled it out of my jacket, already knowing who was calling.

"Anything?" Sofiane asked the moment I answered.

"No, I'm still waiting," I checked my watch to find it was already a few minutes past midnight. "He's running behind schedule," I explained, aiming my attention on the back door again.

After my father had dismissed me the night of Alice's accident, Azara had covered for me for the rest of the night so I'd be able to stay by my sister's side. But with my father there, I'd gone straight home instead and began my search.

Knowing I was working with limited resources, I'd immediately rang Sofiane for help. He'd showed up at my place thirty minutes later with his encrypted laptop and got straight to it. It didn't take long before we discovered that the intersection where the accident took place had no CCTV coverage.

So while Sofiane had gathered all the footage from the surrounding businesses and streets, I'd gone to the scene to have a look at it in person.

It had only been a few hours after the accident, but when I'd gotten there, it was as if nothing had ever happened. The area was eerily quiet and the only evidence left were the tiny shards of a broken headlight, carelessly discarded to the side of the road.

An overwhelming wave of guilt had threatened to take hold of me, but I'd buried any and all of my feelings somewhere deep in the back of my brain and focused on the job at hand. My father reminding me that I couldn't afford any distractions had stirred up what I'd been ignoring for too long.

I'd deluded myself into thinking there wouldn't be consequences, that I'd be able to have the best of both worlds and it would all somehow work out.

But I'd kept so much of myself hidden from Azara, how the hell did I ever think this could work? How could I believe that my responsibilities wouldn't eventually catch up to me and that I wouldn't have to walk away from her?

Of course, I knew that from the first time I kissed her, the second, and all the times after that, that I was too involved. But the more time

I spent with her, the more everything else blurred until my sole focus was narrowed in on her and how I could make her mine.

But that was the thing about making selfish decisions, wasn't it?

Bad things always followed, no matter how high they made you feel.

So, as much as I'd wanted to run after Azara when she'd shown up at my door last week, the cold, unforgiving truth of my reality and its ticking clock hit me like a freight train.

"I just checked the single camera at the entrance again. He went inside exactly two hours ago. Shouldn't be much longer," Sofiane said, pulling me out of my thoughts.

"Let's hope so."

A sudden clatter echoed off the grimy walls of the alley and instinctively, I drew my gun, aiming it toward the source of the noise. But instead of coming face to face with a threat, my barrel was trained on a scruffy black cat, standing right in the middle of the path, its dark eyes staring directly at me.

I let out a sharp sigh and lowered my weapon, tucking it back into the waistband of my jeans. "I'll call you back," I muttered to Sofiane as I waved a hand to shoo the feline away. But it didn't budge. It just stood there as if it was glaring at me.

"Just don't get caught," he warned, fully aware of what would be at stake if I did.

"Have I ever been caught?" I shot back at him before ending the call and slipping my phone back into my pocket.

Simons should be coming out any minute now. Whether he'd stumble out on his own, drunk, or he'd be thrown out for causing trouble.

Something we'd discovered he often did.

After I'd gotten home, Sofiane and I had spent the next forty-eight hours sifting through the countless hours of surveillance footage because whoever had been driving, had been careful to evade the cameras in the perimeter.

Until we finally found a blurry image of the car that matched the description the witness at the scene had given to the police officers. But, of course, things didn't turn out that simple. When we'd tracked down the car's owner, it had turned out to belong to a seventy year old retiree who'd reported it stolen a few days earlier.

And that brought us back to square one.

Sofiane then shifted his search to map out all the possible routes the stolen vehicle could have taken while I worked on tracking the witness that had helped my sister. I'd needed a better account of the events since the officers at the scene had done a poor job at it. But they hadn't taken any proper details from the girl, and the number they had on file had turned out to be a wrong one.

Which hadn't been surprising considering how poorly documented my sister's accident had been. But that was par for the course with law enforcement.

No matter how much money you threw at them, if it didn't serve their own agendas, they could care less about some reckless driver on the loose since no one had been fatally injured.

Even then, unless it was one of them, they never really put much thought into it. Especially not when it came to people like us. Which only reminded me of why the House had been created in the first place and why I had to uphold its legacy.

This wasn't about me.

It had never been.

It was far bigger than what I wanted and I'd do well to remember it.

Eventually, after days of endless frustrations with nothing but dead ends to show for it, Sofiane and I had caught a break.

We'd tracked the car to a petrol station. Sofiane then worked his magic, hacking into their cameras and capturing a photo of the driver. And unlike the effort he'd put in to evade surveillance on the road, he'd quickly shed off any of his anonymity for a pack of beers and a lottery ticket.

His carelessness had set off a quiet alarm bell in the back of my mind, but I'd brushed it to the side, too focused on getting to the bottom of this. My father had been constantly harassing me asking for updates and I had to give him something concrete.

Besides, within minutes of running the image through a police database, we found his name and looking into his background, his negligence wasn't so out of character.

Walker Simons. Twenty-seven years old, unemployed and up to his neck in debt that he'd only made worse every night by frequenting Marcus Blackthorn's place. Simons owed thousands of dollars to the loan shark, and despite his mounting debts, he came here almost every night only digging himself deeper in financial ruin.

The stray cat abruptly scampered behind a dumpster just as the back door of the pub swung open, followed by a body being unceremoniously thrown onto the street.

"Take your filthy hands off me," Simons shouted, struggling to get to his feet. He wobbled a few times before finally managing to stand. He lurched toward the door, but the tall, burly security guard slammed it shut before he reached it.

"My money," Simons bellowed, hammering his fists against the door like a toddler not getting his way. "Just one more round."

When there was no response to his pleas, he kicked the door in frustration, swearing as his foot connected with the steel door. A pained groan filled the night air as he fumbled for his phone and started walking down the street in the opposite direction.

I unmounted my bike, and headed straight for him, the anger I'd been holding onto for the past couple weeks slowly boiling to the surface.

Each step I took fueled it even more until there were only a few steps separating us. Simons was so caught up in trying to turn his phone on that he hadn't noticed me right on his tail, his sense of self-preservation completely inhibited.

The screen lit up for a brief moment before he dropped it onto the pavement with a curse. I slowed my pace, grabbing my gun and coming up behind him. He bent down, wincing with the movement, but the moment he came up, I slammed him against the wall.

My forearm pressed up against his neck. He flailed, trying to take a swing at my head, but his struggles instantly weakened when my gun found home against his temple.

The stench of his breath burned my nostrils as an ounce of his survival instincts finally seemed to kick in. "Wait," he choked out. "I'll give you money, just don't—"

"I'm not here for money, I want answers," I gritted out, trying to keep reign of my wrath. I pressed my forearm harder against his throat and I watched his face morph into different shades of red with cold apathy. He'd left my sister laying on the cold pavement, why should I give him any mercy.

I wasn't planning on killing him, but he didn't need to know that.

Fear was always a great source of motivation and I'd use it to my advantage. Besides, this was much more entertaining than a simple bullet to the head.

"I-I'll" he started, struggling to get his words out. Panic dripped off his skin as he tried to finish his sentence. "Give. You. Anything." He moved to claw at my arm but thought better of it when he remembered the cold muzzle pressing against his skull.

I waited until a purple hue washed over his fair skin tone before I eased my hold on his windpipe. Simons gasped, his chest heaving as he tried to fill his lungs with deep breaths. "I'll tell you anything you want, just—" he wheezed. Tears welled in his eyes as his bottom lip trembled. "Please, please don't kill me."

I didn't expect much from him, but this was almost pitiful.

His eyes flicked to the side as if someone would come to his rescue, but there was no other sign of life. I thrust my forearm forward to bring his attention back.

"Why did you do it?" I said, ignoring his plea and cutting straight to the chase.

"I don't know what you're—" I moved the gun and shoved it into his open mouth, clicking the safety off and letting my finger hover over the trigger.

"The woman you hit on Bradford and Queensbridge."

Realization sparked in his eyes and he sputtered around the barrel. *That's more like it.*

I slid the handgun out of his mouth and placed it under his chin.

"Speak," I commanded.

"I swear I didn't want to do it," he blubbered, snot dripping from his nose and his breaths coming in ragged gasps. "T—they gave me a thousand quid in cash with a photo of that girl. I needed the money, mate, so I didn't ask more questions."

My head spun with confusion but I kept my face impassive, not wanting to show him any signs of hesitation on my part. A thousand questions whirred through my head. Who the fuck would be after my sister? But most importantly, *why?*

She had no connections, no leverage that would warrant anyone hunting her down, let alone leaving her injured with no demands. If anything, they'd come after me.

Yes, my father had made plenty of enemies over the years as a lawyer, but he worked in corporate law for god's sake and none of them would even dare come after any of our families.

Our society might not know how deep their influence truly ran, but they knew not to cross with anyone associated with the Atlas name.

Not in business, and certainly not in private.

"What did they look like?"

"I—I don't know," he stammered, his voice quivering. "The envelope was left at my nan's front door and I—" Simons choked as I cut off his air supply once more. "I got a call from an unknown number later that night and the automated voice on the other end ordered me to do as I was told or they'd come after me," he panted. "I swear, I didn't want to do it. Please, you've got to believe me!"

Simons was reeking of desperation, the weight of his poor decision finally sinking and it wasn't hard to see he already regretted getting involved for what he thought would be easy money.

He could be lying, hoping I'd spare him if he cooperated, but I'd developed a finely tuned radar for bullshit and he was unfortunately telling the truth.

Now, what I'd thought would be the end of weeks without answers, only seemed to have morphed into more questions.

And I didn't have any of the answers.

Simons must have taken my silence as an opportunity to continue to plead his case when he spoke again. "I still have it," he offered, sniffling. "The—the photo. I still have it. They told me to keep it on me. I didn't understand why but—"

"Where is it?" I asked, interrupting him. His voice was really starting to grate on my nerves and if I had to hear him talk any longer, I might just shoot him to shut him up.

"Inside pocket of my jacket. Right one.

I released my hold on his throat, but kept my gun firmly pressed under his jaw while I retrieved the photograph. If he tried to run, one bullet shredding through the flesh would lead to his death.

It was a printed black and white picture of Alice taken from one of her social media platforms. She was smiling in it, just like she always was. Alice was stable now and recovering at home now, but it killed me to know that she'd been such an easy target.

My job was to protect her and I'd failed.

Simons wasn't of any more use to me, so I released him and stepped a few back.

"Don't tell a word of this to anyone," I warned him. I didn't tell him what I'd do if he dared go against my word. I didn't need to.

I lowered my gun and shot his right kneecap. "That's for my sister." A guttural scream tore through his throat as his body began to sag to the floor. I aimed and shot at the other one. "And that's for wasting my time."

Then, I left him in a pool of his own blood and urine, walking back to where I'd been parked. I climbed on my bike and readied myself to leave. I only had a few minutes before the place would swarm with police officers but I only needed a few seconds.

I turned the piece of paper to find a single word printed in generic black font that would likely be untraceable. But I hadn't expected any different.

What I didn't expect was to find a name written at the back.

Sabiri.

I didn't know what it meant, but I knew the person who might.

I ONLY HAD TO KNOCK once before Albert opened the door.

"Seungwon?" he said, shocked to see me here this late, and in the middle of the week no less.

I hadn't announced my visit, but the moment I saw the name, I needed to talk to my father. I didn't care that it was almost one in the morning or that I had to be up in the next four hours to go to work.

"Where is my father?" I said, stepping inside.

Albert shut the door behind us with a quiet click. "Mr. Young is working in his office, why—"

"Thank you," I interrupted, already moving toward the main staircase.

I didn't bother removing my coat or taking my shoes off. My mother would have a fit if she knew, but right now the only thing I had on my mind was talking to my father. Thankfully, my parent's as well as my sister's bedroom were on the other side of the house, so the commotion wouldn't disturb either of them in their sleep.

She'd already been so worried since Alice's accident, I didn't want to add anything more to her plate.

"Seungwon," Albert called after me, but I was already hurrying up the stairs. The lift might have taken me there faster, but I needed to burn some of the tension I'd been holding on the ride over here before I exploded in my father's face.

I'd debated the entire time whether it was a wise decision to come here at all. Part of me wondered if this was all part of a test before my Ascension. The Elders were notorious for testing their legacy's loyalty to the House to determine whether we'd crack under the pressure and betray what we were meant to protect .

The boys and I had plenty of stories to share in that regard.

My father hadn't put me through one of his tests, not since I was in medical school. His meter of morality wasn't the most angelic one, but how completely *fucked* would my father have to be in order to hurt his only daughter as a pawn.

When I finally reached the third floor, my anger was still sizzling in my chest as I headed for his office and entered without bothering to knock.

"Father," I greeted him, my tone clipped as I strode toward him.

He looked up from the stack of papers he was browsing through, his eyes flicking up to meet mine. "Seungwon," he said, his voice measured. "What are you doing here at this hour?"

I didn't want to jump to conclusions until I heard it from him, but he was acting like he'd been expecting me and it didn't help settle the edge I was feeling from tonight's unfolding of events.

I placed the now crumpled picture of Alice on his desk with a firm thud. "I need answers."

His gaze briefly flickered to the photo of his daughter then back to me. "Why are you showing me a picture of your sister?

"Why don't you tell me?" I shot back. I was trying to remain calm, but his impassive demeanor was only adding fuel to my frustrations.

He sighed, the exhale slow and deliberate, as if I was merely wasting his time with an idle request. He let go of the papers and folded his hands in front of him.

"I don't have time for your games, son. You're the one showing up in my office at an ungodly hour, *demanding* things. So either you tell me exactly why you're here, or you can see yourself out."

I clenched my jaw. "I found the man behind Alice's accident," I began, but he cut me off before I could get another word in.

"About bloody time."

"I'm not finished," I retorted, my patience rapidly running thin. Normally, I wouldn't be so abrasive in the presence of my father, but I didn't have time for pleasantries. There were too many unanswered questions and I needed to know what he was keeping from me.

"I found him," I continued, "and he gave me this." I jabbed a finger at the picture. "Why don't you take a look at the back?"

He fixed me with a hard look, before letting out an exasperated sigh and flipping the piece of paper. His gaze flickered to the bottom, where the bolded name was. His usual calm composure faltered for a moment, before he steeled himself again in his chair and looked at me again.

"What is that?" he asked, feigning cluelessness but I'd studied my father long enough to know he was lying.

"That's what I came here to find out," I replied, my voice steady, but my words were laced with a bitterness I couldn't hide.

"I have no clue why he gave you this," my father said flatly, his gaze cold.

"Really?" I said incredulously, a bitter laugh escaping my lips. "You don't? Why do I have a hard time believing that?"

Tension rose to a suffocating level as he stood from his chair, his eyes never leaving mine. "Leave," he commanded, his expression turning unreadable.

The word hit me like a slap in the face, and I froze. I stood there, unmoving, not sure whether I was more angry or confused at his sudden detachment.

"Leave?" I repeated, the voice feeling like sludge in my throat. "You haven't even given me an answ—"

His stare bored into me, colder than I'd ever known it to be. "I do not owe you answers," he said, his voice, sharp and final. "I'll take care of this moving forward. Now, go."

"No," I snapped, baffled by his swift dismissal. I'd spent three weeks, barely holding it together, and had pushed away the only woman I've ever loved because I wanted to abide by my duty and *this* was what

I got in exchange.

A simple brush off?

My chest heaved with anger, frustration and most of all, disappointment.

I didn't trust in my father for many things, but I at least thought this would be different. That he wouldn't send me on a goose chase only to dismiss me like I was a stranger and not his son.

I opened my mouth to argue, but I knew better than that.

So, with one final look, I turned on my heel and did exactly as he'd asked.

I left.

But he wouldn't have the last word.

This wasn't over.

I would still Ascend, but it would be on my terms.

Not theirs.

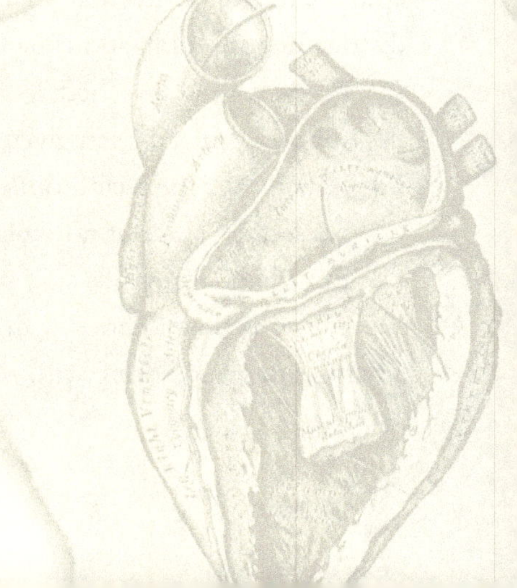

CHAPTER 34

AZARA

NO MATTER HOW MUCH TIME had passed, this day never got any easier.

If anything, it felt like the opposite.

Every year without her seemed to bring a fresh wave of pain, more painful than the previous one. And with the way things were with my dad and Zayd off in Morocco, spending his winter break with our cousins, the loneliness that I'd usually manage to bury beneath a pile of distractions and obligations had nowhere to hide this time.

I'd even tried to schedule a shift so I wouldn't have to spend the day at home, but I'd been given a warning about the number of hours I'd worked over the past month.

Something about it not being healthy.

But I hadn't cared.

This was how I coped with things, by working more and harder—anything to avoid sitting with my feelings and letting myself sink into oblivion from the weight of them.

I knew how to forget. That was easy.

But living with these overwhelming feelings of grief and loss? That wasn't something I was equipped to deal with or wanted to handle.

A therapist would probably have a field day with me.

I'd spent the day trying to busy myself, hoping the constant motion would keep the thoughts at bay. But now, with the sun setting and having already scrubbed every inch of my flat as well as rearranged my furniture a dozen times—only to place it back the way it originally was—I found myself back where I started this morning.

It was in times like these that I really wished I had a hobby.

I could go for a run, but it was getting late, and the earlier light dusting of snow was now thundering from above, so I quickly abandoned the idea. I picked up my phone to send the girls a message and see if they'd want to come over. But as I opened our group chat, I was reminded from the latest message that Hazel was in Ireland with Eddy's family, while Nakia was in Paris for some rare painting she'd been chasing for months.

I really regretted not taking her up on her offer to go with her. I'd finally wrapped up my seven years of surgery training last week and hadn't taken a proper vacation since I started working at Amanar, so getting time off wouldn't have been a difficult request.

But being in the city of love had been the last place I wanted to be in.

Not when Michael and I still hadn't really spoken or seen each other since I'd left his apartment that day. It wasn't like we could avoid each other since we worked together, but whenever I did see him, he was rushing to somewhere else. He even sent any communication either via email or Marcella relayed the information.

I'd tried to be understanding, that he probably blamed himself for what happened to Alice because that's exactly what I would have done if anything ever happened to Zayd.

But a month was a long time and it felt like whatever was happening between us had just been carelessly thrown to the side with no regards to how I felt.

I'd tried not to dwell on it too much, and I hated myself for caring.

I'd never been anyone's priority before and he'd made me feel like I was his.

That he cared how I felt, as much I did for him.

I'd never had that before.

I'd never been chosen, but with him, for the first time, I felt like I had been.

I knew, deep down, that his reaction wasn't intentional. Something had scared him off, but it wasn't my job to make excuses for him or find reason for his silence.

And yet, when I looked down at my phone again, my finger hovered over his name.

Azara, don't, I tried to reason with myself, but against my better judgment, my fingers began typing out a message. Only to end up deleting every iteration because what would I even say?

Hey, how have you been?

Or.

You haven't answered any of my messages, but my mum's dead, and I need you.

I let out a frustrated groan and threw my phone on my bed with more force than necessary.

You're being ridiculous, Azara.

Warring emotions I couldn't even begin to untangle battled inside my chest. The weight of this past year, these last few months, weeks, this day bore down on me, suffocating me with no relief in sight.

I squeezed my eyes and focused on taking deep breaths before I spiraled into a state of panic I'd have no way of clawing myself a way out of. I needed to have a word with whoever had invented feelings because having to fight with something intangible was utterly draining.

This was precisely why I'd always stuck to simple. No strings. No attachments.

It was effective, uncomplicated.

Because attachment meant that there was a chance for someone to leave. It gave them a chance to walk away or… die.

And once that happened, because inevitably, it always did, I'd be left with pain.

I pushed past the ache in my chest and made my way upstairs to brew myself a cup of green tea. I sipped it slowly, the warmth grounding me a bit, as I moved to the couch, planning to spend the rest of my day binge-watching films so I could lose myself in someone else's life and forget about my own for a brief moment.

I'd just settled on watching my favorite Samia Farès drama film when there was a knock at my door. My brows furrowed for a moment on who it could be when I remembered I'd ordered myself takeout, too tired to cook tonight. It came earlier than I'd expected considering I'd only placed my order ten minutes ago, but I wasn't about to look a gift horse in the mouth.

I placed my mug on the table and was about to open the door when I remembered how I looked. I untucked my *gandoura* from the sides of my underwear and smoothed the strays curls of my messy bun back before finally answering the door.

Only it wasn't a delivery driver with my Chinese takeaway. No, instead, there he was, standing on my doorstep in a black jumper and trousers, a dusting of snow clinging all over him.

I blinked, thinking I was hallucinating, but when I opened my eyes again, Michael was still there. The air in my lungs became thin when his gaze slowly met mine for the first time in weeks, but I managed to push through it.

"What are you doing here?"

It wasn't the warmest of greetings, but it wasn't like he deserved any better.

Michael was quiet for a moment, his gaze fixed on me. The expression on his face transported me back to the night of Alice's accident. When I held him in my arms, trying to soothe him from the guilt and shock of seeing his sister in that state.

I'd seen him in passing at work, but this was the first time in weeks where I'd really taken a look at him. He looked exhausted, his eyes were tired and the scruff along his jawline was longer than I'd ever seen it.

I wondered if he was okay, before I chastised myself for caring. He wasn't my responsibility. He'd made that abundantly clear.

"I wanted to see you," he finally said and the breath in my lungs stalled at hearing his voice. My heart stuttered, then hammered painfully against my ribcage, as if it wanted to break free and close the rift he'd created between us, but I firmly reminded it of its place.

I let out a pained sigh, shaking my head. "I think it's a bit late for that." I stared for a moment longer, before I closed the door.

Once I heard it click shut, my body sagged against it, exhaling a breath I hadn't realized I'd been holding in. I'd almost convinced myself he'd been a figment of my imagination, a cruel torture my mind had conjured to toy with me because, earlier, I'd almost gave in and told him I needed him.

But then his voice came through the other side of the door. It was softer this time, and ladened with aching desperation.

"Azara, please… just let me in."

I squeezed my eyes shut, torn between what I knew I should do and what I wanted to do. I *shouldn't* let him in. I should walk back to the couch and carry-on with my evening as I'd planned.

But, god… a small, selfish part of me wanted to forget about these last few weeks and let myself sink into his arms, seeking the comfort I'd been craving all day, one that I'd learned over the last months only he could give me.

I heard a slight shift on the other side, and for a split second, I thought he was leaving. But then he spoke again. "I'll wait here until you let me in."

"Michael, just go home. There's nothing for you here."

In the grand scheme of things, we were never anything more than two people who had to work together. Real couples broke up every day. They mourned what once was and eventually learned how to live without the other, until one day, it didn't matter anymore. They eventually forgot you were a part of their story and they moved on.

That's what I had to convince myself of. This was just another chapter, and though it felt different than any I'd ever been on, he'd forget, and we'd all move on.

But the words had barely left my lips when he replied, "Everything is."

My head dropped back as I closed my eyes, the weight of his response washing over me. I could barely hear myself think over the thundering beat of my pulse.

Everything is.

I tried not to dwell on them, because words were meaningless unless they were made tangible. So why did my stupid heart skip a beat at them? Why did my body ache to know what he meant by that?

I walked away before I caved. I sipped on the now-cold tea and tried to distract myself. But it was pointless. I couldn't focus on anything and although I was locked inside my house, his presence invaded every space.

I could hear him still sitting on the cold, hard floor, shifting occasionally as if he was searching for a comfortable position.

I sat there for what felt like an eternity, until the images on the screen blurred, the dialogue muffled in the background because all I kept hearing was his voice in my head.

Everything is.

The film was about halfway through when I heard voices outside my door.

I frowned for a moment, before I heard Michael say, "Thanks, mate. You can leave it with me. I'll hand it to her once she—"

I was at the door in an instant, yanking it open just as the delivery driver was handing Michael the large paper bag containing my fried rice and spring rolls. I yanked the takeaway bag before Michael got a hold of it and held it hostage. I wouldn't put it past him to use it as leverage to make me talk to him.

The young man flicked his gaze between the two of us, unsure what situation he'd walked into. He eventually just shrugged and made a hasty exit.

"Thank you," I called out to the teenager before retreating back inside my flat, not bothering to spare more than a fleeting glance at Michael. But just as I was about to close the door, Michael wedged his foot in, blocking my attempt.

"Move," I muttered, my fingers tightening around the bag of food while my eyes stayed glued to the floor, desperate to avoid his gaze for fear of giving in.

"I can't, I don't want to," he replied, his voice pained but determined. "Look at me," he added, his hand reaching out to make me, but I jerked away from his touch.

"Why are you still here?" I asked impatiently, meeting his gaze.

Frustration simmered beneath my skin at his insistence. Where had all of this been two weeks ago when I showed up at his place? He was the one who'd pushed me away, so why was he expecting a different treatment from me now?

Why couldn't he just leave?

"I told you," he replied, his eyes never wavering from mine. "I needed to see you."

My arms shot out to either side in exasperation. "Great. Now you've seen me. Goodbye."

With that, I moved to slam the door shut once again, but he was quicker and pushed his way inside my home. "I'm not leaving," he said, his voice firm.

I froze, my eyes widened in disbelief. "Like hell you aren't," I snapped, stepping forward in an attempt to get him out. "You need to leave."

But he didn't move. Instead, he shut the door and locked it behind him. "Not until we talk," he said, slipping off his coat and draping it over the console by the door.

"No."

"Yes," he insisted, slowly taking a step toward me.

I shook my head. "No. You don't get to do this." My voice rose, but I couldn't stop it. I could feel the heat of my irritation crawling up my neck, the weight of it pressing against my chest. I'd been holding on to this for too long, and now there was nothing I could do to stop them. "You don't get to ignore me for two weeks and come back demanding we talk when *you* pushed me away. Not when you threw me out and didn't even give me the decency of a conversation."

"Azara." My name was a sigh.

I closed my eyes, my throat tightening. "Michael, please leave," I said, my anger splintering into exhaustion. It'd already been a day, and

I didn't want to deal with this.

When the room fell quiet, I held on to the hope that he'd leave. But instead, his hands came on my shoulders and snaked up my neck until his hands were tangled in my hair.

I squeezed my eyes further and a deep sigh rattled my chest at his touch.

"I'm sorry," he murmured, his voice thick with regret. His grip on the back of my head tightened, pulling me closer as he pressed his forehead to mine. "I'm sorry that I fucked up and shut you out when that was the last thing I'd ever want to do."

I didn't know what to feel, what to think or how to react. Since I'd left his apartment that night, I'd silently wished to hear these words, but why had it taken him so long to tell me this?

"Why should I believe you?" I asked, my voice barely above a whisper. I still couldn't look at him. I was too afraid to meet his gaze, of what I might find there.

But my will was barely holding and the longer he was near me, touching me, the more my resolve was wavering.

Michael exhaled a shaky breath. "Because I l—" He abruptly stopped himself and I held my breath as the unspoken words hung in the air.

I felt him pull away, just enough that I could feel the weight of his eyes on me.

"I didn't know what to do then," he paused, tilting my head up.

His thumbs reached up to brush across my cheeks before gently moving over my eyelids as if he was willing them to open. He was so close, I could feel every rise of his chest with each breath. I could almost hear the way his heart thundered against his ribcage.

His breath ghosted across my lips as he uttered his next words. "I know what I want. I've always known, I was just too bloody stubborn to let myself see it."

My eyes fluttered open despite my best efforts, and the moment I met his gaze, it was as if time slowed to a crawl. Every second seemed to stretch into an eternity as his gaze filled with emotions I didn't dare naming yet.

Emotions that mirrored my own.

I'd never felt so strongly about anyone before. The intensity was so foreign, so overwhelming, that I was still trying to grapple on what it all meant.

I'd always walked a clear path and I was so certain this was how I wanted my life to be. I moved from one day to the next, blind to what more life had to offer because it was easier that way.

And I had liked it. Or at least I'd thought so.

Until this man with dark eyes and an uncanny ability to irritate me to the point of wanting to strangle him came into my life and destabilized everything I've ever known, sending me tumbling over the edge.

"I want you, Azara."

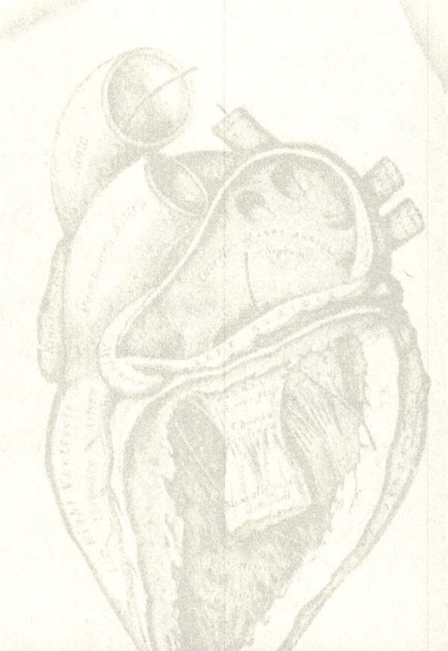

CHAPTER 35

MICHAEL

THE WORDS HUNG IN THE air between us, my breath catching in the silence as I waited for her response.

There was so much more I wanted to say to her, a different set of three words I wanted to confess, but I didn't want to tell her how much she owned me before I got a chance to tell her everything.

Not before I had the opportunity to show her every aspect of who I was.

I just hope she'll accept me.

Our gaze lingered on each other as I held her, hoping to bring her back to me. I'd regretted letting her go the moment I didn't stop her from leaving when she'd showed up that morning two weeks ago. I'd wanted to tell her everything at that moment, but I'd been too focused on my father's words that I'd made the mistake of letting her think I didn't want her there.

But I was done doing what I was dictated to.

I'd made my choice.

And I wanted her.

I'd figure everything else out later.

"I want you too," she confessed softly, her voice barely audible.

Silence descended again around us as the weight of her words registered.

"You do?" I said breathlessly, my heart was thundering in my chest.

Ever so slowly, she nodded. "Yes."

"Do you forgive me for being an idiot?"

She rolled her eyes, but there was a small smile blooming on her lips. "Yes."

My shoulders sagged with relief as I brought her mouth to mine, just barely brushing my lips to hers. Her mouth opened on a short gasp and I watched her brief hesitation melt away when I finally snuffed out the remaining distance.

I kissed her with everything that I'd been holding onto for the last year.

It was slow.

Purposeful.

And I hoped my unspoken words from earlier were conveyed with the way my lips moved over hers.

I found myself quickly lost in her and all of my senses narrowed in on her.

Azara Ziani was utterly intoxicating and I desperately wanted more.

"Say it again," I whispered against her lips, a little dazed.

"I want you too."

I closed my eyes, basking in her words as they washed over me, loosening every muscle in my body. I brought her closer, only to realize that she was still tightly holding onto the delivery bag like it was her lifeline and she needed it to ground herself.

With one hand, I grabbed it from her and tossed it gently on the floor.

"My food," she protested, but my hand came to rest against the right side of her neck. "Later," I said before kissing her again.

I hauled her into my body with my other arm banded around her waist, desperate for her warmth. Her hands grasped at my shoulders as I lifted her into my arms, allowing her legs to wrap around my waist.

I walked us toward her living room and my lips only broke away from hers when I dropped to the couch with her legs still around me. I wanted to do so many things to her, but this time, I wanted to take it slow.

My hands grazed up and down her arms, visible goosebumps flourishing underneath my fingertips. I tucked a long strand of her curly hair behind her ear and I let myself just admire her.

Everything about her felt carved to perfection for me to get to look at for the rest of my life. I hadn't done anything to deserve her, but I'd make sure I'd savor every minute I got.

"What is it?" she asked and my palms found her face again to keep her eyes on me.

"You're just so fucking beautiful, Azara Ziani," I said before pressing a soft kiss to her lips, my hands moving down her body to rest against her waist.

She brushed my hair back a few times, shaking her head. "You're not too bad to look at either."

"Was that a compliment?" I asked, grinning.

"Don't get used to them," she replied, rolling her eyes. But her smile mirrored my own and my heart skipped a beat at the sight.

Azara Ziani didn't smile very often but whenever she did, it was disarming.

"Come here."

This time there was no hesitation when she kissed me. She tasted like green tea, home and perfectly mine. My tongue pushed between her lips, and the sweet noises she made when her tongue tangled with mine sent warmth pooling down my spine.

"I love the way you feel in my hands," I muttered on her lips, my hands sliding under the colorful tunic she was wearing and skating over the expanse of her skin as I reveled in its warmth.

My willpower had barely been hanging on by a thread ever since our first kiss, but it turned to dust when she grinded her covered pussy against my quickly growing erection.

I moved my lips down and kissed along her jawline. Once I reached the spot behind her ear that I knew drove her wild, I nipped at the skin there before sucking on it.

"And I love the way they feel on me," she moaned, her back arching as she moved her hips back and forth with more urgency. Azara gripped the hair at the back of my neck and pulled my mouth back on hers.

She was dry humping me and I'd never felt anything better. Her hands dipped beneath the hem of my jumper and my body trembled with need under the feel of her fingertips skating over my skin.

"Azara," I breathed, my hands gripping the side of her thighs. "I want you," I panted against her mouth, toying with the outline of her panties and I could feel how wet she was. "I want to be inside you."

My request was almost a whine, and I probably sounded desperate but I didn't care. I'd surrendered myself to her the moment I'd laid eyes on her and I never wanted to go back to a life without her in it. She was the only woman I'd ever wanted and the only one I'd ever give up everything for.

Hopefully I won't have to.

She kissed me hard and our movements suddenly turned frantic.

Our mouths parted only for a moment so she could yank my jumper over my head while I discarded her tunic, tossing the pieces of clothing somewhere to the side.

I pulled back slightly and my mouth watered at the sight of her bare chest. Her breasts were tipped with small brown nipples that begged for my attention. I wanted to press my lips to her skin, to slowly take my time and savor every inch of her body until I reached that place between her legs that brought me to my knees.

The image of her pleasuring herself at the gallery had often plagued my dreams. She was like a work of art and I couldn't wait to be the one wringing pleasure out of her this time.

Azara rested her palms on my heaving chest. Her eyes roamed over the expanse of my tattooed skin, her hands exploring every bared inch, before her heated gaze locked with mine.

"What is it, baby?"

"You're just so fucking beautiful, Michael Young," she admired, mirroring my words from earlier.

I felt my cheeks heat at that. I'd never been called beautiful before and it was the best compliment I'd ever been given.

"You're cute when you blush," she teased, gliding her hands down my front. She reached for my trousers and the sound of her undoing my belt buckle cleared some of the spell she'd put my brain under, just enough for me to remember that she didn't know.

"Wait," I said, my voice strained as I gently placed my hands over hers. "There's something I have to tell you."

I hadn't planned for anything to happen tonight, but I'd already made my decision before I even came to see her. I'd fight for this, for us.

I'd fight for her even if it meant I was risking my own life.

"What is it?" She looked at me, uncertainty flickering across her face and I immediately wanted to take it away.

I brushed a thumb over the frown line forming on her forehead before cupping her cheek. "It's nothing bad, just..." My voice trailed off and swallowed thickly. I wasn't ashamed of what I was about to tell her, but I was suddenly feeling vulnerable to confess it.

"I'm a virgin," I finally admitted, my eyes carefully watching her as surprise filled her gaze. But it was only there for a moment, before her gaze darkened with something almost primal.

"Then it'll be my utmost pleasure to be your first."

And my last. But I'd keep that last part to myself.

The moment the words left her lips, she leaned in to kiss me again, this time with a renewed fervor. My fingers tangled in her hair while her hands fumbled to undo my trousers. She pulled them down with my underwear and I lifted my hips to assist her.

My erection sprung free and it practically wept when her delicate hand wrapped around me. A strangled moan tore through my lips at seeing her hand around me. She'd touched me once before, but *fuck*, the feel of her hand on me this time almost made me come right there.

"Your cock is so pretty," Azara praised, taking me in. A laugh bloomed in my chest, but it was cut short when her thumb grazed along the wet tip and she squeezed.

My head fell against the back of the sofa as she tugged on my length a few times. Her lips trailed kisses along my jaw as her fist continued to grip me.

"Azara," I groaned, my hand wrapping around hers to stop her exquisite torture. As if she could hear my unspoken plea, she released me and shifted above me just enough to remove the final barrier that separated us.

Everything around us shifted, the air in the room growing headier, hotter and my blood simmered with need. Her hands came to rest on my shoulders and she hovered her wet cunt right above the tip of my cock.

"Azara… please," I moaned when our eyes met, my hands coming up to grip her hips. If she waited any longer, I was worried I'd combust from how much I wanted her.

But my needy whimper was all the encouragement she needed before she gripped my cock, gliding it over her wetness and lining me up with her entrance.

"I have an implant and haven't been with anyone in a very long time."

My reply that I trusted her died on my tongue when she lowered herself onto me.

We both watched as her cunt swallowed the head of my cock and my breath stuttered when she sank down.

"*God*," I shuddered, my voice strangled. My head felt lightheaded as her perfect pussy stole my virtue inch by inch and it was the most erotic picture I'd ever witnessed. It made me wish I had a camera to film it or that this was happening at my flat so I could rewatch it perpetually.

Because seeing Azara's cunt take me until I was buried in her almost made me come undone right then and there.

I closed my eyes for a brief moment, wanting to bask in being inside her. My dreams came nowhere close to what reality felt like. The way her cunt choked my cock was otherworldly and nothing could ever top being with her like this.

It wasn't just being inside, it was being *with* her. It was her intelligence, and her wittiness. It was the way she was never afraid to put me in place or challenge me to be better.

It was her and how she made me feel like I had a home to come to between her arms.

"How does it feel?" I heard Azara ask.

I opened my eyes to meet hers and my heart threatened to explode. "I don't think any words would be good enough to describe how good you feel. But I need you to move."

My words seemed to trigger something in her because she lifted her hips, before she slammed down. She repeated the motion again. And again. I almost saw stars with how fast and frantically she was riding me.

But I needed her closer, desperate to feel every part of her bare skin against mine.

Strangled sounds escaped from my throat as I wrapped my arms around her back, clinging to her as hard as I could to help ground myself, wanting to soak this moment in, but there was no point.

I buried my face in her chest as we were both driven by all-consuming hunger and there was no more room for restraint for either of us.

"You're taking me so well, *gumiho*," I groaned into her skin. "I want us like this, me inside you, forever."

"Yes," she cried out. She then placed a hand behind me for leverage and increased her pace, riding me unrelentingly.

One of my hands snaked between us so my fingers could work over her clit. "M-michael," she gasped, her other hand fisting the back of my head and tugging my face tighter against her skin.

We fucked each other, my cock filling her, stretching her to fit around me perfectly. While my moans were stifled between her breasts, hers mingled with the sound of our bodies coming together, flesh against flesh, creating a poetic anthem that fused itself in my brain and would become my favorite melody.

Air grew scarce and I felt my orgasm approaching with a frightening speed. I'd had enough years to learn how to control myself, but with her cunt squeezing me so tightly, it was becoming harder with each second.

My hand that wasn't working her swollen sex slid up her spine, landing in her hair. I lifted my chin and pulled her face toward mine to find her eyes.

I needed her to look at me. I needed to see the look in her eyes when she came. "Baby, tell me you're almost there," I choked out, mustering a breath. "I want to come inside you at the same time you come all over my cock," I commanded, my fingers working her clit faster.

"I-I am," she stammered.

Our gazes never wavered from one another as our orgasms climbed, higher and higher, her pussy tightening around my length. "That's it, Azara. Come for me, *please*. I need you to…"

Her shout bled quickly into a keening cry, and her shameless sounds sent my own release careening over the edge. I came hard, lightning bolting through my entire body as my release exploded inside her.

After riding our waves of ecstasy for a few moments longer, we came down at the same time, breathless. I softened my grip on her curls and she melted over me, her forehead finding mine.

Her eyes were glazed over, and the smile that spread across her lips sent my heart into a stuttering heartbeat.

"Azara Ziani, that was…" I started, unable to find the right words.

She huffed out a laugh. "Yeah, it was."

I didn't want to move, but when she shivered in my arms, I said, "Come on, let's get you cleaned up."

After a shower that went on far longer than I'd intended for because I couldn't resist lathering every inch of her body and making her come twice more—once on my tongue and another time around my cock—she'd changed into a large, loose black shirt, while I opted to sleep bare. My clothes were upstairs, and I was too exhausted to bother retrieving them, when I usually slept naked anyway.

I was laying on my back, the weight of Azara's soft body nestled into my side, our limbs tangled together in a way that felt like we'd been doing it forever. We'd been laying here for a while now, none of us saying a word, and I'd never felt so… at peace.

It wasn't until Azara came into my life that I'd realized just how unsettled I'd felt for so long. For years, I'd been a guest of my own story, drifting through the monotone cadence of all the things I was expected to be.

But when I met her, I wasn't an Atlas, or a son or a doctor.

There was no pressure to perform or to be perfect.

To be what everyone wanted me to be.

Azara Ziani wanted me for who *I* was, not what I offered.

She was the first one to truly see *me* and I never wanted to let that go.

Her breathing was slow and steady, the rise and fall of her chest against my body grounding me, but I could feel the slight tremor in her fingers as they traced lazy circles on my chest. Her light touch was soothing, but distant, like she was lost in her own thoughts.

"What's on your mind?" I whispered.

She was silent for a few breaths. "My mum died fifteen years ago today," she finally answered quietly. The words settled in the air around us, and my heart squeezed, aching to find ways to be there for her.

I'd known about her mother's accident and that today was her death's anniversary when I showed up here earlier. It was what made me hesitate about whether or not I should show up here, but when I'd gotten a notification on my computer that she'd been typing me a message before it disappeared, I knew I had to come.

Even if we didn't have the conversation I owed her, I wanted to be there for her.

Azara and I were different in so many ways, but we shared one thing in common when it came to big emotions.

We either ignored them or simply brushed them off.

I'd always been too afraid to ask for help, even when I needed it the most. There was this petulant voice inside my head that reminded me how much of a burden I'd be if I opened up, if I let anyone in and asked them to be there for me. So, I'd deemed it easier to internalize how I felt, to hide behind a smile on my face and carry on.

Or at least my version of it.

Her attempt at reaching out showed me she'd thought about letting me in, but with how I'd treated her and her reluctance in asking when she needed someone, she'd preferred not bothering anyone and shouldering it on her own.

So I'd decided to show up because I wanted to be the soft place she landed when she needed it.

I turned my head to look at her, but her eyes were cast down, focused on the circles she was still tracing against my chest. "Azara," I said on a soft breath.

"It was a long time ago, and I'm fine now."

I brought my hand up to brush her hair back over and over. "You're allowed to miss her. To feel sad even if years have passed," I replied quietly.

I didn't know what it was like to necessarily lose a parent in the way she had, but I didn't want her to think that grief had an expiration date. That if enough time had passed, it would just go away. Because that was the funny thing about grief, some days were easy and you were able to carry on, while others tugged you back to the day you'd lost the person you loved all over again.

Azara took a shuddering breath and finally met my gaze, her eyes filled with unshed tears.

"I wish she was still here every day," she confessed, a tear escaping and trailing down her cheek. She quickly brushed it away and averted her gaze. "I'm sorry, it's stupid, I know. I shouldn't be crying, but she was the best part of my days and I miss her so much."

I found more tears falling down her cheeks and my stomach dropped. It was killing me seeing her like this and I wanted to erase all of her pain, but I knew it was never that easy. There were no words that would make this better or make it hurt less.

"Hey, hey, hey." My hand trailed from her hair to her face, resting against her cheek to make her look at me again. "You're allowed to cry about it. About anything. There's nothing wrong or stupid about it."

She let out a deep breath and let go of what was probably years of bottled in emotions. I wrapped my arms tightly around her, kissing her hair and along her forehead as she cried in my arms.

"I'm right here, love," I whispered against her temple.

I kept fluttering kisses across her skin, her cries softening with each one until they were fewer and further between.

When she looked at me again, my heart soared at the sight of this beautiful woman that I hoped would agree to be all mine.

"Thank you," she murmured softly.

"Being there for you is never something you have to thank me for," I said earnestly as I reached up to gently brush her hair out of her face and pressed a kiss to her forehead.

When I pulled away, I found her smiling at me, small and tender, and I experienced another layer of what I felt for her reach out from me to her.

I was so utterly, and undeniably, in love with this girl.

Her vulnerability called for mine, but I pushed the feeling away before I consumed me, afraid I'd confess everything I'd been keeping from her.

It wasn't the right time, yet.

"Tell me about her," I asked her, offering her a small smile of my own.

We stayed like this, whispering into the quiet night as she shared about her mother's favorite things and what she was like. She did so until her breathing softened into a softer cadence, and I never imagined the day where Azara would be curled against me, falling asleep in my arms.

Despite the unknown that lay in front of us, I quietly whispered the three words I'd been holding onto for weeks now, until I, too, fell asleep.

Hoping I'd get to tell her everything in the morning.

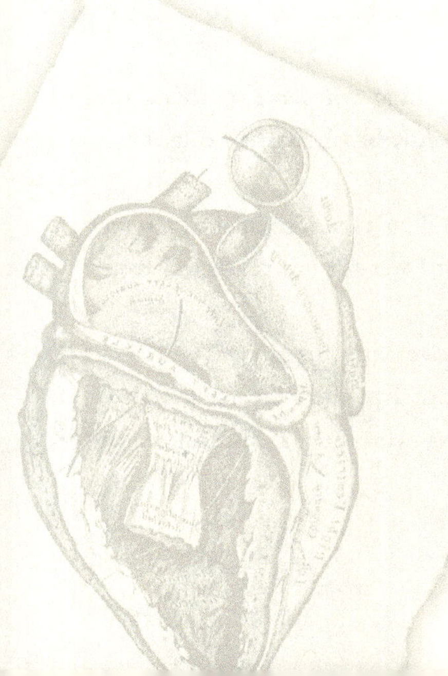

CHAPTER 36

AZARA

I WOKE UP THE NEXT day to an empty bed.

The faint scent of his cologne still lingered on the rumpled sheets but Michael's side of the bed was cold, almost like last night hadn't happened. We'd slept together for the first time only for him to leave without saying goodbye.

A pang of disappointment settled in my chest. I shouldn't have expected him to stay, but after last night, after everything he'd said, I thought things were different now.

I want you, Azara.

Being there for you is never something you have to thank me for.

His words acted like a balm to wounds I didn't even know I had. I had great friends, a family that loved me, but I never realized how much I held back on how I felt for fear of either disappointing anyone or feeling like a burden because my emotions weren't their responsibilities to deal with.

Asking someone to hold me, to be there for me when I was at my lowest had always been something I never dared to do. I always felt like I'd be leeching onto their energy by unloading on them my deepest and darkest thoughts.

It had always just been easier to be that person for everyone else.

But Michael had shown up when I'd needed it the most and never wavered in *wanting* to be there.

For the first time since my mother's passing, I'd had someone I could hold on to. Someone who took such gentle care of my vulnerability that it didn't feel like a weakness to open up.

Tell me about her.

I couldn't remember the last time I'd been able to talk about my mother so freely without restraints or fear of sharing too much. With my father, there was never room to discuss her because he'd always shut it down. I'd tried for years and was always met with the same result. With Zayd, I only shared the positive memories so he'd have even a fraction of the experience I'd gotten with her, without weighing him down with how hard it had been for me to lose her.

But with Michael, I'd been able to share the good and the bad. From how much of a vibrant force she had been to how devastating her loss was.

Being able to talk about her had proved to be more therapeutic than I could even fully grasp yet. For so long, I'd clung to the negative aspects of her passing so much that I'd denied myself the space to truly grieve for her.

I'd never had enough time with her, and the longing for more had inhibited me for so long, the weight of it hadn't allowed me to realize that grieving her didn't have to be a bad thing.

Grieving wasn't linear or one-dimensional. It could be both happy and sad, hurtful and beautiful. My mum had been one of the best parts of my life and not letting myself feel her loss only held back all the unexpressed love that I still had for her and that I could hold onto instead.

My fingers grazed the cold sheets where he'd been, the reality of him walking out bringing insecurity rearing its head, only for them to close on a small torn piece of white paper. I sat up in bed and picked it up to open it.

Went to grab breakfast. Don't miss me too much ;)

What people said about a doctor's handwriting was unmistakingly true; because I stared at the scribbled cursive, and it took me a few seconds to decipher everything he'd written.

But his note had its intended effect and sent a wave of warmth and relief to wash away the previous insecurity and disappointment that had crept in at finding Michael gone.

I swung my legs over the side of my bed and stretched, basking in the delicious soreness in my muscles and between my legs.

Last night had been more than I could have imagined it to be. Nothing about what we'd done had been sweet or gentle, and to be honest, I'd completely forgotten that I was taking his virginity.

Sex had never felt like this before.

I'd been so consumed by him, by my hunger for him and my need to have him closer that all my mind could think about was how to get closer to the precipice before diving head first into the pleasure.

Neither of us held back and it was the best I'd ever had.

But it hadn't been just sex.

Last night I'd felt cherished.

Wanted.

Free.

And I wanted more of it. More of him.

Of *us*.

I never thought I'd let myself fall in love with anyone, given the fatal weight I'd attached to it, but with Michael?

It was the easiest thing I'd ever done.

There had been no room for overthinking or weighing up the consequences. Falling in love with him had been as effortless as performing surgery and nothing had ever felt like that.

It came as naturally as breathing.

I'd be lying if I said I wasn't afraid to tell him because what if he didn't feel the same? What if these last few months, and last night, meant more to me than they did to him?

But despite my usual tendencies to distance myself from the concept of love, I trusted Michael. I trusted *myself* with Michael.

He'd shown me what it was like to be loved. Sure, he'd sent me over the edge more times than I could count, but I'd never once had to question his intentions or motives toward me because of how transparent he'd been about them.

Foregoing making my bed, I washed up and changed into warmer loungewear. I'd had Michael's warmth last night, but my flat was currently freezing. I really had to fix the heaters before the coldest temperatures hit us.

I turned up the thermostat and headed upstairs. Finding the living room a complete mess from what had transpired last night, I moved to tidy it up when there was a sharp knock at the door.

A newborn anticipation shot through me as I swung the door open, but where I was expecting to find him, there was no one there.

My brows furrowed as I looked out into the hallway, only to find it eerily empty.

Strange.

I briefly wondered if I'd imagined the knocking, but just as I was about to shut the door, something caught my eye on my doorstep.

A large manila envelope sat on the welcome mat but what drew my attention immediately was my name, stamped in bold black letters across the front.

A chill ran down my spine, and the hairs on my nape prickled as I bent down to pick it up. The package appeared innocuous—apart from the fact that it had my name on it. I turned it over, checking for a return address, only to find none.

My instincts were warning me to get rid of it, but the strange pull of curiosity about it being addressed to me overthrew caution. So against better judgment, I closed the door softly behind me, leaving it unlocked for Michael to walk in, and padded into the living room, sinking onto the sofa.

I tore at the seam and retrieved the stack of papers.

My stomach plummeted when I flipped through the photographs. The images were disjointed snapshots of Michael in various parts of the city, outside the hospital.

And... here?

My confusion deepened as I tried to understand what it all meant, but the empty contents of my stomach threatened to surge up when I landed on the last one.

A picture of me, naked, on top of Michael, both lost in our own world and oblivious to who might be watching. The profound intimacy I'd experienced last night had now been tainted, reduced into a perverse mockery.

My throat grew tight as the air in my lungs suddenly thinned, and I couldn't breathe.

Who had sent these?

Who had *seen* them?

If these were to fall into the wrong hands...

My heart hammered in my chest, and another wave of nausea

swirled in my gut.

Trying to focus on being pragmatic, I examined every photo again, my mind struggling to grasp what I was looking at, and why I was sent this.

Why was someone following him? Why were they following *me*?

I was an ordinary, overworked surgeon.

This had to be a sick joke.

I grabbed the envelope again, finding it still heavy. I shook the content out and a small, black recorder tumbled on my lap. Grabbing it, I found a note taped on it and unfolded it. It contained a small paragraph typed out in a neat black font, but the signature at the end made my blood run cold.

Dearest Ms. Ziani,

It has come to this author's attention that secrets have been kept from you, and as one who deals solely in truth, I find it in my very duty to set the record straight.

In the following recording, you will find all of the answers you've been seeking.

With utmost sincerity,
The Gilded Truth

The notorious gossip columnist never addressed their issues to anyone directly, but I couldn't afford to dwell on that, nor the unease swelling in my chest.

My fingers trembled as I reached for the recorder. The device felt frigid in my palm, the weight of it pressing down on me as I pressed the play button.

The room was quiet for a moment, before it filled with the sound of a voice I recognized instantly.

Michael's.

But the warm voice I'd grown accustomed to had been replaced by one of a stranger's.

"I think we can both do each other a favor and stop pretending by dragging this charade of yours out."

A brief silence followed, punctuated with the rapid thuds of my heart. Almost as if Michael was baiting me and whoever he was addressing. I wondered who it was, but the rest of his words not only answered my question, it sent horror consuming every fiber of my being.

"I know you've been falsifying reports for NyxMedica so they wouldn't lose their UKCA mark. They've been paying you handsomely in exchange for this hospital to push and endorse their devices."

"You've been altering patients' records by adding the use of NyxMedica's devices into procedures when it wasn't the case to improve their success rate, overriding access logs and making sure your name never appeared in any of the notes once you'd made your 'adjustments.'"

"This contains every altered patient file you've meddled with. While this, has all of the statements for the bank account you opened in your son's name."

"Since there's no point in you denying any of this, here are your options. You'll either resign as medical director and from your position on AGH's board, or this all becomes public."

"The choice is yours."

I didn't know how long I stood there, rewinding the recording, over and over, each time desperately hoping for a different outcome.

But it always ended the same.

The man I'd fallen in love with, threatening my father.

A storm of emotions spiraled inside me from the sudden turn of events until one emotion rooted itself in my chest.

Betrayal.

My phone pinged from somewhere but my heart was hammering so violently against my ribcage, I couldn't hear anything but the sound of my battering pulse deafening in my ears.

You'll either resign as medical director and from your position on AGH's board, or this all becomes public.

His words were stuck in my head like a broken loop, each one drilling deeper. A burning sensation spread behind my eyes while I replayed the last year, each memory twisting into a nightmare.

The dinner date, the soft words whispered during late nights in the closet and all the moments in between.

Last night.

Had he… had he been pretending this whole time? Was his goal to lower my defenses so I'd be an easier opponent and he'd get to my father more easily?

I'd never needed anyone. I had myself to rely on and it had always been enough.

Or at least, that was what I'd been telling myself for years until I'd met Michael and I'd discovered how liberating it was to have someone by your side.

But I should have known better.

I *did* know better.

I'd buried my heart for the longest time, sheltering it from the pain that inevitably came from heartbreak and this was exactly why.

Because the moment I'd allowed myself to believe that love wasn't a painful feeling, that it could be carefree and exhilarating, it was shattered into oblivion.

Because the moment I put my trust in something as fickle as love, reality stomped on it and showed me its true colors.

The door to my flat creaked open, the sound sharp in the quiet room.

"Azara, I'm back," Michael's voice called out as he clicked the door shut behind him. "The line at the shop down the street lasted forever, but I got us—" His voice faltered and I felt the suffocating weight of his presence standing a few feet from me.

"Baby, what's wrong?" he said, his voice full of concern. The term of endearment that normally would have sent a flurry of warmth rushing through my body, now created a painful crack to rip through my chest.

He placed the paper bag with what I assumed had our breakfast inside on the table next to the evidence of his deceit and my grip on the recorder tightened as though it might somehow offer me protection from what I already knew deep down.

Yet despite that, a part of me was still holding onto a small, desperate sliver of hope that this was all some mistake, and Michael would offer a perfectly reasonable excuse.

But when I finally lifted my gaze to meet his, and watched his smile dim, only to be replaced with a flicker of guilt, I knew.

I knew it hadn't been a mistake.

And the love I'd felt for this man had been all but a fabricated lie.

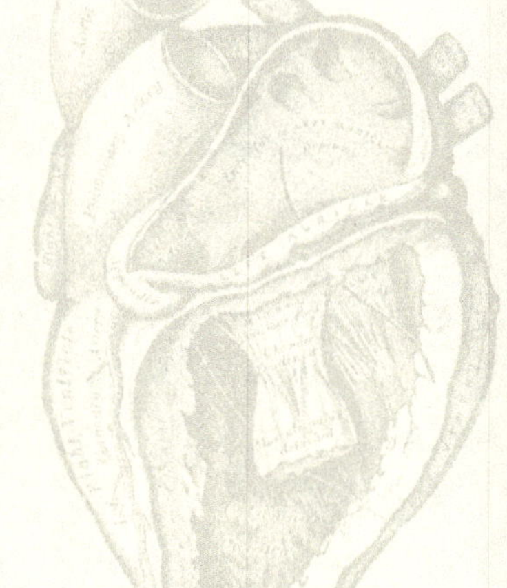

CHAPTER 37

MICHAEL

"GET OUT."

Her command sliced through me and a chilling sensation creeped into my gut, tightening like a noose at the distress written all over her face.

My eyes flitted down briefly to the photos spread out on the coffee table in front of her. I only caught a glimpse at the contents of one, but it was enough to piece together the possibility of why the woman I'd held in my arms last night wasn't the one standing in front of me anymore.

"Not until you tell me what's wrong." I was well-aware it was a stupid thing to say, especially with how damning the pictures laid out in front of her were, but I was willing to try anything if it meant it bought me more time.

If it meant the chance to explain.

A bitter laugh escaped her lips, the sound hollow and empty.

Instead of answering, she held up a small device I hadn't noticed in her hands before. I didn't have the opportunity to ask her what it was before the sound of my voice filtered through it.

I felt every ounce of blood drain from my face when my eyes met hers again after the last words I'd told her father before he resigned cloaked the room around us. Time slowed into an excruciating pace, and panic clawed at my chest at the implication of what this meant.

No. This can't be happening.

Everything between us had been tangled up in a web of lies and half-truths and it was all coming crashing down. But I was supposed to have more time. I was supposed to tell her everything once I dealt with the House. I was supposed to be able to make things right and then be with her after my Ascension.

But wasn't that the cruelty of hope? To have it dangled in front of you, only to watch slip away when you finally reached for it.

I had no idea who had given her all of that information or or how it landed in her hands, but right now none of it mattered.

Azara was more important.

Time resumed its normal course, but the dread I felt remained.

I took a step toward her, desperate to bridge the space between us, but she shot up from her seat, putting distance between us. She only stood a few feet away, and I could still smell her perfume that had lulled me to sleep last night.

But with the way she looked at me, she might as well have been miles away.

"Azara," I said, my voice low.

"Michael, I said *get. Out.*"

"No," I said firmly, unwilling to let go. "I'm not leaving until we talk." My words were reminiscent of what I'd told her yesterday, but this time they held more urgency.

"Oh, so you want to talk," she retorted, shaking her head in disbelief. "Then answer me this," she added, a roughness edging her words.

"Anything," I replied, desperately clinging to any sliver of hope that somehow I'd be able to buy myself enough time to fix this.

But I was deluding myself. Just like I'd been from the beginning.

"Why did you do it?"

Her question was simple enough, and yet the weight of it threatened to crush me.

My throat worked with a hard swallow. "I did what I had to do."

A heavy silence lingered in the space between us as I waited for her to react to my veiled confession. Regardless of how badly I wanted to tell her everything about who I was and what I was involved in, I couldn't just yet. I was ready to risk everything to have her in my life, but I needed to wait until I could leverage things to my advantage.

If I told her too much, too soon, I'd risk putting her in jeopardy.

"Leave," she said, but her voice was eerily calm and controlled this time.

Too controlled.

But I caught a glimpse of the anguish flickering between the cracks.

And I only had myself to blame.

I was responsible for putting it there and I'd never hated myself more.

"It was never my intention to hurt you." I managed to get out, my throat feeling like sandpaper.

"*Hurt* me?" She spat the words and their venom slithered across my heart like a serrated blade. But her next words struck me like a slow poison. "Michael, you *used* me."

She let out a humourless laugh as she looked away from me for a moment before her eyes burned into mine, pinning me in place.

"I spent months seeing my father lose himself," she continued, her voice shaking despite her best efforts to hold it steady. "I thought to myself that maybe it was somehow my fault. That I was failing as a daughter because I couldn't fix the situation, that I couldn't fix what was wrong with him. Only now to realize that it was all because of you."

Her confession struck me like a physical blow and I was unmatched for its force.

I could feel the tremor in my hands as I tried to reach for her, but there was nothing there for me to grasp. My hand fell to my side when her hurt expression slowly morphed into indifference and I watched the walls I'd managed to finally get through grow taller with every passing second.

"Azara," I pleaded, my voice cracking under the weight of everything I wanted to say.

"Get out of my house," she demanded.

Raw panic flooded my lungs at seeing my window of opportunity thinning. Logic had ruled every one of my decisions, but there was no more room for it.

"Just give me a chance to explain," I said desperately, this time when she remained silent.

I'd planned to wait until after my Ascension to confess all of my sins, but fuck it. If my punishment was death, I'd flay myself open in front of her if it meant not losing her.

I needed her to listen to me. I needed her to forgive me. Deep down, I knew I didn't deserve it, but it didn't stop me from reaching for her again and wanting to hold her until she let me back in.

"I don't want to lose you."

She shrank away before I made contact. "You already have."

A strange pressure burned at the back of my eyes as my heart cracked under the weight of those three words. Three words that were the nemesis of the ones I'd wanted to tell her. The ones I'd dreamed of hearing from her.

"Please." My voice cracked and something wet landed on my cheek, but I didn't give it attention. Not when I was watching the woman I love slowly slip further away from me. "Don't do this, *gumiho*. I l—"

"Do *not* say it," she said, anger flooding her voice. She squeezed her eyes shut. "Do not fucking say those words to me. Don't lie to me more than you already have."

The air went still in the aftermath of her accusation except for the sound of my heart breaking further at her thinking that my love for her and the way she completely consumed me could only be a lie.

I tried to claw out of the darkness saturating my lungs, but it was impossible to thread through the pool of shame and regret for what I'd done.

My duty had never felt this wrong.

Not when it became the catalyst of losing a part of my soul.

"How much you own my heart could never be a lie," I confessed, barely recognizing my voice from its rawness.

My shoulders sagged from the weight of her silence. I'd expected it but it didn't prevent the emptiness I felt inside. I let out a shuddering breath, the sharp realization settling in that I might have just lost the love of my life. She'd handed her trust to me and I'd shattered it in ways that might be irreparable.

But as much as I hated it, I needed time to earn it back.

I just hoped that, this time, it wouldn't work against me.

I allowed myself to look at her one more time, one last look at what I stood to lose if I didn't do this right, before I did what she'd asked of me.

I left.

CHAPTER 38

AZARA

TODAY SHOULD HAVE FELT LIKE one of the best days of my life.

But as I headed for the nineteenth floor of Amanar, where the fate of my future here was set to be decided, each step grew heavier than the last.

I'd spent the last week and a half throwing myself headfirst into work.

More than I ever had before.

I knew it wasn't healthy, but I never claimed to be the perfect picture for coping.

The more I worked, the less I thought about him and the last thing I wanted was to think, breathe or see anything related to Michael Young.

Even if that was easier said than done.

Thankfully, for once, he'd respected my wishes to leave me alone. I didn't know how he'd managed it, but I hadn't seen him since he walked out of my apartment.

Of course, I heard the staff talk about him in passing, they never missed an opportunity to share just how amazing of a surgeon and colleague he was. But beyond that, I hadn't even run into him by accident.

Ironic, considering how often that had seemed to happen at our beginning.

But perhaps that had been part of his plans all along. To infiltrate every aspect of my life, until my world pre-Michael was a distant memory.

I stepped off the lift and into the sleek, polished hallway. A jarring contrast to how my life felt at the moment.

The doors to the conference room loomed ahead, and I felt my heartbeat quicken the closer I got to it. My stomach had been in knots for days now, but I felt like I might actually be sick.

The weight of everything that led me here seemed to weigh on me all at once, but I compelled myself to remember what had brought me here in the first place.

I'd poured the last decade of my life into this job.

Long hours. Sleepless nights. Emotional unavailability.

I'd done everything by the book.

So everything would be fine.

Right?

Then why did I feel like I was heading toward my execution?

I pushed the eerie feeling away and rolled my shoulders back, smoothing my hands over the white long-sleeve shirt and black tailored trousers I'd changed into after my last surgery. I'd hoped the gesture would soothe the nerves that had been gnawing at me since I woke up this morning, but it didn't help.

Azara, you got this, I told myself and although I'd usually believe it, I would be lying if I said my confidence wasn't wavering. And I hated it.

I'd never doubted my abilities, never lost confidence in what I could accomplish, but after what happened with Michael, I'd replayed the entirety of the past year over and over again, questioning everything, until I'd been too exhausted to think and had fallen into a restless sleep.

Only to wake up the next and do it all over again.

On the third day, I'd even driven all the way to my father's to speak with him, only to sit in my car for hours, staring at a place someone I clearly barely knew lived in.

How could he have done this? *Why* had he done it?

My emotions swung from sadness to anger and back again after what the recording had revealed and I just couldn't bring myself to face him. I'd had a thousand questions and didn't know where to begin.

In the end, I'd turned my car around and had left.

By the time I'd made it home, the bone deep exhaustion that had been weighing down on me for days had flipped a switch inside me. I had a position to secure, and if I kept thinking about how my life had been radically turned upside down, I'd never make it out in one piece.

Maybe my decision had been selfish of me, but I'd worked too fucking hard, given too much to others and put myself last so many times, that I didn't want to do it anymore. I was done with tiptoeing around what I wanted, what I needed for the sake of everything and everyone else.

So, I'd shoved every thought of Michael, my father, the pictures, and the note from *The Gilded Truth* to the very back of my brain to be dealt with later.

I'd barely made it to the conference room where the decision would be delivered, when I felt a prickle of heat on my neck.

I was afraid to look up, but there was no point in avoiding facing him. I knew he'd be there, he awaited the same decision as I did, but a small part of me had wished they wouldn't call us in at the same time.

My pulse quickened to a threatening rhythm as I slowly lifted my gaze toward where he stood at the end of the corridor. My heart almost stopped beating when my eyes landed on him.

I hadn't seen him in so long, and as hard of a job I had done to not think of him and his betrayal, my stupid feelings for him threatened to resurface.

How much you own my heart could never be a lie.

I'd replayed those words so many times in my head, it was almost embarrassing.

I didn't know much about love, but I knew that love shouldn't hurt.

Love could be messy and hard, but it should never be painful to the point that your heart bled from how the person that had been supposed to protect it, wounded it.

Oxygen grew scarce with each step he took toward me. My chest tightened, until a sharp, physical ache settled deep inside, when he stopped just a few feet away.

Michael slipped his hands in his trousers, his throat flexing with a hard swallow. His eyes flickered with uncertainty and guilt as they searched my face for something I was no longer willing to offer.

Panic surged inside me from the fear he'd try to talk to me, but a giant breath of relief flooded my lungs when the door to the conference room opened.

"You're both just on time," Thompson said, his voice cool as he appraised us. He then zeroed his attention on me, not wasting any time. "Dr. Ziani, if you'll follow me."

I couldn't decide whether going first was a good or bad thing, but there was no time to dwell on it. Instead, I plastered my most jovial expression on my face and followed him inside, where the twelve board members greeted me.

They were all smiling at me—all except for James Kay. Which was unsurprising after the events of Nakia's exhibition. I took a seat at the other head of the table, trying not to focus on the weight of their scrutinizing gazes.

My hands itched to pick at something to calm my escalating nerves, suddenly very aware of being the centre of attention, but I reminded myself that this was what I did best.

Perform under pressure.

Though, to be honest, the operating theater was a much more soothing environment to me than being under the attention of twelve people who held the next big step in your career in their hands.

After a moment of silence, Dr. Alexander, the hospital's CEO, cleared his throat and cut straight to the point. He began explaining what my duties would be as medical director, alongside my role on the board as an executive director.

I'd already known all of this since my father had held this very position since I'd started working here after graduating medical school. Still, I nodded along, offering the necessary affirmation that I understood the responsibilities I was about to take on.

It meant I'd be spending less time operating, but if it meant shaping how the hospital was run, I was willing to give up some of my hours in the theater for this.

Besides, my father had managed to balance both, and the board had promised a possibility to revisit our hours once we settled into the role.

My nerves began to settle the more they reviewed my performances over the years, explained how much of a valuable impact my work and teaching sessions had on new doctors and how impressed they were by how much I'd accomplished over a short period of time.

It's going to be fine, I told myself, smiling with relief as their words continued to affirm everything I'd worked for.

Dr. Alexander paused for a moment, allowing his praise to sink in.

But then, just as I was beginning to breathe easy, a whisper of doubt crept into the back of my brain, trying to warn me, but it wasn't quick enough.

"But," he continued, his tone shifting, "we've decided to move forward with another candidate."

My heart plummeted straight into my stomach.

"It was an extremely tight vote and.." the CEO's voice continued speaking, but everything around me faded into a blur. I didn't catch the rest of his explanation.

I sat there, dazed and struggling to process what had just happened.

I knew there was a chance I wouldn't get it, but…

Ten years.

Ten years of hard work reduced to nothing.

"Thank you for the consideration," I said numbly. I wasn't sure if they were done talking, or if they'd already dismissed me, but at this moment, it didn't matter.

All I wanted to do was get out of this room and go home.

I stood, my legs slightly unsteady beneath me, but I held myself tall as I walked out of the door. And as if things couldn't get worse, I came face-to-face with an expectant Michael.

His face fell when his gaze met mine.

If things were different, I'd think he was disappointed that I didn't get it.

If things were different, I'd believe he was sorry.

If things were different, I'd crush my body to his and find solace in his arms.

But things *weren't* different.

I stared at him for a moment, wondering how I hadn't seen through his act.

What had it been about him that had made me throw caution away? Had made me forget why I'd put up walls for so long when it came to love?

It wasn't like I hadn't believed in it, I'd witnessed its beauty with my parents.

Until it was cruelly ripped away from them.

I supposed it was in my blood for love to always end tragically.

"Congratulations Dr. Young," I finally said, my tone flat. "You got exactly what you wanted."

Then I brushed past him and walked away.

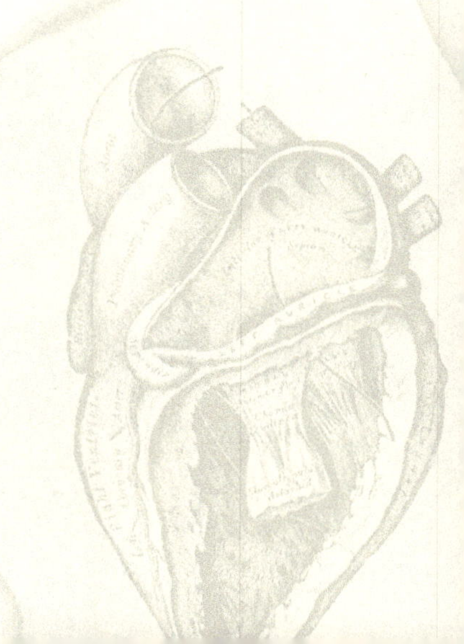

CHAPTER 39

MICHAEL

SHE WAS WRONG.

I didn't get what I truly wanted.

CHAPTER 40

AZARA

I WAS ON MY FIFTH rewatch—today—of my favorite Samia Farès film when a loud bang rattled my door.

I'd planned on ignoring it, seeing as I hadn't ordered anything or was expecting anyone, but then Nakia's voice bellowed from outside my flat.

"Azara, open up. We know you're in there."

I lunged for the remote, hastily muting the TV, hoping I'd done it quickly enough to make them think I wasn't home.

It had been five days since I'd lost the medical director position and I'd been dodging their texts ever since. I knew they'd been worried about me after I'd broken the news to them, but I hadn't wanted to talk about it.

And I still didn't.

After leaving Amanar that evening, I'd gone straight home and had jumped into bed until I'd had to get up the next morning, put on a brave face and go to work pretending as if nothing had happened.

Everyone at the hospital had tried their best to put on cheerful faces around me, but I'd heard their sympathetic whispers and had caught their sidelong glances whenever I walked into the ward or an operating room.

And I *hated* being pitied.

I hadn't gotten the job I'd dreamed of since I'd first started out as a surgeon.

But *fiha kheir*[23]. One closed door didn't mean it was the end for all.

At least, that's what I'd been trying to convince myself of over the last few days.

Until today.

Today, I'd wanted nothing more than to fuse myself to this couch, sit in complete darkness, binge films and eat my weight in food—well, until my blood sugar said otherwise.

I froze and held my breath, the silence stretching out until Nakia's voice rang through the door again, louder this time.

"Azara, don't make me break down this door."

I groaned, dropping the remote. Nakia was strong and could definitely hurt someone twice her size, and while she wouldn't actually be able to break down the door, she'd keep going until I gave in.

With a sigh, I slowly rose from where I'd spent the last ten hours, the faint glow from the TV casting a dim-lighted path to my front door. I cracked it open, just enough to see Nakia and Hazel's concerned faces staring back at me. Before I could say anything, Nakia shoved past me, Hazel quietly following behind her with a shy smile.

"Why are you sitting in the dark?" Nakia asked, already making her way through my apartment, flicking on every light she could find.

I winced from the onslaught of harsh lights. "Because I can," I

---

23 *Arabic phrase that means "there's goodness in every situation"*

muttered, quickly squeezing my eyes shut.

I waited a bit for the sting to subside, before finally opening them to find both of my best friends standing in the middle of my living room.

But what I hadn't noticed before was the three large garment bags Nakia was holding and the oversized tote slung over Hazel's shoulder.

"What is that?" I asked, a little wary.

"What we're doing tonight," Nakia replied with a sly grin.

"Which is…?" I placed one hand on my hip, the other cupping my mouth.

"We're going to the masquerade ball."

"No."

"Yes."

"No, I'm not going anywhere," I shot back, motioning to my previous, comfortable Saturday night set up of snacks, blankets, and a half-empty bottle of wine on the coffee table. I wasn't scheduled back for work until Monday and had planned to not move from that spot until then. "As you can see, I already had plans,"

"You were sulking," Nakia deadpanned, tilting her head to the side.

"I was not—" Nakia shot me a look, silencing my retort.

"Fine," I muttered, slumping my shoulders. "I *was* sulking, but I'm still not going anywhere."

I crossed my arms in defiance, but Nakia wasn't having any of it.

"Besides," I added, trying one last time to make my case, "I have nothing to wear."

"Then it's a good thing I came prepared," she said smugly.

I sighed. "Look, as much as that sounds like a *brilliant* idea"—it didn't—"I'd much rather stay home."

"And we'd much prefer you come with us," Hazel chimed in, her voice soft but insistent. "We won't ask you to talk about what happened, because you'll bite our head off, so we'll wait until you're ready. But we can't, in good conscience, let you morph into this…" she trailed off, glancing down at my clothes and around my apartment, scrunching up her face.

My place isn't that bad, I thought to myself as my eyes quickly scanned the living area. But then I grimaced when I spotted the mountain of dishes in the sink, the takeaway boxes and empty snack wrappers littering the coffee table in the living room, some of it even scattered onto the floor.

"I've just been busy with work," I grumbled, lying to defend myself.

I hadn't found the energy to do much other than work, eat and sleep. Even showering had been optional these days.

Nakia exchanged a look with Hazel before shooting me a pointed stare. "Hazel's being nice, but I *will* drag you out of here if you don't change into this amazing gown I'm letting you borrow," she said, thrusting one of the garment bags at me with far more force than necessary.

She let go too quickly, and I barely managed to catch it before it hit the floor.

I let out a heavy, resigned sigh, then as a last-ditch effort, I reluctantly brought up the one and really *only* reason I wasn't going anywhere near that ball. "Michael will probably be there."

The mention of his name hung in the air for a moment, thick with the weight of everything I'd been avoiding. Although whispers of him often brushed against the edges of my thoughts, I'd done a pretty good job at ignoring them.

It helped that I hadn't seen him since I'd walked out of that conference room five days ago. As soon as he'd been appointed by the board as the new medical director of our department, he'd stuck himself into my father's former office to deal with what my father had left behind. The interim replacement had only been able to do so much, so now Michael was expected to clean up the rest.

Or at least, that's what I'd overheard my team talking about right before I'd walked into surgery.

"So what if he's there?" Nakia said, her voice carrying a hint of disdain. I hoped for Michael's sake, he never had to face her or she'd probably murder him. "You're going to hide in here because of him? Azara, my love, fuck him and not in the 'he's the hot doctor' way this time."

Hazel let out a nervous laugh, and I rolled my eyes at Nakia's remark.

"I'm not hiding," I lied, though deep down I knew I was. Avoiding him meant I didn't have to be reminded of everything that went wrong. "You know I don't love those events, and watching Samia Farès play a woman infiltrating the family who killed her twin sister is far more entertaining than a high-society ball."

"You're coming," Nakia persisted, ignoring my objections entirely. She draped the other garment bags on my dining table—the only piece of furniture left unscathed—and pointed at Hazel.

"Get her ready while I take care of this mess."

"Nakia," I protested, looking to Hazel for support, but she merely shrugged. I stood firmly in place, staring Nakia down, but I knew it was pointless.

When Nakia set her mind on something, it was a lost cause to fight against her decision. That woman was as stubborn as they come and always got what she wanted.

I let out a long breath, defeated. "Fine, I'll go," I muttered. "But you owe me," I finished, wagging a finger at her.

"Yeah, yeah. Now off you go," she said, dismissing me. She pulled her short goddess braids back with a claw clip and got to work loading my dishwasher.

"I hate you," I replied.

Nakia's booming laughter was my only response before Hazel grabbed my hand and tugged me downstairs toward my ensuite bathroom.

Seeing Michael wasn't on my list of priority, but I shouldn't let his potential presence dictate how I went on with my life.

Like Nakia had said, so what if he was here?

'SO WHAT' HAD BEEN A terrible idea.

We'd just walked into the ballroom, and already, I was regretting my decision to come. There were too many people, too many noises, and just too much of everything.

The ballroom itself was unlike anything I'd ever seen. Ivy and delicate vines snaked their way along the walls, and lush plants lined the perimeter, their deep greens and soft hues creating a breathtaking backdrop.

And the giant three-tier marble fountain centerpiece was truly what stole the show. Water gently cascaded into a beautifully crafted stone basin, the surface dotted with floating lotus flowers, while vines weaved around each tier.

Yet, although the atmosphere was meant to be serene, my nerves crackled inside my body like a live wire.

I longed for the comfort of my mountain of blankets and cheap red wine as we threaded through the parting sea of guests who'd adhered to the Botanical Garden theme with their exquisite floral gowns, and tailored linen suits, their faces hidden behind ornate masks of petals, vines and some even had butterfly designs weaved into them.

We were stopped by a few guests as we made our way to the bar, each one offering compliments and asking who'd designed our gowns. Nakia did all the talking, as she'd gotten them for us, praising the merits of Britain's most talented up-and-coming designer, Natalia Armas.

Each dress had been inspired by a different flower and designed with it in mind—tulips for Hazel, orchids for Nakia and wisterias for me. The structured bodices of our dresses were each intricately embroidered with the respective blooms, which then seamlessly cascaded into layers of tulle that mimicked their soft, flowing petals.

The gowns had been so meticulously crafted, I almost felt guilty wearing mine. They looked like pieces of art and would normally cost a fortune, but Nakia's grandmother had been the Spanish designer's mentor ever since a serendipitous encounter at *Lalla* Latifah's shop a few years back when Natalia had moved here.

When we finally reached the bar that had been transformed into a secret oasis with an ivy-covered backdrop, I let out a sigh of relief.

It was empty save for an older couple sitting at the far end because most guests didn't bother with waiting at the bar since servers impeccably dressed in various shades of greens circulated around the room with gin and herb-infused cocktails served in pastel-colored tumblers and champagne flutes.

"See? This isn't so bad," Nakia said, after ordering us one of the infused cocktails they were offering.

I shot her a glare, though under the intricate mask I wore, designed to match the wisterias on my dress, I wasn't sure it came across quite as I'd intended it.

"How long do we have to stay for?" I groaned, leaning my forearms against the sleek, polished wood of the bar that was covered in soft green moss, fairy lights woven through it and casting a soft glow over its surface.

"We've only been here for ten minutes," Nakia deadpanned.

"And yet it's felt like hours, so my question still stands."

Nakia rolled her eyes just as Hazel placed a gentle hand on my right arm. "Look we can leave anytime you want, but just try it, yeah?" she said with a comforting smile, her deep dimples making an appearance.

I could never bring myself to say no to her when she looked at me like that.

"Okay," I sighed just as the bartender returned with our drinks. Hazel's light brown eyes sparkled with triumph before we each grabbed our respective drinks and turned to face the crowd.

Watching the rich mingle amongst each other was always a fascinating spectacle, but tonight, unlike last year, I found no amusement in it. Even when Hazel and Nakia started gossiping on either side of me, I couldn't bring myself to join in.

Instead, I sipped on my drink and swayed side to side to the different orchestral renditions of some of this year's hits and older R&B classics. I was in the middle of humming along to a saxophone version of "Can We Talk" by Tevin Campbell when a cello player joined in and the music seamlessly transitioned into the first notes of a song I knew all too well.

I used to love this song—and I still did for the most part—but it was now tainted by memories I'd much rather forget. I shot back the rose flavored gin that had been my steady companion for the past hour, the sourness sending a shiver down my spine.

I moved around to ask for another round, trying to escape the rising pressure in my chest, when a sudden rush of awareness made goosebumps pepper across my skin. My entire body prickled to life and there was only one person who had the infuriating power to do that.

Don't look. Don't look. Do not *look,* my mind screamed at me, but my heart was a glutton for punishment.

My gaze darted over the crowd until it inevitably caught on Michael.

And he looked… devastating.

His hair was neatly styled back, emphasizing his chiseled features, and his dark brown eyes burned into mine with an intensity that drowned out the sound of my thundering heartbeat and held me captive. My hand gripped my empty glass so tightly I was afraid it would break, but none of that mattered.

He didn't deserve an ounce of my attention, and yet…

All of my attention was zeroed in on him.

On the single unruly strand that had fallen across his forehead, making my fingers itch to brush it back in place.

On the way his broad shoulders filled the cream linen suit, perfectly fitting him in a way that made my breath lodge itself in my throat.

But most importantly, on the regret—or guilt, I couldn't tell the difference anymore—broadcasted all over his face.

The longer I looked at him, the further the pain that had found a home inside my chest seared sharper.

How much you own my heart could never be a lie.

His words were so far engraved into the folds of my brain, I could still *hear* them.

There was something else he tried to convey with his gaze, but before I could decipher what it was, a sharp intake of a breath snapped the invisible thread tethering me to him.

I blinked myself back to reality and glanced to my side where the sound had come from. I was met with Nakia's horrified expression and the dread in her eyes froze me in place, a chill creeping up my spine.

"What is it?" I asked, my anxiety clawing its way up my throat.

"Azara." She'd said my name so quietly, it only heightened the sense of impending doom that was washing over me. Her gaze fell to her hands, and confusion joined the anxiety swirling in my chest as I followed her gaze.

She was tightly holding a piece of ivory paper that hadn't been there before.

My brows furrowed as I took it from her, the sensation of the cold paper against my fingertips sending a jolt through me. I stared down at the gossip sheet in my hands, my heart threatening to give out inside my chest as the sentences started to blur the more I tried to read.

But I didn't need to read every word. Just the few I'd been able to make out were enough to know what this was about.

Adnan Ziani. Arthur Nyx.

Bribes. Corruption.

The earlier pressure took over and I couldn't breathe.

Could barely process if this was real or a twisted figment of my imagination. In an instant, I was transported back to just a few weeks ago when that same wave of devastation had collapsed over me as I'd listened to the recording that had shattered my perception of everything I thought I'd known.

The daming details about my father's actions I'd rewinded so often they blared in my mind everytime I shut my eyes, the same ones I'd only learned about merely two weeks ago, were now splashed across the page of *The Gilded Truth* and distributed to the masses like a cruel joke.

I'd seen the author disseminate the wealthy and corrupt over the past several months, but I'd never thought I'd ever be caught in the crossfire of their new victim.

A low ripple of whispers spread across the room as my eyes caught on the last line of the column.

Michael Young.

The voices around me seemed to fade as my gaze found him again. Holding an identical issue to the one I'd inadvertently crumpled under my fist.

He stood across the room, in the same spot I'd found him in just a few minutes ago. But this time, his eyes were wide with shock, his expression almost mirroring the one I was sure was reflected on my own features.

A flicker of uncertainty flashed across his face and my brain found itself caught in a whirlwind of wild theories.

Why would the gossip columnist privately send me the information beforehand only to publicize it a couple weeks later? Was *he* responsible for this?

I didn't know if he *was* behind this coup, but right now, reason battled with the dull ache settling in my chest, adding another mark to the betrayal that had cut so deep I worried I'd never find a way to come back from it.

"I'll be right back," I told no one in particular, barely managing to keep my voice steady. The weight of everyone's eyes on me bore down on my chest and smothered my supply of oxygen. Faces in front of me began to blur as the pressure heightened and my pulse quickened. "I need to use the restroom."

"Do you want us to come with you?" I heard one of my best friends ask, but I couldn't hear them over the sound of my heartbeat roaring in my ears.

I didn't answer. I rushed out of the ballroom, desperately needing to be anywhere else. The buzz of resuming conversation, of people already onto other topics, blended into a hollow sound as I pushed through the crowd.

I was gasping for air, my chest constricting with a feeling I hadn't experienced in years. The last time I'd felt like this, I'd walked into the house I grew up in, bursting with excitement with matching shirts for my parents in hand to announce I'd gotten into my top medical school, only to have that happiness shattered when I stumbled on a horrifying image that still haunted me every year on its anniversary.

I'd barely made it to the corridor when I heard him call out my name, "Azara."

My heart skipped a beat as I realized I'd been walking the opposite way from the restrooms. I tried to walk faster, and rounded a corner, hoping it'd give me an escape.

Only to be led to a dead end.

I could retrace my steps and find somewhere else to hide but he was already here. I could feel him watching me and carefully drawing closer, the sound of his shoes rubbing against the concrete.

I spun around and found him standing just a few feet away, breathing heavily and still holding that bloody column.

The sudden surge of anger that engulfed me was unlike anything I'd ever felt before.

Gone was the sadness of how things had turned out.

Gone was the longing for things to be different.

All of it had been snuffed out and anger conquered.

"Did you do this?" I demanded, my words coming out ragged.

"What?" he asked, taken aback.

My chest tightened as I spoke my next words. "Do you hate me so much you'd expose my father like this? Wasn't blackmailing him to resign enough? You had to ruin his name too?"

His face tightened at my accusation. "What? *No*, I didn't—" He faltered as he gripped the back of his head. "I could never hate you," he added, his voice cracking at the end.

The agony dripping from his words traveled through my entire body and threatened to submerge me so I let out a humorless laugh to drown the pain scorching my chest. "I don't even know why I asked. Why should I believe anything you say anymore?"

He reached for me, but I flinched away from his touch and a flash of pain crossed his features as his eyes softened, filling with anguish.

"I know I haven't given you a reason to, and this is possibly the worst thing for me to say right now, but I just need you to trust me. I need you to trust me until I can explain everything. I wish I could do it, but that would lead to consequences I can't even bring myself to think about."

He ran his hands back and forth over his head and let out a frustrated groan.

"I don't hate you." Michael's voice grew hoarse. "There's not a universe that could ever exist where I could even fathom hating you. I want to say *so* much more but—"

"You need to leave," Nakia's voice cut through the air, her words harsh and final.

I looked past his shoulder to find her just behind him, her face set in a scowl and her eyes blazing with a protective fury.

Michael kept his attention on me, a series of unspoken words filtering in the chasm between us that he'd created.

"Don't make me repeat myself," Nakia warned, her voice unwavering.

The heavy cloak of a suffocating silence fell over us until Michael's face fell, his shoulders slumping in defeat.

Without another word, he left.

Again.

As soon as he was out of sight, Nakia moved toward me, placing a steadying hand on my arm while Hazel appeared at my other side. I didn't know whether she'd just showed up or she'd been here all along.

"I've got an idea," Nakia said, the sudden shift in her tone almost making me forget why we were standing here.

I glanced over at her, brows furrowed, and found her quickly typing something on her phone before looking back at me.

"Your last idea led us here," I muttered, a weary sigh escaping my lips. "I'm not really in the mood to hear any more ideas right now."

"Just trust me."

I hesitated. My trust had been so battered recently, it made it hard for me to believe anyone, even her. But this was Nakia. In the thirty years I'd known her, she'd always fiercely protected me.

So, despite my wariness at her sudden new idea, I grabbed her hand and followed her out of Anzar.

"A RAGE ROOM," I SAID, utterly dumbfounded, as we stepped out of the taxi.

Nakia had kept her lips sealed for the entire twenty minute drive. I'd come up with a few ideas of wherever she was taking us, but Smash Labs hadn't even crossed my radar.

My gaze traveled from the red neon sign down to where the girls stood at the front of the brick building.

"And in these gowns?" Hazel questioned, a brow raised, and I glanced down at my dress because she had a point.

Nakia just shrugged at her concern. "They're just clothes. Now, come on," Nakia urged, holding the front door open with her foot and gesturing for us to hurry up.

Hazel and I looked at each other for a moment before we followed Nakia's lead. The place was open 24/7 as it said on the sign above the front desk, but it was mostly empty save for the single worker behind the counter and the few clients shuffling out of their sessions.

Unfazed by the curious stares, Nakia pulled out her Centurion card and slid it across the counter. "Give us your largest room and book us an unlimited session."

The man flicked his gaze to the credit card before looking at Nakia, his brows pulled together. "We don't have—"

"It wasn't a question," she replied firmly. There was a brief moment of hesitation before he took it and processed the payment before handing Nakia her card back with a trembling hand.

After watching the fifteen minute safety video, we each donned protective gear—facial shields, and gloves—and changed from our heels and into boots they'd provided for us.

The terrified worker didn't even dare ask us to change out of our dresses after Nakia glared at him. He simply closed the door of the room he'd escorted us to on his way out.

My gaze roamed over the space, taking it in. Baseball bats, sledgehammers and an assortment of other tools were hung on one of the walls while three large tables were gathered in the center of the room. Each was stacked high with glasses, dishes, and other various trinkets I couldn't make out from where I stood. There were even smaller televisions, computers and printers dispersed around the room.

Nakia appeared at my side and handed me a wooden bat.

"Let it out," she simply said.

I eyed her for a moment, before deciding to grab it from her. Destroying things wasn't really something I did, I usually fixed them. But maybe I should give this a try.

I'd heard about people paying to come here and vent their stress and anger by smashing breakable objects.

I turned the bat over in my hands as I walked around the room, eyeing the dishware and electronics around us. I didn't know where to start or if this was even a good idea, but when my eyes eventually caught on a small recorder, one eerily similar to the one that had been sent to me, all of my emotions from earlier erupted to the surface again.

My pulse drummed louder as I approached it.

I didn't even take the time to take a deep breath before my grip around the bat tightened and I swung it over my head before slamming it down. I did it a few more times, imagining it was the one I kept in my bedside table drawer, until the small device was in tatters.

But it wasn't enough to expunge the growing pressure inside my chest.

So instead, I grabbed a fistful of my dress and charged toward the table with a pile of dishes. I was about to take my bat to it, when the sight of a sledgehammer filled my vision.

I let go of the bat in my hands, the wooden club clattering to the floor, and took the tool. I didn't pay much attention to who had given it to me when I hit the plates again, and again, and again, until they all splintered into dust.

After that, I vented my frustration on anything that crossed my path. Nothing was safe as I took every ounce of anguish I'd kept locked inside, and released it.

I don't hate you.

I smashed a vase.

There's not a universe that could ever exist where I could even fathom hating you.

I threw the sledgehammer and reached for another bat before turning my attention to the screen of a television until it was barely recognizable.

I just need you to trust me.

How could I trust him after he'd shattered it into jagged pieces. The bitter taste of betrayal, anger and hurt all wrapped into one still lingering in the back of my throat as I kept swinging, reveling in the shower of glass and ceramic, until there was nothing left for me to break.

Only then did I stop.

I sank to my knees, and my bat clattered to the floor somewhere near. My chest was heaving, so I placed my gloves hands on my thighs as I tried to regulate my ragged breathing. But my throat felt raw and my sight grew blurry the more I looked at the chaos I'd caused.

At how it mirrored what I felt inside.

Suddenly, everything inside me burned and I felt suffocated under the weight of the protective gear. I needed it off. Now.

I threw the gloves aside and tore off the facial shield, letting it join where I'd sent the gloves off. I tried to blink to clear my vision, but it didn't work.

Instead, something warm and wet slid down my cheek. It was such a foreign sensation that I didn't want to touch it.

I was afraid of what it might trigger if I acknowledged it.

Afraid that I wouldn't be able to stop it.

"We're right here." I heard voices say from afar. Warm hands—familiar hands—wrapped around mine, their fingers interlacing with mine.

"I'm fine," I instinctively said, but my voice was so hoarse, I didn't even know if my words were even comprehensible.

"It's okay not to be," someone said and I recognized it was Hazel.

Another tear fell.

I knew I hadn't been fine in a very long time, but it was always easier to pretend I was than to sit and contemplate what it looked like not to be. I couldn't afford not being okay, people relied on me.

Not being okay meant I couldn't be there for them.

A sob threatened to wrack my chest, but I swallowed it down.

"It's okay to let it out," Nakia said this time.

Her words had only meant to be reassuring, but instead, they cut through me so deep, the gates I'd been fiercely protecting for years were ripped open. My shoulders slumped and the exhaustion of everything I'd held back for so long caught up to me.

My emotions had been beaten down raw and I didn't have the strength anymore to hold it together like I'd done for the last fifteen years.

Every fear, frustration and heartbreak broke free and poured out of me.

I cried for the first time in what felt like forever.

I cried until my chest hurt and my head screamed at me to stop.

I cried until there was nothing left inside me to give.

I didn't know how much time had passed, but when my tears slowed, I let my head fall on Nakia's shoulder.

"I'm sorry," I said, my voice cracking through a lingering sob.

Hazel tightened her grip around my hand. "You have nothing to apologize for."

"What she said," Nakia echoed.

I peered at our reflections in the mirrored wall in front of us. We looked ridiculous in our expensive gowns surrounded by the aftermath of my wreckage, but the sight shifted something inside me.

It made me realize that I'd spent so long being adamant on sheltering myself to avoid getting hurt, it only led me to foster a home for something far worse.

Something that would eat me alive if I let it continue on to fester.

I'd kept my emotions at bay for so long, thinking that was the answer. That if I just held on tight enough, that it would become the perfect solution to controlling everything and I wouldn't feel or get hurt.

But the truth was, I'd already been hurting and most importantly, I couldn't control everything. No matter how hard I'd tried to.

My mother's accident hadn't been my fault.

My father's dejection following her death shouldn't have been my responsibility.

I'd taken on so much on my shoulders that I hadn't stopped to think: What about *me*? What about being okay—happy—for *myself*?

By focusing so much on controlling every variable, I'd inadvertently suffocated myself in the process. I'd let its poison slowly wrap around my heart and suppress my feelings until it ate away at me from the inside out and became too much to bear.

I'd been breaking myself all along and I hadn't even realized it.

But I didn't have to stay trapped in a prison of my own making.

Although broken things couldn't be mended, they could foster something else.

New beginnings.

Change was terrifying, but it was also inevitable.

And maybe, just maybe, I was finally ready for it.

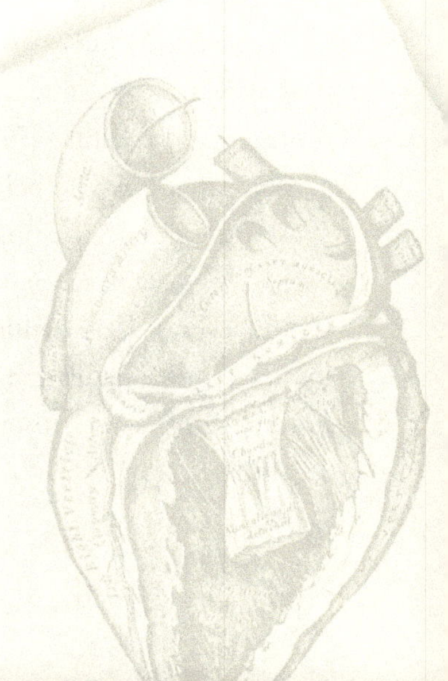

CHAPTER 41

MICHAEL

"HOW MANY DRINKS HAVE YOU had?"

My gaze moved up to see Sofiane slide into the seat across from me, placing his worn computer bag onto the table. He still wore a tailored suit which told me he'd got off work and came straight here.

I held my tumbler up. "Just the one," I replied.

It was a Monday evening and I'd been at Rubis Rouge for the past several hours, nursing the same drink. I worked early tomorrow morning and couldn't afford a hangover.

Not that it would help numb my sorrows or quiet my mind.

Nothing did. Trust me, I tried.

A server with tanned skin, and wavy brown hair came over to see if Sofiane wanted anything to drink or if I wanted a refill. Her face looked vaguely familiar, but she must have been the one who'd brought me my drink earlier, though I hadn't been paying attention to much recently.

She came back a few seconds later with his bottled water, before telling us to let her know if we needed anything. Once she left, Sofiane's gaze lingered on her for a few seconds before he turned his attention to me.

He eyed me for a moment before he spoke. "How," he hesitated, "how's the new job?"

I knew he wanted to comment on how I looked like I'd only slept a few hours in the last three weeks—which was the case—but unlike Amar, Sofiane didn't broach uncomfortable subjects unless absolutely necessary or he was forced to.

"Do you really want the answer to that?" I asked curtly, glancing back at him with a raised brow.

He winced at my tone and began toying with the cap of the water bottle.

I immediately felt bad for how short I'd been.

I sighed. "It's been busy, like I'd expected," I replied before he apologized for overstepping. I twirled the remaining amber liquid around in my tumbler. "I've had to catch up on months of untouched paperwork and handle some pressing budget issues," I added, hoping the voluntary concession would make up for my brusqueness.

"That sounds like a nightmare," Sofiane commented, his expression apologetic.

"Yeah," I sighed, though it was nothing compared to the nightmare my mind had been a prisoner of.

I knew being a medical director wouldn't be the most thrilling job, but I hadn't expected to be glued to a desk almost everyday. I missed operating, but if I was being honest, I missed *her*.

I missed being *with* her.

Walking away from her once had been torture.

Doing it a second time had ripped me apart.

Except the punishment of losing her was entirely my fault.

I was the reason I'd spent the last month in unrelenting hell where everywhere I turned, she haunted me. Where every little thing I came across or thought of reminded me of her and I hadn't been able to find peace no matter what I did.

But I deserved it.

I'd done this to her. To myself. To *us*.

I often thought about how her life would have been better if I'd just stayed away. If I'd just done what I'd been supposed to and completed my Order without wanting to ingrain myself in everything that involved her.

But then I wouldn't have met the best thing that had ever happened to me.

I caught glimpses of her whenever I came out of her father's office—well *my* office now, and every time I wanted to run after her. To fall to my knees, confess everything and beg for her forgiveness.

Except it wasn't the time just yet.

I hadn't followed the rules before and look where it got me.

As much as it destroyed me, I had to stay away until I'd fixed everything else.

Starting with why Sofiane was here.

I glanced above his shoulder and did a quick scan of the room. The pub was largely empty except for a man that seemed to be in his fifties and was on his eighth drink of the night, and a few other miscellaneous customers that seemed to be regulars.

We could have gone to Azel, but after the fiasco of the masquerade ball, it was better to avoid it. Although I'd done everything in my power to contain the gossip mill after *The Gilded Truth*'s latest issue by collecting every issue and threatening anyone if the content left the ballroom, it didn't stop the prying eyes that followed such a scandal.

It was a small blessing that the damning issue hadn't made it to the general public, but the damage had already been done. Reputation was everything in our world and anyone of importance had been present that night.

My name had briefly been mentioned, but it was nothing compared to what the author of the column had exposed about Adnan Ziani and his unsavory connection to Arthur Nyx.

I was just about to ask Sofiane if he'd found anything while analyzing the issue I'd given him since neither him nor Amar had been present that night, when the latter finally showed up.

"Hello boys," Amar greeted us, slapping his hands down on Sofiane's shoulders with a cheeky grin. "Miss me?"

"You're late," I told him, shooting him a look as Sofiane shrugged him off.

"Only by a few minutes," he replied and I rolled my eyes as he settled into the seat next to Sofiane. "Alright, what'd I miss?"

"Nothing yet," I answered. Before he commented on how I'd just admonished him for being late when nothing had been discussed, I leaned back against the booth and got straight to the point.

"Tell me either of you have good news."

Sofiane hesitated for a moment, his fingers absentmindedly fiddling with the strap of his satchel. Letting out a small sigh, he pulled his laptop out. "I don't know if you'll consider this good news," Sofiane started, sliding on his glasses. He tapped a few keys on his keyboard before turning his computer screen toward me. "But I found this."

Multiple tabs were open with different sections of the issue I'd given him displayed. Some were enlarged, while others were side-by-side comparisons with other issues of the gossip column that had been published over the last fourteen months.

My gaze shifted from the screen back to him with a raised brow.

"What am I looking at?"

Sofiane tilted his laptop slightly so that Amar and I could both see.

"At first glance, the issue from the masquerade ball seemed just like any other. But when I studied its content and prose, I noted some discrepancies. You see here." Sofiane pointed at one of the side-by-side. "The writing style is almost identical but the real author is very peculiar with the string of words they use. In all thirty seven issues, they've never strayed from their intentional prose. Until this one. "

He paused, giving a moment for the information to sink in. "It *could* very much be a coincidence," he added, "but I highly doubt it."

"He's right," Amar chimed in. "I couldn't retrieve any fingerprints or DNA, but I analyzed the paper and ink used for printing. Although remarkably similar, and almost undetectable to the untrained eye, the fibers in the paper and the pigment in the ink are different from anything released in the past."

"So you're telling me this was a copycat?"

They both nodded in unison, confirming my suspicions.

After I came home from the ball, I'd spent the entire night reading that column over and over and I couldn't shake the nagging feeling in the back of my mind that something was off.

So, I'd immediately gotten to work and called them in for reinforcements. I'd hesitated at first because although it wasn't an Atlas related-matter, it was close enough to potentially warrant a visit from The Fixer or worse our fathers.

But I'd taken my chances, and so far, we'd been in the clear which meant one of two things. This was a completely isolated incident or our father's were watching from afar.

Either way I didn't care.

I'd get to the bottom of this—with or without their approval.

My birthday was only days away and there were certain things I needed to clear up before I could complete my Ascension.

And it started with whoever this impersonator was.

The Gilded Truth had been the cause of many's downfall, but I refused to let it be mine.

Or Azara's.

"Someone was responsible for the masquerade ball but it wasn't *The Gilded Truth*. Whoever did this, it was personal," Amar echoed what I'd been thinking.

I fixed my attention on Sofiane. "I need you to find who did this."

"I can keep looking, but it'll take me some time."

"We don't *have* time," I shot back, frustration creeping into my voice.

He tugged his laptop back to him and adjusted his glasses, pushing them higher up his nose. "I understand that, but I've already spent almost three weeks on this, and still haven't found anything. I'm excellent, but I can't perform miracles, Michael." Sofiane's tone remained soft, but I could hear the undercurrent of displeasure in his voice.

My irritation wasn't aimed at him, but I hated feeling out of control. Not being able to get to the bottom of this would mean losing the love of my life.

I was prepared to give up anything. But not her.

Never her.

"How long?"

Sofiane shrugged uncomfortably. "From a few weeks to a few months? But it could take me longer."

I sighed heavily and rubbed my temples, the aura of a headache blooming on the horizon. This was far from what I'd hoped to hear, but I knew I couldn't rush him. If I had a choice, I'd devote myself to helping him hunt whoever this was, but time wasn't on my side with my

Ascension looming closer.

As much as I despised being patient, it seemed that I now had no choice but to wait and move to the next thing on my list while I looked for another angle to pursue and Sofiane worked on deciphering this.

I sighed, standing from my seat. "Just keep me updated," I said, my knuckles rasping against the wooden table between us. "I have something to take care of."

I grabbed my wool overcoat from next to me and slid out of the booth. I walked briskly to the exit, the evening air cool against my skin as I made my way to my Rolls-Royce parked out front. I climbed inside and made the thirty minute drive to the only thing I knew with confidence I could take care of.

During the entire ride, I turned over every detail of the situation in my head, hoping to find a connection I might have missed.

If the author of the latest issue wasn't the original writer, then why target Azara's father? Why would they want to lay out his crimes for everyone to see when they'd done it privately just a few weeks prior?

Were they after Nyx? And if they were, why attach Ziani to it?

Arthur's actions were incriminating enough that involving the doctor didn't make sense. NyxMedica had already been under investigation by the authorities for medical negligence and fraud, the column only drew more attention to the engineer's fraudulent activities.

I kept sifting through the information when a hypothesis struck me like a bolt of lightning. Once I parked in front of the townhouse, I pulled my phone out of my pocket and dialed Sofiane's number.

He picked up on the first ring. "What is it?" I could hear Amar's voice in the background, which meant the two were still together.

"Remember what I found on Simons?" I asked, stepping out of my car and walking toward the front door.

"Yeah, what about it?"

"Do you still have it?"

He hummed in agreement.

"Get Amar to test it while you see if you can find any connections," I said before hanging up. It might be a long shot, but it was worth looking into.

After dealing with Simons, I'd stopped by Sofiane's flat to make a copy of the original picture of my sister, as well as the note that had been left with Simons, before confronting my father about it.

Just in case, I had thought to myself.

It was a good thing that I didn't trust my father implicitly and had known he'd shut me out before I started asking too many questions. His threat from weeks ago might have held weight then, but an Atlas didn't yield.

It was time for me to step into my rightful role.

I shelved those thoughts for later and knocked on the red door three times. The last time I'd been here, the circumstances had been entirely different and I'd had a singular goal in mind.

Take him down.

This time, I hoped that the man I once saw as an obstacle would accept my help, even if I was responsible for his current predicament.

The door swung open, and the father of the love of my life stood before me, astounded to see me on his front steps.

"What are you doing here?" he asked, his voice laced with suspicion and growing indignation.

"We need to talk."

CHAPTER 42

MICHAEL

"WHY ARE YOU HELPING ME?" Adnan asked, just as I began going down the front steps.

I turned around and faced him. His expression was still wary of my presence here, but he was much more relaxed than when I showed up less than an hour ago.

Our conversation hadn't been long—nor did it need to be—but I'd gotten what I'd needed from him. Now all I had left to do was help clear his name. I wasn't sorry for completing my Order, and he'd been responsible for his own demise, but without this, there'd be no coming back for what I wanted in the end. He didn't know about the House, but my motives had nothing to do with being an Atlas.

I looked him squarely in the eye. "Because I'm in love with your daughter."

My heart twisted painfully at the confession. I'd known for a long time now that I was in love with Azara, but I'd never said the words out loud or admitted them to anyone. I'd always imagined that Azara would be the first to hear them, but there was no point in hiding the truth from him.

His eyes widened at my admission, a mix of surprise and disbelief flashing across his features. "*My* daughter?"

I nodded once. "Yes."

His jaw set into a hard line and protectiveness hardened his features as he crossed his arms tightly over his chest. "What makes you think I'd ever give you my blessing?"

I slid my hands in the pockets of my coat and didn't shy away from his sharp gaze. "I don't need your blessing. I only need hers."

His eyes lit up with indignation at my response, but there was a hint of respect hidden beneath his apparent disapproval.

Azara's father might hold significance in her life, but to me, only her opinion mattered. I didn't owe him anything and I was already doing more than he likely deserved.

But seeing the anguish on her face at her thinking her father's situation had been her fault when it had been mine had broken my heart. And I'd do just about anything to make things right for her.

"I should leave before they get back."

Azara and her brother were out for the evening to watch some sort of musical, and the last time I'd checked her location, they were on their way back.

Despite how much I longed to see her, I doubted she wanted the same.

Especially here of all places.

I'd made it to my car when I remembered the one thing I needed to make sure Ziani did for me. I turned back to glance at him. "I don't want her to know," I called out before he closed the door.

His brows pulled together. "Why?"

I didn't want Azara to think that I'd helped her father in some calculated attempt to win her back. It would be a lie to say I hadn't considered using it to my advantage, but it wasn't fair or right to do so. I wanted to make amends and deserve her forgiveness by my actions toward *her*, not by any favor that I could do for her.

But I kept that to myself.

Without another word, I climbed into my car, the engine roaring to life as Adnan retreated back into his house. I didn't pull away immediately, and instead lingered in the driveway as I replayed our conversation in my mind and what I'd learned. I had a week left before my Ascension, and wanted to wrap this up before then.

Otherwise it'd be too late.

I was about to dial Sofiane's number when an eerie sensation crawled up the back of my neck. Before I could place it, something sharp pricked my neck. My hand flew up instinctively to find out what it was, when a wave of drowsiness hit me, dulling my thoughts and slowing them to a crawl.

My hand grew heavier while a tightness gripped my lungs. My head lolled back, my breaths growing increasingly shallower with each passing second.

Through the fog, I heard someone mutter something before my vision faded to black.

THE FIRST THING THAT HIT me was the smell—like wet earth and mildew.

The staleness in the air clung to my lungs and made it hard to draw in a proper breath. There was even a faint, bitter chemical scent that made my stomach churn so I squeezed my eyes and wrinkled my nose, hoping to somehow dissipate the smell, but it was no use.

I groggily stirred, but they must have injected me with some sort of sedative because a dull throbbing headache drummed against my temples. Even my body felt like it had been dipped in concrete, my muscles stiff as I tried to regain sensation that was slowly beginning to creep back into my arms and legs.

I slowly opened my eyes to gather my surroundings but there was a black hood over my head, keeping me from seeing where I was or if there was anyone in the room with me.

"Where am I?" I muttered, the words coming out slurred with how dry my mouth was, like I'd swallowed sand.

I forced myself to push past the dizziness and figure out what happened.

The last thing I remembered was leaving Ziani's place and getting in my car. After that, everything was dark. Was he behind this? A retaliation after what I'd done. But that wouldn't make sense, it would be stupid of him after I offered to end his entanglements with Nyx.

Just as I started to gather enough of my bearings to figure out how I got here and more importantly, how I could get out, a blaring sound echoed in the space around me.

"Young Seungwon," I heard my name over my pounding headache. "Welcome to your Atlas trials."

My what?

Was that where I was? The House?

This didn't make any sense. My Ascension wasn't for another week, why was I already here? What about my job? People would wonder where I'd gone off to without notice. Besides, I'd never heard or read anything about trials.

A lot was kept under wraps until we officially became members, but we'd been briefed about the night of our Ascension.

Completing our Order was meant to be the only thing we were expected to do.

But I should have anticipated this.

After all, we'd always been taught not to trust everything and question things.

This should have been no different.

I tried to move but quickly realized my hands were shackled in front of me and I was in nothing but my underwear. I shifted uncomfortably, the cold metal of cuffs digging into my skin, as I attempted to break my wrists free, but suddenly, hands grabbed me from behind and yanked me to my feet.

I wanted to fight them, but thought better of it. It was smarter to save my strength for whatever was about to come from these trials. Whatever that meant.

And this was the House. Any sign of resistance would probably have me terminated and I didn't make it this far to die now.

My cuffed wrists were brought above my head, the strain pulling on my shoulders, before the hood was pulled from my head. I took in a deep breath, but the damp smell was so pungent, the phantom taste settled on the back of my tongue.

I moved to peel my eyes open, when a blinding spotlight blared right at me. I winced, blinking several times, waiting for my eyes to adjust.

I wasn't exactly sure where I was, but I knew it was somewhere inside the House. They wouldn't have brought me anywhere else for this.

I stood on a sunken circular platform in the middle of a two-storied stone chamber. There were empty tiered-wooden benches around me and I was strung up to a metal structure like a witch about to be burned at the stake, my bare feet barely touching the floor.

My body was pulled so tight, my muscles were screaming for relief. I looked up and felt my hands growing numb from the frigid temperature and how tightly the metal cuffs were digging into my skin from the new position.

Unlike the room I'd been in before, this one was weathered by time and the acrid smell that overpowered my senses suggested this place had been witness to countless atrocities.

And I was about to become another one of its victims.

"Let the trials begin," the same voice from earlier called out, just as a figure emerged from one of the arched openings ahead of me, a creaking sound of wheels joining the echo of their footsteps.

At first, the blinding glare made it impossible to make out who it was. It wasn't until he stood a few feet away from me that I recognized him. I'd only seen the man once before, but once had been enough to never forget his face.

He looked older, his former black hair now peppered with streaks of grays, but the jagged scar that spanned from his right brow to his hairline was still there.

His presence had been discomforting when I was nineteen, but being the entire subject of his attention now was slightly terrifying.

I couldn't make out what was displayed on his cart, but it didn't matter. It might even be better if I remained ignorant of what was in store for me.

The Fixer's cold, steely eyes were fixed on me with a piercing intensity. I waited on bated breath for him to say or do something, but he just stood there. Hours may have passed of him simply staring at me because I'd lost count after counting to thirty-seven minutes.

The torture of waiting for what came next was almost as painful as the physical strain of the position my body was hung in. My muscles were screaming in protest from being forced to remain outstretched.

My wrists ached from the cold iron as the metal dug into my skin. My head throbbed with each heartbeat, fatigue washing over me and threatening to take me under.

But I knew I couldn't fall asleep or move to alleviate some of the pain.

I wasn't sure what type of test or trial this was meant to be, but I shoved any distractions of my body's response to this waiting game to the back of my brain and focused on staying awake and not faltering from his gaze.

I waited and waited until *finally*, he moved. I almost sighed with relief, but I swallowed it back before it escaped my lips. Wishfully, I wanted this to be the end of whatever this was meant to be, but I knew it wouldn't be this easy.

Without averting his gaze from mine, he reached for a needle on the cart and headed right for me, his movement slow and deliberate. My instincts screamed at me to fight against my restraints, but I didn't move.

Just like I hadn't for the entire standstill.

When he stopped in front of me, I braced for impact but nothing came. At first.

Then the sharp sting of a needle bit into my thigh.

I swallowed a curse as I tried to maintain my composure. "A warning would have been nice," I commented, forcing my voice to remain steady as if that didn't bloody hurt.

He didn't respond. He never did.

He merely stepped back and resumed his previous position.

My worry didn't have time to take root as I wondered what he'd injected me with, because soon the room I was held in started to shift, and everything around me softened at the edges. Like I was drifting away from my body and becoming an observer to my upcoming predicament. Even my previously sore limbs felt light, distant, as if they belonged to someone else.

And I slowly became too disoriented to realize he'd injected me with ketamine or to question why. Just a few minutes later, I got my answer when the Fixer returned with a scalpel in hand, the cold gleam of the blade catching in the glaring light

Then, he started what I assumed was the trial the earlier overhead voice mentioned.

Each strike to my torso was followed by a fresh shallow cut on my lower abdomen. I could still feel the pain from his ministrations, but it almost felt distant. As if it was happening to someone else. And I didn't know which was worse. Feeling the pain or being so detached from it, I couldn't gauge the extent of the damage I was sustaining.

I tried to maintain my focus on what was happening, but every time a semblance of clarity washed over me, he injected me with another dose.

Agony became an elusive concept and the ordeal stretched on to a point where every second that passed twisted into a slow crawl, but my perception of time was too distorted to grasp how long it lasted.

Until it finally stopped.

The moment the Fixer stepped back, I heard a clicking sound above me and my wrists were released. I crumpled to my knees, but I barely felt the impact of the cold concrete against my knees.

My visions blurred and my head swam with the remnants of the last dose still coursing through my veins. My eyes fluttered, my eyelids growing heavier with each passing second, until hands dragged me off the stage.

At a certain point, I was pulled onto something soft, but it barely registered in my disoriented state. My head lolled to the side, as I was wheeled away to god knows where

Right before everything faded away, I caught a glimpse of three masked figures, standing motionless behind where I'd been held and I could feel their gazes intently aimed at me. For a brief moment, I wondered if they'd been there the entire time.

Until darkness swallowed me whole.

I SMELLED THE BLOOD BEFORE I opened my eyes.

The copper scent was so thick and oppressive, I couldn't draw a single breath without the metallic taste choking my lungs. As a surgeon, I'd gotten accustomed to the sight and smell of blood.

But this… this was different.

Every inhale only deepened the dread of the gory scene that awaited me and I fought against the bile rising up my throat from the pungent smell. I braced myself and blinked away the grogginess until the room came into gradual focus.

I didn't know how much time had passed since I'd last been here—it could have been a few hours or days—but I was back in the same stone chamber again.

This time, however, I found myself clad in scrubs, my cuffed wrists tethered to the floor, and right before me, no more than ten feet away, were two bodies restrained to operating tables with a towering monitor between them, its glaring red countdown ticking down from fifteen minutes.

My eyes widened at the grisly sight, but my instincts immediately kicked in, my brain quickly catching up, and assessing the situation. Surgical drapes covered them from chin up and waist down, each mangled body hooked up to monitors and IVs, but no screens were switched on.

I stood up, grimacing from being knocked about, and tugged at the chain, testing how far I could move, when the same deep, distorted voice from however long ago it was—one I was growing to resent—halted me in my tracks.

"Choose."

What?

I furrowed my brows in confusion, my mind struggling to make sense of what it was asking me.

"Choose," it repeated, more insistent now. Then, the monitor in the middle blinked and an entire minute was shaved off in an instant.

I stood there for a moment, frozen, because it couldn't possibly be asking me to choose between the two.

"What? No," I retorted to whoever was listening, my voice rising as I tugged harder on the chain. "Let me out. I'm not—"

"Choose," the voice growled, the sound reverberating against the stone walls and taunting me with its command.

The timer blinked again and another minute was deducted.

"Alright, alright, okay," I spat, as I watched the seconds go down. "I'll choose, just stop." Fifteen minutes was barely enough to make a proper assessment and I was down to less than thirteen. I couldn't afford angering whoever was in charge of this twisted game.

But I didn't even know who needed my help more. I had no insight on their conditions, no knowledge of their medical histories, no idea what injuries they'd sustained or what their vitals signs and results of diagnostic tests were.

My pulse quickened as the urgency of the situation pressed down on me and it felt like the walls were closing in on me.

Twelve minutes.

Shit. What kind of trial was this? I'd been called out in the dead of night more times than I could count to stitch up strangers—sometimes in conditions far worse than these—but this was sick and went against everything I believed as a doctor.

How do you make the right decision with no information? What if I chose wrong or worse one of them was already dead?

Michael, get a bloody grip. You're a doctor, for god's sake.

I steeled my shoulders and forced my gaze to flick back and forth between the bodies, trying to glean any hint that might help me decide, but their bodies were in such bad shape, it was difficult to assess from my vantage point.

I didn't want to fucking do this, but the uncertainty of what would happen if I didn't choose wasn't something I wanted to find out. Especially if it meant neither of them receiving any medical attention.

Eleven minutes.

I made an instinctual decision. "The one on the right," I shouted.

The moment the words left my mouth, my restraints clattered to the floor and a blaring, shrill beep pierced the air, breaking through the silence like a jagged knife.

Both monitors flickered to life.

The sight of the readings relayed that both were in critical conditions, but my stomach lurched when the patient on the left's heart readings transformed into the dreaded straight line of asystole.

Without hesitation, I rushed to his side to begin CPR and formulate a plan with the limited resources that were laid out for me. I'd barely made it to his side when the floor beneath him opened up and with it the patient vanished.

I stood there, stunned for a moment, starting at the empty space where the patient had just been seconds ago. The screen next to me flashed and when I glanced over at the countdown again, two more minutes had been deleted.

"You've got to be kidding me," I gritted out.

I had less than nine minutes now to help the other patient before whatever the fuck happened after the timer ran out. If it wasn't someone's life at stake, I wouldn't entertain this.

But I didn't have that luxury.

I snapped my focus back to the remaining patient. There was so much fucking blood everywhere, coating the floor in thick, dark pools. I couldn't even see their face, since it was trapped under some sort of locked contraption.

This is so fucked.

I swiftly donned a mask, and gloves then assessed him as best as I could given the limitations. I checked his vitals, then his chest for any trauma before reaching for the stethoscope to listen to his heart.

I glanced at the clock.

Eight minutes.

I shut my eyes for a brief moment, drawing in a deep breath, fighting to steady my racing pulse. I needed steady hands and a sharp mind to do this because one wrong move and I'd kill him.

I let everything around me fade away—the relentless ticking clock hanging over my head, the shrill, incessant beeping of the monitors, the oppressive silence suffocating the air. Until all I could hear was the slowly steadying drum of my own heartbeat.

You've done this a thousand times, I told myself, though a small, lingering voice in the back of my mind retorted that I'd never done it blind *and* in a non-sterile environment like this one.

Because of course they'd have all this bloody equipment, and no ultrasound.

Dragging the small cart with supplies behind me, I quickly identified the key landmarks, sterilized the area with whatever antibacterial cleanser I found, then draped it with sterile towels.

His condition was deteriorating at a frightening pace, and there wasn't any time for anesthesia—not that I had time to look for it. I hoped, for his sake, that he was sedated or this would be much harder. I was flying blind, relying entirely on years of experience, and prayed to anything that was up there that my differential was accurate.

With no time for hesitation, I drove the needle in and reached for the syringe, carefully attaching it. After positioning the needle where I needed it to be, I began aspirating.

The ticking countdown seemed to stretch into an eternity as I watched the syringe with bated breath. For a moment, I wondered if I'd made a mistake when blood-tinged fluid filled the syringe and my shoulders sagged with relief.

With no catheter to help, I kept aspirating until *finally* his blood pressure and heart rate improved. After finally pulling the needle free, my hands gripped the side of the table and I exhaled a breath I hadn't realized I'd been holding.

I glanced at the clock beside me, noting I'd made it with ten seconds to spare.

Ten bloody seconds.

A flood of what ifs rushed through my thoughts as I watched those final ten seconds slowly tick away.

What if I hadn't been right?

What if there were complications and I'd killed whoever this was?

What if I hadn't made a choice and had let the clock run out?

The countdown eventually flickered to zero, marking the end of this second trial.

Then, the screen went dark for a few moments before bold, glaring red text flashed across it.

Congratulations, Seungwon. You've made it to the final round.

I sighed and averted my gaze when the overhead lights reflected off the small ring on my pinky, the engraved *yaz* gleaming back at me.

It was meant to symbolize being a free man and breaking the chains of how this society had treated people like us.

Suddenly, despite the exhaustion that weighed on my shoulders, a fresh wave of determination surged through me. I had no idea what this final trial would bring, and if the previous two were anything to go by, it would hardly be a walk in the park.

But it didn't matter.

I'd set my mind on completing my Ascension on my own terms. And although I hadn't had a choice in the outcome of the last two, I was determined to make this one matter.

No matter the consequences.

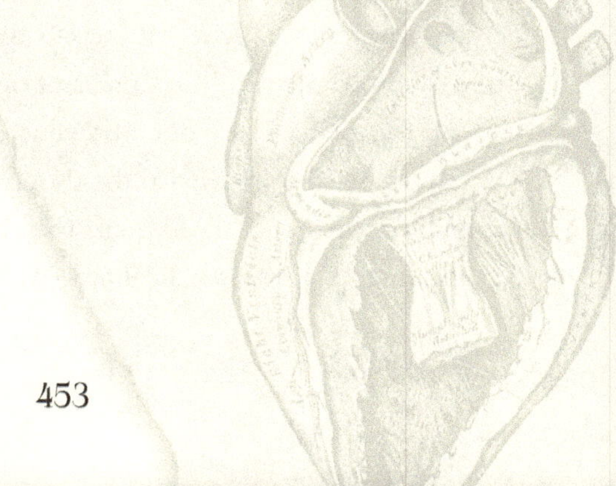

CHAPTER 43

MICHAEL

I WASN'T SURE HOW MUCH time had passed since my last trial, but unlike after my first encounter with the Fixer, I'd been kept awake this entire time.

A few minutes after I'd completed the pericardiocentesis on the stranger, said Fixer had appeared with a black hood that had been placed over my head before he'd ushered me down to wherever this cell was.

I'd been kept prisoner in this cold, cramped space of concrete with no windows and a single steel door, shrouded in endless darkness most of the time. Except when someone sporadically pushed water and a piece of bread through the small slot on the door, but not consistently enough for me to figure out a timeline.

My stomach grumbled at the thought. I couldn't recall the last time I'd had a proper meal. Although the shallow cuts and the bruises on my abdomen were slowly healing—which suggested I'd been here for nearly a week—my body was exhausted, sore and sleeping on a glacial, unforgiving floor certainly wasn't helping matters.

And to top it all off, I was still wearing the same soiled scrubs from the procedure, the bloodstains and lingering stench a reminder that I had no idea whether either patients had made it through.

But that hadn't been the only thing on my mind.

With all this time spent in the dark, with nothing but my own thoughts for company, I couldn't stop replaying the events of the last year and how wildly different things had turned out from what I'd mapped them to be.

I couldn't stop thinking of what I'd imagined being an Atlas would be like and how the reality was nothing like the vision I'd built in my mind.

But more than anything, I couldn't stop thinking about her.

About the last time I'd been able to hold her in my arms before everything came crashing down.

About what would happen after all of this was over.

The sound of the door unlocking dragged me out of my ruminating thoughts. A sliver of dim light filtered through the gap and I stiffened, waiting for someone to come in and drag me to whatever final grim task awaited me.

But nothing came.

I frowned, and pushed myself up, confusion settling in. I waited a moment longer, my pulse drumming to life, before I cautiously reached for the door and eased it open further.

When I peered outside, there were no signs of life or the distant echoes of retreating footsteps which only heightened my unease. My eyes strained to adjust to the faint lighting as I stepped into the dimly lit corridor to investigate why they'd let me out now.

Squinting down the long, narrow corridor, I found that it stretched in both directions, but only one end was bathed in light. I opted to go down that way but it wasn't until I closed the door behind me that I spotted the garment bag hanging on the other side.

I unzipped it, the sound cutting through the stillness around me, and inside was a three-piece black suit that was perfectly tailored to my size, alongside a pair of dress shoes. There weren't any notes or instructions, but it was clear that I was expected to change into it.

So, I did.

I undressed and swapped the dirty scrubs for the designer suit, though given I hadn't showered since being taken from Ziani's front steps, it hardly mattered. I probably still smelled dreadful.

But then again, I knew this was only for the sake of appearances.

I placed the dirty scrubs inside the bag and closed it, assuming they'd dispose of it. Then, after adjusting the black tie, I ventured down the tunnel, the sound of my breathing echoing against the stone walls.

Anticipation crackled against my skin like a live-wire, my chest growing tighter with every step I took toward the unknown that awaited me. As I neared the end, the scent of smoke filled the air. I followed it for a few more moments until the corridor spilled into a room I'd seen before.

The same one where I'd received my Order last year.

It was as though everything had been frozen in time, except now, I was walking into it, willingly—or so to speak.

My gaze traveled to where the Elders stood in a semi-circle behind the raised circular altar at the far end of the pool, just like they'd been last year. They were cloaked in their long black robes, their faces obscured by an Elder's mask, moonlight spilling over them from the tall, arched windows behind them.

Although I'd seen this room once before, it didn't make its grandeur any less overwhelming. The atmosphere carried more weight this time around, but I reminded myself that I couldn't show them any weakness or hesitation.

So I focused my mind on the one thing I knew could keep me grounded.

I had no idea what would unfold tonight, but at the end of it, I'd ensure Azara could be mine. So, with that sole focus in mind, I casually slipped my hands behind my back and stepped down onto the main floor. I moved toward them, until I stopped at the edge of the pool, opposite to them.

"Young Seungwon," my father, who stood in the middle, said, his voice deep and commanding. "You have been summoned by the House to fulfill your Ascension." He gestured for me to come forward with a nod. "Please present yourself to your Elders."

I raised a brow, unsure if I was expected to step into the pool wearing this suit that was worth more than what I made in a year. Before I could question it, a soft mechanical whirring filled the room. The surface of the water rippled and, in an instant, it was replaced by a sleek, solid floor.

I stepped forward, and the tension in the room grew more palpable with each step I took toward them. I closed the distance between them and I and halted less than five feet away from them, the flames of the raging fire from the altar licking my skin.

Only then did I spot the imposing, weathered cover resting in the middle of the altar.

The Book of Aman.

I'd heard about it all my life, even studied parts of it. But I'd always wondered what it looked like, since none of us were allowed to see or touch the original until our Ascensions. But there were more important things at play and I didn't have time to dwell in awe at the century-old relic that contained every secret the House held from the origins to our

Code, along with records the generations before us collected on the most powerful figures this world came across.

And people have gone to unspeakable lengths to get their hands on it.

"As an Atlas," my father continued, his voice low and measured, "you will vow to wield the power granted to you with unwavering loyalty, honor the legacy of those who came before you, and protect the secrets of our bloodlines. Do you wish to proceed?"

Without a moment's hesitation, I answered, "Yes, sir."

I couldn't see my father's expression, but there was a subtle shift in his posture, his squared shoulders sagging ever so slightly with relief. I wouldn't be so confident if I were him, but I'd wait until I broke the news to him.

I knew better than to make demands yet.

He gave me an imperceptible nod before declaring, "Welcome to your final trial."

His words brought a noticeable shift in the air and my heart drummed louder against my ribcage. The last time I stood in this position, I'd been engulfed by the floor so I braced myself for what was to come.

The sharp sound of a door creaked open on my left, followed by the distinct squeal of wheels turning sliced through the heavy silence. I fought the urge to look at what was being rolled into the room, knowing it would betray the mounting anxiety in my chest.

When no scent of blood or stench of a decaying body filled the air, a small wave of relief washed over me. But it wasn't enough to ease the tension fraying at the edges of my nerves.

Eventually, the Fixer came into view, pushing a stainless-steel stretcher with something lying upon it. But it wasn't a something.

It was a *someone.*

From my periphery, I watched him halt by the raised platform, carefully lifting the body from the stretcher and placing the woman's unconscious body onto it.

The older man then stepped back, bowing slightly in the direction of the Elders, before turning to leave with a quiet precision. The door thudded shut behind him and I briefly glanced at the woman lying at my feet.

A hood was drawn over her head, obscuring her identity, while her arms and legs were respectively bound with rope. Her tawny skin glistened under the dim light, and dark hair cascaded past her shoulder, long enough to partially cover her bare breasts which were exposed beneath the sheer fabric of her ivory dress—one that looked eerily like a wedding gown.

What on earth is going on?

Her chest rose and fell with slow, steady breaths and she didn't appear to be injured so I couldn't make sense of why she'd be here or what this trial was meant to be.

Women weren't allowed inside the House. Ever. The only exception had been my grandmother when she was brought here to take her oath.

Confusion swarmed over me, but I forced my expression to remain unreadable. Instead, I kept my composure, remained quiet, and focused my attention back on them.

I wrung my fingers behind my back, waiting with bated breath for whatever was to come next, when one by one, each Elder shed themselves of their anonymity, their masks and robes now at their feet.

My father, Belkacem and Ouali all stood in front of me, all dressed in matching suits—identical to mine—except for the deep red ties they wore. Each folded their hands in front of them and my father's gaze bore into mine as he spoke his next words.

"All members of the House must remain virgins until their

Ascension is complete," he said solemnly, reciting rule number IV from the Book.

The hairs on the back of my neck prickled. There was no way he knew I wasn't a virgin anymore, but the underlying implication in his words sent dread pooling down my spine.

"Once he becomes an Atlas," my father continued, "the Ascended must marry a suitable and approved suitor by his Elders."

I stilled, the gravity of his implication settled on my chest like a boulder, suffocating me and squeezing the breath from my lungs.

"Young Seungwon, and Simone Peters are to be wedded tonight, as decreed by the House, and the union must be consummated with the Elders as witness. She will be—"

His words became distant, drowned out by the erratic pouding of my own heartbeat, the sound rushing in my ears.

Married? Tonight?

The heavy wooden door, the same one the Fixer had disappeared through, opened again, and in walked a blindfolded priest being carried inside by our fathers's handyman.

Realization that this wasn't a bloody joke hit me like a ton of bricks. My earlier anxiety quickly transformed into something much more potent and visceral.

Oh, fuck no.

I knew it was within my duty to marry someone the Elders approved of, but that wasn't meant to happen until next year and I had a plan tonight to remedy that.

Why the sudden urgency?

But most importantly, I wasn't marrying anyone who wasn't Azara.

The trembling priest was brought to stand beside me, the black hood still drawn over his head. His hands were shaking as they gripped the worn leather of a sacred book.

My eyes flickered back to my father, and I realized I must have cursed the words out loud judging by the lethal glare he pinned me with. Normally, I'd go out of my way to steer clear of his disapproval, but the surge of revolt I felt spilled over and incinerated any trace of caution.

"I am not marrying her," I said, my voice unwavering.

"Do not mistake your final trial for an option," my father said, his voice as cold as a blade. "Do you need to be reminded of the consequences of going against the House's wishes?"

I heard the threat in his words. He would have to kill me if I defied orders, but I refused to bend. Especially not on this.

"I am not marrying her," I repeated, more resolute this time.

The room fell into an uneasy silence, but my father's eyes only hardened. I could feel the other Elders' disapproving stares, but I kept my gaze locked on my father's.

I didn't particularly want to die, but the very thought of being with anyone else sent pain shooting through me.

My father's jaw tightened at my opposition, but beneath the hard exterior, I saw the faintest flicker of fear in his expression. It was subtle and only there for a brief second, but I planned on using it to my advantage. I'd planned to wait until I took my oath to bring it up, but if I didn't act now, I wouldn't put it past them to have their beloved Fixer drug me and I'd wake up tomorrow as this Simone Peters' husband.

I'd thought I'd have a bit more time to gather enough information to corner them into meeting my terms before I Ascended, but the sudden kidnapping and being imprisoned in a dark cell for a week had thrown a wrench in those plans.

Now, I could only hope that the name would be enough.

I took a step forward, and met each of their eyes with a brief but deliberate look before I said the name that had been lingering in the back of my mind since I'd confronted Simmons: "Sabiri."

Immediately, every Elder in the room stiffened. They tried to recover quickly, but it wasn't fast enough for me to miss it. The name hung in the air like a curse, and for the first time tonight, the uncertainty emanated from their side.

I knew I had their attention, and I'd use it to get exactly what I wanted.

I was playing with fire, but like I'd said before, I didn't care.

I'd rather die than not be with her.

"Michael," my father warned, but I still didn't relent.

"I will complete my Ascension, but I won't abide by this marital union. I will also be granted my choice of bride, and she's to be briefed about the House."

I was pushing my luck, but I needed to be able to tell Azara everything. I'd already kept too many secrets from her and if I wanted a real chance at being with her, she had to know about the House— about all of it.

Our relationship had been built on lies, but I didn't want our second chance to be tainted by the same deceit.

That was if she even spoke to me after I told her everything.

But that would be a problem for later, and I'd do anything in my power to get her back. No matter how long I had to work for her forgiveness.

She'd be mine in the end. I'd make sure of it.

"Absolutely not," my father growled, his typically composed demeanor finally cracking under the weight of his indignation.

"You will grant it to me," I replied. "Unless of course, you'd like the boys and I to dig into why you were so adamant about me not asking questions about whoever this *Sabiri* is."

My bluff was reckless, since the name alone should be enough to get me the leverage I needed. It was clear they didn't want us uncovering whatever it was that this Sabiri represented, but I had no intention in digging further into this Sabiri—not yet, anyway.

I only wanted one thing.

And the sooner I got this over with, the faster I could get to her.

Belkacem and Ouali exchanged looks with my father, their expressions full of barely concealed outrage. Their masks had slipped and it was obvious my father hadn't shared with them my visit from a few weeks ago.

My father's sharp gaze flicked between them and me, his lips pinching together tightly, his frustration mounting. I hadn't defied my father in a very long time, and he hadn't expected me to push back like this. He eyed me, intently, searching for any sign of weakness to use against me.

But I wouldn't give him the satisfaction.

"You realize what you're asking?"

I nodded once. "I do."

There was a long, drawn-out pause. The air between us thickened, my heart hammering in my chest, but I didn't look away.

"Very well," he said, his tone bitter, barely concealing his fury. "Step forward."

"I need to hear you say it," I insisted. An Atlas never went back on his word and I wasn't willing to lose the upper-hand on a technicality.

My father exhaled sharply, his anger flaring up with each passing second. "This union is officially dismantled and you will be granted the choice of your bride. But we still will require to vet her before she's sworn into the House."

"That won't be a problem," I said. "Azara Ziani is my choice and I would like clearance to read her in."

The silence that followed was deafening and every minute my

father didn't respond stretched even longer. I could tell he wasn't surprised by my choice, but his irritation toward me hadn't eased.

"You have our blessing," he finally said and I exhaled a deep breath, one I felt like was overdue for weeks.

"Come forward and kneel," my father ordered as whoever this Simone Peters was and the priest were ushered away by the Fixer. Once they were out of sight, I took a single step forward, and knelt before the altar as instructed.

The fire surrounding the altar flickered out as my father reached for the Book of Aman. "Atlas, you've officially completed your trials. You must now take your vow to the House," he said before handing it to me.

I carefully took it from him, and I could almost feel the weight of its power in my hands. Bound in brown leather, the exterior was cracked and adorned with dark, intricate symbols.

A shiver ran down my spine as I opened the Book, my eyes roaming over the pages yellowed with age. I flipped to the last page where every Young had binded his oath. A page right before seemed to have been ripped, but I brushed it off to the book being weathered and focused on the task at hand.

Although this was my first time seeing it, we'd been taught the steps to complete our Ascension so many times, they were ingrained in our brains. So I grabbed the dagger that was attached to the back of it and layed the Book in front of me.

I met my dad's gaze. I knew he wasn't happy with what had just transpired, but surprisingly, there was still some pride in the way he held himself.

This wasn't how I'd ever expected my Ascension to be, but I wouldn't change a thing if it meant getting Azara in the end.

At least, I hoped I would.

I pushed the thought away for a moment, took a deep breath and began what I'd waited thirty-three years to do. "I, Young Seungwon, will my life to the House," I proclaimed as I held the dagger against my right palm.

Gritting my teeth, I dragged the blade down, just deep enough to draw blood. The sting was barely noticeable as the blood welled from the wound. I placed the used knife to the side and removed my ring from my left hand.

I held my right hand over it and watched my blood drip onto my ring, the fluid filling the divot of the engraved symbol. Then I impressed it under my name in our legacy tree.

"Young Seungwon," I heard my father say through gritted teeth. "Welcome to the House of Atlas."

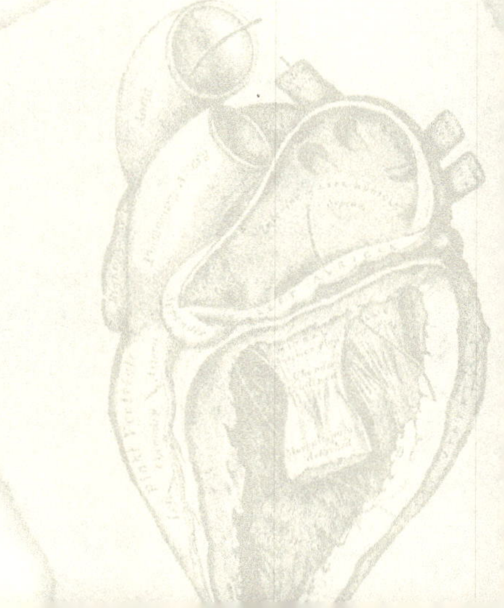

CHAPTER 44

MICHAEL

"DO YOU THINK HE'S DEAD?"

The distant, muffled voice softly broke through the haze as I drifted in and out of a deep sleep. There were more hushed whispers before I felt a sharp, painful pressure throb in the center of my forehead.

My heart leaped in my chest as I shot up, scrambling until my back hit a headboard and making me realize that I'd been placed in my bed with no recollection of how I got here.

Again.

I really need to reinforce my security measures.

I blinked a few times, disoriented, until the world around me came into focus and I found Amar sitting on the edge of my bed. Sofiane, on the other hand, leaned against the doorframe, his arms crossed over his chest and his legs crossed at the ankle.

Thankfully, whoever had brought me back to my place had had the decency to change me into more comfortable clothes and I wasn't still dressed in a suit or left naked.

"What the hell, mate?" I managed to croak, as I rubbed my forehead to assuage the sting. "What did you do that for?"

"You weren't moving so I just assumed," Amar replied, with his attempt of an apologetic smile, but his amusement at the situation overpowered it.

I narrowed my eyes at him. "I was sleeping, you idiot. Besides, you couldn't just shake me or check my pulse like a normal person?"

He shrugged. "Flicking you seemed like a better option, and look, it was effective."

I shook my head and aimed my glare at Sofiane. "And you let him?"

Sofiane held his hands up. "I tried to stop him, but when does Amar ever do what he's told?"

"Never," we both said in unison.

I rolled my eyes. "What are you two even doing here? I might have to fire Mamadou because this is the second time you both show up unannounced," I groaned.

I would never let Mamadou go, but the man had to be stronger when it came to Amar's persuasion skills. They both were on my approved lists of visitors but I might need to remove them if these yearly birthday visits became a habit.

"Last night was your *big* day. We just needed to make sure you survived and we wouldn't have to die because you messed up," Amar explained nonchalantly.

Sofiane's eyes widened, as he crossed his arms over his chest. "There's no we. *You* did. You showed up pissed drunk at my place to pick me up, and I wasn't letting you drive all the way here."

If Sofiane hadn't said anything, I wouldn't have noticed the dark circles under Amar's eyes or the faint glassiness shrouding his eyes.

"Semantics," Amar said, brushing him off with his hand.

"Always the pain in my arse," I muttered as I reached for my mobile that had been left on my nightstand. It was almost nine in the morning and I had a few missed text messages from my mom and sister wishing me a happy birthday, the boys and I's group chat, but I focused my attention on the last two.

Both were from Lucia, Ziani's former assistant who'd become mine when I took on the role last month. She was welcoming me back from my holiday in Spain and reminding me of the weekly board meeting.

It didn't take long for me to realize that the House had organized my being off the grid for an entire week well in advance and had made the necessary arrangements. Thankfully, I'd been to Spain a few times in the past, so if anyone asked about my trip, I'd be ready with a believable answer.

I had about an hour before I was due at the hospital, and I needed a proper shower to scrub off the lingering stench still clinging to my skin. I couldn't exactly show up like this, especially when I planned on speaking to Azara.

She hadn't talked to me in nearly a month, and I really needed that to change. My heart ached every time I saw her and couldn't reach out for her freely. Every time she looked at me, and the lingering gaze she once gave me was now replaced by one of resentment.

Earning her trust again and winning her back would take time, but I was prepared for whatever it took.

As long as she gave me the chance to.

I wouldn't have enough time to find her before the board meeting, but she'd be the first and only thing I'd devote my attention to afterward.

"Now that you've got proof of life, I need you to move," I said, though it was more for Amar's benefit than anything. If it were up to Sofiane, he'd be at work right now, not here babysitting Amar. "I have a meeting to get to."

"I will, but not until you open our present," Amar replied with a mischievous grin.

I already dreaded what he might have gotten me, especially since the look on Sofiane's face made it clear he hadn't had a hand in choosing it.

Amar stood up, reached into his pockets, and placed a small object in my palm, his other hand gripping my shoulder. "Happy birthday, mate."

I flipped my palm over to reveal his birthday gift: a familiar foil-wrapped square packet. Yeah, Sofiane definitely hadn't been involved in this.

"Amar," I groaned, narrowing my eyes at him.

He chuckled. "You're thirty-three now. It's the perfect gift."

"Get off me, man," I tsked, shrugging him off and tossing the gift at him as I got out of bed and headed to the ensuite bathroom.

That only made him laugh harder as he caught the condom just before it hit the floor. "You'll have to let us know how it feels when you're no longer a virgin," he teased as I turned the shower on.

I strode back toward my bedroom, my fingers curling around the sides of the doorframe. Amar flashed me a suggestive grin while Sofiane, still standing in the same spot, covered his face with his hand, clearly weary from Amar's antics.

"I will do no such thing," I shot back. "Now, leave."

Both of them knew about my involvement with Azara, but I'd kept the details of that night firmly under wraps. It wasn't for them to know. Not now, or ever.

Amar's expression shifted, his eyes lighting up with sudden curiosity. "You shagged her already, didn't you?"

I pushed off the doorframe and strode toward him with deliberate intent. My hands landed on his shoulders, spinning him toward the door in one smooth motion, and I gave him a firm shove, ushering him out of my room.

"You have, haven't you?" he called over his shoulder, a knowing grin playing on his lips.

Sofiane stepped aside as I gave Amar another shove. "You cheeky bastard, you—" His words were abruptly cut off by the resounding slam of the door in his face.

Once inside my bathroom, I quickly discarded the white tee and black joggers I'd been changed into, tossing them aside to dispose of later, before stepping into the shower.

The scalding water hit my skin, and I tipped my head back, letting it stream down my face as I reflected back on the last twenty-four hours—and on *her*.

I tried to recall what had happened after I'd officially become a part of the House, but my memory faltered, offering only a hazy image of my father's face, twisted into a grim smile before everything faded to darkness.

But it didn't really matter how or when I'd made it back to my flat.

My Ascension was complete.

Becoming an Atlas came with its own set of responsibilities, but the full extent of its power would only be granted to me when all three of us had Ascended. That gave me a few years of freedom—or at least, the closest thing to it I'd ever get—before I'd have to dedicate myself entirely to the House and bear the weight of its decisions.

I had blood on my hands and a century of legacy to uphold on my shoulders. My life came with its fair share of complications, but I was determined to fight for her.

I just needed her to let me.

Once I'd scrubbed the grime of the past week off my skin, I dried off quickly and slipped into a clean pair of black trousers and black shirt. I then grabbed my coat and made the five-minute walk to the hospital.

I might be getting ahead of myself, but for the first time in over a month, as I walked into Amanar, I felt an unfamiliar glimmer of optimism.

Not wanting to get my hopes up just yet, I pushed the fleeting feeling aside and stopped by the cafeteria before heading upstairs. I still had about thirty minutes before the board meeting, and I hadn't had a coffee yet.

I was in desperate need of one if I wanted any chance of making it through the day.

I stood in line behind two younger doctors—general practitioners, judging by their navy scrubs. Both had tanned skin and seemed familiar, but after working with so many people over the years, they all eventually blurred together.

There were a few people ahead of us, so while I waited my turn, I pulled out my phone and checked my inbox for any urgent emails. I was in the middle of replying to one when their conversation caught my attention.

"I still can't believe Azara's leaving," the woman murmured.

At the mention of her name, I froze, my brows furrowing. I glanced up from my phone, and although I only caught the doctor's profile, I could still see the sorrow that clouded her expression.

Shaking my head, I turned my attention back to my phone and resumed typing. There were countless doctors in this hospital who could share the same name, and surely, I'd just misheard them because I'd been thinking of Azara.

"After everything that happened with her dad, I don't blame her. Besides, she's not moving to a different country. You'll still be able to talk to her," the man next to her replied.

I paused, letting his words sink in, as dread coiled in the pit of my stomach.

They had to be wrong. There was no way my Azara was leaving.

"Excuse me?" I asked, stepping closer. Both of them glanced at me over their shoulders. I'd noticed the resemblance between them before, but their name tags—Zainab and Houssam Haddad—confirmed they were related in some way.

The woman's eyes widened in surprise, while the man shot me a quick, assessing glance.

"I apologize for overhearing your conversation," I continued, forcing my tone to remain calm. "But I couldn't help but catch the mention of an Azara leaving, and I just wanted to make sure you weren't referring to Dr. Ziani."

The two exchanged glances before the girl responded in a wary tone. "No, that's who we're talking about. Today's her last day."

The confirmation hit me like a blow to the chest and the earlier dread morphed into a full-blown panic.

Today? Her last day?

No. No. That couldn't be right.

They had to be wrong.

She wouldn't be leaving.

I would've known. I was technically her boss for fuck's sake.

"Are you sure?" I asked, my voice betraying the panic that was surging through me. I clung to the hope that this was a simple misunderstanding and that she'd tell me she'd made a mistake.

But she simply nodded.

She said something else after that, but I didn't catch it. My mind was spinning as I brushed past them, storming out of the cafeteria and heading straight for the lifts.

I bumped into a few people coming out of the emergency room, but I didn't care.

All I could think about was finding Azara.

This had to be some kind of mistake.

By the time I reached the lifts, my heartbeat was hammering in my chest. I jabbed at the button, my impatience growing with each second the doors didn't open. The illuminated numbers above the doors flickered, but they weren't moving fast enough. I pressed the button again, and again, hoping somehow it would help speed up the process, but it was still stuck on the bloody eleventh floor.

My panic mingled with frustration that bubbled up inside me.

Fuck this.

I wasn't waiting a second longer.

I had to find her.

Now.

With a swift turn on my heel, I rushed toward the nearest staircase. I pushed the door open and took the stairs two at a time. I hadn't thought about how far the operating theaters were, but I didn't care that I'd have to climb thirteen floors.

I just needed to get to her before she left.

I thought I'd have more time to talk to her, but I should have learned my lesson the last time I'd lost her.

I wouldn't make the same mistake again.

By the time I made it to the tenth floor, my legs were screaming at me to stop and my lungs were gasping for air, but I gripped the railing, and pushed harder.

Three more floors to go.

With a final burst of energy, I reached the thirteenth floor. My chest was tight from the exertion as I threw the door open. The ward was eerily quiet, save for the few scrub nurses and orderlies who glanced at me like I'd sprouted another head.

I didn't pay them any mind, and instead headed straight for the large white board where all the scheduled surgeries were listed. My eyes scanned the names frantically until I found Azara's.

I checked the time on my watch only to realize that her surgery had ended fifteen minutes ago. Without a second thought, I rushed to Theater B, clinging to the faint hope that, by some miracle, she hadn't already left, or that her surgery had run longer than expected.

"Please", I whispered under my breath as I neared the operating theater. I just needed one thing to go right for me today.

I pushed open the double doors to the scrub room, and a strangled exhale of relief rushed from my lungs when I saw her emerging from the theater.

Alone.

"Azara," I panted, my voice strained.

She looked up, and when our eyes met, the fleeting sense of relief I'd just felt was instantly replaced by something far heavier, something that pressed against my chest and made it harder to breathe.

She stared at me for a long moment, the silence stretching between us like an unspoken barrier, before she removed her surgical mask and moved to wash her hands.

"Can I help you with something, Dr. Young?" she finally said, and my heart pinched at her cold, indifferent tone.

I used to love it when she called me Dr. Young, and she'd ruined me the moment she called me Michael. Now, I'd never despised my name more than I did in this moment.

"Were you going to leave without telling me?" I still held to the hope she wasn't really leaving. I wanted to hear from her that the doctor from downstairs had gotten the wrong information, and this was just some twisted joke to get back at me.

Another breathless, painful silence filled the chasm between us.

"I've gone through the appropriate channels for my departure," she said, her tone still so distant. "There was no need for you to be—"

I didn't let her finish because we both knew her response was a complete load of nonsense. "Don't do that," I said, roughness edging my words.

She closed her eyes, taking a slow, deliberate breath, before looking at me again. A simmering fire danced in her brown eyes. "Do what, Dr. Young?"

"Act like we don't know each other, or *mean* anything to each other."

She let out a bitter laugh, one that echoed around the room and wrapped around my heart like a vise. "But we don't, Dr. Young."

The vise crushed my heart so tightly, an unbearable pain seized my chest. I hated that this was how things turned out. As if these past few months had never happened and we were back to being complete strangers.

"We do. And would you stop calling me that? It's Michael to you."

She shook her head, a slight tremor in her hands as she crossed her arms. "Why do you keep doing this?" she demanded. "Everything about whatever this was," she motioned between us, "was a complete lie. I don't understand why you are so relentless in keeping up this charade?"

I swallowed hard, forcing the lump in my throat to dissipate.

"It was never a lie."

We never were.

No matter how much I'd tried to convince myself otherwise, I knew things would never be the same the moment she barreled into my life.

I just didn't know how back then.

Chance moments had the power to change the course of your life, and she'd been the best unexpected event to ever come into mine.

"I had to do it," I continued, my voice faltering as I tried to find the right words. I…" I exhaled a shaky breath and brought my hands up to grip the back of my neck, hoping it'd help steady me.

I was allowed to read her in, but I'd never done it before. I didn't even know where to start or how much to reveal. But this might be my only chance to explain.

I stole a quick glance through the large windows, confirming we were alone as I saw the last housekeeper finish up and slip out through the other exit door. With a sigh, my hands fell to my sides, and I started from the very beginning.

"I'm part of what is called the House of Atlas. Over the last century, the three families involved in the society, including mine, have been tasked with producing a single male heir to take over when they each turned thirty-three. But only if they complete their Order."

I was well-aware she could walk out at any point, but I pressed on, my words spilling out faster with each passing second.

"Earlier this morning, at four minutes past midnight, I turned thirty-three and taking your father's job was my Order."

I told her about the bribes her father had taken, the ultimatum I'd given him and how lives, mine included, had been at risk if I hadn't done what had been necessary. I told her about how we were looking into *The Gilded Truth*, where I'd been over the last week and how I'd made sure her building and the surrounding areas were now secured so that no one else would ever invade her privacy again.

The only thing I'd left out was the reason behind her father's ties to Nyx. They weren't my sins to confess and he would tell her if and when he wanted to.

When I finished, her complexion had drained of color, and her gaze was fixed on the floor. I wanted so badly to wrap my arms around her, to hold her and comfort her, but I remained still as an excruciatingly long silence ensued my confessions.

"Why?"

I frowned, confusion sparring with the anxiety roiling in my stomach. Of all the things I'd expected her to ask, that hadn't been one of them. "Why what?"

Azara lifted her gaze to meet mine, the earlier fire now doused with unshed tears. "Why did you do it? Why is this *House* so important that you ruined my father and used me to do it?" Her voice cracked and my chest caved from the anguish in her tone.

I couldn't change what I'd done and I didn't regret Ascending, but breaking her heart would forever be my biggest regret.

"Because people that look like us, like you and me, we were never given a seat at the table back then. The House made sure we'd always have one, and I couldn't end that legacy—no matter how much my heart fought me against it."

As a suffocating tension pervaded the space between us, I saw her eyes flitting with a thousand emotions while processing my reply.

Please, baby, let me in, I silently pleaded.

"My shift's over. I have to go," she said, incinerating any sliver of hope I had left.

She moved to make her way to the doors, and fear gripped my lungs. I stepped into her path, my heart pounding furiously against my ribs.

"You can't leave."

A pained sigh escaped her lips. "Let me go."

Something inside my chest stretched past the point of painful. I instinctively placed my hand over my heart, willing it to stop hurting, but it didn't. The exchange of three words often had the power to change the course of a relationship, but I hadn't expected these to be ours.

"I can't."

My eyes bounced between hers, and I saw every ounce of effort she put into maintaining a straight face and remaining emotionless. But I could see beneath the cold demeanor. I could see that despite how much she was fighting to keep me at arm's length, she didn't want to,

But maybe that was wishful thinking on my part.

Hoping that I still had a place in her heart and with time, she'd let me back in.

So, for the first time since I'd walked in here, I moved toward her.

But she stepped back.

And then again, until her back hit the wall and I reached for her, my hands trembling as I grabbed her face.

My eyes burned as I whispered, "I could never let you go."

Her face twisted in torment, and she turned her head away from me. But then, as if her body betrayed her resolve, she leaned into my palm, closing her eyes as she drew in a shuddering breath.

For a fleeting second, I thought I'd slipped past a tiny crack of her armor, but just as fast, she ripped my hands off her. "I have to go," she whispered, her voice barely audible, before slipping out of my reach completely.

Desperation surged through me, and before she reached the door, I grabbed her wrist, her name leaving my lips in a strangled cry. "Azara…"

The three words I'd longed to say to her were caught in my throat. I wanted her to hear it, *needed* her to know how much I loved her.

But I didn't want it to be the reason she stayed.

I wanted her to give me a chance because she wanted to.

I wanted her to give me a chance because she wanted me. Because she wanted *us*.

She hesitated, just for a moment, and I almost thought she'd turn around. But instead, she shook her head and pulled free from my grasp, her hand slipping from mine with a heartbreaking finality.

Then, without another word, I watched the love of my life leave with my bleeding heart in the palm of her hands. My shoulders slumped as I stood there, a wave of hopelessness threatening to take me under.

I felt like the world around me had been sucked away, leaving me only with the hollow echo of her absence.

Letting her go went against my every instinct. Every fiber of my being screamed for me to chase after her, to fight with her until she forgave me. But I knew, deep down, I wouldn't be able to get through her.

At least not right now.

I could only push her so far and I'd already done too much.

She might be leaving, but I wouldn't let her go.

I couldn't.

I'd fight for her even if it meant I'd have to beg and plead for the rest of my days.

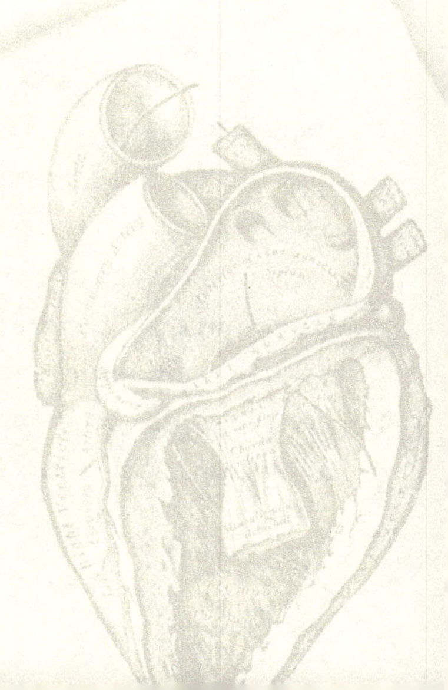

CHAPTER 45

AZARA

One month later

I'D ALWAYS BEEN AFRAID OF change.

The mere thought usually sent me into a spiral. I found solace in the stability of a routine and rarely veered from what was familiar to me. But after everything that had happened, I'd needed a fresh start.

The walls of Amanar had grown suffocating and I'd been so trapped in my own thoughts that each day blurred into the next. Not only had my mind become the last place I wanted to be in, but it had also started to affect my work—and I simply couldn't allow that.

Being a surgeon had given me a sense of purpose after losing my mum. Surgery was what I escaped to when I needed it the most, and it was so deeply woven into who I was, that to feel disconnected from it because of the incessant whispers and the constant pitying looks from my colleagues, became unbearable.

My instincts wanted me to retreat into the safety of what I knew and block it all out. But after I'd battered my frustration in that rage room, I'd made a promise to myself—a promise that I'd do better by myself and stop brushing off how I felt because it was easier.

Then one morning, my phone had pinged with a new email notification, a lifeline thrown my way when I'd least expected it. It had been the first good news I'd had in a long time, and although leaving Amanar had never been in my plans, taking the lead consultant role at Orion University Hospital had been a no-brainer.

Of course I'd missed the ease that came with working at Amanar, since I'd spent years there, but no one knew me here—and that meant I could be whoever I wanted to be.

My father's legacy—or should I say, now, his tainted legacy— no longer loomed over my head as I led my own department. And, most importantly, after a month at Orion, the spark I thought I'd lost had returned.

"Dr. Ziani, wait up," called a voice I'd grown accustomed to, as I made my way to the doctor's lounge, my shift finally coming to an end.

It was nearly 6:00 p.m., and unlike the usual late nights I'd had at AGH, there were some perks to not working at the biggest trauma center in the city—such as leaving work on time on a Friday evening.

I turned around to find Kaz, one of the ICU nurses, heading toward me. Starting over and working with strangers had been a bit daunting, especially after spending the last ten years with the same group of people. But Kaz had been one of the first people I'd met here, and he'd made me feel immediately at ease.

"Everything all right?" I asked, hoping this wasn't an emergency that would keep me longer. Not only was it my weekend off, but I had a plate of couscous—courtesy of Nakia's grandmother—waiting for me at home, and I was really looking forward to a quiet night in after the long week I'd just had.

"Yes, everything's fine," he said with a small smile. "I just wanted to see if you'd like to join us for happy hour at The Old Harp tonight?"

The Old Harp, just across the street from Orion, was the staffs' favorite local pub. Kaz had invited me almost every Friday since I'd started, but although I appreciated the offer, the thought of socializing made my skin itch.

I shook my head with an apologetic smile, but before I could reply, he did it for me. "You have other plans," he said with a shrug, flashing me a boyish smile. "It was worth the try."

"I'll see you on Monday," I said with a chuckle before I waved him goodbye and headed for the lounge.

After changing out of my scrubs, I slipped on my coat, grabbed my bag from my locker and made my way out. I was almost at the hospital lobby when my personal phone rang. Digging through my tote, I pulled it out to see Nakia was calling.

"What's the best way to kill someone without getting caught?" she said the moment I answered her call.

I laughed, shaking my head. "I'm a doctor, remember? Not a serial killer."

"*B7el, b7el,*" she replied with a heavy sigh. Nakia wasn't really one to complain, so I knew if she was calling me this irritated, someone must have really gotten on her bad side.

"What happened?" I asked as I pushed through the revolving doors.

A cold, biting breeze whipped across my body, and I shivered, pulling my coat tighter around me. Although it was only the beginning of March, we'd had a few unseasonably warmer days this week, but it seemed winter was reluctant to let go just yet.

Nakia launched into her rant, but her words faded as an all too familiar prickle of heat raised the hairs on the back of my neck.

Please, no.

I didn't want to look up, but my stupid curiosity got the better of me. My heart rate quickened as I lifted my gaze—and there he was.

He was the absolute last person I'd expected to see here, and yet, sitting on one of the benches at the front of the hospital, wearing a grey wool coat over a black suit, was Michael fucking Young.

"You've got to be kidding me," I muttered under my breath, squeezing my eyes shut. When I opened them again, he was still there, as if fate had decided to mock me. "Nakia, I'll have to call you back," I told her, shoving my phone back into my bag.

The sensible thing to do would have been to walk right past him, to pretend I hadn't seen him. But he'd already spotted me, and there was no way out.

Even if I wanted there to be.

He stood as I approached, and my breath caught in my throat at his proximity.

"Hi," he said softly, and I had to stop myself from flinching at the sound of his voice. Seeing him had made my stomach somersault, but hearing him was like a pummeling punch to the gut—a painful, familiar ache I'd been trying to bury for weeks.

I hadn't seen him in over a month and the sight of him brought with it a mix of anger and anguish, battering against my ribcage. The constant tug-of-war between my emotions had given me more headaches than I could count. I'd done my best to push him from my mind, to erase the sound of his plea for me not to leave, to pretend that his confession about the House and everything it entailed had never happened.

A bloody secret society. I couldn't have made it up even if I'd tried.

Though it was easier said than done because that was the

maddening contradiction of loving someone, wasn't it? The constant battle between two polar emotions where your head knew what was best, yet your heart stubbornly clung to the tattered remnants of what once was.

Thunder rumbled in the distance as I asked, "What are you doing here?" It was probably a silly question, since this was a public space, and he did use to work here, but this was *my* space now.

Michael's eyes searched my face for something I was no longer willing to give. But unlike the last time I'd seen him, he didn't falter at my sharp tone, nor did he look torn by the confrontation.

No, this time, he looked almost… resolute.

"I'm here for you."

Ignoring how his words sent my pulse thundering in my ears, I rolled my eyes and tightened my grip on the strap of my bag. "Listen, I'm not interested in whatever game you're playing," I replied, hoping my voice sounded steadier than I felt. "So if you'll excuse me, I have somewhere to be."

I stepped to the side to move past him, but he blocked my path. My frustration bubbled up, stronger than the pain that came with seeing him again. I moved to the other side, but once again, he placed himself in the way.

"Michael," I warned, letting out an exasperated breath.

"It isn't a game," he said firmly. "It never was."

"Michael, I swear to you, if you don't move…" My threat hung in the air between us, the rumble of thunder growing louder. For a moment, I thought he might back off.

But then his next words rooted me to the spot.

"I love you," he said, releasing a deep breath, like he'd been holding on to those words for far too long.

I drew back at his confession, and I swore my heart nearly gave out. There was a time where all I'd wanted to hear from him were those three little words—words that would have changed everything.

Loving someone always seemed like the last thing I wanted to do. But not with Michael.

With him, it was the only thing I could think of.

Through everything we'd shared, I'd begun to look forward to the moments where I'd fall more for him. I had let myself open up my heart to the prospect of a future I'd never imagined for myself.

Because he'd made me feel safe.

He'd made me feel loved.

He'd made me feel whole.

Until everything fell apart.

Hearing those words would have changed everything. Now, they only brought me immense pain—the kind I'd tried to ignore for weeks.

The sky opened up, and large droplets of rain began to pour down on us.

"I love you, Azara Ziani," he repeated. "God, I've loved you for months now, but I've just been too bloody stupid to let you know how I felt. I didn't know how or when to tell you, because I was waiting for the perfect moment. But I realized too late there's no such thing as the perfect moment to tell the love of your life that they're it for you."

The rain crashed down harder with each word, soaking us both, but I barely noticed. His eyes shimmered with emotions, and my chest constricted until my lungs screamed for air.

His words left me momentarily stunned, before my anger flared back to life. Because what the fuck? How dared he tell me he loved me? I'd spent the last two and half months stowing him and all of my feelings away, only for him to show up and undo all the work I'd done to move on.

"You don't love me," I gritted through my teeth, shaking my head.

"You lied to me, and manipulated our entire relationship. How can you call that love? You don't hurt those you love, you protect them. You protect their hearts, but you *broke* mine."

By the end, my voice was barely above a whisper and my body trembled. Whether it was from the cold rain or the force of my emotions, I couldn't tell.

But at this point, it didn't matter.

And I hated it. I hated that I couldn't get a hold of myself, hated that I couldn't just shut it off and act unaffected by his words. Because the truth was, I *was* affected by his confession.

It stabbed through like a stake to the heart, leaving my vulnerability bleeding in front of him. I felt tears well up, my eyes and nose burning, but I swallowed them back.

He instinctively took a step forward before he caught himself, his eyes softening as if he tried to convey what he couldn't do with his touch.

"I know I hurt you, Azara," he said quietly. "And I'm not expecting you to welcome me back with open arms. But I do know that I'm willing to fight for you. No matter how long it takes. I'll be here every day, waiting for you."

I heard my heart splinter in half. I wanted to believe him, but I'd done it once already, and look where we ended up. It'd be foolish of me to put my trust in him again.

It didn't matter that I also loved him, and in a perfect world, our confessions would have been at the culmination of a perfect moment. I'd have fallen into his arms, and we would have lived out our happily ever after.

But this wasn't a perfect world.

Not every love story ended in a happy ending, and this one was no exception.

"I'll file a restraining order against you," I said, my chest heaving, trying to breathe through the pressure building inside me. Seeing him once was already too much, but the thought of seeing him every day sent me into a spiral of panic.

"Then, I'll be however many feet away from you that I need to be."

I sighed, emotion clogging at my throat. I couldn't do this back-and-forth anymore. The exhaustion of it was taking over and I just couldn't—

He pulled one hand out of his coat pocket, and I recoiled instinctively, thinking he was about to touch me. Hurt flashed on his face for a brief moment, before he reigned it in and handed me a white envelope.

It had today's date scrawled on the back of it in black ink. Rain began soaking the paper, so I reluctantly took it, pulling it under my coat to shield it from the downpour.

At least that's the excuse I was going with.

"What is it?" I asked, my pulse hammering in my chest as I looked from the envelope clutched in my right hand to him.

"Last time, you said you didn't know who I was. Although, I'd argue that you're the only one who truly knows who I am, I hope that these letters help with that."

He paused for a moment, and my heartbeat slowed under the weight of his earnest expression. I hadn't even realized he'd mentioned *letters*—plural.

"I'm not giving up on us, Azara," was the last thing he said before he walked away.

CHAPTER 46

AZARA

Three months later

MICHAEL LIVED UP TO HIS word of showing up every single day.

I had no idea how he'd managed to get ahold of my schedule, or how he even balanced it with his own hectic one. But no matter the weather or the hour I finished work, he was always there—sitting on the same bench, waiting for me with a new, dated white envelope much like the first one he'd given me.

The very one I'd kept tucked away in my bedside drawer, unopened. Just like all of his other letters.

At first, I pretended he wasn't there, walking past him without accepting the envelopes he extended. But every time, the letter I'd refused would find its way under my front door the next time I woke up.

I'd given him a week, two at most, and I was certain he'd grow tired of whatever he was trying to achieve.

Spoiler alert: he didn't.

Even when it rained for an entire week, he was at his post, umbrella in hand and waiting for me. Each day, he had a new letter, and each day, he silently walked me from the hospital to the metro station I took home.

He was there, but he never pressed for conversation, which, as much as I hated to admit, I appreciated.

By the end of the first month, I caved and started accepting the letters because the thought of having him so close to my home—the last place where we'd been together—became too overwhelming to ignore.

Nothing was forcing me to keep them, and I could easily have thrown them away. Or even burned them. But there was a small, perverse part of my heart that clung to each handwritten note, as if they were the final thread connecting me to him—one I apparently couldn't bring myself to sever.

It made no sense. I'd told myself I'd let him go, just as I'd asked him to let me go, but I felt him everywhere.

Even when I couldn't see him.

It stirred a maddening dichotomy within me, one that made me equally want to scream at him, and open the door to let him back in.

By the end of the second month, my resolve began to waver, and I came dangerously close to reading his letters. But I held back. Because, despite the fact that he'd kept his promise, and showed up every day, I wasn't sure if I could trust him.

More importantly, I wasn't sure if I could trust myself.

I'd always prided myself on my intuition, on my ability to know who to trust and what to do in any given situation. But Michael's betrayal, coupled with my father's secrets, had cut so deep, and while

I'd tried to heal, in my own ways, doubt still lingered in the recesses of my mind.

Because if two people that I'd entrusted with my heart could hurt me the way they did, how could I ever trust myself with anything?

Yet, by the end of the third month, the reasons I'd held on to for not forgiving him, for not being with him, were becoming harder and harder to justify. They were being slowly overpowered by the feelings I still harbored for him, feelings that, instead of fading, grew stronger with each passing day from his consistent efforts in showing me that I *could* count on him.

Even on my days off, he left me a letter, slipped carefully under my door. Today's was sitting on my coffee table. I had been in the midst of preparing dinner—*rfissa*, Nakia's favorite, as the girls were coming over for a Sunday girl's night—when it had arrived.

I finished tearing the *msemen* into smaller pieces when a knock echoed at the door. I glanced at the time, my brows pulling together since it was only 4:00 p.m. and I wasn't expecting them for another hour.

Perhaps one of them was early.

I grabbed the tea towel from the counter and headed for the front door. Peering through the spyhole, my heart skipped when I saw my father standing on the other side.

"*Baba?*" I said, anxiety swarming inside my chest as I opened the door. "Is everything okay? Has something happened to Zayd?" My pulse quickened as I fired off each question.

Sensing my rising panic, he placed a reassuring hand on shoulder and squeezed it. "Hey, *benti*, everything's fine. Zayd is at Nabil's house to study—though I doubt they'll do much of that."

I let out a long, relieved sigh. "God, *baba*, you scared me." Shaking my head, my heartbeat simmered down from the previous rush of anxiety, but then I realized I had no idea why he was here. I frowned. "Wait, then what are you doing here?"

My father never dropped by unannounced. If this wasn't an emergency…

He dropped his hand and stuffed it into his pockets. "Can't I visit my daughter?" he teased, but despite the lightheartedness he tried to convey in his tone, his throat flexed with a hard swallow and his eyes flickered with uncertainty.

I knew my father well enough to know something was off. Our relationship wasn't like it used to be, but I'd never seen him this nervous.

"Of course you can," I scrambled to say. "I just—" I hesitated before stepping aside to let him in. "Come in."

He entered, bending down to remove his shoes and place them neatly by the door, beside mine. Since it was early June, and the weather had been fairly decent recently, he only wore a light cashmere jumper and dark jeans.

He straightened up, inhaled deeply, and asked, "*Kataybi rfissa?*"

I glanced back at the kitchen where the large pot was cooking, then returned my attention to him. "Yes, Nakia and Hazel are coming over in a bit. I'll make a plate for you and Zayd to take home."

"Thank you and I won't be long, then," he said, before walking with me to my living room.

We sat next to each other on the sofa. A long silence lapsed in the space between us, and I wrung my fingers together, my nerves building again as I watched him, his eyes fixed on the floor. After what seemed an eternity, he took a deep breath, pushed his glasses up his nose, and turned to face me.

"I'm not very good at this," he said, his gaze shrouded with vulnerability. "So, please be patient with me while I try my best to say what I came here to say."

My dad wasn't an emotional person. I'd inherited that from him. So seeing him like this was unsettling. But I wanted to give him space to say whatever it was he came here for.

"Okay," I said, gentle and quiet, hoping my nerves wouldn't bleed through.

"Your mum…" His voice faltered, thick with emotion. He swallowed hard and cleared his throat before continuing. "She was the best thing in my life. I fell in love with her when we were kids. I knew I was hers the moment she cursed at me for not letting her play football with us on the streets."

He smiled, a wistful laugh escaping him, as if he was transported back to that exact moment. I'd heard the story many times when I was younger, but I hadn't heard it in years.

Not since she'd passed.

"Mamak, she was so headstrong, you know," my dad added, looking at me.

I swallowed against the growing clog of emotions stuck in my throat. "She was," I managed to say. Mum had the biggest heart, but if she set her mind to something, nothing could change it.

A tear silently slipped down his cheek, and the sight was like a blow to my heart. The last time my father cried was the day we found out about the accident. After I'd found him on the bathroom floor, tears streaming down his face, I'd taken Zayd from him and had gotten us to the hospital to see her.

He'd cried so much when the doctors had taken us back to see her that I thought he'd never stop. But after I'd made the arrangements, and we'd gotten home that night, it was as if he'd depleted his capacity to cry.

He hadn't shed a tear at her funeral or any time after that.

I gently placed my hand on his, letting him know that it was okay to let it out. I knew better than anyone what it felt like to keep everything bottled up, and I didn't want him to keep doing the same.

He gave me a sad smile and continued. "She was my person and losing her was unbelievably hard."

"I know," I whispered, feeling heat growing in the back of my eyes and my throat growing tighter with each passing second.

He nodded a few times, his gaze softening. "You do, *benti*. You do. Because you bore the brunt of my pain." He cleared his throat. "And I'm sorry I wasn't there for you after her death. I ran and let you shoulder the responsibility of taking care of yourself and Zayd. Of me. I saw how much it was weighing on you, but it just felt so much easier to let you handle it. You were doing such a better job than I thought I could. But I s-should've tried harder. I'm your father, and… I'm your father and it was my responsibility to take care of you."

His free hand rested gently on my cheek, wiping away the tears I hadn't realized had fallen. "You and your brother are the best thing your mother gave me, and I'm sorry I didn't prioritize you."

"Dad, you did your b—"

"Azara," he interrupted, his voice hoarse. "You don't have to make excuses for me anymore. I wasn't a good father for many years, and I made a lot of mistakes. Stupid mistakes. But I hope you'll let me try to redeem myself."

He looked at me earnestly, despite the redness rimming his eyes and his tear-stained cheeks that I was sure matched my own. "I know I haven't said it enough, but I love you, *benti*. I hope you know that."

I opened my mouth to respond and reassure him that of course I knew he did, that there was no redeeming needed, but the only thing that came out was a broken sound as he wrapped his arms around me, pulling me into his embrace.

My dad and I weren't affectionate people or really expressed our love like my Mum did so freely. So this, having him be so open, so vulnerable with me—the way she would have been—both broke my heart and soothed it at the same time.

"I love you, too, *baba*," I eventually murmured into his embrace, my breathing slowly steadying.

He pulled away, gently wiping the tears from my cheeks. "Your mum would be so proud of you," he said with a small smile. "I am."

I placed my hands over his. "I know," I whispered through a sad smile.

I'd always known my dad was proud of me, but hearing him say it out loud felt… comforting. We still had so much to talk about, but for the first time in a long while, this felt like a step in the right direction and gave me hope for our relationship.

He looked at me for a moment longer, and I could tell he wanted to say more, but instead, he drew me close and pressed a soft kiss to my forehead, before letting me go.

"Right," he said, rubbing his temples. "We need to stop this. My therapist says crying isn't a bad thing, but it's giving me a bloody headache."

I frowned. "Your therapist?"

He shrugged casually. "Yeah, he's a bit stubborn and grumpy, but he does make some good points," he explained, like him being in therapy was nothing out of the ordinary.

I let out a burst of shocked laughter. "I can't believe you're in therapy."

"Neither can I," he muttered, waving it off. "But someone made the suggestion, and, well, the bastard was unfortunately right," he grumbled, more to himself, just as my timer went off.

"I'll need to hear more about this therapist," I said with a small laugh as I stood up from the sofa. I didn't know who'd encouraged him to seek therapy, but I'd like to personally thank them. "Would you like one large plate, or shall I plate one for each of you?" I asked, heading into the kitchen.

Luckily, I'd made extra. My dad wasn't exactly a culinary expert when it came to Moroccan food. He only knew how to make two things, so whenever I cooked traditional dishes, I always made sure to have enough for them as well.

"Two plates," he said quickly, followed by a laugh. "Your brother will eat half of it before I even say '*bismillah*.'"

While I waited for the shredded *msemen* to steam in the couscoussier, I stirred the stew and checked it was done before grabbing two shallow plates. I was in the middle of assembling my brother's plate when my dad suddenly said, "What's this?"

"What's what?" I glanced over my shoulder, my heart leaping into my throat as I watched him pick up the letter I'd left on the table.

"Oh, that's nothing. Probably just some junk mail," I said, attempting to sound nonchalant, despite the rising panic in my chest. I hastily finished plating the food, wrapping it in foil, desperate to divert his attention elsewhere.

Logically, I knew he wouldn't open it, but right now, all I could focus on was that my father was holding whatever it was Michael had written for me today. He didn't know about us, and I'd prefer to keep it that way. He hadn't mentioned it, and I didn't want to bring it up—not after the fresh progress we'd just made.

And especially with how much of a tangled mess everything still was.

He stood from his seat, that damn envelope still in his hand. "Is it from him?"

I packed the hot plates in one of the grocery bags I kept under my sink and made my way back to him. "What?" I replied, confusion mixing with my anxiety as I handed him the bag.

Thankfully, he placed the letter back on the table to grab the bag from my hands. I let out a faint sigh of relief, but it was quickly snuffed out by his next question.

"Is it from Dr. Young?"

I froze, my heart hammering in my chest. I'd never told my father about Michael so how on earth did he suspect it was from him?

"I…" How was I supposed to respond to that?

Yes, father. The man who blackmailed you out of a job was the same man I fell in love with while you were at home, completely miserable.

I still had a hard time looking my father in the eye every time I saw him after the masquerade ball, where everyone had learned what he'd done.

My father pushed his glasses up his nose—his tell when something made him uncomfortable—and looked away for a moment before meeting my gaze again.

"I know about you and Michael."

My heart sank the moment the words left his mouth as my mind spiralled, bombarded by a thousand questions.

What? How? Since when?

"I… I don't understand," I stammered, struggling to wrap my head around what he'd just revealed.

"Young came to see me four months ago, and as you can probably imagine, I wasn't exactly thrilled to see him. But I'm glad he did."

None of this made sense. Why would Michael go see my father?

He took a deep breath, gathering his thoughts before continuing. "When you asked me last year why I resigned from Amanar, I wasn't entirely honest with you. Well, I didn't give you a reason, really." He gave me a rueful smile. "Though leaving wasn't entirely on my terms, I only have myself to blame for it."

"What happened?" I asked, wary.

I remembered that day as though it had happened yesterday, even if it felt like a lifetime ago. At the time, I'd desperately wished for him to talk to me, but the grim look now taking over his face made me question whether I still wanted to know the truth.

Not when I knew it had something to do with Arthur Nyx.

I had thought about broaching the subject countless times over the past few months, but our last serious conversation had ended horribly, and I didn't think I could handle another rejection from him.

He sighed heavily. "After Mum died, I was in a really bad headspace. Did a few things I'm not proud of… and I needed money. Arthur and I went to uni together, and what I thought was a helping hand from a friend at the time, turned into something much bigger. Something I couldn't stop, no matter how hard I tried to."

"I… I don't understand." My mind was trying to connect the dots, but all I had to go on with was the remnant of what I remembered from *The Gilded Truth* issue at the masquerade ball. I'd been too stunned that night to absorb much of the column, and after we left Anzar, there had been no copies to be found.

"He needed the numbers for his device's approval," my father continued, his voice small. "So I gave them to him."

I shrank back, the gravity of his confession becoming clearer.

"What about the patients?" I asked, incredulously. "The father I knew would've never done something like this."

I waited for him to deny my conclusions, but instead, his face twisted with regret and my stomach lurched at his confirmation. "Nyx threatened to come after you and Zayd if I ever went public with what he was doing. I didn't care about risking my job, but I couldn't risk you both. Not when I was already miserably failing as a father."

"We lost mum," I whispered, the weight of the words heavy on my chest. "How could you possibly do that to another family?"

"I did what I had to do," he said, his voice raw with guilt.

I struggled to process what he was telling me. To grasp that my father would put people's lives in danger. Especially when one of those lives had been someone on my operating table—someone I'd almost lost if I hadn't caught the bleed in time.

"No one actually used the device on patients," he added quickly, as if somehow it would make this any better. "I just documented that they did."

"But you couldn't guarantee that, *baba*," I replied, my voice rising. Anger and fear swirled inside me. "*I* almost lost a patient because of that bloody stapler."

"Dr. Adams proceeded without my consent. He was let go after that incident."

My mind reeled with the magnitude of the situation. We always heard that people would do anything to protect their loved ones, and although on one hand I could understand my father's motive, on the other, this wasn't just morally wrong, it was illegal.

"This is a lot, *baba*," I said, my voice strained.

"I know, *benti*," he replied, his voice low and filled with sorrow. "Like I said, I'm not proud of what I did and if I could go back and change things, I would."

His words hung in the air, their reality of it all settling like a boulder in my gut.

"What will happen to you?"

"Nothing," he replied quietly, shaking his head once. "Michael… he offered to take care of things."

I blinked, unsure I'd heard him right. "Michael?" I echoed, disbelievingly. There were a hundred questions running through my mind about what 'taking care of things' meant, but only one slipped out. "Why would he do that?"

There was a brief silence before my dad answered, "I think you know why."

My heart squeezed painfully in my chest at the implication.

I love you, Azara Ziani.

The words echoed in my mind so vividly, it was almost as if I could hear him say them. His voice reverberated the words over and over in my head, until they bled into my chest, finding their match in the quiet ache I'd carried there.

There was no point in pretending my feelings for him didn't reflect his.

I loved Michael.

I loved the way he showed up for me even when I didn't ask.

Especially when I didn't.

I loved the way he looked at me, like I was the only person in the room.

I loved the way he pushed me to be better.

But was that enough?

"You're overwhelmed," my father said when I didn't answer. "I'll go because I don't want to make things worse. But I'll just say this one last thing. You're a lot like me, *benti*. You busy yourself to forget. When your mum died, I thought that if I worked more, if I kept busy, it would solve everything. That maybe, the more I worked, the more numb I'd become, and the pain of her absence wouldn't hurt anymore. But we both know that never works. It's only a temporary solution, because the pain... it always comes back."

He came to my side and pressed a kiss to the side of my head. "Don't make the same mistakes as me. Although Michael wouldn't have been my first choice for a son-in-law... he's not all bad. But most importantly, he wants to do right by you."

My father lingered for a moment longer but I hardly registered his goodbyes or when he left, the heaviness of his words lingered in the room, suffocating.

Don't make the same mistakes as me.

He wants to do right by you.

The ache in my chest deepened, and I didn't know what to do with all of this new information. I couldn't bring myself to move, or speak, as I stood in my living room.

My eyes eventually traveled to the letter sitting in front of me, today's date staring right back at me.

Last time, you said you didn't know who I was.

I hope that these letters help with that.

I'm not giving up on us, Azara.

The emotional rollercoaster I'd been on over the last months, coupled with my conversation with my father had taken its toll on me, and I had no clue what I wanted anymore. My resolve to let Michael go had already been waning, but my father's words weakened it even further.

I swallowed past the knot of emotion in my throat and did the only thing I could think of. I grabbed the white envelope and headed downstairs to my bedroom. I still had a little bit of time before I was expecting Nakia and Hazel, so I opened the drawer I'd kept at bay over the last three months.

Ninety days.

Ninety letters.

One for every day since he'd told me he'd loved me.

Not that I'd counted.

After taking them out, I sat back in bed, picked up the first letter and started reading.

CHAPTER 47

MICHAEL

IT WAS NEARLY 8:00 P.M. when I made it to Orion.

Azara was nearing the end of her shift, according to the screenshot of her schedule Kaz had sent me every month since she started working here. If it hadn't been for his help over the past three months, I'd never have been able to pull this off.

Despite the devastation I'd felt at her leaving Amanar, discovering she'd be working here had been the first moment of relief I'd felt since all of my veiled lies were uncovered.

I'd reached out to Kaz immediately and although he was initially reluctant to essentially spy on her, he became more than eager to help when he saw the desperation on my face and of course, when I offered him the only volume of Osama Tezuka's Black Jack he was missing.

Being an Atlas often came with its perks.

The cool evening air brushed against my skin as I walked down the pathway to Orion's entrance, and I immediately regretted not wearing a long sleeve. Not wanting to be late, I'd come straight here from work, so I hadn't had time to change from the navy T-shirt and black trousers I'd worn all day.

I pulled today's letter out of my pocket before sitting on what had become my wooden bench. I ran a hand over my face, the whispers of my exhaustion creeping in. I leaned back and closed my eyes for a moment. I hadn't had much sleep over the past few months—not since I'd left her apartment the morning she'd learned the truth. Throw in my new job and the regular visits here, and sleep had become a rare luxury.

Not that I cared.

I'd spend an eternity awake if it meant I had the chance to be with her again. That was what kept me going every single day.

That she'd give us a chance.

Because I didn't want to imagine a world without her in it.

I didn't know how long I'd been sitting there, head tilted back, eyes closed, when I felt someone sit beside me. I opened my eyes, ready to tell them to leave before Azara came out, but the words died on my lips when my gaze met the prettiest shade of brown I had ever seen.

Azara.

I blinked, wondering if I had fallen asleep and was dreaming. She never really acknowledged me when I handed her the letters, let alone sat next to me.

"Hi."

My next breath fled my lungs.

I was almost afraid to speak. Afraid that if I did, the illusion of her so close to me, of her beautiful face gazing at me with an expression I hadn't seen in far too long, would vanish.

She looked nervous, but she was also smiling.

At me.

She's really here.

My Azara was sitting next to me.

"Hi," I finally said back, my voice barely a whisper.

Hope bled inside my chest, but I immediately scolded it to stay away. I'd waited for this moment so many times, and I didn't want my desire for it to overshadow whatever was about to happen.

Because what if she was here to tell me to stop?

I'd told her I'd fight for her every day, but what if it wasn't enough? What if I'd hurt her so deeply she couldn't see past it?

I didn't want to give up, to give her up, but if she told me there was no coming back, I'd have to.

Even if I'd never be the same after.

It was killing me not to touch her, not to tell her how much I missed her, but I was letting her take control of whatever this conversation was meant to be.

She shook her head. "I should have come up with a plan," she said with a soft, nervous laugh. "Or even rehearsed what I was going to say. But I didn't know what I was going to do until I saw you sitting here. Like you always do."

"I promised you I would be," I said, my voice thick. "I'll always be here, Azara."

"I know."

There was a brief pause then, one where we both looked at each other, apprehension filling the space between us as I waited for her next move.

"My dad came to see me yesterday," she said, and a sudden wave of anxiety surged inside my chest.

"What did he say?" I asked cautiously.

"He told me everything."

My heart pounded against my ribs, unsure of what that meant. Did he tell her about what he'd done, why he'd done it? Or did he tell her that I'd gone to see him? That I'd taken care of Nyx, and he'd never be a threat to her family or anyone from his prison cell?

Her smile faded a little, and I braced myself for the worst.

"I was really overwhelmed with his confessions, and it's going to take me some time to wrap my head around what my father did. But before he left, he said something that I couldn't stop thinking about. It made me reflect on what happened. On what you did. And what it means for us."

Us.

It was the first time she referred to me and her as a union, but would it mean the beginning of it or the end? My breaths grew shallow, and the fear of losing her—one that had been in the back of my mind—resurfaced. The air around us felt heavier, and just when the silence stretched to its breaking point, she spoke again.

"I read your letters." Her voice soft, her gaze burning into mine.

I'd considered many ways to win her back, but I quickly discarded all of them when I realized that she wouldn't care for fancy gifts and flowers. She would have probably donated the former and thrown away the latter.

So, I'd gone back and forth for days coming up with new things, but her last words to me had replayed over and over again until it had dawned on me.

I'd been hesitant at first because I'd never written anything to anyone before, but the moment I picked up a pen, the words had poured out of me.

They were also the only way I could talk to her these days, and writing them had almost become therapeutic.

The letters covered everything from my life growing up and my favorite graphic novels to how terrified I was of pigeons. And of course, many were filled with how I felt about her. How she made me feel like the most important person on the planet and that being with her was the first time I'd felt seen.

She already knew me better than anyone, but I wanted to show her that I didn't want to have any secrets between us. I wanted her to trust my word, to believe that I'd always stand by her side consistently, no matter what.

"I meant every word," I said quietly, my voice barely audible.

I didn't know if she'd ever read them. I thought she'd probably thrown them away or even burned them. But I kept writing them, holding on to the hope that, maybe one day, she might.

"I know," she said again, but this time, she cupped my face with one hand.

A small shudder of relief wracked through my body as I leaned into her touch, overwhelmed by the sudden feel of her soft skin against my stubble. It slowly started to ease this indescribable ache that had taken a permanent root inside my chest the moment I lost her.

Her thumb brushed across my cheek, and I exhaled a stammering breath. "I don't agree with what you did, and we have a lot to talk about, but there's something more important I need to tell you."

I held my breath as I waited for her next words.

"I love you."

I froze, disbelieving for a moment. "Yeah?" I asked, when the words finally registered, every fiber of my being desperately hoping that I'd heard her right, and that she wouldn't take them back.

She framed my face with both hands, and brought it closer to hers, her eyes flicking between mine. "Yeah," she said, her voice steady. "I've loved you for a long time. Even when I didn't want to."

A smile tugged at the corner of my lips as I curled a hand around the back of her neck, bringing our foreheads together. I took a deep breath, and it felt like the first real one in a very long time.

"Say it one more time."

"I love you," she breathed, her smile warm and bright.

My heart soared as I pressed my lips to hers. The kiss was gentle, almost tentative, but it still left us both breathless when we pulled away. I could kiss her forever, and I intended to—for the rest of my life.

I wrapped an arm around her waist, drawing her closer, still in disbelief that the woman I loved was back in my arms.

Azara looped an arm around my neck, brushing my hair back a few times. "I missed your hair."

"Wow," I said, placing a hand above my heart. "After all this time, and you only missed my hair?"

"I guess I missed you," she shrugged, but the bashful smile spreading across her lips betrayed her.

Laughter rumbled in my chest, the bright feeling shooting through me like a burst of sunlight. "God, I missed you so fucking much," I said, pressing another soft kiss to her lips.

I finally had everything I'd ever wanted right in front of me and I never wanted to let go.

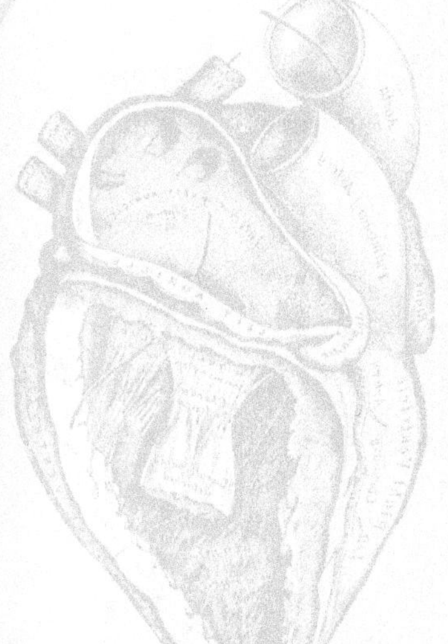

EPILOGUE

MICHAEL

Three weeks later

IT WAS LATE BY THE time I finally made it home.

I'd had a terrible day, and the only thing that would make it better was her.

She had a way of always making everything better.

"Azara?" I called out softly as I stepped inside my flat, hoping she wasn't already asleep. She'd finished work earlier this evening and texted to say she'd be staying the night, even though this place was as much hers as it was mine.

I'd hinted at her moving in permanently since she was here most days anyway, but we'd only officially been together for three weeks, and didn't want her thinking I was rushing things.

Even though I *really* wanted to.

"In here," she called, her voice floating over the gentle sound of a bath filling.

I placed my messenger bag on the kitchen island and made my way upstairs, following the sound of the running water. When I stepped into the ensuite bathroom attached to my bedroom, I found her with her feet propped on the edge of the tub, water spilling between them as her fingers trailed lazily through the milky water that barely covered the top of her breasts.

She looked almost ethereal, and the thought that she was all mine made my heart soar. She turned to look up at me, offering me a warm smile that made its way straight to my heart. There was something to be said about having her attention that made me feel invincible.

I forced a smile as I walked toward her, but she saw right through it.

"Bad day?" she asked gently.

I crouched down and pressed a quick kiss to her lips. "An absolute nightmare," I replied, my exhaustion from the day bleeding into my voice.

I'd been inundated with meetings and logistical issues to deal with, on top of losing two patients from post-op complications.

Death was unfortunately an inevitable downside of our line of work. We couldn't save everyone—it was naive to think otherwise—but it didn't take away the grief we felt when we lost someone.

"Come here, baby," she said, beckoning me to join her.

Wordlessly, I stripped out of my clothes, tossing them on the floor before turning off the tap and stepping into the massive tub. She sat up, patting the water in front of her. The water rose dangerously close to the top as I lowered myself in, but I didn't care if it spilled over. I would never pass up an opportunity to be close to her, and right now, I really needed it.

Once I was settled, she brushed my hair back, pulling my head gently against her chest. I let out a long sigh, the tension of the day slowly melting away. She kept playing with my hair as I sank deeper into the water, getting lost in her presence.

It was like coming home, where no words were needed.

Where being together was always more than enough.

These past three weeks had been something out of a dream, and I'd never felt more at peace. Yes, we'd had difficult conversations about everything that happened with her father, about the House, and what our future would look like, but she was still here.

She wanted me, and everything that came with me being a Young.

"Move in with me," I blurted, tilting my head to look up at her. I'd been thinking about it for weeks and I was tired of dancing around it.

Her fingers paused, and when she didn't answer immediately, I started listing all the reasons why it made perfect sense. "I know it might be early days and probably sounds a bit mad, but you're already here most days, and my place is closer to Orion, so you wouldn't have to commute as much. Plus, I'm an excellent cook and just… I really want to make this our home. Or we can move to yours, or anywhere you like."

After the longest pause known to man, she raised her brow and asked, "Are you done?"

"Yes," I said, my shoulders tense.

Please, say yes.

"Good," she replied, her eyes twinkling with amusement. "I was already going to say yes, but watching you nervously try to convince me was rather endearing."

My eyes narrowed at her mocking me and so, the only appropriate answer I had was to splash her.

"No, you didn't," she gasped and I couldn't help but laugh at the look of outrage on her face. Before I could register what was happening, she threw a retaliatory splash straight at my face.

I ran a hand over my face, and we both burst out laughing, my heart swelling with so much joy I thought it would explode. I twisted in her arms and firmly grabbed her face in my hands.

"God, I love you so fucking much," I said, before closing the gap and pressing my lips to hers. The kiss started off slow, just a soft brush of our lips, but when one of her hands found its way to my throat, it transformed into something more potent.

My body ignited with urgency; and I needed more.

But just as things were beginning to heat up, the shrill ring of my mobile sliced through the air, echoing off the walls. I ignored it at first, until the ringtone I'd set for Amar finally registered. I wanted nothing more than to return to our peaceful, warm bubble, but Amar wasn't exactly known for adhering to social constructs.

I groaned, eyes still closed for a moment as if I could will the interruption away.

But my phone rang again.

"He'll just keep calling if I don't answer," I muttered against her lips. Reluctantly, I pulled away, letting go of her face and stretching out my arm to reach for my trousers. I fumbled around, until I found it.

"What is it, Amar?" I said, already irritated. "It's midnight."

It was only 11:00 p.m. here, but he was in Paris for the weekend to celebrate his last birthday—his words—since next year he'd get his Order. Sofiane and I had both told him how terrible of an idea it was, but Amar insisted that if he was about to be tied down for the rest of his life, he wanted to go out in style.

Whatever that meant in Amar terms.

I just really hoped his call wouldn't require me to fly out to drag him out of whatever mess he'd gotten himself into this time. It was the first weekend Azara and I both had off work, and I had every intention of making the most of it.

"I'm going to marry this girl," Amar's voice bubbled through the phone, dreamy and far too cheerful.

"What?" I muttered, confused.

I'd expected him to be drunk, asking me for money, or worse, calling me from jail.

Not to talk to me about one of the girls he'd set his eyes onto.

He sighed. "Michael, you don't get it. I just met this girl…"

I pinched the bridge of my nose. "Look, mate, unless this is an emergency, I'm a little busy. But we can totally talk about it tomorrow." Without waiting for a response, I hung up and tossed the phone somewhere on the floor.

It pinged with a barrage of text messages, likely from him flooding our group chat about whoever this girl was, but I'd check on him tomorrow.

I turned my attention back onto something far more important.

Azara squealed in surprise when I lunged for her, water flying everywhere as I pulled her into my arms, and kissed her again, a peaceful warmth crackling under my skin.

I never imagined I'd get the chance to experience what it felt like to really love someone, to have my own happy ending.

But this, with her. It was the best thing I'd ever felt.

And I couldn't wait to make more memories and create our own version of forever.

THE END

If you're intrigued about what's to come in the Sons of the Atlas and who the next book is about, then keep reading for a sneak peek…

INTERLUDE

My frustration boiled over, and before I could think better of it, I swept everything off the coffee table in front of me—papers flew like confetti, pens scattered to the floor, and my bloody computer crashed onto the wooden floor with a sickening thunk.

"Fuck," I groaned, running my fingers through my hair and immediately regretting my outburst.

I wasn't one to lash out, but after more than a year of sleepless nights, juggling two jobs alongside my studies, chasing endless dead ends, and desperately trying to stop Michael from Ascending, I'd failed. Miserably. A bitter taste settled in my mouth because failing wasn't something I was used to.

I only had a single goal this year, and despite the car accident, despite the documents and forged societal paper exposing the old medical director, Young had not only Ascended, he'd even managed to get the girl.

I'd underestimated him. Especially his little friend, but I'd get to him eventually.

My methods had been too cautious, too conservative.

But I wouldn't let that happen again.

With the rage still simmering in my veins, I stalked over to where my computer lay on the floor, praying to whatever higher power might be listening that I hadn't destroyed one of the few things of value I owned. Fifteen years I'd had that machine, and there was no way I could afford a replacement.

Bracing myself, I bent down and reached for it. A small scuff marred the outer casing, but when I tapped the trackpad, the screen flickered to life, confirming it was still working. Relief washed over me as I checked my servers, finding them intact.

I then left the computer on the weathered sofa, the tension in my chest still tight, and moved to stand before my wall that had grown heavier with information since the last time we'd spoken. Although I'd learned a lot over the past year, there were still too many pieces to the puzzle that remained just out of reach.

My time was slowly running out and I couldn't—*wouldn't*—let them win.

Not after everything I'd had to sacrifice.

With a swift motion, I tore down Michael's photograph from its previous central spot, and let it fall to the floor so I could make space for my next target. I grabbed his picture from a previous connection and pinned it where Michael's picture used to be.

Amar Belkacem, you're next.

THANK YOU!

Hey lovely,

Thank you so much for reading Veiled! If you enjoyed this book, I would be grateful if you could leave a review on the platform(s) of your choice.

One review can make all the difference !

Love, Seraya x

AISO BY SERAYA

THE VENDETTA SERIES
A series of interconnected standalones

Nemesis

Ashes

Burdens

THE SONS OF THE ATLAS
A series of interconnected standalones

Veiled

KEEP IN TOUCH

To stay up to date on SeRaya's upcoming projects, connect with her on social media, sign up for her newsletter, or go to her website.

Reader Group: facebook.com/groups/serayaswarriors
Website: authorseraya.com
Instagram: www.instagram.com/authorseraya/
Tiktok: www.tiktok.com/@serayawrites
Goodreads: goodreads.com/authorseraya

ACKNOWLEDGMENTS

Every book I get to write almost feels surreal because I get to book stories that have lived in my brain onto paper and the magic of doing that never gets old!

This book was by far the most challenging I've ever written, but I've never felt prouder of typing "The End."

There are so many people to thank for helping make Veiled was it became, and a few words will never be enough, but let's give it a try.

To my girls, you know who you are—I am eternally grateful for every single one of you. You have supported me and become the family I never thought I'd have. The love and encouragement you have given me is something that I will never forget. Thank you for being there every step of the way, for being my ride-or-dies, and for being some of the best people I've ever known.w

To my DB—I quite literally could not have done this book without you by my side. You've sat with me days on end, talked me off the ledge many times and woke up to my endless voice notes about me not thinking I could do this. There aren't enough words that could express how much your friendship and support have meant to me. Thank you for holding my hand through this entire thing, I love you.

To Kylie, Kristie, Salma R. and Salma D.—I'm so lucky to have people on my team who care about my characters and my stories as much as I do. I am so grateful for your input, and your feedback helped make Azara & Michael shine the way they deserved.

To Kylie (again, because I love you)—There aren't enough words in any language to describe how grateful I am for your help in this book! You've helped me so much with Michael's character and shape the story to what it became. You already know how I feel about you, but I love you and I hope I get to have you by my side for many years to come.

To Rae—Girl! You're the best PA a girl could ask for. You've made my life so much easier over the last yeat and there's no word to describe how grateful I am for you, your friendship and your support.

To Kimberly and the team at Brower Literary—Thank you for your patience, support, and continuously believing in me. I'm forever grateful that our paths crossed and I couldn't do this without you.

To Cat—My genius fairy! You always create magic, and I'm so happy to have you bring my stories to life. I'm obsessed with you!

To Louise—Thank you for making my words shine and making this story the best it could be. I wouldn't have been able to do this without you.

To myself—After endless sleepless nights, and crying over the fear of writing this, of even ever finish writing this, we did it, love.

And last but not least, to you the reader—Thank you for taking a chance on me and my stories. This story was very special to me, and I hope you fell in love with these two just as I did writing them. None of this journey would be possible without you lovelies and I cannot wait to see where we go next!

xo, Seraya

ABOUT THE AUTHOR

SeRaya is a hopeless romantic twenty-something living in one of her favorite places in the world. She loves writing swoony and steamy love stories about fierce and imperfect characters who find their happily ever afters. Her stories may be emotional rollercoasters and she does have a weakness for slowburns, but that never tempers the heat that comes when it ignites.

She's always had a love for writing and is so happy that she gets to share her characters with you!

When she's not frantically trying to make her deadline, she loves being cozied up with a good romance book, rewatching her favorite shows, and discovering new food places.

www.ingramcontent.com/pod-product-compliance
Lightning Source LLC
Chambersburg PA
CBHW031730180726
48283CB00005B/1445